MANNA.

Emergent Literatures

Emergent Literatures is a series of international scope that makes available, in English, works of fiction that have been ignored or excluded because of their difference from established models of literature.

Manna for the Mandelstams for the Mandelas
Hélène Cixous

The Rift
V. Y. Mudimbe

Gates of the City
Elias Khoury

Yes, Comrade!
Manuel Rui

The Alexander Plays
Adrienne Kennedy

Deadly Triplets
Adrienne Kennedy

Human Mourning
José Revueltas

Love in Two Languages
Abdelkebir Khatibi

The Stream of Life
Clarice Lispector

Little Mountain
Elias Khoury

The Passion according to G.H.
Clarice Lispector

An American Story
Jacques Godbout

The Trickster of Liberty
Gerald Vizenor

In One Act
Adrienne Kennedy

HÉLÈNE CIXOUS

FOR THE MANDELSTAMS
FOR THE MANDELAS

Translated and with an

Introduction by

Catherine A. F. MacGillivray

University of Minnesota Press *Minneapolis*

The University of Minnesota Press gratefully acknowledges permission to reprint poetry that originally appeared in the following publications: *Osip Mandelshtam: The Eyesight of Wasps. Poems*, trans. James Greene (Columbus: Ohio State University Press, 1989); *Osip Mandelstam: Selected Poems*, trans. David McDuff (New York: Farrar, Straus, Giroux, 1975), by permission of translator; *Poems of Paul Celan*, trans. and intro. Michael Hamburger (New York: Persea, 1988), by permission; and *Osip Mandelstam: Selected Poems*, trans. Clarence Brown and W. S. Merwin (London: Oxford University Press, 1973), by permission of Oxford University Press.

Originally published as *Manne aux Mandelstams aux Mandelas* by Les Editions des Femmes. Paris, 1988.

Published by the University of Minnesota Press
2037 University Avenue Southeast, Minneapolis, MN 55455-3092
Printed in the United States of America on acid-free paper

Library of Congress Cataloging-in-Publication Data

Cixous, Hélène. 1937-
  [Manne. English]
  Manna : for the Mandelstams for the Mandelas / translated and with an introduction by Catherine A. F. MacGillivray.
      p.   cm. — (Emergent literatures)
  Includes bibliographical references and index.
  ISBN 0-8166-2114-4
  I. Title.   II. Series.
PQ2663.I9M3613   1994
843'.914 — dc20   93-34674
                                                        CIP

Contents

Introduction
"The Political Is— (and the) Poetical"

Catherine A. F. MacGillivray

*And the Lord spake unto Moses, saying, I have
heard the murmurings of the children of Israel:
speak unto them, saying, At even ye shall eat flesh,
and in the morning ye shall be filled with bread;
and ye shall know that I* am *the Lord your God.*

*And it came to pass, that at even the quails
came up, and covered the camp: and in the
morning the dew lay round about the host.*

*And when the dew that lay was gone up, behold,
upon the face of the wilderness* there lay *a small
round thing, as small as the hoar frost on the ground.*

And when the children of Israel saw it, they
*said one to another, It is manna: for they wist not
what it* was. *And Moses said to them, This* is *the
bread which the Lord hath given you to eat.*

This is *the thing which the Lord hath
commanded, Gather of it every man according to
his eating, an omer for every man,* according to *the
number of your persons; take ye every man for*
them *which* are *in his tents.*

And the children of Israel did so, and gathered, some more, some less. And when they did mete it with an omer, he that gathered much had nothing over, and he that gathered little had no lack; they gathered every man according to his eating.

And Moses said, Let no man leave of it till the morning. Notwithstanding they hearkened not unto Moses; but some of them left of it until the morning, and it bred worms, and stank: and Moses was wroth with them.

And they gathered it every morning, every man according to his eating: and when the sun waxed hot, it melted. And it came to pass, that on the sixth day they gathered twice as much bread, two omers for one man: and all the rulers of the congregation came and told Moses.

And he said unto them, This is that which the Lord hath said, To morrow is the rest of the holy sabbath unto the Lord: bake that which ye will bake to day, and seethe that ye will seethe; and that which remaineth over lay up for you to be kept until the morning.

And they laid it up till the morning, as Moses bade: and it did not stink, neither was there any worm therein. And Moses said, Eat that to day; for to day is a sabbath unto the Lord: to day ye shall not find it in the field.

Six days ye shall gather it; but on the seventh day, which is the sabbath, in it there shall be none. And it came to pass, that there went out some of the people on the seventh day for to gather, and they found none.

And the Lord said unto Moses, How long refuse ye to keep my commandments and my laws? See, for that the Lord hath given you the sabbath, therefore he giveth you on the sixth day the bread of two days; abide ye every man in his place, let no man go out of his place on the seventh day.

So the people rested on the seventh day. And the house of Israel called the name thereof Manna: and it was like coriander seed, white; and the taste of it was like wafers made with honey.

And Moses said, This is the thing which the Lord commandeth, Fill an omer of it to be kept for your generations; that they may see the bread wherewith I have fed you in the wilderness, when I brought you forth from the land of Egypt.

And Moses said unto Aaron, Take a pot, and put an omer full of manna therein, and lay it up before the Lord, to be kept for your generations. As the Lord commanded Moses, so Aaron laid it up before the Testimony, to be kept.

And the children of Israel did eat manna forty years, until they came to a land inhabited; they did eat manna, until they came unto the borders of the land of Canaan.

Exodus 16:11-35

It has been said that pure unredeemable evil, on a grand and technological scale, is one of the hallmarks of the twentieth century. Since the atrocities committed at Auschwitz and Hiroshima, many writers and philosophers have been asking the question once implicitly posed by Adorno: How can one possibly write poetry after Auschwitz?[1] Isn't the very effort "barbaric," to use Adorno's word? How can horror be expressed through language? Should one at least attempt to write the inexpressible, even though such an effort will be, according to poststructuralist notions of language and literature, a lessening?[2] Questions like these participate in a long tradition of reflection on the subject and scope of poetic language, at the site where such concerns coincide with more contemporary queries about ethics and history.

In her writing from the 1980s, Hélène Cixous takes up these very challenges, of late so urgent in Europe and North America. She has described herself thus:

> *On the one hand there is knowledge*
> *and on the other there is belief. This*
> *year in my seminars I've been talking*
> *a lot in terms of faith, but I realize*
> *this is something to fear. It's a term*
> *one must use with caution, because*
> *above all I wouldn't like to fall into*
> *religiosity, pseudo-mysticism, etc. I*
> *"believe," and I insist on believing. I*
> *insist as well on a certain number of*
> *values. When I work, I situate my*
> *work between poetics and ethics. I*
> *express myself poetically, but I think*
> *in relation to the world. This is a*
> *state of being which is both*
> *historical and cultural.*[3]

As always, Cixous takes part in the debate in a way that is peculiar to her.[4] A constant interlocutor and thorn in the side of a certain current in contemporary French thought, Cixous has consistently placed herself in the position of the displacer, of the winged thief, *la voleuse*, in relation to the very discourse whose agenda it is to displace and deconstruct. As Cixous said recently, her question is not how to write *after* Auschwitz, but how one writes *in* Auschwitz.[5] And her answer to this and other ethical and philosophical questions has always been the act of writing itself, a writing of the unwritable that celebrates and insists on its own being in the world. "What is important for me is the almost impossible to write."[6]

It should therefore come as no surprise to anyone who has followed Cixous's rich and varied body of work to find that in her writings of the mid-to-late 1980s, in her own attempt to express the inexpressible, as well as to perform, by writing, the difficulties of that very expression, Cixous has chosen contexts that are else-where (or, as in the case of *Manna for the Mandelstams for the Mandelas*, no-where: a prison, a place of exile, and an African u-topia)[7] — outside the European center. Her recent texts, including her ventures into the theater, have performed a double gesture: Cixous has moved toward what is for her a relatively new genre, and also toward a renewed and refocused inscription of her political commitment. I am referring to her epic plays, written for Ariane Mnouchkine's renowned Théâtre du Soleil: *L'Histoire terrible mais inachevée de Norodom Sihanouk, Roi du Cambodge*, and *L'Indiade ou L'Inde de leurs rêves*,[8] and to the new poetic praxis that is at work in *Manna for the Mandelstams for the Mandelas*, which I am honored to have been asked to translate and present. I have undertaken these two tasks in a characteristically Cixousian spirit: not as "critic," but for my own pleasure and as gift, a giving for reading (*donner à lire*).

Manna for the Mandelstams for the Mandelas, which grew out of a short piece Cixous wrote as her contribution to a volume dedicated to Nelson Mandela and edited by Jacques Derrida and Mustapha Tlili,[9] is inscribed against richly populated panoramas, what Cixous refers to as "epic" backdrops, namely, those of contemporary history and a certain theatrical tradition. The Mandelstams and the Mandelas, like the Sihanouk, Gandhi, and Nehru of her plays, are "real" people, significant historical figures of our own time, whom Cixous has been possessed to write about at the level of myth or legend. As she puts it in *Manna*, "If it sees the light of day, this book will be the fruit of a haunting." Written in the form of a long and legendary mythic prose poem, *Manna for the Mandelstams for the Mandelas* draws from African folklore traditions and presents its own, novel, totemic animals, such as the ostrich, retuning the tenor of the totem, not in the analytical spirit of Freud's *Totem and Taboo*,[10] but in order to pay poetic homage to a non-Western storytelling tradition.[11] It is a prime example of what Catherine Clément has described as a "feminine" way of (re)writing history. "[I]t is a history, taken from what is lost within us of oral tradition, of legends and myths — a history arranged the way tale-telling women tell it. And from the standpoint of conveying the mythic models that powerfully structure the Imaginary (masculine and feminine, complex and varied), this history will be true. On the level of fantasy, it will be fantastically true: It is still acting on us."[12]

And indeed, we can marvel today at the magic that must have been at work to have produced such a text, written starting in 1986, just three years before the walls of the two hells presented here, Nelson Mandela's prison cell and a Russia still under the shadow of Stalinism, succumbed. Such an incredible coincidence compels us to wonder what truly is the relation of "reality" to the realm of poetry. Should we conclude, as Kafka is said to have done upon seeing Picasso's futuristic images, that the artist acts like a clock that goes too fast, already seeing and feeling today the shapes of things to come?[13]

Few other works by Hélène Cixous embody more distinctly than *Manna* the complex and fruitful relationship she has found between the poetical and the political. This poem takes a political stance in relation to human suffering and to questions of redemption and sacrifice in writing, questions so crucial in this, our century, by exploring and performing the difficulties of its own tradition. It is a written text that asks, How to write? How to write of the Mandelas and the Mandelstams, of Anna Akhmatova and Steven Biko? How to regain what is gone, so that "nothing will have been lost"? Language cuts, captures, caps unconscious energies; feeling and experience become words and lose their corporeal origins: the signified is sacrificed to the signifier. As soon as one writes, one substitutes, one represses the living, symbolizes the absence of the living thing. And yet, "there is also the necessity of inscribing to resist death, effacement, silence."[14] This is what Cixous's texts teach us. Hence she persists in writing, is compelled to try to tell these contemporary stories, so full of grief and dolor.

Manna is also a love story, the tale of two epic loves, studded with allusions to the literary tradition of the long poem treating hell and human struggle, which includes texts like the biblical story of Job, Dante's *Divine Comedy*, and Milton's *Paradise Lost*. Traveling by text to South Africa and the Soviet Union, this tale is a commentary on the poetic nature of the political gestures made by the man of action, Nelson Rolihlahla Mandela, and by his devoted wife, Nomzamo Winnie, and on the inevitably political nature of the poetic works of the Russian poet Osip Mandelstam, whose poems had to be saved from oblivion by his wife, Nadezhda. Nadezhda reconstructed Mandelstam's poems after they were banned and burned, and kept them safe in her memory and on scraps of paper she hid for nearly thirty years, until they could finally be published, beginning in the 1960s outside the Soviet Union, and in the 1970s within. Thus these two twentieth-century couples, Osip and Nadezhda, Nelson and Zami,[15] join the long line of literary love stories and mythic couples, like Penthesileia and Achilles, Antony and Cleopatra, Tancredi and Clorinda, favored in Cixous's writings over the years.

In Russian, *nadezhda* means "hope," and as Nadezhda Mandelstam and Winnie Mandela brought hope into their husbands' lives, *Manna* too is a story of hope, of the oasis of paradise that can still exist, even in the darkest hell. Cixous has given a partial explanation as to how she thinks this paradise possible:

> *The common lot of people is to think*
> *and to experience that in human life,*
> *the tragic always wins out over the*
> *comic. But I myself am not like that.*
> *I do not think that tragedy is the*
> *winner. I think there is something*
> *stronger than tragedy. It isn't*
> *happiness of course, it's thinking, it's*
> *thought, which is stronger than*
> *everything. That is why I have*
> *spoken of Etty Hillesum.[16] She was a*
> *young Dutch journalist, who wrote*
> *in an extraordinary way, within the*

precincts of despair. She was on her
way to Auschwitz, and she knew it.
. . . This means that in the worst kind
of hell there's something stronger
than hell, the singing of human
beings against hell, in spite of hell,
through hell.[17]

This is what the Mandelas and the Mandelstams have in common, this resistance to loss, to banishment and imprisonment, to time spent in the other hells of our "century scarred with camps": the gulag and apartheid. "[T]hey all refused to submit to a brutal and morally corrupt authority."[18] As the text tells us, they are "two men who do not know each other, but the same sorrow knows them."

Springing from their stories, interlacing with the places and scenes told by the books *Part of My Soul Went with Him* by Winnie Mandela, and *Hope against Hope* by Nadezhda Mandelstam,[19] comes Hélène Cixous's *Manna*, a text that is neither pure poetry nor pure political history, but a hybrid weave of poems, anecdotes, scenes, images, historical "truths" (themselves always figurative representations of what one names "reality") embroidered on and expanded by poetic fiction. Echoing the expression used to describe the correspondence between Tsvetayeva, Rilke, and Pasternak in 1926, Cixous has called *Manna* a *correspondance à trois*. The poet Cixous takes up the texts two other women have left us, in a writing with others and from other texts that has always characterized her way of writing, perhaps more than anything else, and writes a modern myth of separation, loss of paradise, descent into the lower world, and of the human struggle to maintain in prison what is left of the earth and sky.[20] The

Cixousian sky, central metonymy in *Manna*, is not the Blanchotian *ciel désastré*,[21] nor is it the sky of Mallarmé, with its alphabet of stars (although it holds more in common with the latter than with the former).[22] It is the starry eternity with which Osip Mandelstam measured events and time, and the sky of Dante's *Paradiso*, as the epigraph to *Manna* tells us. In canto XVIII of the *Paradiso*, the spirits form themselves into successive letters and spell out the opening words of the book of Wisdom: "Love righteousness ye that be judges of the earth." In *Manna*, the sky has turned into a prisoner's earth, full of verse traversing the universe, swarming the sky as worms swarm the earth.[23] And there are also worm-eating birds, flocks of them flying, north to south, cold to warm, following the same seasonal rhythms and juxtapositions as we do, reading. Among the main "metonymic metaphors"[24] of *Manna* is metaphor itself, transport glimpsed in the Mandelstams' trains and the constant flights of birds, with which the book also ends.[25] Form and content merge in Cixous's use of metaphor in *Manna*, and in the relation of transference, another kind of transport, she has as poet toward the Mandelas and the Mandelstams. She works on trance, *la transe*, as transport, on "the passage from one to the other, on continuity, on the possibility of exchange."[26]

These two explorers of hell, and their two times, two wives, and two continents, are linked in other ways as well. For instance, Winnie refers to Brandfort, her home in exile, as "my little Siberia,"[27] Mandela the politician was forced to resort to metaphor in his prison letters in order to get his message through,[28] and Mandelstam the poet's metaphors were read as political whether he strictly meant them to be or not. And then there are the dates, such as May 1: the date of Osip and Nadezhda's first meeting in 1919 and of their separation in 1938; on this same date many years later, Winnie Mandela spoke at a rally in South Africa. She was wearing an ostrich-feather hat, and Cixous was struck by her, struck as if by lightning, struck as if by writing. Cixous said of this encounter: "Why [write about] Mandela becomes then a question of why Winnie Mandela. . . . There is an avatar. This avatar could be called the triumph of Life. . . . I saw Winnie Mandela for the first time, as I have written. One day I turn on the television and I see an extraordinary woman . . . an absolutely sumptuous woman, about whom I sense that she is for me a double of those women who move me by their apparition in person and as metaphor. . . . I hear that it is Winnie Mandela. There was a conjuncture, a primal scene . . . it was like a completely poetic vision. Thus springs forth like an explosion of poetry something that nonetheless presents itself as political."[29]

A comment made by Cixous in an interview I conducted with her in 1988 situates her outlook at that time. In 1980 she wrote a text she called "Poetry Is/and (the) Political."[30] In the 1988 interview, she mentioned that were she to write a similar text again today, post-Théâtre du Soleil, she would call it "The Political Is — (and the) Poetical." I would like to propose this shift, taken up again by the title of this preface (or rather, by my translation of the French title, wherein I introduce a dash in order to indicate a back-and-forth movement between the two poles, a dash that does not exist in the original), as exemplary of the movement of the Cixousian oeuvre across the 1980s.[31]

Toward the beginning of that decade, Cixous insisted on the radically revolutionary force of the materiality of poetic language itself, and on the political gesture inherently made by every poetical text. As the second version of the title suggests, later on she began to explore the poetry and the semiology of politics, the ways in which free poetic thought and political freedom feed one another, and in which certain political gestures pay homage to poetical ways of reading the world and to the poetry of existence. In Cixous fictions of the last decade prior to *Manna*, the common question was how to write women's pleasure, without all the *jouissance* being lost in the lingo (not to mention, alas, the translation). In *Manna for the Mandelstams for the Mandelas*, the movement from the poetical toward the political is sensed also in the shift from this previous problematic of pleasure to one of suffering, though they are both implicated with each other, the one always being sought *chez* Cixous in and through the other.[32] The tension between these two remains dialectical, but the balance has teetered. And the shift implies that wisdom today can be found elsewhere than in the seminal texts of modernity's philosophic traditions. Wisdom can be sought too in the politics and poetry of the individual's strange and nightmarish relation to history. (—History, Stephen said, is a nightmare from which I am trying to awake.)[33]

A Site of Contrasts

Manna is couched between extremes: paradise and hell, earth and sky, white and black, frozen Siberia and the hot plains of South Africa, sweltering Johannesburg and bleak Moscow. Hélène Cixous has described how in writing *Manna*, the Mandelas' and the Mandelstams' differences came together. "One story feeds the other, one story makes love with the other. Maybe this is a typical trait of feminine writing, I don't know, but *Manna* is really a lovemaking of texts that intertwine and grow from one another."[34] The book begins: "When the terrestrial earth is lost, the celestial earth remains." The sky is earth for the exiled: it is the only outside one can see from one's prison cell. "*L'exil fait taire. L'exil fait terre.*"[35] It is the earth that is our home, but in *Manna*, the relationship to apparent polarities involves seeking the extreme point where the one glides into the other. Cixous has said, "Perhaps I resist exile, which is fundamental and initial for me, by working incessantly at reuniting. I sense that when I write, nothing satisfies me more than to reunite extremes, to reunite the orient and the occident, the north and the south, black and white, the icy cold and the boiling."[36]

When we have no terrestrial home, when we have lost the fertile, matrical earth as home, when as birds we have no more nest, the sky becomes our earth. And the ostrich, the only bird that cannot fly, becomes the emblem of all birds, of birdness itself. Likewise, following this logic of melding contraries, even in hell there is the human voice.

The text is littered with examples of this type. These are not simply sterile exercises in the art of paradox, but fruitful mixes from which new relations are born. In *Manna*, we are asked to contemplate the shocking idea that there can also be a bit of heaven about hell. I would contend that this upheaval of polar opposites also suggests the type of privileged relationship of *contiguity*, of metonymy, Cixous would like to insist exists between the political and the poetical. And at the center of this mix is writing, writing as metaphor, as dream of contiguity, as act of resistance, writing as, simply, persistence in the face of its own implausibility.

I believe it is in part these "metonymic metaphors," appearing in some form in virtually every Cixous text, that render her "unreadable" to many in the Anglo-American feminist tradition. Her poeticization of politics does not fit any established political pattern, but instead aims at being inspirational, destabilizing, and politically evocative. And I would argue that the categories of the creative and the evocative are as important to a feminist politics as those of the "epistemologically useful."[37] Cixous is a poet, and approaches all questions in the guise of the poet, searching in politics and history for the underlying structural patterns of political thought itself, rearranging these structures according to the laws of her poetry, to produce an altogether other politics, which often goes unrecognized as such. I wonder if this is due in part to the importance politics plays in relation to the feminist project. As Diana Fuss has put it, "It is politics . . . that is essential to feminism's many self-definitions. It is telling, I think, that constructionists are willing to displace 'identity,' 'self,' 'experience,' and virtually every other self-evident category *except* politics. To the extent that it is difficult to imagine a *non-political* feminism, politics emerges as feminism's essence."[38] Essential or not, how can we define the political in Cixous's work? It is not, according to traditional notions of the political, an effort at reorganizing life in the polis. It could be considered a politics of myth or a notion of myth as politics, a political rewriting of the myths that are central to us or a call for a more central positioning of myths we must bring back from the margins. (I have something particular in mind here, and will come back to the use of myths in Cixous's writings in the section of this essay entitled "Poetry, the Fruit of Sacrifice." I am not, nor is Cixous, putting out a call for a new politics of myth based on ideas of nation or community, that dangerous relation to myth described so well by Jean-Luc Nancy and Philippe Lacoue-Labarthe in their book *The Inoperative Community*.)[39] Or, as Verena Conley has argued, "In Cixous, the poetic functions both aesthetically *and* strategically. Its aim is to undo a homogenous, dominant discourse that hides its will to power beneath eternal, conceptual truths. Poetry is not opposed to politics; it is more political than a so-called political discourse, itself already part of another system."[40] Precise definitions still seemingly escape, and so I again invoke one of Fuss's arguments, as reminder before a reading of Cixous: "Politics is precisely the self-evident category in feminist discourse—that which is most irreducible and most indispensable. As feminism's *essential* component, it tenaciously resists definition; it is both the most transparent and the most elusive of terms."[41]

All told, this is a propitious moment for *Manna* to appear in English, given contemporary feminist concerns in

North America and England with how to speak, write, and read class, race, and sexual differences, and with how to make political and theoretical discourses from the place of, with a space for, these differences. As a part of this endeavor, there has been a turning to strategies usually associated with French thought operated by certain feminist writers,[42] and in the texts of these Anglo-American women and men we read a call for a plurality of voices, for alterity within subjectivity, and for political solidarity within differences. In keeping with this commitment, some feminists have grown both suspicious and weary of identity politics, having come to see these as fundamentally posited on an indivisibility and stability of the subject that in these poststructuralist times seems specious. These are all notions, long held by French feminists like Hélène Cixous, that have taken on renewed significance of a tactical, practical kind within the Anglo-American context. Therefore, the time for a new cross-reading appears to me to be at hand. I agree with Gerald Hill when he writes in his article entitled "*Bardés d'apotropes*: Anglo-American Responses to 'Le Rire de la Méduse' ":

> The translation from French
> "density" to American empiricism
> [has] involved to a significant (if, for
> my own rhetorical moment,
> exaggerated) degree a warding off of
> the "evil" (the "dangerous charms"
> the "vamp") within the "French
> thought" . . . later writers, beyond
> evil, [can] come back to a writer like

Cixous and re-enlist her brilliant rhetoric.[43]

It is my hope that the publication of *Manna* in English will participate in this rediscovery.

Celestial Food — Terrestrial Torment

The Bible tells us that God sent down manna from heaven, to save the Israelites who would otherwise have wasted away in the wilderness. Manna is celestial food that helps us weather the times of terrestrial torment: prison, exile, and other configurations of malevolence. In the word "manna" we can also hear the word *mana*, the force to which good fortune is attributed in Polynesia.[44] In hell or in the desert, we must make do with "the remains"; we must feed ourselves from the leftovers, and this is our good fortune. In *Manna*, the Mandela wedding cake and the Mandelstam farewell candy are the two most obvious forms of manna present, the wedding cake symbolizing deferred spiritual union that results in a union, through separation, of difference, and the candy, received through a train window when the Mandelstams are on the move toward Voronezh, symbolizing anonymous solidarity with the exiled poet: "This book then will not be without sugar, without eggs, without spices, without succulence. Nor without famine, nor without desert. It is the cake's story that is sweet and nourishing. The cake itself might be rancid, but its essence is inalterable, I believe.

"Thanks to the existence of the cake, the courage to write this book came to me: that there be pastry in hell, not merely torment, is what allowed me to advance sentence by sentence but not without shyness in this sweetened hell. I entered it then through the kitchen, with one soul, shy, and the other soul, audacious."

There are other sources for the reader's nourishment as well, namely, in the unfoldings of Cixous's writing. The word *manna* worms its way into *Mandela*, which glides like a bird to *Mandelstam*, all of which further recall the French words for almond and lover, *amande* and *amante*, as well as the German words for almond and stem, *Mandel* and *Stamm*. *Stamm*, like its English equivalent, can also be used to indicate origin, for it means "tribe" too. *Amande* resembles *Amandla*, which is the Xhosa word for "power," a word Mandela would shout to the crowds at his trial, and they would respond: *Nwagethu*, "to the people." The list of associations goes on and on, *l'être-là* (being there), *le mandé-là* (summoned there), *mandorla* (mandoline, and the title of a hymnlike poem by Celan to the almond, hence to Mandelstam as well);[45] one can also see in the French for manna, *manne*, a feminine version of the English word *man*. The almond is a fruit that perfectly embodies this bisexual being, symbolizing as it does "a kind of maternal seed,"[46] a nut that is both seed and milk, shell and kernel, hard outside enclosing a milky center. In this way, the almond is the perfect Cixousian symbol for the bisexuality of the poet, bisexuality referring here, as always in Cixous's lexicon, not to sexual practice, but to a libidinal economy that affords both masculine and feminine drives. And the almond recalls another coupling, the coupling, new to the Cixousian text, of pleasure and pain. "In the bitter kernel the milk seed. The almond is there, in the bitterness. That is the Mandela secret: the manna. Manna come from the heavens hidden under the earth. It has a taste of necessity. *Amandla!*" Finally, *Manna* is too, as Milton knew, a symbol for language.[47] The word *manna* in Hebrew means "what is that"; so the Israelites were saved from starvation by eating "what is that," a mysterious food that recalls all the mysteries of language.

The title is not the only textual food in *Manna*. Language is also clearly marked as nourishment, in, for example, the play on the French word for line of poetry, or verse, *vers*, which also means worms, favorite food of birds, the letter-eating animals of this text, which search for worms like the poet searches for words. And for once the English offers us felicitous wordplay. Words for birds are worms, warm food plucked from the earth or sky, which they stud like stars, or is it like verse? Once filled with worms, birds become poems, searching for a place to land, a scrap of paper or a piece of sky. And we must add, worms are both earth-friendly and friend of the maggot: worms devoured the biblical manna left too long untouched, as they will devour us also after we are placed in the earth, thereby completing the food chain. Here the configuration food, life, death, and language is replete.

And so on, a chain of signifiers that unrolls horizontally as well as vertically. The words of *Manna* suggest one another phonetically, musically, visually, at once metonymically *and* metaphorically, rather than on the level of a hierarchy linking sense and symbol in an asymmetrical couple. This is a commonplace of Cixous's poetics. To quote Katherine Binhammer's excellent article "Metaphor or Metonymy? The Question of Essentialism in Cixous":

> *Cixous subsumes the two [metaphor*
> *and metonymy], insofar as the*
> *metaphor that is not a metaphor is a*
> *metonymy. . . . In defining the*
> *metaphor that is not a metaphor as a*
> *metonymy, the traditional opposition*

*of metaphor and metonymy is
displaced.*[48]

One sense hides and at the same time suggests another beneath it, but in Cixous's use of language there is no central, proper origin, no forever missing and deferred (phallic) signifier in the Lacanian sense, only endless multiplication and extension, words played off of one another heterogeneously. Cixous implodes the binarism that has traditionally been posited, first by Jakobson in linguistics, then reinscribed by Lacan into the psychoanalytic vocabulary, as existing between the opposed axes of the metonymic and the metaphoric, as well as redressing the "hierarchy of two meanings" Jakobson spoke of as existing between a metaphor or a metonymy in relation to its primary, "context-free" referent. Although Jakobson also spoke of a "poetic function," which would be a more complex relation of the metonymic and the metaphoric and of primary and secondary meaning,[49] chains of chiasmal creations seen in a use of language deemed poetic, Cixous subverts the notion of the poetic function as a repetition of equivalence, by introducing *différance* through displacement into the equation. Her scansions are not of the "I like Ike"[50] variety, but are instead a proliferation of signifiers that are "put into play, but never arrive at a final telos or meaning."[51] "Metonymic metaphors" do not merely stand in for a missing term, but produce "a surplus of meaning,"[52] transporting meaning beyond the known. This type of play could also be qualified as partaking in part of the Joycean tradition, and indeed, as we know, Joyce is an important inhabitant of the Cixousian literary universe.[53]

Furthermore, food has always been central to the Cixousian practice of poetry as nourishment, and she has insisted on food as an appropriate topic for poetry. This stems partially from her explorations of what would be a feminine *économie libidinale*, underpinning an *écriture féminine*.[54] One major pulsion driving this feminine economy,[55] according to Cixous, is the psychoanalytically defined orality phase. Posited by Freud as infantile and therefore inferior to the "adult" stage of phallic genitality,[56] orality is recuperated and reinstated by Cixous as representative of an *other* economy, most easily accessible to biological females because of their socialization, but by no means essentially limited to them. As Deborah Jenson puts it in a note to her essay "Coming to Reading Hélène Cixous" in *"Coming to Writing" and Other Essays*, "the female body is the place from which metaphors of femininity originate, but it has no copyright to them."[57]

In addition to being a rewriting of the oral impulse described by Freud, texts by Cixous are entwined with the theories of language attributed to psychoanalysts Nicolas Abraham and Maria Torok. These theories of the *bouche vide/bouche pleine* (empty mouth/full mouth) acquisition of language are in opposition to Lacanian theory. According to Abraham and Torok, language would occur not as a cutting short of the imaginary fusion of mother and child, after the intervention of the symbolic name-of-the-father, but as a crying out for reparation in response to separation from her, a feeling of emptiness in the mouth that the child seeks to fill. Abraham and Torok describe it thus:

> *This cry is first of all experienced as cries and sobs, deferred filling up, then as occasion for calling, way of making appear, language. . . . The passage from the mouth full of breast to the mouth full of words is*

effectuated through experiences of
the mouth emptied.[58]

In French, the word *breast* truly is a mouthful (and is one of the many examples of loss on the level of multiple and undecidable sense in this English "version" of *Manna*), calling up as it does a whole list of signifiers: *sein, sans, sang, signe* (breast, without, blood, sign), not to mention the verb *sein* (to be) in Cixous's mother tongue of German, as well as the multiple meanings in French of the word *sein* itself, which can commonly indicate not only breast but womb, heart, and center. In the Cixousian lexicon the breast is at the core of Being (*le sein* is/*das Sein*). Orality then is linked to the maternal, to nourishment in relationships that leave the other intact, nourishment that is neither a cannibalism nor melancholic incorporation, and is most often a thirst. Or it is an Eve-like tasting of the tree of knowledge, an eating so as to know the interiority. As Cixous put it in her essay "The Author in Truth":

> *[In] the first fable of our first book*
> *. . . we are told that knowledge could*
> *begin with the mouth, the discovery*
> *of the taste of something. Knowledge*
> *and taste go together. . . . the*
> *struggle between presence and*
> *absence, between an undesirable,*
> *unverifiable, indecisive absence, and a*
> *presence which is not only a*
> *presence: the apple is visible, is*

*promise, is appeal—"Bring me to
your lips"; it is full, it has an inside.
What Eve will discover in her
relationship to concrete reality is the
inside of the apple, and this inside is
good. The Fable tells us how the
genesis of "femininity" goes by way
of the mouth, through a certain oral
pleasure, and through the nonfear of
the inside. . . . our oldest book of
dreams relates to us, in its cryptic
mode, that Eve is not afraid of the
inside, neither of her own nor of the
other's. The relationship to the
interior, to penetration, to the
touching of the inside, is positive.
Obviously Eve is punished for it, but
that is a different matter.*[59]

The oral drive, then, is the Cixousian economy's paradigm for a certain stance in relation to pleasure and to the law, and for the birth of language, whence writing. Words and writing will be part of a chain linking alimentation to dissatisfaction and on to verbalization. Language, like the apple, comes to the aid of satisfaction and pleasure, and is thereby an oral nourishment, a manna. In *Manna*, we have a cake that can't be eaten, a candy that says farewell, and *la bouche pleine de paroles* of the exiled poet, who even in death has his mouth full, of verse and worms.

OM[60]

The Anglo-American reading public is perhaps more familiar with our world-famous contemporaries the Mandelas than it is with the Mandelstams;[61] I know I was. Among the greatest pleasures for me in preparing the present volume was the discovery of one of this century's greatest poets, in any language: Osip Mandelstam.

Mandelstam was born to a cultured Jewish family in Warsaw in 1891 and grew up in Saint Petersburg. He took his university education abroad, first in Paris, where he studied with Henri Bergson, then in Heidelberg, from 1909 to 1910, and finally in Italy, where he became devoted to Dante. He began writing poetry in the years just before the Russian Revolution and published his first collection, entitled *Stone*, in 1913. Both this collection and his second, *Tristia* (1922),[62] convey "a sense of an oversaturated existence" and express, according to Joseph Brodsky, "the slowing-down, lasting sensation of Time's passage . . . using all the phonetic and allusory powers of words themselves . . . [where] the words, even their letters . . . are almost palpable vessels of Time."[63]

Mandelstam was associated in his lifetime with the movement known as Acmeism, as was his great friend and colleague Anna Akhmatova, another major Russian writer of this period, who also appears as an important figure in *Manna* (and indeed, the book ends with Nadezhda Mandelstam and Akhmatova, walking and bickering their way down Pushkin Street).[64] Acmeism was a Russian literary revolt against what its proponents saw as Symbolism's tendency toward mysticism, empty musicality, and lack of concreteness.

The Acmeists wanted a return in poetry to the tangible and actual things of this world, to poems that would take their strength "from contact with the earth."[65] We can understand why Cixous, long interested in the works of Brazilian writer Clarice Lispector, whose texts chronicle the small, the slow, and the everyday thingness of things, would find herself drawn to the verse of Osip Mandelstam. Indeed, the Acmeists' slogan "Down with Symbolism! Long live the living rose!" is inscribed in terms readers of Cixous and Lispector will recognize. Mandelstam himself is said to have defined Acmeism first in an essay in 1922 as the "organic school," then, in 1937, as "a homesickness for world culture."[66]

After the Russian Revolution of 1917 Mandelstam found himself disliked and mistrusted by the authorities, because he refused to embrace in his art a specifically ideological, pro-party agenda. This was considered a highly political and subversive gesture in and of itself, in a country of which the great poet Alexander Blok has said, "Literature is a more vital force in Russia than anywhere else. Nowhere does Word become Life, nowhere does it turn into bread or stone as it does with us."[67] As a result of his fall from favor, Mandelstam found himself less and less able to publish, and he was eventually faced with governmental censure,[68] and with the years of trains and exiles, of birds and shabby shoes, chronicled in *Manna*.[69]

Following a five-year period of relative silence in the 1920s, which he called his "deaf-mute" period,[70] Mandelstam produced some of his best poetry, first in 1930, during a prolonged visit to Armenia with a group of biologists, and then during his exile with Nadezhda in Voronezh, from 1934 to 1937. The verses from *Armenia* were the last to be published in Mandelstam's lifetime, after which his work was definitively banned from publication. The Voronezh verses were only to be published many years after his death. The poems of these two cycles attest to the survival of art and human consciousness, at a time and in a place where both were under attack.

Although he did write his most notorious poem, the curious and cryptic epigram correctly assumed to satirize Stalin,[71] as a (suicidal) protest, Mandelstam's cry resounds most often as a nonideological one, against injustice and for poetry. He was apparently neither strongly for nor against the Russian Revolution (and I say apparently because so much of his poetry is ambivalent and willfully obscure in its complexity), but seems to have seen it first as potentially promising, later as just another, harsher, existential reality. His resolve in the face of party pressure to conform seems more a spiritual, structural one than a political or rebellious stance. Any instinct toward self-preservation was ceded to ethical concerns, and in his verse Mandelstam offered insights that were heroic and risk-taking in their acuity. He was an "interpreter of the apocalypse"[72] and thereby was perhaps the *most* "political" poet in the Russia of his time, "the epoch of tyrants" as he called it, referred to in *Manna* as the musicless, mustached age.

Mandelstam has been called an "inner émigré," someone who felt so deeply alienated from his time that he turned to a conception of human existence based on eternal modes of being and perception, and, on the most elementary human level, toward the near and the known. In this way, he belongs in the Cixousian category of the poet as (inner) exiled and wandering Jew, a poetic paraphrasing of a line from another Russian poet, Marina Tsvetayeva, taken up by Celan and later by Cixous.[73] He is also a representative of what has been called "Cixous's interest in individuals who move outside the Law. . . . It is as . . . an outsider who opened a crack in the system . . . that she represents Osip Mandelstam."[74]

As a poet, Mandelstam was not attempting to be a representative of his nightmarish age or of his generation (and yet he was, in the deepest sense, both); rather, he saw his lineage as stemming from the eternal poets of world culture, such as Homer and Petrarch, Ariosto, Dante, and Racine, seeking "to find a poetic tradition that would speak beyond the priorities of the contemporary moment."[75] References in his poetry are most often those of classical European literature and the Judeo-Christian tradition of the Bible. The Voronezh poems, however, written in exile and published posthumously, as were his very last poems, are starker and more revelatory than his previous highly erudite work, less strictly metrical, and unusually short, often only seven or nine lines long. They were written in three notebooks over a three-year period, in three short spurts followed by months of relative silence. Biology, physics, and cosmology have entered into these later poems,[76] which often deal with the pain of separation: from physical love, culture, language, inspiration, and from life itself.[77] They are, as *Manna* indicates, less traditionally literary than past poems, and more like birds' songs, chirping nervously and flying high. And yet they are still very structured, searching in symmetry to make tragic sense of Stalin's system. With regard to the Voronezh period, it has been pointed out that "what interests Cixous . . . is [Mandelstam's] reasons for returning to poetry at a time when the social and political stakes in doing so were so high."[78]

After the time in Voronezh followed only one year of relative reprieve, until Mandelstam's last arrest and exile in 1938. He is thought to have died at the end of that year in a Vladivostok prison barrack. The Vladivostok camp was being used at that time as a transit area, "where prisoners were held temporarily before being sent on to Kolyma."[79] No one has ever been able to reconstruct either Mandelstam's last days or his last attempts at verse, although many legends of all sorts have sprung up, including some that deny his official date of death and others that tell of a mad poet, reciting poetry to his fellow prisoners until the very end of his life, which came quickly. Nadezhda was not allowed to follow him on this second exile, and it is widely believed that her absence greatly contributed to the rapidity of his demise.[80]

Poetry, the Fruit of Sacrifice

At first glance, the political poets in *Manna* appear to be the men Nelson and Osip, and this represents another unusual transformation in Hélène Cixous's literary world. As she has taken up subjects of an increasingly historicocultural nature, she has turned her ear from heroines to heroes, for it is men who have made official history and culture, up till now. And yet the heroes of Cixous's writing are always ambiguous, bisexual beings, inscribed as men who contain both maternal and feminine drives.[81] For instance, Cixous's Nelson Mandela is coded as being more maternal than paternal to his people. The chapter entitled "The True Portrait of Nelson" portrays the political hero as a male mother, "the man with milk," a delicate hippopotamus who tries to save a wounded gazelle, and when he cannot, takes the gazelle's head into his mouth in an attempt to revive her expiring soul with his *souffle*.[82] Nelson is also shown symbolically offering his body up to his people as nourishment, as manna, so that, like the Hebrews, they can succeed in their journey across the desert of apartheid.

Manna, then, is not merely a celebration of traditional roles, but, as I have indicated, a reflection on the ambivalent and slippery nature of these very roles. And, as with the language of politics, it is poetry that greases the poles of the language of gender roles. For instance, in the chapter entitled "The Marriage Proposal," Zami and Nelson share a rare moment alone on the veldt. "And there at the end, at the utmost edge of the world, standing side by side draped in a lone mantle of light, were a lion and a lioness, or else a lioness and a lion." Language as code causes one to write automatically "a lion and a lioness." But language can as well be a means for change, for disruption of the ordinary and the cementatory, inscribing and thereby reminding us—but they might be "a lioness and a lion."[83] And so it is throughout this tale, causing the subtle reader to wonder, Who is the writer? Whose voice is it, wife's or poet's? Who sacrifices what, and for whom? Or, as the text puts it, in a scene where Zami is discussing her impending marriage to Nelson with the Ancient Ostrich, who tells it to her like it is:

" 'And to end I'm going to tell you the gravest part of this story:

'This life will be your sacrifice.

'But the problem with sacrifice is that nobody knows what it is. Who sacrifices who is sacrificed to what by whom no one will tell you.

'The laws of sacrifice exist but no woman and no man can explain them. All we see is the blood. But whose? As soon as there's blood it's mine, as soon as there's blood it's yours.

'If you can't understand me that's because I'm talking to you about the incomprehensible. Do you understand?'

Obscurely and without understanding Zami could feel the blood flowing out like her body's tears, without being able to stop it.

'We women we're against our own sacrifice, but how to avoid it? We women who are a mix of mother and son?' "

Relations in *Manna* are obscured: inside to outside, Nelson to Winnie, Osip to Nadezhda, memory to forgetfulness. Sacrifice, after all, though most often the plight of wives, has also been the plight of poets, whose sacrifices have been made in the realm of "real life."[84]

In the landscape called *Manna*, the women appear to be the heroines of their husbands' stories, but Zami and Nadezhda were also writers.[85] Indeed, in *Manna* Nadezhda is portrayed as playing Virgil to Mandelstam's Dante, a writer in her own right and the one who leads, not the one who follows. Nadezhda and Winnie also serve as figures of Isis, remembering their dismembered men, giving them a chance for rebirth through them. And the unfolding of the textually woven tissue that is *Manna* is as well an unfolding of the heroinism of Winnie Mandela. As Verena Conley has put it in her most recent book on Hélène Cixous: "New riches are born of pain and the story of absolute love in the face of hatred or *apart-hate* is carried off in the conundrums of history. What could have been an ordinary love story did not take place. Winnie Mandela lost an ordinary kind of paradise to gain an extraordinary one made up of spiritual riches."[86] As it was for the heroes and heroines of Greek tragedy, misfortune is a distinction, a sign used to mark those who surpass the human scale.

The text tells us that in the register of myth or tragedy, women often choose whatever sacrificial gestures are necessary in order to remain associated with life, love, and trust.[87] We see how, through sacrificing herself as centralized identity and locus of desires longing for their own, proper, fulfillment, Zami of Bizana constructs Winnie Mandela, international political heroine. The figure of Zami functions as prime example of an attempt to negotiate the poststructuralist dilemma of feminism's relation to the subject.[88] As Diana Fuss has put it in her crucial book *Essentially Speaking: Feminism, Nature, & Difference*, "How do we reconcile the poststructuralist project to displace identity with the feminist project to reclaim it?"[89] Winnie, powerfully integrated signifier and identity, takes her place in the realm of politics by deconstructing Zami as privileged origin of subjectivity. And in order to do this, Zami must become mother to herself, must learn to nourish herself, because Nelson is first and foremost mother to his people. This state of affairs is made clear when they first eat together, and again the metaphor is one of nourishment. Nelson takes Zami to an Indian restaurant, and neither of them manages to eat much: she because the chicken curry he has chosen is too spicy for her to swallow, too overwhelming, and he because he is constantly interrupted by his people, who desire him in a virtually cannibalistic way. Later on in the story, Zami's heroism will once again be posed in terms of the production of nourishment, when, like the Christ of the loaves and fishes, she will be asked to make a meal for ten out of one mere pork chop.

In some sense, the Cixousian notion of sacrifice too, another continuing preoccupation in her oeuvre, has changed in *Manna*. A central female figure of sacrifice for the Western literary tradition is Eurydice, who has been analyzed by Blanchot as symbolizing the (female) sacred, the essential night that must be sacrificed for the (male) poet to be able take on his identity and task as creator.[90] "He is Orpheus only in the song: he cannot have any relation to Eurydice except within the hymn."[91] Indeed, the Latin epithet that characterizes Eurydice in Virgil's version of the myth is *moritura*, "she who is going to die." In *The Space of Literature*, Blanchot informs us of the primacy of this myth for his own conception of the literary space, when he tells us that the section entitled "Orpheus's Gaze" is his book's center.[92] Blanchot, like Cixous, works much on the question of what it is to be a poet, but unlike hers, his answers entrain the myth of Orpheus, "the equivalent in letters of the oedipal myth in psychoanalysis,"[93] as primary metaphor. In the chapter mentioned here he states, "Writing begins with Orpheus's gaze."[94] And as we know from the myth, this gaze is deadly. For Blanchot, Eurydice is the figure toward which art, desire, and death are all traveling, but it is only through a detour, the gaze of Orpheus, his backward glance that kills Eurydice, that any of these three forces can be approached or approach each other. In the Blanchotian construction of the myth, Orpheus wants Eurydice

in her distance, with her closed body

and sealed face—wants to see her not
when she is visible, but when she is
invisible, and not as the intimacy of a
familiar life, but as the foreignness of
what excludes all intimacy, and wants,
not to make her live, but to have living
in her the plenitude of her death.[95]

Hélène Cixous has said in discussion that "to write on, to talk on women, on the corpses of dead women, is one of the recurrent motives in Blanchot's texts,"[96] and one of her own first attempts to dislocate the supremacy of the Orpheus–Eurydice myth was in her book *Illa,* which opened the decade in question in this essay.[97] In some ways, *Illa* can be read as a companion text to *Manna. Illa* is a text of the earth, whereas *Manna* is a text of the sky. Both are about absence due to separation, and about the heroic creation of a new reality principle in the face of devastating loss. "In a strange reality, on another scene, the 'presence' of the other body is felt even after 'separation.' "[98] In *Illa,* Cixous explores the Ceres–Proserpina myth and offers it up as enabling countermyth, as the genesis myth of a "feminine writing."[99] As we remember, Ceres' daughter Koré is abducted one day by Pluto, king of the lower world, while she is picking flowers in one of her mother's fields. In this world she receives her name of the father, Proserpina, and because she has eaten a pomegranate seed after nine days of refusing hell's nourishment, she is doomed to live out a third of her life in the lower world as Pluto's queen. During this time each year her mother, Ceres, goddess of the harvest, withholds her gifts from the earth, thereby transforming it into a frozen desert of wintry mourning.

The critical impulse to penetrate a text, an impulse that becomes especially aroused in some when the text is a difficult and mysterious one, an impulse that is not a reader's desire to taste but a critic's desire to master, is teased and rebuffed by the texts of Cixous in wily and subtle ways. I mean to say: it is always more complicated than that. Although the comparison I have just offered between the Blanchotian and the Cixousian comings-to-writing holds some interpretative water, there are other layers. The text *Illa* itself, although *about* the privileging of a pre-Oedipal paradise of presence, a female relationship once described as "women-as-beings-of-proximity [who] are still back in, or must go back to, 'those times' when knowledge is, was, not predicated on distance and sight but has the immediacy of smell, taste, and touch,"[100] is written *after* the rape, after the father's abduction and naming. In another way, what Cixous is proposing is a triple feminine subject from which to write: "as mother, daughter, and absent mother."[101] Writing even *with* presence is nevertheless based on a certain absence, and because language always presupposes absence, as I have tried to demonstrate by calling on the Abraham and Torok model, writing is always an *après-coup*.[102] Pre-Oedipal experiences were not symbolized in their time because they occurred before language, and so instead became mere traces in the unconscious. Writing is the inscription of these traces, the memory of them made linguistic. This pre-Oedipal culture, buried by "man," must be recaptured by "woman," in order for the *her* in her to come to creating.

The joyous exploration of the pre-Oedipal continues in Cixous's other fictions of the 1980s prior to *Manna*. *With ou l'art de l'innocence* is in part about a being *with*: with child, in a childhood before the law. And *Le livre de Promethea* inscribes the pre-Oedipal as linked to freedom, joy, and an innocence beyond ignorance. In *Promethea*, Cixous negotiates a writing with presence, reacting against the absenting nature of writing itself, both practically and linguistically. In her recent book *Hélène*

Cixous: A Politics of Writing, Morag Shiach traces yet another lineage: "In its analysis of the transformative capacity of a relationship of love, . . . [*Manna*] can . . . be related to both *Le livre de Promethea* and *La Bataille d'Arcachon*."[103]

The figures of Zami and Nadezhda, however, hint at a further twist in the Cixousian topos relating absence, presence, and creation, and one that is truly new for Cixous. In *Manna*, unlike in *Illa*, separation leads not to winter but to creation and nourishment in spite of absence, against absence, not because of it. This distinction is crucial, for, thereby, Zami's and Nadezhda's heroinisms are a tribute to life in the season of hell. Their survival is what they generate, like a writing, from absence.

Hélène Cixous has been accused of taking her metaphors literally, in a manner whereby metaphor is swallowed whole, as it were. I submit, however, that it is Cixous's critics who have disingenuously chosen to take her "metonymic metaphors" of the body literally, and then, in an act of circular logic, hastily accused her of subscribing to an anatomy-is-destiny position with regard to language.[104] The act of poetry according to Cixous is always a struggle against this type of reification, and her remetaphorizations are attempts to symbolize the specifically feminine part of the human imaginary, so long kept silent. In *Manna*, one of the major mythic re-creations is that it is not death that is delegated to the other, as in the Orphic myth, but life. All of Cixous's fictions are living vocal monuments to memory as fidelity and hope, and none more so than this one. The "reality principle," described by Freud in "Mourning and Melancholia"[105] as "gaining the day" in a successful work of mourning, is not common currency here; Zami's and Nadezhda's calls are invocations and not mere evocations, always still believing in the possibility of the other's true return. The Freudian postulate that sees denial of death as psychotic is contrasted with the courage of Zami's undying hope and Nadezhda's unfailing memory. In the figured language that is Cixous's, ladies-seen-waiting are often linked figuratively to women waiting for and giving birth, living through a pain that will lead to life. The heroic gesture of immense strength that is the effort to create a reality of presence in spite of absence is metaphorically linked to the maternal body, a body figured by Cixous as so full of life and nourishment that it cannot accept death into itself at all.[106]

The other matrix of *Manna* is the ostrich, that unknown and tragic heroine, unknown because she is forgotten and has gone unrecognized, tragic because in the movement from prehistory to history, the ostrich lost her bird-being. *Manna* is dedicated to the ostrich, and Winnie Mandela appears for the first time in the text under the sign of the ostrich, wearing a hat covered with her feathers. In this text, the ostrich appears as another Cixousian variation on the figure of Prometheus, a figure who has given fire, light, and justice to humanity, and paid for these with her very own being. The ostrich is figured here as the primordial origin of Africa, never recompensed for her troubles, but willing to sacrifice herself in a gesture of commitment to trust: the ostrich is described as having sacrificed her wings rather than surrender to mistrust. Such a commitment to trust signifies certain death for she who trusts, but continued life for the force of trust itself.

———

I have tried to point to *Manna* as embodying five major trends of the Cixousian oeuvre in the 1980s: the attempt to answer, through writing, the cry of how to create culture after Auschwitz; the shift from the politicization of poetry toward the poeticization of politics; and, in order to accomplish these projects, the use of a strategy of hybrid pollination between the two poles of oppositional logic. I have also traced briefly the Cixousian problematics of orality and sacrifice, from *Illa* to *Manna*. I have yet to explore fully a final term I would like to touch: the impact on her fiction of Cixous's writings for the theater.

"The Body and the Story of Someone Else"

Most notably, the 1980s were the theater years for Hélène Cixous. I am referring in particular to the two major plays already mentioned, both written for and performed at the Théâtre du Soleil in Paris: *L'Histoire terrible mais inachevée de Norodom Sihanouk, Roi du Cambodge*, which is about events leading to the domination of Cambodia by the Khmer Rouge in 1975 and the terrible massacres that followed (often referred to as the "killing fields"), and *L' Indiade ou L'Inde de leurs rêves*, which deals with the struggle for Indian independence from Great Britain and the subsequent partition of colonial India into present-day India and Pakistan. Both these plays, and playwriting in general, have clearly informed the writing of *Manna*. It was through her work with the theater that Cixous turned her eyes and ears toward the other's continents, and *Manna* continues this trend in fiction, just as it also continues the difficult project of writing about real historical moments and personages. Cixous portrays this process using theatrical analogies:

> *Actors write with their bodies. I do*
> *the same type of thing when I write*
> *about others. It's very vertiginous.*
> *We both become somebody else, it's a*
> *maddening experience. . . . You have*

to live another life. You have to get
up, and instead of putting on your
own clothes, you put on the body
and the story of someone else.[107]

As Cixous pointed out in her famous manifesto "The Laugh of the Medusa,"[108] what has been called by others *écriture féminine* posits the writer's body as one of the sources and origins of her scriptural impulses. According to this relationship between writing and the body, a rapport with any figure other than the author's many "I's" must nonetheless pass through her body in some way. This is a circuitous operation that Cixous shied away from in most of her poetic texts of the 1980s, but which she approached during the writing of *Manna* with some attraction and curiosity.

In creating *Manna*, then, Cixous encountered this problem common to contemporary, post-*nouveau roman* fictional writing: how to introduce that elusive and problematic category of the fictional character into a textuality carved from the disruptive authorial territories of body and unconscious? Cixous's writing has most often been both fascinated and frustrated with the plural and provisional quality of her own author's "I's," and by maintaining the delicately balanced, near but not too near relation to the other for which she has striven, in an attempt to avoid writing toward assassination and appropriation. A poetic writer such as Cixous, cognizant of the slippage in problematic that occurs upon trying to mingle another's desires, voices, and identities with the desires, voices, and identities of her own multiple and sometimes competing "I's," must necessarily be suspicious of moving toward the more easily locatable play of differences between discrete fictional characters, and away from insisting on the differences within (one's nonunitary) subjectivity itself. And in fact, the personages appearing in *Manna* are rather more like oneiric "figures" than like "characters" in any traditional sense.

The effects of such a metamorphosis are vibrantly present in, among others, the scene of sensual love that takes place between Nelson and Winnie Mandela in *Manna*. A woman writer limns making love to the body of a woman, Winnie Mandela, from the "eye" of Nelson, in astonishingly convincing and violent detail. Cixous herself described the perils of writing this particular scene in a talk she gave in 1988 at San Francisco State University:

> *Manna* is the first book I've written
> where real characters appear in a
> piece of fiction, and I'm glad to have
> tried to do that. I had to write, for
> the first time in my life, in the third
> person. This was a terrible experience
> for me because I both enjoyed it and
> at the same time always had the
> feeling that at each step I might be
> deceiving myself, I might be lying in
> spite of myself, because the third
> person is so far away. Very often,
> then, I had to come back to an "I." I
> had to say "I" as Mandela, I had to
> say "I" as Mandelstam, which was
> very difficult to do, with men of
> course particularly. Because a man

like Mandela, for instance, has to
have his body to survive. . . . At one
point I did write in the first person
as Mandela, and in a scene of sexual
enjoyment. How I did it I do not
know. It was a bit dreamlike.
Afterwards, I had to conclude that of
course it wasn't complete, I couldn't
do everything, but I think it must
have been homosexual; that is, it was
my own knowledge of a woman's
body that I could transfer to
Mandela's body. That was very
strange. But I do not think I lied in
doing that, I think it is the woman in
Mandela—because he is also a
woman—who really inscribed this
scene in the text.[109]

Cixous has attributed her ability to operate this sort of
metamorphosed identification in *Manna* to her experience
writing for the theater:

Everything you do changes your way
of writing, your acquired

craftsmanship, or your wisdom. It's
true that creating characters is
something I hadn't done before with
fiction. I didn't even know I could do
it. After writing for the theater, I
suddenly realized I could create as
many characters as I wanted to. The
question I knew within came to the
surface again strongly: why didn't I
write characters into fiction? Why
did I resist? It made me think that in
my next work of fiction, which
turned out to be Manna, *I'd like to*
treat real characters in my own kind
of poetical writing, which is
something very different from writing
for the theater.[110]

Cixous further illuminates the nature of her resistance to writing the fictional other, and here we see that it is in the exploration of this resistance that the dual problems of how to write the unwritable and how to write the other coincide:

It's purely moral. I do not like to tell
lies, or say things I'm not absolutely
sure of. . . . When something is

*rooted in me, when I know its source
to be myself, I am absolutely sure
that it won't be wrong, it won't be
falsified. I am the guarantor of what
I write. Perhaps I have a
philosophical or a metaphysical
leaning. I'm not interested in working
on characters that don't carry
essential human themes. . . . I think
this is what I have difficulty with in
fiction, it isn't really my scene for
such reflection. Finally, however,
I did accomplish that type of
reflection in* Manna, *and I was able
to do it because I had chosen
characters who for me are
outstanding. The Mandelas and the
Mandelstams are examples of
humanity.*[111]

It has been pointed out that the type of fidelity referred to here and elsewhere in Cixous should not be confused with realism, but "more accurately approached as the problem of making figurative the 'vision' of the writer."[112] As in *Sihanouk* and *L'Indiade*, universality serves as a bridge linking the author's particular multiplicity to the historical figures chosen as textual and theatrical subjects, carrying these contemporary characters over to the territory of Shakespeare's heroes.

Through Hell, I Glimpse: Paradise

And what of the impossible task with which I introduced this essay? How to write of history, after history, in history? Part of our modern dilemma stems, I believe, from an incapacity for thinking (about) evil. We have remained for the most part helpless in the face of radical evil. Is this in part because contiguous to the death of God has been the loss of his alter ego, the Devil? Hannah Arendt has argued that far from being a devil's handiwork, modern evil springs merely from banality. Perhaps; but in *Manna* there is a "religious substance" present, as there is in Hélène Cixous's writings in general.[113] Let us turn again to Deborah Jenson:

> *"Soul" is one of many terms that are*
> *generally banished to the*
> *metaphysical broom closet these days*
> *but that Cixous gifts with a*
> *reincarnation, in the sense of a*
> *reconstituted relationship to the*
> *body. The soul for her is an*
> *"ultrasensual substance."*[114]

In *Manna*, the Devil, like the human soul, has been reinstated, as has his habitat. Here he takes on many shapes; one of the most fearsome is the many-headed hitler[115] of the chapter entitled "The Visit from the Ostrich." In the following passage from this chapter, Zami dreams of a body-to-body battle with hitler:

> *The battle against the demon lasts*
> *and will last a hundred years. With*
> *her own hands with furious fingers*
> *she saws away at evil stalk by stalk.*
> *Twists and saws, with a disgusted*
> *power. There is something dirty and*
> *immemorial in the limp persistence of*
> *the Old Man. As though he were*
> *obstinately persisting at deserving*
> *hatred throughout centuries of*
> *centuries because that is what he*
> *enjoys. Pig following upon pig*
> *interminably. Will I never see the end*
> *of them? . . .*
>
>   *If it were a man one could kill*
> *it; but the hitler is a numerous*
> *innumerable pig with an*
> *undiscoverable soul, if it even has*
> *one in it, and so we will have to*
> *stomp on it and saw away at it and*
> *carve it up and trample it down for*
> *hours maybe and for generations, for*

it is only at the price of this deadly
digging that we can hope to arrive at
the root of evil.

Poetry participates in this slaughter, or attempts to. And this attempt finally is to my mind one of the very definitions of poetic writing in the twentieth century, and is a party to the constant unresolved encounter between language and the inexpressible. Poetry is not a substitute for politics or for life, but can it not be its handmaiden, or even its heroine? Although we could say that poetry does not really speak the unspeakable, it gives at least the illusion of doing so in its song, its antidote to silence. Cixous expresses this when she explains what she is hoping to accomplish, in all her audacity:

What would the naked intolerable
be? It would be the vision of charnel-
houses, the naked charnel-house,
bones, the grimace of the
concentration camp. These are things
which the individual must go on a
solitary pilgrimage to contemplate.
We must go to Auschwitz or to what
remains of the Cambodian charnel-
houses and wrap ourselves up in
meditation on these remains. But this
is without language, obviously it is
done in silence, and it isn't art. Once

there is art, of whatever kind, there is transposition, there is metaphor, and language is already metaphor. . . . the word placing itself on that which would otherwise be only silence and death. This is a huge problem, it is the problem of the poet. Can a poet permit him- or herself, and does she have the strength to speak about that which has been reduced to silence? Wouldn't this be blasphemy? Isn't it a necessity? Isn't this exactly what we must attempt to do, knowing all the while the paradox, knowing there is a price to be paid on both sides: something is lost but something is safeguarded. This is the question I am always asking myself. My choice has been made, after all I have decided to try to speak about what takes our breath away. Because more than anything else, I am suspicious of silence. There is such a thing as a respectful silence, there can be a silence that sings, but I'm suspicious of human silence.

1

In general, it is a silence that
represses.[116]

It is especially contingent on women writing as women, as it is on writers presenting all repressed voices, to speak out over silence. One may wonder, as Cixous herself does in *Manna*, in what register and with what "right" she came to write this text. "How shall I dare to speak of all these events which apparently haven't happened to me? And which are superiorly cruel and superiorly gentle, superiorly to my experience. How shall I dare to speak of a black destiny, me, whose destiny is apparently white?"[117] Such questions and concerns can be explored in the reading, and as has been pointed out, "the reader [of a Cixous text] is always free to jump in the circle or to turn away. Who is affected, when and where, may depend on one's sex, cultural origin and/or memory."[118] This reader for one receives and retransmits *Manna for the Mandelstams for the Mandelas* as a stand against silence, a voice offering that hopefully will "make the reader vibrate."[119] For, what the text tells us of its protagonists is true too of itself: "everything that comes into their voices is saved."

Hélène Cixous is a poet whom some in North America (as in France) have seemed to want to silence, and have "judged in a reiteration of our Anglo-American tradition with its own system of clichés,"[120] at times merely serving the market forces of what in this country is called the Academy, at others mostly due both to a misreading and to a virtual nonreading of her enormous oeuvre.[121] But just as the repressed so often returns, so will the paradise proposed in poetry continue to be brooded and hatched, for those who wish to approach it. This, then, is what Cixous has accomplished in *Manna*: a certain paradise is regained; what once was lost is found again, not by going backward, but by going forward, to a "second paradise."[122] This second paradise is not for the sentimental; it is for those who have struggled through hell, and made it to an *other* side. Nor is it a place, but rather a space, the space of writing. As Verena Andermatt Conley has put it, "Perhaps, the very key is that one is never 'home,' but constantly exiled, wandering, looking for the key to paradise. The exiled poet hopes to find paradise through writing, but the key is in the *writing* and not in the recovery of a place."[123] *Manna* bridges that space, and is, for all of us who choose to taste it, a remembering, a transforming, and a food called hope.

Translation or Transformation?

> *The translator must assure the survival,* which is to say the growth, *of the original, which, insofar as it is living on, never ceases to be transformed and to grow. It modifies the original even as it also modifies the translating language. This process— transforming the original as well as the translation—is the translation contract between the original and the translating text.*
>
> —Jacques Derrida[124]

Any "translation" of a text by Hélène Cixous tends by definition more toward a transformation of her work, a fixing of what in French is in constant "larcenous flight." I have tried hard to ferry this text across from the French to the English shore, but I fear the form has not been ferried properly, or rather, that the ferried form is altogether other than the French.

In the case of *Manna*, the translator's challenge is due less to the level of undecidability, present in most texts by Cixous to a much greater degree, and more to the level of poeticity at which the text functions. I have chosen occasionally to "trespass" the closely literal translation tendencies usually the most effective when dealing with a Cixous text, in the interest, here, of poetry. I must confess as well to a love of Latinate cognates that some might find "un-American"; I found myself unable or unwilling to cure myself of this predilection, partially because, to quote the consummate Cixous translator, Betsy Wing:

> *A major risk for a translator is the tendency to make a text so "readable"—so "natural"—in English that the words are effectively domesticated and, entering a realm of banality that is frequently the one Cixous seeks to displace, lose the psychic density essential to a poetic text.*[125]

In some cases I can cite contextual or textural reasons in defense of my imaginary choices. For instance, I have translated the French verb *rester* consistently as "to remain," rather than as "to stay behind" or some other more colloquial solution, because the play on *rester* and its substantive *les restes* is constant throughout the text. Maintaining the more exact English couple "to remain" and "the remains" seemed important to me. A similar logic can be found behind my choice to maintain the verb "to pass" and its many variations in English ("to pass by," "to come to pass," "to pass through," "to surpass," "to pass away") perhaps more often than some readers find comforting. The French text is replete with the verbs of this family, particularly the verb *passer* itself, and this is, it seems to me, one of the unifying verbs and notions of the entire text, linking up as it does with the problems of "passes" and "passports" experienced by the Mandelas and the Mandelstams, respectively, as well as with the abundance of birds passing above, the passing over borders, passing trains, and the passage of time. I have also chosen frequently to opt for the use of the gerundive in English, as I consider it to be a very Cixousian tense, and indeed, Cixous herself has written that she feels its lack in French.[126]

Hélène Cixous writes for the ear, with a sense of music seldom equaled.[127] Studying *Manna for the Mandelstams for the Mandelas* on the level of signifiers and phoneme chains, one sees and especially hears a constant flight or concert of visual and auditive patterns. Many of the rhyming and rhythmic structures that absolutely teem in this text cannot be rendered exactly, and I have not tried to do so. What I have attempted to do is to create an English "version" with its own voice, its own breathing and rhyming rhythms, its own alliterative constellations, an assonant English text for the ear also.[128] (And in this English translation the ear is seen and heard often, in words like earth, heart, years, tears, fears, in the hearings, appearings, and disappearings scattered all over the text.) To this end, I have studded the text with as many rhymes and alliterations as I could, wherever I could, in an economy of alternance between loss and recuperation.

For example, the following passage was rendered in such a way as to create three internal English rhymes:

Pour bien courir tous les sentiers de

*l'Enfer de ce siècle, combien de
souliers me faudra-t-il user, se
demandait Osip, avançant juste
derrière Alighieri, ne lâchant pas le
maître d'une semelle, maintenant
qu'il avait un passeport pour la Cité
Dolente.*

*To really travel well all the roads of
this century's Hell, how many shoes
will I have to use, Osip wondered,
advancing just behind Alighieri, not
letting a sole come between him and
the master, now that he had a
passport for the Doleful City.*

Or, an *alexandrin* in French can sometimes be rendered by an iambic pentameter in English, as in the following example, in which *le soleil se mettait lentement à genoux* becomes "the sun was sinking slowly to its knees." The additions here of an "extra" or "equivalent" richness in English serve, I hope, in a small way to "make up" for losses incurred when ferrying across another beautiful *alexandrin* like the following: *l'ancienne peur de ceux qui meurent à contrecoeur*, which in English becomes simply: "the ancient fear of those who die reluctantly."

The voice breathing life into this English version is, of course, that of Hélène Cixous coursing through me, but I was also influenced by my readings of English translations of the Mandelstams' works, the Winnie Mandela book, the contemporary Bible and *The Divine Comedy*, just as Cixous was traversed by her readings of these same texts. I believe the overall effect of this multivoiced approach to be one of rendering more closely an equivalent poetic weight, since certain of the other poetic functions have been lost, as I have described. There is also a plural modality operating in this text on the level of nouns, which I have chosen to maintain, and so the reader will encounter not only happiness but happinesses, not flesh but fleshes, musics rather than merely music, and so on. Universal nouns reminiscent of allegories appear as multiples here.

I cannot stress enough the extent to which the rules of French versification are everpresent in *Manna*. Cixous explains: "For *Manna* I constantly told myself: the fictional genre must interchange with poetry, I wrote it almost all the time as a poem. I needed what the poem procures for us: a beyond language. That which the poem makes us hear, its own music plus the echo of that music. What is important for me is that echo, the beyond music. What is left us of the poem is not only the interior of the poem, not only its message, or simply its literal meaning, it is this beach, this bank, this shore, between its music and silence. Poems are surrounded by silence. Books are not surrounded by silence, they are so long, they proceed, you are at the interior of the book; with poems there is always a border, and you must hear this border too."[129] The form that is *Manna*'s, then, that of the long prose poem, urged me to include certain syntactical rhythms and patterns that are not generally associated with contemporary English prose, but are most definitely associated with poetry in English. As many of us are unaccustomed to reading much poetry, we have tended to forget how supple English syntax can be. The creation of a translation offers, I believe, an opportunity to infuse the host language with the blood of a new writing, which often is also a reminder of already existing possibilities. In preparing this translation, I have tried to remind myself of and let resonate all the varied richnesses of my own tongue.

In *Manna* there is a use of syntax and tense that is particular to French and more so to Cixous, as if she were attempting to follow the quirky flow of thought processes themselves by constantly changing tense and tranforming order. For instance, in French one can place the grammatical object at the head of a sentence, thereby giving it a place of privilege, but this is less easily done in English. Sometimes I have maintained similar structures anyway, at other times I have rearranged the clauses to more closely resemble "everyday English." In terms of verb tense I have stayed close to the French, because it seemed to me that the quirkiness of the sudden shifts was as strange in French as it would be in English, and because I felt the comment being made in this manner regarding the slippery nature of time, in this text that crosses so many times, was important to the reading experience.

Another innovation I have chosen to maintain is Cixous's preference for the conjunction "and" over all others, and for balance in her sentences. For instance, she will often propose a sentence that defies the traditional logic of grammar (and the logic of thought since Descartes) by doing away with the tendency to set seeming opposites against one another grammatically. She will speak of someone "who wants to run across the water and does not run," of a cotton cloth, spread out to dry on a meadow, "that hides and hides nothing." There are no "buts," "yets," or "howevers" here. Juxtaposed states exist simultaneously and are connected, as opposed to being opposed, to one another. As Katherine Cummings has put it, referring to Shoshana Felman's work on the grammatical copula, "As the mark of supplementarity in language, 'and' undoes oppositions and destabilizes power relationships that have been established historically between subjects in order to effect their mutual coinvolvement or coimplication . . .

'and' consistently demands movement of and between terms."[130]

Another trace of Cixousian style I have generally maintained is the way in which terms are almost always repeated, thereby acknowledging the importance of each term and its idea, and the importance of each separate clause. Cixous doesn't write: "You don't want to believe me but you do." Instead, she insists on writing: "You don't want to believe me but you do believe me." Or: "I know I'm going to marry his white struggle and his black struggle," and not: "I know I'm going to marry his white struggle and his black."

Ultimately, I remain unconvinced by the argument that a translation must attempt to be "the same" on all levels as its original. As I consider this in any case impossible, I do not feel uncomfortable with the idea that a certain haunting and even awkward strangeness remind the reader that this is, after all, a foreign text, an "equivalence in difference" as Jakobson has called translation,[131] that she or he is encountering. Although the highly fluent, (overly) easily readable translation into English has traditionally been the one to be lauded and applauded, I have seen too many instances in which the achievement of such an English version has been at the utter expense of the original. I prefer to stick my neck out in a different direction. To a certain extent, what the French have delineated as *écriture* (and Jacques Derrida has called Cixous's texts the most important contemporary examples of this term according to his definition of it), is always on the side of the uncanny. I have striven to allow in my "voice choices" as many *coups d'écriture* as I could. Certain turns of phrase I have chosen, such as the many expressions using the verb "to pass" that I mentioned earlier, are consummately English, although fallen somewhat into desuetude.

Finally, let us hope the translators of the 1611 King James Bible were right when they wrote: "Translation it is that openeth the window to let in the light; that breaketh the shell, that we may eat the kernel."[132] If so, then translation too, like *Manna*, can be a way to see the sky and a means to a substitute food, and to the extent I have managed to crack the window and the nut, something will not have been lost.

Much has been written regarding the problems inherent in writing a preface, particularly for a text that confounds critical discourse. I have figured my essay here as another level of translation, and, as with most translations, it is regrettably a less rich oversimplification of the original to which it refers. To attempt to fit a Cixous text into the critical categories of themes or historical developments is to do a certain violence to the complexity of the weaving, as such a writing cannot and will not be captured or pinned down. This is perhaps the fate of all expository attempts. But a pre-face is also a presentation, in all senses of that word, in the form of an echo or an accompaniment to the poetic text. And so I present *Manna*; I make a present of it to the reader, and I hope to have rendered it more present to you.

I would like to thank Anne Berger, Hélène Cixous, Peter T. Connor, the participants at the University of Virginia's conference "Exploring the Unexplored" on September 26, 1992, Susan Sellers, Ann Smock, my reader Betsy Wing, and especially Melanie Fallon and Marguerite Sandré, for reviewing various or all sections of the translation for me. They have offered felicitous solutions to perturbing problems, and have saved me from many mistakes. I would like to thank Sigrid Berka, Alexandra Bloom, Peter T. Connor, and Ann Smock, for painstakingly reading and making valuable suggestions regarding drafts at various stages in the writing of this preface, and Bertrand Augst, Verena Andermatt Conley, Melanie Fallon, Deborah Jenson, Zita Nunes, Camillo Penna, and Avital Ronell, for their general counsel and their encouragement of my efforts at explication, often, I feared, a fundamentally doomed endeavor. I would like to give special thanks to Roland Ganter for having provided me with all the computer-related and other practical assistance I so often needed, as well as with a comfortable atmosphere, full of time and nourishment, in which to work, and to Hélène Cixous for her encouragement of my work and her intellectual mentoring, which now spans more than a decade. Thanks finally to my research assistants, Melanie Fallon and Tesha McCord, for their help in the preparation of the notes that accompany both this essay and the translation itself.

E come augelli surti di rivera
 quasi congratulando a lor pasture,
 fanno di sé or tonda or altra schiera,
sì dentro ai lumi sante creature
 volitando cantavano, e faciensi
or D, or I, or L in sue figure.

DANTE, *Paradiso*, Canto XVIII[1]

Dedication to
the Ostrich

When the terrestrial earth is lost, the celestial earth remains.

No more plateaus of perfumed skin, no more hills raced up and over by horses and gazelles, no more waves swept and rowed by branches, no more streams, their bellies full of animals,

There remains the earth above, the boundless sea, its belly full of stars

The airy earth remains, all traversed by birds.

In Voronezh[2] of the four winters, OM was living his last winter, remains of a great poet chased from the earth, chased like the starling by the storm, cast here, there, below, no, no

1

more below, above, beyond, no hope, no rest, no companion no compassion, the world is a bad caving in,

Living on nothing, on the remains of memories, on the remains of fingernails, the remains of terrestrial tissue, on the remains of language once numerous and proud, today laid waste, a man with a worn-out name, with a heart consumed by the cold, the banishing hurricane, raging thoughts,

And into his verse only stars would come this last winter only stars would still come and certain birds.

(Until at the end of this last winter came a day without light, and Osip Mandelstam upon lifting his head saw only a sky swarming with worms of verse.[3] And all the birds and all the stars remained in his verse)

Happily there are birds, without which exile would be infinite, the desert would be uninterrupted, there would be no more dams to the deluges, no more hope at the boundaries of hopelessness,

and hell would not only be infernal but wintry and congealed.

Happily, when there are no more letters, no more bridge, no more mail, all wires are cut, and when man arrives in a place deprived of all space, that roars like the sea in a squabble of contrary winds,

there are the cranes up above who go on singing their lay, and, forming a long line in the air, rend the distance with their riotous wings

there are the swallows that go on losing and finding their nests again, making and undoing the fabric of our lives,

And in a single song of Hell crowd together at least ten species of tender gracious birds, the indispersible remains of warm stolen lives of flight

We need doves to cope with the worst.

Ultimately it is to the ostrich bird that I would like to dedicate this book,

The ostrich is the most discreetly tragic living being of all prehistoric creation. The ostrich is a bird that is not a bird. It is the greatest bird in the world.

The History of the world began in Africa. At the beginning of Africa was the ostrich. The ostrich has a destiny. This destiny is tragic and tragic: it is comparable in misfortune to well-known tragic destinies, like that of Oedipus, that of Achilles, that of Prometheus, but especially to the destinies of forgotten heroes.

The worst misfortune of the ostrich is that almost everyone is unaware that the ostrich had a destiny. We have forgotten the truth, the myth, the goodness of the ostrich.

The ostrich is an unsung heroine. Without the ostrich, for millennia there would not have been in Africa either human being, or justice, or light.

When man was still but a tiny chilly wildebeest, a clawless animal, a wingless bird, a rootless tree, a motherless suckling, the ostrich was a great bird like a tree, with wings more powerful than the eagle's and a pensive gaze. Her entire being radiated order, strength, and justice. Her immense innumerable feathers were all of the same length. At noon they were light and cool like the morning mist. In the evening they became warm and thick like a fox's fur. Seeing the ostrich flying among the mountains one had to believe the gods existed, and they were good. But seeing the wildebeest stark naked and trembling could cause you doubt.

The whole History of Africa began thanks to the ostrich's sacrifice. It is she who saved the human creature, it is she who revealed the secret of fire: it is the ostrich who gave a gift of life, of intelligence, of light, to the weakest of animals, the human animal.

The ostrich gave us the keys to the world. And in exchange — she paid. We wrenched her own keys from her.

Her beautiful feathers of fairness were clipped and paralyzed. She was condemned to prison, she lost the air, the clouds, the happiness of seeing the earth from the celestial viewpoint of birds. She became the bird that does not fly. The bird in vain. The plaything of the gods.

But that's not all. She lost everything, and she gained nothing. She didn't gain men's gratitude. The sacrifice effaced.

Only the Egyptians in the time of the pharaohs were faithful to the ostrich's truth. Their kings always kept flyswatters trimmed with ostrich feathers, to make the air of justice and inner light that the ostrich gave to humanity flow through the heat of their palaces.

The free ostrich is now extinct. Today African ostriches are chickens raised in huge henhouses for their eggs and not for themselves. One ostrich egg makes an omelet for a dozen people. In South Africa one eats scrambled ostrich egg for breakfast.

The ostrich has always trusted. Trust is the cause of all misfortunes and all joys. A life without trust is a night without stars. Whoever accords her trust to human beings must also at the same time accord her forgiveness. For her trust will be betrayed, her eyes will be gouged out, her wings will be clipped, and never grow back.

But whoever accords her trust to no one, whoever gives herself up to trust as one surrenders to incomprehensible and mysterious life, whoever puts her trust in a magic bottle and entrusts it to the sea, whoever yields to trust without expecting any recompense, shall be recompensed.

When Samson forced himself to accord his trust he was betrayed, naturally, and just as the distrust hidden in his trust had anticipated. It is a rather complicated story to tell, but anyone can understand it, for we have all betrayed our own and been betrayed by our own, just as we betray ourselves.

But when Samson was plunged into darkness at Gaza,[4] without eyes, without wings, and his ankles in irons, then his soul soared in the flight of the ancient ostrich and lifted itself beyond human walls up to the moon. And there above reigned a radiant trust. You have never seen a day as dazzling as the one that rose in that night. That is why Samson left the ruins of life smiling with joy.

Another name for Samson: Nelson.

The ostrich hides her head in her coat so as not to see the furious face of Brutus. This is how she protects her look of trust. Was the ostrich betrayed and assassinated? Or did she give herself up to death out of a love for trust?

The truth of the ostrich is that she preferred to die trusting, rather than to outlive trust. One might think she died of trust, but she died so as never to have to witness the assassination of trust.

I insist on protesting against the calumny the ostrich has been victim to: the ostrich does not hide her head in the sand when there is danger. It is we who close our eyes from fear, and pretend the ostrich no longer exists, since behind our stingy eyelids we can no longer see her.

The ostrich has extremely piercing sight, she can see so far away she always feels very alone, far ahead of our nearsightedness.

The ostrich is noble, powerful, courageous, and peaceful. The roar of the angry ostrich is a magnificent warning. The ostrich is the lion's possibility. But nonviolent. The Mandela family counts among its royal ancestors the first descendants of the ostrich. It is a line of majestic angers, controlled by the will to not destroy.

Moreover, equality of the sexes has existed from time immemorial amongst ostriches. Males and females take turns watching over all the eggs and all the children of the community.

This book would like to be a declaration of love to the forgotten ostrich, to this fire-giver and to all the fire-givers who pay with their wings so that human beings can see a bit more clearly in the dark.

To those who have been punished for having disrupted the uniformity of the night. Punished by a night without stars. To the seers deprived of the light of day, to the prophets of hope, to Nelson Mandela, who is being kept in a cage for having flown so fast ahead of his time.

To the poets who had the strength to not drop their pens in the heart of times without future. All that still remained of tomorrow held alive and sheltered in their frozen hands. To the women, to the mothers and sisters, without whom there would be neither flight nor ascension nor erection nor resurrection. Nor Divine Comedy.

And to all the winged avatars of the prophets, all equally free and uneatable: eagle, lammergeier, griffin, goshawk, vulture, kite, crow, sea gull, sparrow-hawk, swan, pelican, cormorant, stork, heron, hoopoe, ostriches of every genre and every species, signs, letters of augur flying across the voices of space and time.

This book is going to think a lot about Mandelstam, who while I was being born was dying and writing in star-filled snow to tomorrow's address and no one and never

And to think at the same time about Mandelstam and Mandela, two men who do not know each other, but the same sorrow knows them.

From Voronezh depart poems, which, descending the stairs of the universe, blindly divine and seek the one who does not know himself to be sought and divined.

From one continent to the other birds are passing, shouting with glory above our lands. And they are heard, these cries, they are received by unknown ears. All I know is that from one hemisphere to the next, pity takes a deep breath and moves on.

Mandelstam, Mandela, almonds in the bosom of the world,
Tomorrows sheltered in the century's shell,
Whoever has an ear must hear the future ripening within the walls of bitter time.

If I write in a broken way it is because I am in the process of contemplating in me the South African landscape. It is a landscape that takes my breath away. It is so ancient and so untamed. There is so much sky and so much earth and so little man. Minuscule, stirred by the wind, intimidated by the flocks of mountains suspended above the bush, judged weighed measured by the white bones which the creatures human and animal have abandoned just anywhere upon leaving, in the middle of the immortal continent, I see the world of before and after me. I see my mortality. And I see the time of forever. Whoever sees the African space perceives eternity.

I see her violet and innumerable nipples that nourish no one. I see her oceans of golden earth. I see my own little bones, invisible from the hilltops, no bigger than milk teeth. I see the beautiful, powerful carcass of a buffalo, reposing without anguish beneath this too much eternity. Ah, I nestle my tiny remains near the tranquil skeleton. And it is with the intoxicating sensation of the infinitely small within the infinitely great that the calcareous fragment that I am sets herself to thinking. Thoughts born in Africa are grandiose and sloped like those that come to us in a cathedral. They go from the lowest to the highest. They start at nothingness and cast themselves into the sky, hoping to find a port. I am nothingness flown over by flocks of migrating birds.

The wind blows very hard. Thoughts change forms and color like huge clouds. Sometimes they are clear and close to me, and I see them distinctly like stains of paint on the body of a young Xhosa[5] initiate, and I seem to be able to decipher the most ancient secrets. Sometimes they retreat suddenly to infinity, all the way back to where one cannot tell anymore where the sky begins where the earth ends, if it is the earth that mounts in the light or the mountain chain that kneels to sleep. Into my sky cloud silently palaces, giant barges, battles, temples, whales. All is vision. The air reveals. One believes one is seeing the unthinkable. To believe in seeing is such a joy.

The ostrich's feathers are black. They are of a brilliant whiteness. A white ostrich feather was standing on the goddess Maat's[6] head while she watched over the weighing of souls in Egypt.

The feather is white but I see it as a brilliant black. At the back of my eye the goddess Maat weighs the colors of day and night.

On May 1, 1986, Winnie Mandela was wearing a black hat, of black straw, a milliner's hat, and the hat bore long black feathers thrown backward by the wind. Beneath this hat, a great black woman who looked larger than nature. The hat attracted everyone's gaze. It was an extraordinary hat. She spoke before one hundred thousand African strikers.

The crowd was extraordinary. And what was most extraordinary was that in this crowd all you saw was her. I had never in my life seen such a hat. Such a glory. Such a pride. Such a woman. Such a victory. Those feathers were the future. This was clear to everyone. Winnie Mandela began to speak. She said: Nelson Mandela says: I am in prison. My people are

8

not free. But how could I lose faith, when I know that the future is ours. In prison I am free. Everyone looked up. At that moment a flight of birds went by very very high in the sky just above the crowd, but so high that at first no one saw a thing, all one heard was their cry rending the air, and suddenly there they were, and everyone saw the immense black majestic V descending slowly toward the plain, then climbing again, climbing again, and blending finally with the light of that day, yes it was the future and the one hundred thousand strikers saw it, just as I saw Winnie Mandela's hat.

Winnie's hat is her standard, her crown, her sword, her black horse, her panache, and her shield. At home, Winnie wears a brightly colored scarf. And she is called Zami.[7] At home she is even bigger, because the house is so small, but once the hat of glory is taken off, it is quite clear that Winnie is in reality an enlargement of the little girl Zami, from Bizana.[8] These are the same eyes that can see over walls and mountains. And she does not watch where her feet will land.

Her feet pace a soil at the bottom of my breast. If it sees the light of day, this book will be the fruit of a haunting. I want so much to tell the story of Winnie Mandela. Because for several seasons, thanks to her, what is stretching out in me is Africa. Not the non-African Africa out of which I came, the Africa of the North, but the other one, the ancient one, the first, the one I felt beginning behind my back when I was little. And now, without my being able to defend myself, she has won me over, invaded and overwhelmed me. I am resting peacefully. I want to lie down burning and astounded and dry and heavy and of a golden color. How this came to pass I do

9

not know. It happens in the depths of my body behind thought, there where me stops governing and gives way into world. Me is the door to Africa. Past the door, everything mysteriously immense. I carry the traces of animals on my soil, along my roads over which for days all that passes is the sun, the rare shadow, and with a leap the antelope. And it's as though a memory I haven't had since birth is given back to me. Thus am I returned to the age when the separation of animals and men had not yet been accomplished, when Creation was complete, when we ate each other without hatred, when we weren't ashamed to be naked, and when each was in the elegance of her own skin. So much so that had I been in the bath with Zami, I would not have started to wonder if she saw me naked white or if she were wondering if I saw her naked black, nor if I should see her black, nor if I were able not to think of the color white and the color black, nor if skin had a memory of eyes and teeth, nor if I should think of the past, of the present of the future, nor if she were thinking that I was thinking all this, and so wondering weighing till the water that washes all cleanses my spirit. I would have been in the bath, without thought, with pleasure, without the shame that is the shame of human beings, without the shame that is the skin's malediction, and I would have bathed myself with my sister, a magnificent gracious corpulent woman, in the black-white water of golden whiteblack gleams.

And to think that so much misfortune and fatality have existed for so many centuries just because so many men are afraid of the night and of their mother's womb.

Happily there are, all the same, some people who love their mother's womb! And who know: white comes out of black and black comes out of white. All teeth are white and the pupils of all eyes are black.

Now I've said enough on this subject.

———————

How will Zami have one day entered my cold core, my inner north? And I find her giant and much bigger than me, in me.

By a stroke

By a stroke of words, of voice, of face,

By a sentence that pushes my heart head over heels,

By the song of three lines that fling the soul into the sea

By a look that doesn't look at me, that passes before me and continues on, pensively, interminably, flowing toward the back of the world, by a gaze that travels far away, toward what I cannot see and would like to see, by the stroke of a wand, of feathers, of magic teeth, you strike and enter me, rending Unknown, opus or woman, poem or poet, like a blade that cleaves my forehead and does not hurt me

Zami entered me by the stroke of a hat. Then she went away like a bird in winter. But when I heard her tell the story of the wedding cake, it was then that I ceded her all the space in my soul and she entered forever without harm and as though she were at home, and as though her story were my own grand mother returning to sing to me the most familiar lieder, in the kitchen returning as usual back from among the dead, as soon as I ask her sing again and tell, one more time. It is an imperishable, grandiose, and familiar story, like a quote from Dante, cruel and musical and painfully familiar.

Sweet and nourishing on the tongue is the bitter plaint molded by Dante, my grandmother.

E come li stornei ne portan l'ali

nel freddo tempo, a schiera larga e piena,

così quel fiato li spiriti mai,

di qua, di là, di giù, di su li mena;

nulla speranza li conforta mai,

non che di posa, ma di minor pena.[9]

Presently I am going to tell the story of an extraordinary cake. The story of its life. This book then will not be without sugar, without eggs, without spices, without succulence. Nor without famine, nor without desert. It is the cake's story that is sweet and nourishing. The cake itself might be rancid, but its essence is inalterable, I believe.

Thanks to the existence of the cake, the courage to write this book came to me: that there be pastry in hell, not merely torment, is what allowed me to advance sentence by sentence but not without shyness in this sweetened hell. I entered it then through the kitchen, with one soul, shy, and the other soul, audacious. And there in the middle of the kitchen, the great black Egg was smiling, the Lady of the divine panache and on her head the sun for tomorrow.

In the kitchen amid the white chickabiddies Zami broods Africa, and on her head is tied the white scarf imprinted with gold and silver suns. She turns on herself and shines. He, meanwhile, turns on himself in the vault of stone. Around him the wall is dead bone. In his midst, his own house, his continent.

In their midst, the hard joy causes distance to boil in its cauldron. Distance expires.

Without a telephone He calls: "Be my bird of the sea, and come to me in a flap of black wing, come, Zami, blade of Love, cleave the sky's sands, cleave the veils of time, come through the hundred fissures in the world's concrete come, cross over, come my army of the sea, my dove of war, and set yourself on the suffering egg of my chest, brood my heart Zami, where tomorrow sprouts."

Whoever has a sublime ear hears plainly these voiceless words.

How shall I dare to speak of all these events, which apparently haven't happened to me? And which are superiorly cruel and superiorly gentle, superiorly to my experience. How shall I dare to speak of a black destiny, me, whose destiny is apparently white?

Once upon a time there was a man who had been told in childhood the marvelous story of Abraham put to the test by God, losing his beloved son and finding his beloved son again, in the midst of life losing life, and once dead finding life again, and all this, death, life, death, passing by like the hard heels of God on a single heart, and all this all alone beneath the heartless feet of God, for God has no heart, has no need to have a fragile human organ, and all this, this crushing, this extirpation of joy, this transplantation of the heart, without trembling, but not without hiding all his tears from the father of the world. This story was so terribly beautiful that the child became crazy about Abraham. Grown up, he had only one desire: to see Abraham. His entire life became a taut bow, an immense tension of his soul attempting to see with his eyes, however they might be, of air or of flesh, the one no eyes had ever seen—since God alone saw Abraham put to the test, God who has no eyes.

So you see, this man, ancient and sometime child, wanted upon aging to be the child seeing and understanding the incomprehensible, which only the new child, whom thought has not yet woven into its web and inspected, can see.

And he spent his life growing old in reverse and trying each one of the millions of paths that Abraham laid out with his slow and solitary step upon our docile earth.

I am then neither the first nor the only one to die of the desire to approach the sublime stratum that stretches above my height. I hear their feet walking wistfully on the sky's floor.

And I too I am dying and living of the desire to see the absurd unimaginable face of the person who hopes in hope, after the setting of hope, who believes without the aid of reason, whose soul flies in reality just as I know how to fly in dreams, who gives birth every day to a new hope, then night kills the child and swallows it up, but in the morning each day's hope sees the light of day.

And I too I try each morning to make my way, climbing in the direction of those I have no hope of ever overtaking; but I don't despair of climbing and imagining in their direction.

The ancient and sometime child had only one desire, the impossible: to have witnessed these events without witness. He had the desire but not the hope.

And I too with the absurd eyes of she who wishes to behold the hidden, I want to be present at that to which I'm not a witness. And above all, I want to bring my heart up close to the fire where the Devil didn't throw it, and give it an inkling of the martyrdom it will never know. Why? Because a life without the intuition of absolute grief is a life without light without water without salt without miracle and without bliss. And because "why was I born this color and not another?" is a question I do not want to forget to ask myself from time to time, and that I often forget.

At Voronezh perished, without crucified mother, without mute father, without olive trees without stone without tree, all was under a sheet of snow, no one knew who,
Mandelstam, unknown to the passersby.
And no one to cry out to why have you forsaken me
Without last word without last breath without last anger
No one knew when
Perished lost and unknown, and become

No one
A foreign snow cradled him
Only a snow knows

Unhappy the dead from whom we have stolen not only their life but also their death; they die forever without reprieve.

This book is an attempt at compassion. Only an attempt, for I am capable of going to the foot of the olive trees, but I will never manage to feel in my feet the nails Sergeant Visser drove into the feet of old Willie Smit, in spite of the supplications and tears. Only the supplications pass through my heart. I hear and do not feel, I weep and do not bleed. The next day my tears come no more. I have spent all I had.

Without a witness, how to die our death how to suffer our suffering? I need you to give me my suffering and my death. I need you to give me my pleasure. May my sufferings be mine, and my pleasures also!

I am not great enough to suffer even my own suffering alone. Whenever suffering has befallen to me I have suffered to the utmost, as well, as terribly as possible, and sometimes with the help of hollering, but this was never enough. One day I lost my father. The whole world caught fire. Curled up, I couldn't take my eyes away. Between my father and myself: fire. Alone, I watched. I hollered. I suffered greatly from not suffering enough. I had a puny and fake voice. I was suffering, suffering, and all the suffering remained above me, inaccessible, majestic and indestructible, like a suspended ocean that did not drown me, that I could not drown. Until I stopped shouting and resigned myself to suffering softly.

But at least I know a little how to suffer from suffering and from not suffering.

And I also know things one knows from having been a tiny child living before the too great universe. Even without knowing we know them, we know them, these unknown and future sorrows. Whoever lives knows the worst even without ever meeting it. For having seen my whole family die in a concentration camp several times in dreams, I know to what depths the sword can hollow out the heart in a single secular minute. Absolutely suffer absolutely one minute I know how. But then I wake up and I know no longer.

I also know that everything that occurs in dreams can occur in reality. For we only dream true. I know unknown sorrows, for my heart is fruit of the human tree. I am the fruit of unknown good and evil. A same blood burns in each human heart.

But I am only speaking here of sorrows of the heart. I know nothing of the sorrows of solitary flesh. Ah, bodies are terribly separated from each other whenever it is a question of suffering in the body's dough and down to the hidden meat. The worst part of crucifixion is being so infinitely alone in one's body. Because no one can understand, not even God, not even the mother.

The road that leads to dying is deserted, my brother.

God-the-Grief grounds and silences me.

If only I could take you in my arms, my child, my crucified one, if only I could hold your passion in my arms, that would be a consolation to me, suffers the mother without arms, without succor. Double is the dolor.

The mother who watches the crucifixion and lowers her eyes, the mother who cannot console herself for not being able even to console, I cannot look her in the face.

I watch her secretly. I cast a furtive glance and forthwith retrieve it, mute, struck with a shameful reverence. I do not accompany the woman who cannot accompany. And all here is solitude and silence. The rivers swallow their floods.

—All is you, silenced. And yet You is alone.

The sobs remain chastely in the chest. The words remain in the throat.

In the region where the Double Dolor burns, immediately, ash is the word. And it is exactly here that the poem is needed. Here where all is silenced and stopped, the impossible song must be invented.

To watch the fire devour the world, to stroll in the swamps of infernal Hell

All we cannot do, must be done.

To make the stones speak, on which there is nothing more inscribed, this must be done. Otherwise it is true that none of the lost dead shall ever survive.

The only chance remaining to the dead whose death we have stolen is the rock on which one day we may stumble.

If we have no ear for what the rock, become naked, smooth, mute, tells us, then all that has been silenced and assassinated will die again.

The ones who have died alone on the frozen boulder will die again for eternity, thus there will have never been a Prometheus, if we do not lay our hand on the stone, so as to blindly read the tale of solitary death.

All rocks recount Prometheus, and our forgetting of Prometheus.

Stones, ashes, high walls, fields of mud, bits of paper, barbed wire, here are our books, everything is written, everything silently shouts. May the reader come forth, may the ear, the hand come forth to hear so much silence.

When Alfios Sibisi was tortured on March 1, 1962, in the Dundee countryside near Natal[10] (But I shouldn't recount this here, so as not to cause too much anguish) . . .

It is not the pain that hurt him, it was beholding wickedness face to face, and having the devil as witness.

As for Alfios Sibisi, I know nothing of him save this name and the date of his death. Neither his age nor his face. I know the list of tortures, in order, I know the club, the nails, the ladder, the chains. I know he didn't cry out. All night he wept, he was heard weeping.

And the price of the ax he did not steal was: £1.5.9. Through his nostrils, his ears, his throat, through his esophagus, his entrails, his anus, he gave the ax back, in tears in blood in flesh, and in vomit.

But this, no one can understand.

— Your suffering is beyond my strength

Your solitary face is beyond my gaze. And meanwhile, crouched, my runny nose between my knees, rolled up under the rock of Dolor, I try to lift up my insufficient soul toward You,

You, innocent initiate of atrocious mysteries, you, living inhabitant of insane hells.

You, meat hung alive on night's hooks.

I glance toward you, wretched ordinary man lifted up to the divine by the all-powerfulness of misfortune. I cast just one frightened glance toward A. Sibisi, who entered skinless into the region of mysteries, for I cannot look him in the face.

"Where I am nailed, no nor any ordinary man has ever gone, from the high frozen exile where I am attached no one has ever descended. An interminable abandon holds me separated from the earth. You who do not follow me, you do not see what I see,

"Countless deserted, lifeless, endless mountains encircling my two human eyes, and there is no echo.

"And there in front of me, sole movement in the immobility, comes and goes sole presence in the abandonment, the sore with the iron teeth.

"Where I am planted, only pain and suffering stir.

"And up there is not one more word."

18

Mute the angel of God. No appeal. The knife falls on the young man. God did not follow A. Sibisi.

It is not the pain that hurts, it is seeing absence face to face, and not crying out. So as not to hear the silence.

Up there, in a strange land, where no one has ever gone, I am, I follow.[11] Null, naked, and annulled. Strange clouds, cover my excoriated body.

The path leading to absolute solitude needs to be traveled. Someone up there is crying, I have the impression it was me. But I cannot find the path

---

Until early morning, no one has found, no one has come. Quartered on his ladder, sole witness to the end of the world, he said: oh my cherished mother, today I go away.

And in the end a wild and savage solitude carried him off, with his mother in his breast. Then A. Sibisi himself finally abandoned A. Sibisi. He let him fall.

And all was finished and forgotten.

The ladder was found. The ax was not. Sibisi could just as well have dispensed with being born. Being born not to be is what occurs in this country.

Stories like Sibisi's I do not know how to recount. I remain at the bottom of the ladder that leads to the heavens of echoless sand. I only feel them while they are slipping away, weep for them while losing my tears, and then, so as to live, forget them.

So it goes; not only do we have to kill in order to live, kill the echo, we also have to silence ourselves and die, all this to remain, across earth, across blood, alive.

But I am not here to weep, and even less so to make others weep. Happily, Zami's story contains numerous radiant instants, even in deepest darkness.

———————

Zami is Winnie Mandela's name, when she isn't sleeping but nestled in the night, she waits, her eyelids attentive, her eyes half-open, and reaps even the most distant promise of footsteps, she waits, hours pass empty, her ear greedy, breathless, she hears the beloved not coming, not coming, not coming in the night strained toward his coming, all is carpet for his feet, tapestries for his passage, until at the extremity of waiting, just before the end, he comes, "Zami! Zami!" he calls, and already he is rapping on the windowpane, let the pane be blessed and the emptiness filled, and the wound healed. At dawn. And at the dawn blessed yesterday, Nelson Mandela's name was Rolihlahla.[12]

Yesterday he might have come. Nights without him were full of footsteps.

Yesterday, twenty-four years ago, nights without him were full of him,

All traversed by bridges, by tracks, by lanes, by alleys, on which he would arrive, he could arrive, he arrived endlessly, even when on that night he didn't arrive, he was coming, he was going to come.

Nights, full of fits of fear, full of flowers of fear.

Full of threats that are dreadful to joy.

But twenty-four years have passed without one full night of waiting blessed, and pregnant, with a secret day. Nights now are without the joy of fear.

For twenty-four years Zami has called out to Rolihlahla every night without expecting an answer at the windowpane, and at the windowpane the voice has not called out Zami! Zami! The voices have already been separated for twenty-four years and for many years as yet unknown. But each night they burn, call out to and remember each other, and the memory of the answer answers mutely here, and there, Zami and Rolihlahla.

All that is really missing is noise, water, earth, air, air drunk avidly, and sleep after suckling. Fire reigns. It alone is fed.

Now, in this instant, she is calling to him, and it is the call that is the answer.

———————

Rolihlahla and Nomzamo engendered Zenani and Zindziswa they engendered the baby Zaziwe and the baby Zamaswazi, and after that they engendered Zinhle and Zoleka and after that Zondwa.

And when Nelson writes to Zami from prison he calls her Dadewethu.

And on the island Nelson is called Madiba according to his clan.[13]

Whereas they are called Kruger, Botha, Voerster, Visser, Krebs,

Who has placed the milk names to one side, the iron names to the other, no one can say.

All is just, all is unjust.

Face of Abandon

The evening I started to read the story of Steve Biko,[14] the world's floor caved in like a terrified face, breath lost I immediately wanted to stop, I could not, neither pursue, nor stop, the sad book held me, my eyelids biting my eyelids, eyes constricted, refusing I advanced, a tidal wave of blood rose up inside me, recoiling I surrendered, the book was rising toward me, its neutral voice surrounded me, I could have closed it I could not, with my back to the night I succumbed, page after page, the book was praying in my ear, listen oh listen oh how not to listen to what I do not want to hear,

certain books bewitch us by the pain they inflict upon us, there was in the horror a superhuman charm

What I flee surrounds me, when I wanted to exit, there was no exit, until death I was inside, in spite of myself I followed the book, there was no chance, trembling, like the hooves of the ox that doesn't want to move, up to I know not where, over there, in front, where the Face it doesn't want to see awaits it, up to this page, pulled I let myself be pulled up to the Wild and Savage Page,

And there, nailed to the paper cross, was the Abandoned Face. Such an abandon I had never seen such a dark Abandon. A black fire broke out. I did not look at the Face. Only saw the Abandon blind me. There, suddenly, the book went out, or else it was I who finally wrenched it from me, it, weary, finally opened its teeth and let me go.

And then I ran to the kitchen, the terrestrial and immobile kitchen, and there I drank water, water, I drank to swallow bitter words, water to forget the unforgettable, and to wash I read I read, book after book, I drank books of milk but none flushed the poison from me, nothing cleansed my hands or eyes

O standing in a coffin, how to forget, how to forget forgetting and the unforgettable?

I was standing in the lead gorge, the house was weighing down upon me, and on my chest was the weight of a crushing face. All night long I fell heavily in the stairways of skeleton teeth, with all my weight and without movement as though I were carrying a crushing dead person, my legs couldn't carry me, their cotton stems alive amid derisory leaves were breaking beneath me, all night long I descended I was descending into the coffin, standing and carrying upon me the weight of a giant cadaver,

At two o'clock in the morning I lifted myself halfway up, I thought: I'll drop Africa; the descent continued. At three o'clock I lifted myself halfway up halfway collapsed at three o'clock, at four o'clock, at five o'clock, Africa was making me breathless.

But at dawn, as soon as I opened my eyes, I thought: I want to live too much and my pity is too short, how could I look the country of Abandon in the face, without failing and without falling in a dead faint, like a cadaver. I thought of the dire dreams born of dire thoughts, and of the months trembling beneath latticed skies, and of the exorbitant stars, and I imagined black enraged eyes chasing me from the hell where I dare come knocking

And then I felt that the courage to write, me living a whole part of my life inside a book that impedes breathing, a book where one must constantly carve out windows with one's own fingernails and unearth dead people, this courage I do not have. No one enters prison voluntarily. No one ever bashed his head against a wall voluntarily, at least, as Professor Loubser said, we don't yet know of any example, but it's not impossible that such a thing could happen once.[15]

What decided me was the degree to which I did not have the courage. For one must pass through dread in order to enter the human heart.

It is dread that inspires within me the tormenting desire to write this book.

And it is dread that gave me the quivering courage to contemplate the true Face of Abandon. Without dread bending my soul, I wouldn't have dared.

———————

I looked at you, Face abandoned even by death, even by death, empty breathless Face.

Day lost in this world and in the other
Death robbed, who will be able to say who you were
Abandoned eyes, blind in this world and in the other
No one still lives in the mask of no one, half-open onto abandon

The dead one weeps all alone. Still long after his death, weeps.

All resemblance is lost
weeps, eyelids empty, robbed of the last breath
Lips empty in this world and in the other.

Shell of no one, who will never stop losing his powers of speech. Mask without the life of death, without the slightest trace of the inhabitant. And yet once upon a time, here lived a living face

The mask weeps eternally with lips that will never close again, with surprised lips.

They robbed the dead man. Robbed him of his last word, his last look, his last thought, his last agony. His death.

Never has one seen such a miserable mask, so impotent, so stupefied.

Once upon a time behind these dumbfounded lips lived an incredibly full man.

Through two cracks passes the blank white look of nothingness.

The eyebrows remain, forever anxious about so much silence

Will never be at rest?

The dead man weeps all alone. He still weeps, a long time after his death

"I'm lost. Who knew me? Did anyone know me?"

And the mouth full of air cannot say a word

"Who is it?" remains, dead man condemned to death, dead man lost.

What are you thinking about now, abandoned Face of Steve Biko, what are you thinking about, Withdrawn, far away behind this silence?

Of old this man would dream, his head full of dreams.

Now the ruined night reigns. The emptied night.

Now the deaf night has come, the mute night.

It advances, immovably dead full of nothing, with the immemorial step of the cockroach.

Sleep, Kaffir,[16] sleep, Mozart is dead, in this air and in the other. Not another sound.

No, I do not have the courage to write this book, all I have is the dread. And the contrary desire to forget the Abandoned, to abandon them.

The solution is to think; to stop thinking; and to begin again to think; then to think of something else and so on in this way.

September 6, 1977, the man accused of being Steve Biko lost his powers of speech, he was a man and not a beast, a big man, merry, with a voice forged like a helmet and a shield, and terribly sought after. September 6, 1977, not another word. Mouth dried up.

His eyes full of air, and metamorphosed,

He uttered bird cries. Not mammal cries, not the cries of a wounded horse. Bird cries. His bewildered eyes, lying in wait for the unknown enemy, would cast brief bird glances,

Di qua, di là, di giù, di su

Like a chicken who without knowing knows what she does not know, and knows and knows that a chicken is for eating,

This man uttered bird cries here and there.

How to recount this? How not to recount it?

Since the poet was fleeing, how to relate this metamorphosis without falling?

And day after day, crying out crying out, only these bird cries and never again a single word till the last bird cry and these extralucid chicken looks *di là, di giù,*

"This is not an aviary here, Steve Biko!"

The cries too fell silent.

And no one to say it was a man.

Everything has become inhuman, and no one in the Pretoria prison to say that everything has become inhuman.

———————

When I read this, everything became impossible. Without lips, without voice, my throat constricted, I called out with my memory without words, I called out, help for my faltering thought, to the transparent birds that people the troubled sky of Dante.

Dead doves are falling like tears in the completely airless space of Pretoria.

Had I known, I would not have started this journey in the evening and all alone in my bed. But if I hadn't been all alone and at night, I might have had the strength strong enough to make this book let go, this book that held me by the heart and in terror. I would have gotten out of it and gone off unscathed, and without pity. Luckily, I didn't know when I started the dazzling agony awaiting me. If I had known you were this kind of book, wouldn't I have run away from you, and wouldn't I have lost the chance to grow up?

There are books that have hands to catch me by the hands and by the chin, and that won't let me go

List, list, O, list,[17] Listen oh listen,

and I too hang on to these hands,

I listen oh I listen and I want to hear, speak again, you who hold my heart in your hands like a bunch of grapes,

You who abound in terrible mysteries, I am, following you,[18] I can no longer leave you, what you have tasted, how would I taste it, lend me your pain, shed your tears for me and make me pale from your agony.

I am abandoned, and delivered up to the book of the Abandoned

Abandon carries me off and carried I weep, intoxicated.

Astride Pity, which knows neither cloud nor bit, nor restraint,

I want to go there where dying is man's mirror, to mirror my life in your (my) death.

The best help for whoever travels to the country of the worst pain is to have within reach the thick, very warm body of a person with whom one can nestle, for touching flesh one persuades oneself physically that the human creature is, after all, the best thing in the world.

But the nest of human flesh is what is most rare, for indeed the most classic form of destiny is tragedy, that is to say, the parting of thinking from suffering fleshes.

Without nest, the bird will perish above all from hunger. The nest nourishes.

What pushes all around the prisoner in prison is hunger and its greedy nettles, human hunger, the foremost. Everything is famished, the entire fabric cries famine, mutely. The skin is hungry, skin without hands without words, and the skin that speaks with its palms and its fingers, the isolated and abandoned skin, is only a repeated cry: touch me, touch my breasts, weeping from separation, touch my belly, tortured by separation, touch my thighs, blinded by the abyss, I hunger for human hands, I am devoured by hungers. Ah! mother, the wolf is all around me, gnawing me insatiably. I am eaten by absence.

One can perish from having one's skin so starved. In the too starving absence of Nelson, Zami has fed more than once at the breast of her small children. At night, she would place her suckling baby everywhere, she would press it between her thirsty arms, she gives it her great weaned breasts to suckle, drink, doves, this is my milk, then she places it to press on her widowed womb, taste and lick, unhappy lonely one, this is the weight of my flesh,

yes, it is with the help of the flesh of her flesh that she seeks to dress the wounds.

But he? Has only the wolf, on the island, not the baby. At night, nothing assuages the agony of the flesh that must live without water without milk, without fingers, without respite, incessantly bitten, and without any dying.

He, who has only bitter milk left to drink: thirst
He, uncaressed, unkneaded, untouched
I wonder what invisible hands visit him, and keep his skin alive.

The poet did not know he was dying of this. And yet would burn his wood, and yet would be cold.

Like the last swallow,

Came a slightly crazy question, slightly lost, like the last chick before deserted winter:

"How do you say *nest* in Russian, my friend, I don't remember anymore, I don't remember anymore."

How do you say nest?, he asked the remote Russian friend. He was Rilke again, and not purely unaware that in ashes were spreading his very last stars.

And indeed, all that still came to the windowpane of the poem was a dove, but a strangely foreign one. Barely returned, it would leave again for foreign lands for the absolutely foreign, forever.

And behold, I no longer know how to say: *nest*. Neither in Russian, nor in German, nor in French, the word nest no longer makes an appearance beneath my pen. I have lost the word nest in every language, behold, I am naked. I am outside, thrown far from all bodies, only stone still faintly living and flying, heavily and wingless above no earth,

Last cry heard by no mother in this world.

When the answer arrived, no one heard it. The cold had won.

Who will know now that nest is called *gnezdó* in Russian?

For this is one of those too late stories, with which we feed the tragic tragedies

———————

But all tragedies are not wholly tragic, otherwise they would often end before the end. Without a large portion of the strongest joy, tragedy wouldn't even be possible. Tragedies come to pass at the foot of Paradise, not far extremely far from Paradise, tragedies and their last looks.

A tragedy full of joys, and full of last looks: behold what I shall try to tell.

I would like to say one last thing about Steve Biko. What caused me the most suffering of all the sufferings brought about by his death is not his suffering, it is not his death-throes, it is not September 6, 1977, September 7, September 8, September 9, September 10, September 11, September 12, 1977, which are the names of his death-throe days spent na-ked, chained, his brain in the process of being extinguished, it is not that he spent September 12 in a coma, but stretched out carefully on the floor on a mat, as if they had thought that even in a coma he was going to feel himself dying naked-on-a-mat-on-the-floor, for all these sufferings no longer cause him suffering from now on, they died with his body, which had no more brain. No, what continues to cause me suffering is those who did not die, and whom nothing will kill, and whose names follow: Dr. Lang, Dr. Tucker, and Dr. Hersch, because they contemplated smoking the death-throes of the man whose brain was crushed and who could no longer do anything on purpose, who, without doing it on purpose, let flow like a baby tears drools smiles urines, and tiny bird cries,

And because three times in each day they said all three of them: it's nothing, if not the height of trickery, said and signed: "Get down off your cross, joker." Signed: the doctor.

And behold how, in spite of the crime of having commit-ted a crime three times more criminal than the crime of the assassins themselves, they are still alive on this earth, in this very moment, exactly as though they were born and had just been born from the belly of a human woman, and like me, and like you,—something that takes away from me, personally, a large portion of my taste for life.

I call these three doctors to your attention. They have pushed hatred farther than hatred.

Those who wrote the word "simulation" on the word "martyr," those who, laughing, looked out of the corner of their fat eyes at the murdered man, and laughing thoughtfully at nothing drank three beers to his health,

This is not an aviary here, Cockroach,

Kaffir, you are not a bird

Those who watched him drain away without horror without curiosity without interest without any disguised form of pity, without disgust, without regard, merely watched him, saw, and in the blink of a blank white eye forgot

That this was a big and merry man

And now they have taken off his face and put on him the mask of a dry hollow cockroach,

I name them, in the hope that a huge number of curses is more efficient than a small number of curses.

I hope.

And that in Hell they live on Steve Biko Street.

The Marriage Proposal

There are many nights in this Story. The nights pass very quickly. Everyone hopes in vain to hold them back. As though to see the light of day were each time to lose one's mother. But they do pass. And separation sets in.

There will be many dates in this account. But what there is hardly any of is time.

If the celestial pitiable Great Night did not exist, I wonder what would be left of the Xhosa, Swazi, Tembu, Zulu peoples the Sotho-swana, Venda, Tsonga families.[19]

Deprived as they are of earth, of sea, of movement, of parents, children, books, and of all houses,

So the Night serves them as earth, ocean, and last mother. They fall from her like tears. And it is into her breast they return when they have run their course. But in what a state they come back to her, all these dead children: their limbs broken, their ears torn off, their lips tumefied, their foreheads covered with lumps, their eyelids sad, their backs scored with sores. How harsh life will have been! But not always, just the same. Let's let the Night identify her dead.

The miracle is that the living do exist. I'm going to speak of two people who have never ceased being champions of life, even when we might have thought them dead. And also champions of speed. One has never seen a life rush ahead so precipitously. Even when it seemed to be stopped short and thrown in prison in 1964, it continued this rhythm, for it was also the life of an entire people. As soon as there was no more present the future started up in haste.

As I have announced, there is never any time in all these years.

What I mean by time is the moment. Mandela time hurtles along momentless like a torrent. There are so many events that certain ones are borne away before they have been lived. And never does a moment reach its natural end. Never have Nelson and Winnie succeeded in giving their own end to something they started themselves.

To return to the first beginning:

The first thing they did together almost at the same time was to go out to eat. It was the first time Zami had been to an Indian restaurant,

the first time she had been to a restaurant

the first time she had been with a man, gentleman, stranger, a person she knew even less because very famous and also married and the father of three children she did not know,

the first time with a dress below the knees, borrowed expressly for this time and then never again

the first time that she, Zami, found herself seated across from Nelson Mandela, for how she got there she can't remember.

It was a Sunday. It could have been any day for him, since he stopped working only to take refreshment. But still it was Sunday and it remained Sunday. They hardly ate anything. This is the only thing that wasn't the last time.

It is the last time they had lunch in a restaurant like a woman invited with a man who has invited her. It is the last time she ate chicken curry, because she couldn't swallow a thing after the first mouthful.

But he who adores very spicy chicken curry ate next to nothing, because as soon as he had swallowed the second mouthful, someone who was waiting for him to do so came up to speak to him, and then a second person came and then another till the end of the meal. And during the whole half hour, Zami looked at Nelson's plate and at her watch, and it became a game of swallowing a mouthful between two people and at the end the player truly lost. Almost all the curry remained uneaten.

Half an hour to not eat. Half an hour to go from the restaurant to the car in the same mode, with a person between each step. That's what the first lunch was like.

Zami didn't have a chance (to be with Nelson). And moreover, she didn't even have the chance to see Nelson. She saw herself, with the dress and the spicy hot curry that made her eyes water. And she saw quite clearly each person who used him right in front of her, which she in any case would not have dared to do. He welcomed everyone. But all she managed to see of Nelson was that he was all black. Because of Zami's shyness it became a kind of night in broad daylight. She found him strangely old, like a forty-year-old man. And also forty years early.

He was very far from her, or rather she was very far from him, whereas all the while she could see that in fact she couldn't see him. She was losing weight, she lost the color in her cheeks, she lost all of her last few years, of which she was so proud, and she even lost the strong sensation of charm she usually attributed to herself.

She wilted. And she got angry but timidly. Never in her life had she felt so alone, so secret, so banished, so domesticated, so hypocritical, for she was feeling at least ten feelings at the same time, all melting together. And moreover in public, and in front of this man who did not see that she was hypocritical and alone.

He didn't see a thing. He saw everything except her. She wasn't his daughter. He wasn't anything to her.

And, when she was already seated in the car, there was still another creature who had rights in relation to Papa. It was a mutt, who seemed to know Nelson too. Nelson actually got out of the car just for the dog, and caressed it with hands she suddenly saw as being strong and long and sporting a man's fingers.

If she hadn't been wearing this dress that imparted an awkward strangeness to her, she would have gotten out and disappeared with a bound. This scene didn't take place. But flight remained in her, the whole way home. In the depths of her body was a young she-dog fleeing belly to the ground in the direction of the forest, and while she ran, she constantly turned back panting to see. To see, she felt with a sudden anxiety, if he were pursuing her. If he had understood, he who was the cause of her flight, that he should pursue and catch her. And her heart wrestled with itself. "If you touch me, I'll bite you!" She thought. But he didn't touch her. Unfortunately. And she didn't know what she would have done if he had touched her. He was very tranquil, and she was very trembling, as though there were a hurricane reserved for her alone.

Her life was threatened, and there was no threat. And it was this absence of threat that threatened her like death. In the end, the desire to die is what saved her: for it offended her too much to see herself, she who had still been free and proud the night before and even that morning, fallen into needing this man who wanted nothing from her, who didn't need her, who respected her and kindly offered her his hand. It was the first time in her life she needed. She who hadn't ever loved, there she was, starting shamefully by clutching at a stranger. And without being given or taken, she felt lost.

Luckily, the violence of fear suddenly transformed itself into an icy skin that gloved her heart, for luckily Nelson said: "This has been a lovely day." And under the steady light of these words, the day ceased to grimace like a sorcerer in a hypnotic trance. She hated the word lovely.

He said: "This has been a lovely day." As if he had spoken to her in a foreign tongue, or as if he had just told her farewell, as if a departure had just taken place, and as if she suddenly had a veil of tears over her eyes, all at once she saw him too much and found him a little bit much, a bit much a bit too elegant, a bit too nonchalant, a bit too old, and whereas he was bending toward her she felt a river dry up, a cloud devour the day, and in that same instant she renounced him. Because of this strangely foreign phrase. For a few moments. He wasn't her mother, she thought, with rapid and bitter regret. No. He was a man without cares, he was a mountain indifferent to the winds, he was innocent and he didn't even feel the countless blows she struck against his side with her tiny sword. He was too strong to be able to conceive of the emotion of she who is not mountain. How to prick a mountain?

She was ridiculously small and he was ridiculously large. The ridiculousness was in the disproportion. And all this because of that misplaced phrase. Come from another time. A generation and a world had separated them. A man's phrase, she neighed, mare of the unshod hooves. Would she have ever uttered such a repulsive and well-trained sentence? She who was already shying away so as not to show the curve of her neck?

Great python crouched among your rings, who says my rings are mine, my bones and my men are mine, it is I who have made them, and my blood and my women I have made them also,

I shall escape from you, I shall break your circle with my

teeth and red I shall shoot forth beyond you and fling myself into the bush.

But she said nothing. Pretending to be a woman from the city. As though she were no longer governed by the moon and shaken by the earth's shudders.

Nelson was compliant and content. And having personally no reason to mistrust, he didn't mistrust. And in truth, he wasn't suffering. Since for him there was no cause for suffering. And he wasn't one to invent. Reality was his destiny.

He didn't put his hand on Zami's knee, which would have been, in this moment of convulsion when everything that was happening was immediately twisted and accused, a catastrophe.

I don't know why in this moment Zami was desperately fleeing what she desired. And everything was unruly.

A great fear of hope possessed her. Yes, it was hoping she feared, this is why she was running backward like a madwoman toward the end of the world, her eyes downcast before the terribly desired, Terrible Face.

But Nelson simply looked thoughtfully at her shining knees. Zami immediately catches this look and twists it, telling herself that Nelson is thinking of another woman.

And so, even though she doesn't believe herself, she scratches her heart a little.

In this way, she chastised her own temerity: don't let her go around thinking she was born to be queen. And servant, never. And if her country's mountains had been changed into roads, did she deserve this?

So then he kissed her. For it is in this way that this day should end, according to him. But not her day. He already in union. She in separation.

In the end Nelson kissed her according to her destiny, but she did not have the strength to become a woman, she was too exhausted. She kissed him like a young girl with a broken sandal. Her soul, awkward, in her foot. So much so that she didn't know what there was in this kiss. If Nelson had looked into Zami's eyes at that moment, he would have torn her out of her soil of stubbornness by the root, he would have bitten her lips till she cried tears, he would have broken her wickedness with his wickedness, he would have freed her from her fury, if he had opened his eyes at that moment, she would have let herself fall to the bottom of his heart the way a dove, exhausted by storms, falls like a stone, throbbing, out the window.

But it was the proper ending to this day. He remained his eyes closed, his lips without mistrust resting without haste on her closed lips. And even like this, before the door, his heart was content and without a doubt. The day was over.

He was always like this: without a doubt. This is the secret of his strength. This is his forbidden weakness.

What does not appear in this story of Nelson is hesitation. Beneath the hero's footsteps the road goes straight no turns to the promised period of isolation. This makes life with him without a doubt powerful, and majestic, and triumphant, but hard. For from time to time we need to be impure and tormented; and we need to dream we have lost what we had, in order to enjoy what we have.

On her golden arm the young girl tries a golden bracelet. The bracelet barely fits her. When she wants to take it off, she cannot take it off. No turning back. The road goes in only one direction: forward, forward.

So the story goes, according to the myth, step by step like a sacred ass, without a glance to the left or to the right, and up to the mountain's peak.

Winnie did not want any of this, did not want a story without frightening shadows, without disbelief, without the looks that fly here, there, over all the world, without the salt of life made up of menace and dread. For living, she thought, couldn't simply occur the way in the morning the day and in the evening the night. Living could only be unexpected, she thought.

On top of everything else the pathway through the veldt was slippery and chaotic. A pebble rolls underfoot, her sandal strap breaks: she has slightly twisted her foot. He extends to her his large, calm hand which says: "in the storm, I am roof," and in spite of herself she feels protected.

This return trip was silent but very agitated. In the same car, they weren't in the same moment. He inside the possible, she inside the why. He by the sun, she by the moon. Two lamps in the wind. One lowered so as not to die. The other, miraculously motionless.

And nothing had been said, except: *lovely.* A blank, white word.

———————

Kissed, she would have liked to ask him: "And your wife?" But as eyes swallow back tears and the sun the mist, she swallowed her vain curiosity. Since nothing had been said.

For her, first came words, then fruit. But apparently not for him: fruit right away. Would this budding life be without flowers?

About the seasons too, she was worried.

Or else, is this not about a life? Or else it is a walk in the veldt, leading, she knows not where.

———————

In the heart of South Africa are young girls who have never seen the rain. Only the dust that changes color with the light. Nothing grows. Like a young girl who sees and smells and receives the rain for the first time, and who sheds more and more tears, weeps for the rain, weeps for having never before received the rain, weeps with inextricably mingled rage and joy, weeps with mingled rain and dust, this is how Zami fell asleep that night, as though she were herself the dry and dampened heart of Africa. All is unjust, all is just. Like a young girl who recognizes the rain she is receiving for the first time, because so many times before she has wept in dreams like the sky is weeping onto the earth, finally. Wept the rain.

On this day, the moon is becoming the earth, finally.

The next morning she woke up on her own side, in her own size, her own age, with her own rivers where ran her own powerful and familiar bloods, she hugged herself tight in her own round arms, and relieved to discover herself again, she put on her own dress, which goes down to just a little bit above her very own knees.

She beheld herself in the mirror, proof that a beautiful woman is worth any handsome man, and this is what she saw: for the first time in her life, she saw that she was she. An earth, with its secrets and its promises. And also an army. An army of peace and of war. She saw her gaze marching along, moving off alone across the forests of time. Yesterday insect, hare, hen, today woman with a destination, obstinate black dove. Bound for the universe, this is what she saw.

And the day before yesterday she had still been a schoolgirl, watching the world from the bottom up.

It is without being aware of it that we find the door. The out-of-doors was stretched out before her, with all its nations, its peoples, and its battlefields.

A desire for combat makes her heart throb. Yesterday she had been defeated. And in the morning, up she springs again.

So she had victoriously traversed the ordeal of initiation. Before the tempest's bellowings and white lightning bolts like milk, she had become a tiny trembling crazy disoriented naked hen. She had discovered her own wells of weakness, she had seen how death could easily surprise her, she had met her own smallness, her cowardice, she had perceived her own horizon, she had seen her distant borders, the somber line at the place where her pride became conceit, and above all, crouched in the rugged crevice of a rock, under the divine storm, she had discovered she was a patch of tender panting doughlike flesh, molded from anguish and pain, from whom not only a word but also a nonword, a nonlook, a nothing could wrench a cry. Nothing had come to pass. And yet every part of her was in pain, her heart had ridden all night long, borne by Insomnia, it was a war, and wanting was nibbling at her organs with its little monkey teeth. Thus had she met the other's strength, and under the shock she had stumbled, and rolled into the pit of her very own night. In a single outing, in a single night, what hitherto ignored emotions she had discovered! And completely surprised she was slightly glad, for it was good to get to know evil.

She remembered the first ordeal: she is four years old. This is all she knows: she is four years old and she is running. She was the center of the world out of which she came. The Ancient Ostrich had told her she was born from an ostrich egg. This is all she knows. The important thing was running, tasting the things that seem made for the mouth, spitting out what tastes bad and sucking what tastes good. There are also the other children but there isn't any knowledge, the children hop about, the vermilion worms make violent silent circles before the hens, thin hoops of transparent blood, certain creatures are drawn to one another, and the things that attract her are on the ground. It was the time of trying the things of the earth. And she, who was she? Closed, full like the corn fritter, with paws, feet, and hands. And needing? She knew nothing. She knew nothing except how to drink. Thirst was her only window on the world. Being thirsty was the pathway of her childlike ecstasy. For when she drinks big sweet fresh gulps from the coconut, sweet and fresh, then she feels she has an inside, a gullet and a vessel of delights. Being thirsty was to have, in the vessel, the sun with the shade. And also, one was made of earth and water like pottery. Being thirsty is what is best and most disturbing. For one could become mean, wily, thievish, from thirst. Except when she opened herself to thirst, she was quite closed. Until the day when, by accident, the shell broke.

She is running. And suddenly, as only children know how, she fell. For it is only out of ignorance of the mysteries of falling that children fall so hard, so entirely. This is how she fell completely. Then the brutal acquaintance with the earth's pebbles, and with the net weight of her own person who nevertheless weighed nothing, was made. In the encounter, a sharp stone gashed her knee. And it is here that everything ended and everything began. Seated on the ground, she saw the horror: big drops of blood were coming one after the other out of her very own knee. This is why she uttered such a big cry, she is trying to rouse the gods to riot. Because of the horrible revelation: there is blood in her being, in the little dry vessel that was no one, is red brilliant life that could escape. Help, she cried, and no one to console her, for she isn't hurt, but worse,

She saw:

What came to her was the vision of her contents. Opening up, one saw there was someone inside. Her blood was the outsider, and yet, it was inside her, and her instinctive mission was to keep and care for it.[20]

With furious desperation she understood everything. She wasn't made like a stone, or like a cake, or like a vessel, or even like an egg, in which there was no foreign red. Her destiny is to carry her life's blood, to protect it and to be protected by it. So one could lose one's blood. Stop, she cried.

The blood stopped. This was her first fear of the other that was she. Zami looked at her knee. This is how, she thought, Nelson began to come to me, a long time ago, while I was running on the Bizana path. The scar is still there. For you to enter, my love.

Opposite the school door, at the corner of the tiny lane, was the old man still waiting for next to nothing. How to describe him? He was the tiny thorn in her paw. Being careful not to notice him, she avoided hurting herself too much.

Every day she passes by not far from him, being careful not to.

He is a very old man who doesn't look at her. So she too doesn't look at him, guarding against regarding him. But he isn't on his guard. He's seated at the corner of the lane and does nothing but barely wait and next to nothing. Only a little skinnier and a little older than another. Almost a stone. But he doesn't live there, since she sometimes sees him arriving early in the morning, like the timid ghost of a human. He comes there. That is what he does. Because he doesn't do nothing. Living he doesn't live, but nonetheless he isn't dead, and that is why every morning he comes back and every evening he goes away again. He comes and crouches. And now he is waiting for someone to give him something. Because begging he doesn't beg. And asking for work now how to ask, without being spurned. In front of him a minuscule tin of wax that hopes: if only one day a shoe would come.

There are never any. The tin is a murmur, a prayer: I can still shine. I can also carry a basket if it's not too heavy. Or a letter to the post.

Waiting he hardly waits for anything. And yet he waits imperceptibly, waiting for death. The little tin of wax is all he has left. It is his kingdom and his dignity. Why did I call out, though no one replied? This is what the tin means. Nonetheless, I'll keep on calling.

It isn't the skinniness that wounds Zami, it is the tin. It is . . . hope? If not a taste for hope at least a distaste for desperation. And she hasn't ever had any shoes to shine. And each day she must crush pity in order to live, she must treat it as one treats a cockroach, without pity. For from pity to pity the heart gets to hate.

If only he would beg. But he wants the impossible.

Behold that on this day, she doesn't shy away from him. All of a sudden it is the impossible. She has to look at him. She cannot pass in front of him without stopping. Ah, right away she is seized by pity, an immense powerlessness rises over all of Africa like a suffocating cloud.

—Why don't you die, my child, my old motherless child, why don't you flee this earth?

—Too early, smiles the old man. In a bit, his eyes apologize.

Yes, this is what comes to pass: on the old man's face, a smile like a childhood memory. Passes. Then, without thinking or calculating, or fleeing, or reflecting, or speaking, or fearing, or hating anymore, she gives him all at once a ten-rand coin. And looking at him she begs to give him, she begs the sharing of bitten bread, she begs him for the ten-rand coin, with an uneasy smile, beggingly.

Take and give, old child-mother, take and give me your taking, she smiles surreptitiously. Do you understand, mother-child? do you understand it is me who asks you for pity? Do not spurn me, receive me.

But none of this is said, it all comes to pass in a flash of black wing in a red sky.

Red is the color of the whole scene, since it is a scene about secretly passing from one womb to the other.

And like a bird the old man nimbly nabs the coin, like a bird born for taking what it finds, and also like a child with its two hands held out as if it were receiving fistfuls of nice things from fists. In the two hands held out the little coin has become "all that," it is received like "all that for me," and in this instant she fills with her smallness the immensity of the old need. At least two hands are needed to receive all that. On the faces above the hands was something like the soft glow of a candle.

This moment had deep, transparent roots. And it had come to the surface of time from the bottom of delicate, pensive centuries. Like an imperceptible allusion to possible kindness.

Whenever two human beings meet in the middle of the hostile worn-out world like two secret agents, meet at the corner of a lane and say nothing to each other but their eyes downcast, and just as quickly fade away like in a dream, there is miracle. But this miracle is so tenuous, maybe it is merely an invention, and no one can bring it back.

What has remained of this event is an inexplicable pain in Zami's chest, because of the old man's two hands held out, as if holding on to his childlike age.

How like a mother she felt herself to be, the black schoolgirl with her teeth a flock of sheep, with her young eyes already a thousand years old. And this is also how, through this old man with hands left gluttonous a hundred years after the abandonment, Nelson began to come to her. Through all the sores. Through all the palms. Through the too great droughts and thirsts. And through the inexhaustible thread of hope inside the wizened child. The earth was the sore, its lips cracking. Nelson was the rain.

There are countries of dust and misery where one doesn't know how not to kill the child.

Imagine the child without hunger in the land of hunger, she is five years old, and what she sees in the street: a beggar, a beggar, another beggar, yet another, yet another, she sees hunger without end, and she sees the without, the without eyes, the without a leg, the without an arm, the without a nose, all that isn't dead and isn't without desolation. She, with her legs, her eyes, her hands, her bread, her mother, how will she get past the river of without?

See her over there, she who feverishly divides all she can divide, see her dashing meticulously down the lane, from one without to the other to exhaustion. And before her press the countless withouts of this world.

And now, her hands empty, what to do? Now this is what hell is: the child's fault. The world is her fault. The sickness of the world is my fault. And I do not know how to avoid the crime. I do not know how to bear the other's without without fail. One must stop the river. But the air in the street becomes malicious music. And the child's chest fills up with heavy feelings.

In the end there is no more pity at all in the street. Only an anguish on the heels of an anguish. And there is no angel. No message. No garden: proof of the absolute absence of a gardener. And which is the ant that will turn the desert into garden? What's the use of the small ineffectual kindness? In full light it is night, in full life it is death. Barely outside and I am pruned from wound to wound. What is the use of being born innocent to be assassinated and assassin?

In this way the child Zami continues on with death for an answer, until the day she has the good fortune to discover the Enemy. So it wasn't God, it wasn't anyone? There is someone we must fight, with blood and with iron! But she will never forget the thick air of Hell.

Before the door to the school, someone is waiting for her with a car, from Nelson Mandela. She is being called, he is the one who is calling her and she herself is the one who is called.

She took a deep breath, and what gave her the most pleasure in that second was her victory over herself: she succeeded, in spite of the shock, in not falling back into the hen state. "Luckily I am beautiful," she told herself. And it is as Nomzamo Winnie Madikizela of Bizana first black social worker that she moved toward him. A long dress doesn't hinder her gait at all, a severe shyness doesn't hold her qualities captive. She remembers how she always won first place in running and the long jump at the Umtata sports festival,[21] and it is proudly that she desires the impossible. Thus is she set in motion, and as though she bore a tiger on her helmet's crest.

The car jolts along quickly. Just as quickly she remembers her secret. There is a black pearl encrusted in the bowels of her memory. One chance. One time:

She was in Johannesburg, standing among the people, in the courtroom. The crowd, a forest, began to murmur: Mandela, Mandela. She was the forest, she stretched her body, murmuring, till she finally saw the man, very tall, very black, very solemn, and bearing the name of Nelson Mandela like a lance. She saw him then for the very first time. At that moment there is neither once upon a time nor any other time. She sees him for the first time so tall, so ancient, so chosen, so remote, yes, although incarnate, as distant as a man from another history. He was at the helm of Time, which was slowly flying above the Earth. It was the first time she was seeing him in all his majesty, surrounded by the crowd calling him Mandela, adoring him and separating him from itself and from her too. She looks at him, and thinks nothing. What to think of a planet, what to think of a temple, what to think of a mountain, what to think of a milestone, what to think of a century? Her thought doesn't stir. At the gong of his voice only her blood stirs a little. At the sound of the voice according to the voice. As the center spreads a soundless bloodbeat through space. The words upon his voice are heavy and musical. A warning reigns in the room.

I shall never tell you that I surrounded you from very close, from very far away, from nowhere, dove around a column, and I repeated your name Mandela, without tasting it, without calling you to me, it was before the beginning, before good and evil, all I was then was an atom of Africa attracted by obscure hope.

I have already seen you once, I alone, without desire, without hands outstretched, without pain, pure of you, and you pure of me. I saw us one without the other, before us, before life. This is my secret. This is my cradle.

There once was a strange time when the gods drew the curtain aside. And I alone, I saw. I was outside. And I was saying your name. This scene belongs to eternity. Even you without me I was with you. And everything could not have been.

Zami wanted to have everything, including the moments of nothing, of before and of not as yet.

When there was neither death nor life, nor desire nor envy nor masculine nor feminine, from where did the light come?

Only remains of this day without them: the long explosion of the voice. When there was not yet hen, nor cock, only two motionless eggs in the same sky, without dreams and without imagination.

The car stopped, the combat nearly began again: the man was there, adorned, the earth doesn't bear any mortal more natively proud. More naively, more anciently proud. Neither Nelson, nor Mandela. Man. His gym attire is white, as is all his finery. And behind him a long train of men and of generations. And for two hours, in the gymnasium, thoughtfully, elderly, she has to watch him sweat, from generation to generation, seated on the edge of time, on the sidelines, to watch him flow, while he plays at being, he plays at being, at the game that is only played when one is game and alone, but not without you.

"It's for you I am sweating!" he dedicated to her.

No, it's for you.

Clouds cross her sky, only her sky, for nothing can darken his.

At the end of the first hour, she girds her loins. A letter is rising in her chest in a lava of tears, from the beginning of the world up to her lips. She is going to write it. To vomit it. It would be a door. It would be a gulf. It would be a separation. She would begin by leaving. What stops her is her blood, the song of Xhosa blood, the ancient tender hesitation of the blood before the bones, so white and innocent.

The letter falls in ashes and her blood bears it between her bones. If the inside of the body were not a mix of white and red, of hard and soft, of solid and liquid, fire would scorch the water dead. And the hen would not become a fan of the cock.

But the world must begin and that's the cause.

Yesterday I was a hen today you are a cock. She saw the cock. The cock can't do otherwise. The cock is made for playing the cock. The cock is born dressed as a cock. And his vocation is to sweat before the court. What could be stranger than the cock's ways? thinks the woman. While he sweats according to his genius and his innocence, Zami was thinking, unbeknownst to him as women do, and without saying a word. She sees that he's sweating and does not see. She's thinking about the distribution of destinies, she's thinking about rails and about the obstinacy of trains, about the secret awful presence in each one of us of the first cock of the first hen and of the first eggs, and about the immemorial fresco deep inside the cave. That is what I should scratch. She thinks on the sly.

But what she was in the process of doing, unbeknownst to herself, was letting herself be taken in by the old egg trick. It isn't the cock, it is the shell that makes the hen feel tender, because it is so fragile. By dint of watching him sweat, she became a mother. As it has been drawn in all the caves. It is by his gift of sweat that he obtains her. Neither with flowers, nor with pearls. Man sweats, and woman surrenders, instead of making it easy for her to derail the train.

She thinks and forgets thinks and forgets thinks and forgets and finally forgets, and it is without thinking about it that she surrenders to eternal coquetry. She would have to be a huge hen to make a nest for such a man, so tall, so grave, so naked, so originary. It's a story about confusing light with darkness. I should add that if he hadn't seemed to be her father she would not have let herself become his mother. But there is nothing to regret, for all that could have been is a part of all that is.

Once she had swallowed the letter, she decided to taste him with her eyes, with and in spite of the sweat and annoyance, she who still hasn't seen him without armor, without helmet, without lawyer's suit, without uniform, without gentleman's mask, and all she had seen of him was the mass of his majesty.

Watching him above and beyond thoughts simplified things. For Nelson was undeniable. He weighed his weight in force and fragility. Now he was jumping rope, it was a real fact, and an absurdity, but absurdly reassuring, God jumping rope heavily and lightly, reassuring God. In the end, she was content to see him do all these things she didn't like and that were so undeniable. He wasn't just tall, he was also small, and not just extraordinary.

She scanned her prayer: jump, Nelson Mandela! Sweat, Nelson Mandela. Dance, my child my elephant. I adore you, I adore your baskets. To the point of becoming the first earth on which the first man used to run and plow. We don't know how, Nelson was born to her, outside of her and in her.

He trampled her and didn't hurt her. It is enough to not resist the ritual. And everything becomes normal again. The man jumping is not a lawyer. He's a male. It is normal for the earth to be roused by earthquakes.

She too perspired for him.

An immense attraction weaves the space between them and invisibly holds them together separated beneath the canopy of desire. And already before they know it, the world begins its transformation.

The absurdity of the scene was slowly becoming religious. We climb from world to world. As when, around midnight, the air churned by the elders' dance becomes divine butter. And even she who doesn't believe feels the unbelievable passing, from humid hand to humid hand. Sweat permits passing.

All of Zami's words and the turbulence of their judgment dissipate, and silence rises. The Ancient, the first. The silence is stronger than everything. As it climbs up from the unknown center, it speaks the unknown center, and the coexistence of worlds, one on top of the other, one underneath the other. The gymnasium is also the brush, obviously. And the brush is also the temple of engenderings, obviously. The silence makes this clear. Silence envelops the universe in a delicate pink linen. In the silence we see everything with other eyes, eyes that light up like lamps for seeing dreams in the dark. The future, we do not see the future.

Zami sees the present, the inside of the present. She is beneath the surface now and contains her own depths. Within immobile Zami the other conscience comes and goes and weaves the immense ties. The air in the world's womb is of a Levant pink, the moving pink of dawns. The one that when born puts fire to the day and then dies. The attraction comes and goes like a sea, that from one shore to the other is traveling in itself.

The universe extends in the West as far as his body and as far as my body in the East. And everything that could come to pass was in the inside of us. And between them unfold all the red roads, all the white roads, and all the distances under the black tent.

The distance was good. And the expectation as good as a starry sky.

It gave them a strange foreignness. Zami was looking at Nelson as though she had never seen him before, nor ever seen a man, and was furtively marveling: he runs, he jumps, he sweats, he laughs, and with his fists he strikes the air and what else doesn't he do of the ordinary, strangely ordinary. As if, getting up on her dreamy island, just after the tempest by which all stories begin, she had just lifted the fringed curtains of her eye and for the first time saw: the creature.

"O Temple, beautiful house, kingdom, king, spirit, no, invention real and shiny and black, do you love me?" she thought far from her thought.

No! don't answer! I simply want to release the dove from its place here near me, and may she fly for a long time for a long time asking do you love me, and fleeing asking how is love made and fleeing

Tirelessly pushing away softly that which she desired most in the world.

"Slow down, earth, waters, retreat without haste, man do not answer me, for it is still satisfying to my thirst to wonder if you love me.

Wondering this was already all the vibration of happiness she could bear without shouting.

Yes, I want the sky, but the stars only one by one.

And so, taking ant steps in the sky, and fearing disaster. Luckily the sky was sluggish in the gymnasium, gestures were being repeated, jumps were beginning up again one after the other, and Zami was able to turn the cut stone over in her palm and admire each of its facets, each one equally sparkling. Surprise was beginning again.

"What can he possibly get out of hopping about?" Perhaps it was a way of not touching her, of not saying to her do you love me, of not crossing the distance, of keeping her agitated, uneasy, quivering, of enchanting her.

There was thirst and there was water. The thirst was water. The thirst was an inspiration. And irritation is good. Zami was gathering together everything that was happening to her, quickly, quickly, greedy little girl, seed of woman, delighted by this manna of sensations. Rain! Rain! In two hours' time she received more life blows than in her entire existence.

During this time Nelson smiles as he jumps.

She saw that she would see him always, jumping in front of her and without ulterior motive. Everything became a face. Even the gymnasium. Everything became a memory. In the middle of a storm, peace is born. A peace for always, a high tense peace, stretched taut above all war. Inside the peace one can equally fight and suffer anguish. Upon guessing this, her eyes grew larger and were calmed. They were flat and brilliant as is the sea only in winter, when it is left in peace by the winds.

She let herself grow absolutely still, her eyes steady. Which Nelson perceived immediately and received as a victory. From her flowed the inexhaustible trust of the doe. A pure animal promise of betrothal without any presentiment of death. The doe that eats from the human hand.

And immediately, this calm upset Nelson. As though this softness made her impregnable. So surrendered was she. Nelson vacillated. Because it was easier for him to struggle to have than to have without a struggle. Then a ferocity of irrational desires sprang up all over his body. He wanted more from her than her. He wanted from her a daughter who would be a Zami all raw and soft, that he would tear himself with his own paws from her breast like a fruit, a baby without defense but without innocence, he wanted her womb, the fruits of her womb and at the same time he wanted her at the door to her mother's womb, ravishment and voracity possessed him, he wanted her childhood, her youth, and her old age, her softness and her dryness and to hold her in the palm of his hands and sniff her intact, round, body without orifices, and at the same time to tear with his teeth at her unnested organs, oh! to caress and ravage.

Because of these eyes that held no fear of him, he wanted to tear out all she was entrusting him with, all her liquids and all her dough, and because he could never eat her enough, because even if he clawed at every centimeter of her silk and even if he gnawed at and shattered each little bone, his hunger would never end, a great ache inhabited him.

Behold what in the human garden awaited a man who has a woman for destiny: fire, hunger, and at the end fatigue and at the end the cold. But as Nelson had his people for destiny his ache slowly softened into fire and that was all.

I shall never play at the game with death, my love, this is my regret and my hope. The grand dream of fresh flesh was fading from sight. Right here in the gymnasium the forbidden began. You shall not eat of your wife. And you shall not be devoured by your daughters. For your meat belongs to the people.

Right here at this very hour the door to infernal paradise closes.

———————

Luckily, Zami didn't know on that day to what extent Nelson was uneatable. For all this came to pass on this earth and in 1956. At that time, there was still a bit of present and a bit of bread. And dying of the thirst for love was not yet a sin against the people.

Nonetheless, the notice of banishment is already flying toward her and it will find her. But she is unaware of this and doesn't know it. The gymnasium is clinging to eternity by but a delicate shell. She doesn't know it. That is why she lives these two hours in a state of subtle nonchalance. Life later on will never have this heightened fineness. She allowed herself everything, like those who think they hold the key to eternity.

She allowed herself the slownesses that are luxury *par excellence* in South Africa. The slow soft fores, the delicate forbiddens.

She lets her boat float without steering it. It is in this way we can enjoy the river's skin.

"If you knew," she does not say with her virgin lips, she says with her eyes of tear-filled tongues, "if you knew how in this instant my hands love your humid skin that I do not touch. The length of your chest my earth and upon your breasts and through the thick grass of your flesh my hands pass humid with stubbornness and slowly fall frightened down to your heart. Oh my hands in the light, my hands grab hold of the humid kernel, the singular ovary, the male almond. Do you know that one tomorrow I shall make them, this flight, this dive?"

And as though he had read in the water, for one instant Nelson stops moving, streaming with sweat and silence, and says nothing. It was the last hour.

Inside eternity she is getting frightened. Fear too is a luxurious pleasure. She lets occur to her the ideas that cause the heart to swoon; the idea that she could have never met him, she lets it amass in her head till a night of icy sand falls upon her soul. And till she feels in her flesh what tomorrow will be a life awake without him: a deadly emaciation of the earth, a cow quartered alive, a womb with enucleated eyes, the world drowned in sands.

On this day she recognizes that Nelson has mortalized her. This is a cause for horror. Horror is the humid almond inside love. I want to taste the threats of love and gorge myself with its horrors. But before this day it hasn't yet been said she loves Nelson. At first it is death, need, and sickness she encounters.

And because of him, because he has landed on her breast like a star, because he is here, one foot on the earth and the other not, she can feel what solitude would be.

Arms linked, good and evil come along, and if I have the courage: welcome! all is well. Otherwise there won't be anything.

Pushed by a strong gluttony for life, she brought almost all the terrors to her mouth, she bit into their ardent flesh, and burned herself.

Inside eternity one gives oneself the time to not have and the strangely foreign happiness of taking the longest road home.

Thus, differently, he by jumping and she by crawling, they were heading toward the eternity room exit.

What came to pass in the gymnasium: seeing him run and jump in place like a virgin, innocent man, Zami had completely forgotten that Nelson was already nailed to his own name and branded and called to by the trees and walls, by the feet and hands and by the country's entire skin and by the forests of people wearing the sores of his seven letters, who had brandished him and claimed him before her. And she had but a single voice.

Thanks to this forgetfulness she had used him, with gusto, and an hour before his name.

I saw you sweat in the brush, my beloved, you were standing before the door to the century, still ageless, colorless, and nameless, and no one had pronounced you, no one had yet betrayed and crowned you.

I alone could have killed you you alone could have killed me and we were the most deeply moved the most loving strangers in the universe.

This is the truth: what she loves to love in him is the Beast,[22] without distrust and shameless, the animal who looks and does not lower its eyes, it is the round-eyed lover whom she alone could nourish, perish, revive, and it is the horribly tender almond beneath her teeth once it is undressed, this is what she loves cunningly under the covers, beneath the book, feet naked and without admitting it to anyone not even to her.

And what she doesn't love to love is the name. But she cannot do without it, for the almond is hidden inside the name. The almond is there dressed in all its glory. Now what she loves above all is precisely to undress it down to the kernel of milk. Without all this name to take off, without this innumerable and multiplied name to traverse, how to ever hope of attaining the uttermost the trembling the unhoped for nudity of the first unheard sound, the very first sigh that says: yes. Whereas Nelson is a famous orator, and at the sound of his voice the walls of the tribunal synagogue tremble.[23]

Which doesn't keep Zami from loving her Nelson Mandela, to the contrary, from loving his third person, his strength, and all his glory, and from adorning herself with all his words, with his letters and his ornaments.

This then is the Truth: inside the Truth there is a kernel of soft and tender lying that does not easily separate from the envelope. Whoever speaks the Truth, lies a little.

Truth is a crossing, a hybrid fruit.

When he has just been Nelson Mandela, when he has just come from being him, it is there, at the exit, at the crossing, that she awaits him and she loves him.

I'll never forget the white odor of the gymnasium and

that one extraordinary hour I did not love you, I did not understand you, calmly, astonished, I did not know you, I was sleepwalking on the edge of the abyss, and during this time the seeds in the red earth were germinating to their silent cadence, the mangoes on the mango trees were ripening, what had to happen was happening.

It is not impossible to surprise the genesis of genesis. You must choose a virgin strand, boundless without a trace of wind, perfectly smooth. The sand barely spun. Let no one set foot here. The translucent air of winter reigns, at noon. The pure emptiness is full of birds. At the call of the sun, sex goes back centuries to the winged instant.

Life is: a shoal of a thousand and one sea gulls poised on a shoal of white sand between the earth and ocean. The noise of the air in the universe is a slight vibration: the noise of human silence. This is the silence that allows the sea gulls to breathe the sun, their thousand and one white breasts turned toward the light that fertilizes them from afar. This ceremony takes place in winter in the absence of witnesses. There is nothing but the air the light and, behind the birds subject to the need to live, the world's ocean, agreeing and holding back. Man is not authorized to attend this mystery. A look— the sea gulls hear the slightest glance—and all is scattered.

This is how Zami contemplated furtively, and as if from a distant star, the scene of cosmic preparation. The sun labored in silence.

The gymnasium was the first strand. Zami was watching Ferdinand emerge all sparkling from his Tempest.[24]

The following day the season without present began, the time without time. There were weeks, but not a single moment. There was only a gasping for breath.

Each morning a mountain at the window. A roadless ascent. All that began was neverending. The day was without its evening, the evening without its night, the night without dawn, the dove covered with blood and without rest, going, coming, losing the earth, losing its head.

And the worst for Zami was the absence of parting. Which she did not manage to live, only to suffer and to die.

Parting was not given them. Instead of ending an unthinkable tearing away. It was like this: the female fish harpooned, taken from the water and suddenly abandoned atop the unlivable sand.

Never have there been so many births, so many arrivals, but never so much blood and so many abductions. Nelson never left. Suddenly carried off and without farewell. An absence would fall upon her. If only you would leave, if only the parting came back to me, if it took place in my flesh and beginning with my body, if I could undergo it, if only I could feel the bite and the taste of teeth, and the flesh retreating and crying out, then if I could suffer and eat of my suffering, this would be a consolation. But Nelson barely had the time to go before he was already gone and cut off. What her eyes didn't have was the horrible happiness of seeing him depart and go.

The beginning was taking shape, gaiety took a step, and immediately a disappearance fell on top of her like a funereal net.

Outside of her, outside of him, chased from paradise by a divine kick at the speed of madness. Was it hell just before the door, a thousandth of a second after joy? It was still paradise where she was lying, helpless, trembling, thrashed about by blows, since God allows himself to thrash those he loves, and to deprive them of everything in exact proportion to his love.

And there was the car, but without him. The car was very

faithful even if there was always something wrong with it.[25] It did everything for Zami. It took the place of a lover and of a confidant, it served her as letter, hands, and chest. It was her always lively ideal mother, her friend. At the exit to the school, Zami would wait for him, heart beating. He wasn't there. Sometimes it wasn't there yet, but it was coming, it was coming, across streets, crowds, and forests, she heard it, she heard its hoarse horn from kilometers away, she recognized it from among ten thousand, she will recognize it in another life, in fifty years, and on another continent, the ancient, obstinate voice of fidelity. Puffing and wheezing it comes, it is here, its headlight feeble, but it is inextinguishable, similar to the centenary elephant, similar to the threadbare ostrich, hoarse proof of the endurance of mothers. And inside, the aroma awaits her.

Wings a little closed, nesting on the backseat, Zami smells Nelson. His spikenard, his substance, his fragile, penetrating message. I sniff. I am well and I have so many prayers.

He is in the townships, he is seen in the nameless streets, he is seen in the offices, he is the water in the neighborhoods without fountains, without trees, without streams, he is drunk in dry tenancies, under paper roofs, he is seen in the stations and in the courthouses. She sees him in the newspapers. Everything speaks to her of Nelson. Everything worries and delights her.

Far away from me are you far away from me? Come back and don't come back. One life and the other life.

Sometimes she is crushed in the egg. Sometimes from here she haunts and pursues him over there. You won't finish pleading this defense, I have come to hold you, be quiet or else speak with my tongue in your mouth.

Sometimes she waits to live, on the backseat, her eyes open, fascinated by the fire of time, and life passes watching the blaze Nelson is feeding, branch by branch.

One can remain for a long time watching that burning nothing there is in fire. It's like remembering without memory an absolutely lost scene of which only this magic roaring remains. Day after day everything burns up in a flight of instants become lighter than air.

Is it me you are burning, my love, is it with my living wood, wood that has done nothing, that you nourish this gorgeous nothingness? Thoughts and ashes of thought all that.

He never forgot a thing in the car. Oh my lord and my languor, think of leaving a handkerchief on the seat, a little nothing from you, an indescribable something.

One time he is there in the car, Nelson, in his proper place. Everything became too beautiful and she not enough, too strong and she not big enough, not beautiful enough, and clinging like a she-monkey to each second to each feeling. It was almost unlivable.

Behold the moment. And behold how she just misses missing it, by too much joy. Behold the water, no more lips. The technique! I don't have the technique! I know how to burn, but don't I still know how to drink? These days instead of living, what have I been learning? Time is shooting at me at point-blank range. I will have to learn to live faster than the wind, what book can teach the technique?

At which point he stops the car by the side of a country road and says: "Ray is going to make your wedding dress. How many bridesmaids will you want?"

There it is. The dress was already made. The maids are what remain. Will want? Cried Winnie without a word. Wantrage![26] Wantrage became a strange mute red-winged rage-filled bird. How many maids. See what he asks her. Jumping this time beyond the pages and stories and without turning back. So sure of being followed by your ant, my friend? On all feet.

I would so much like to give you my answer, but I don't know how to get to you when there is neither door nor window nor wall nor fault nor house, only this great wide-open breast, this blank white space without an obstacle on which to knock. And before I even sprout I am hatched and spoken for.

On all feet mouth open runs Zami the ant behind the strange giant fiancé.

What I want is this instant, with all its seconds and all its words. I want the proposal. And to be given a thousand arms two thousand hands and twenty thousand fingers precisely today and not tomorrow, so that I can hold it back by each of its strands, catch it by its stringy hair, live it on my tongue and between my teeth by each one of its flavors.

And mutely cries to the sky: Stop! Stop everything! Stop this instant! This heart! This madman! This day! This hasty fiancé! This gust of wind! This soft ache that is passing over my head, I want to seize it, I want to smite myself with it, to tear myself with it, to scare myself with it, joyfully, but I slip and fall on my knees.

The event has taken place and there wasn't any time. And there wasn't any place. The arrow vibrates and strikes no heart. For there wasn't any heart to expect it, no waiting, no organ, no one's hands held up: instead of flesh for enjoying, there was this bloodless patience, this paper of transparent patience that she—by dint of expecting nothing, after weeks of waiting for the hour that wouldn't come, that ended up not coming—had woven for herself in place of a soul.

Yesterday, she had just triumphed, had just hoisted herself up to hopelessness. At that moment, the horse of fire surges up from between the curtains of heaven, and, bursting through with its neck and withers, tears all this precious paper.

Her joy takes place in her own absence, ahead of her is her horse of fire, life falls before her, the thunder is pink, she is two steps away from god just behind her. Who could bear such a killing expropriation?

Between god and me twice nothing. I am at the threshold to this world.

Will I remember what happens faster than time and higher than place, where will I retain the trace? In what memory more vivid than memory, more sensitive and more black? I smell the aroma of paradise I am one step away from the entrance, one second from eternity, the second turns round me, my hands are missing, my foot is missing, eternity smiles and it has all the time, my moment is missing precisely this one, the singular step, all is except me, poor me, shame is my heavy inhabitant, I am betrayed, under my tongue not a word, under my foot no floor.

At that moment, from happiness and ridiculousness, she catches her foot on a root and trips.

It is the second time. It is the sandal that is the cause. It is the root. It is the scandal of this grace that falls upon her and knocks her silly.

The ridiculousness helped her to act as though it were not grace that made her stagger.

But still, she would have liked to have known if he had divorced, but because of the golden dusk flowing through the heavenly windows, and because of the golden calm of the veldt, she didn't dare to formulate out loud a profane question. And also reasonable. A cooking question, of kitchen and kindling.

She knew only too well where this scene was sprouting: in the absolute that knows no detail, under the canopy of the absolute future.

She meanwhile a little lower, crouched in the dust of yesterdays, surrounded by grand old mothers: ask him about the details ask him about the formulas and ask him about the words. A woman needs words. Man without words, woman without water.

But, she parleyed, surely he said the words it is my ear that failed. She lied to the old women because she was already protecting him, from herself and for herself.

Besides, maybe she wasn't lying, and all the words were in a single word.

In a single word he had not even pronounced.

"Come," he did not say, since he held his hand out to her and everything was in his hand, all the words and all the stories.

—Come, follow me.

—And you think I'm going to follow you?

Nelson was so confident he didn't even turn around to see if she was following him. Now there's a man who gets up in the morning believing and in spite of everything. In spite of Evil, which exists, in spite of the government, in spite of the police, in spite of the past, in spite of human weakness, and because of all the threats, he believes. How could he not believe? The pillar that carries the world's dome, can it envisage bending?

Zami thought with a faint fear that she was perilously approaching the world of faith. I do not want to have to cease to tremble. I do not want to lose the torment of disbelief. Nelson says to the dead man: Come on, get up. And if the dead man doesn't rise? What happens? The end of Africa?

Nelson trusted like a man. If the dead man doesn't rise, that is because the dead man cannot rise. Nelson would see that he could do no better. He pushes his horse to a gallop and to the limit of life. And there he pushes life farther, till it can't go any farther.

And then, by the almost mortal effort of one who tears herself out of the claws of the dream of death, she finally freed herself from the earth, and from the claws of all her inner grandmothers who would have really liked to know if Nelson had divorced, if he was free, and also if he had what it took to pay the *lobola*.[27]

Turning her back on the old oumas,[28] mothers of corn and succulent umphokogo,[29] turning her back on the mothers of the mouth and stomach, she leapt. And with a marvelous bound she went mad.

Across seven nights I have forgotten myself, I'm coming! She renounced all questions and she accepted everything.

She said, "When?" And without turning back to see if he was following her, she said: "We shall eat the first portion of the ritual cake at Bizana." The first portion at the home of the mothers whose memory feeds the entire field of compassion, which in its turn feeds Zami's courage.

And for the second portion it will be time to go to Umtata where the memory of kings subsists.

The wind of time was blowing very hard. Borne by the golden arch of twilight, the world was progressing stage by stage toward its ultimate and mysterious goal. On board Nelson seemed very small. And this precise smallness conferred on him all the grandeur of man. He did not ask her to marry him.

———————

But I do not know if this is because he didn't have a minute. Or because the invitation to the Indian restaurant was already the marriage proposal. Or because Zami had been given to him for eternal wife before their birth.

And she had already answered "when?" the first time she had seen him without his seeing her, he standing amongst the crowd that believed him, in the Johannesburg Courthouse.

In the evening in the veldt the light is so virgin we think we can ask everything of the universe and that everything will manage to begin again before death and before the impossible.

He asked her for everything and its contrary and without a word. He asked her to renounce the life of a married woman and to the contrary not to renounce it in any way and not in any thing. And to start on her way toward him for forever to march to march to meet him across the months without paths and the rivers without bridges, as though he were himself the bridge and the path the earth and the torrent,

And to carry his absence on her back in the Xhosa way as though absence were their child

And to maintain the fire alive even without fuel.

This is what was the most difficult and the most contrary to what she could do: to make a fire without wood.

And she asked him for the same items except for the life of a married woman.

The sun was sinking slowly to its knees.

The road was deserted. The little village of Jerusalem with its white churches and its synagogues that are trying to forget in order to sleep was somewhere to the east, invisible behind the hills.

It was before the army, before the police. Or rather behind their imagination. I mean to say: Zami and Nelson were alone on this earth, with the rest of nonhuman creation, for a quarter of an hour.

The impossible took place one time. The sky spread out to infinity and limitless, nothing could stop it.

Blue and low above their heads it was gold and stretched like a cloth bordering the earth, for it was already day and already night.

And there at the end, at the utmost edge of the world, standing side by side draped in a lone mantle of light, were a lion and a lioness or else a lioness and a lion.

This was their wedding present, on behalf of Africa: the vision, unexpected on this road, of a lion and a lioness — something neither of them had ever seen. Standing side by side they contemplated the mystery of lions, whose beauty is made up of heavy peace.

Lions take their source from the great root of repose that humans rediscover only after making love. In the full of life, calm like lovers during their brief death.

Rolihlahla said: "How beautiful you are!" He had never told her that he loved her. He was looking at the mirror, collectedly.

Nelson softly placed his hand on his wife's left hip and Zami felt all the weight of love. The weighty calm. The peace in the weight.

"How lucky we are!"

They were wrapped in each other's thoughts, collecting and inhaling and impregnating one another, immobile like the lions. Their nostrils more thoughtful more moved than their lips.

The garden began. They were at the center of a passionate chastity.

Ibises, herons, and two-thousand-year-old storks, which time and the weather had turned completely black, were passing by to the west and to the east of their immobility and when they absentmindedly noticed them were unsurprised, knowing from their intimate manner that they were all from the same garden and obeying the same laws.

They looked at each other in silence, like it is forbidden to look at someone, with a slow, delicate surprise, dreaming, leaning over the map of their own strangely foreign country, it is here that I live, it is here that I shall dwell, following the course of the eyes, dreaming the length of the lips, musing on the contour of the cheeks, on the herd of goats, on the always secret always familiar rivers bathing without haste in the calm light of the eyes.

Far away from them, Africa was passing by and without bothering them.

This is how, by passing through the face, they entered smoothly into the warm breast of the inner future. And there, time was spreading out at a single stretch, like a field that shows all four faces of our seasons on its surface at the same time.

The future opened sparkling before their eyes: Zami left the country of yesterday, leaving far behind her her room, her friends, her street, the entire universe blighted by having been the world without Nelson, the past has paled, an effacement has veiled all that would be no more, and tomorrow already she has moved, in a divine transposition, already she has grown accustomed to the Orlando[30] neighborhood where she has not yet ever been, with a prophetic look she is in the kitchen one evening preparing Nelson's meal ten years from now, and behold, she remembers ten years from now already with tenderness the singular day ten years ago, in the deserted countryside where she had not yet begun to live this life of hunger and thirst, when each day is a torture but blessed, when, while she kneads the bread of patience, her gaze fluttering around the clock ten years from now, she remembers in advance that she will remember today past, for all that will be is already and all that is will always be, since in the world created by Nelson there will be no more effacement no more forgetting, only an immense forever beginning future, an immense present forever pursuing itself from today to today. From now on, life will never again cease to remember itself at every instant. An intense future carries her to her old age.

Down below in the dust of today-yesterday were lying the lost, defenseless bones of the men who were black. They didn't see them.

But for quarter of an hour there was not a dead man not a dying man not a single telephone call not a shiver of horror that made it up to their heights. They were without pity, and they didn't feel ashamed to have forgotten the police, injustice, and desolate remains.

They were held in peace, one inside the other, one in the shelter of the other, by means of a moment of immortality.

This was their marriage before the lions and the clouds. And before the car.

This quarter of an hour lasted an entire lifetime. They returned, sliding softly into the car. A birth occurred.

The stable was in the car. And time around them was held still and silent like the Singular night.

At that moment they were each the other's newborn. Each was gazed upon with delicate compassion. For they both sensed that destiny was making an exception by holding back its countless harbingers of anguish. And both thought it right that for ox and for ass they had a lion and a lioness.

Peace was strong, contemplative, and the color of dark gold.

The car was a stable.

And I too without knowing who I was I was breathing forgetfulness and in spite of myself I was hoping against all hope that history wouldn't be what it would be. Like an ordinary woman in childbed in the country from which I write, Africa was resting.

But this is only a dream.

There is no witness to this ceremony. And what I know of it myself I have seen in dreams.

The truce lasted two hours. Between forgetting and pain slides eternity. Eternity very narrow on the surface, but in depth, eternal.

That day, two hundred and thirty people were arrested in Jo'burg for lack of passes. And those arrested were waiting for Nelson Mandela to come and wed them all, and lead them on forced marches to survive, merely to survive.

An entire army of the arrested, hungering for hope, nourished on anguish.

The True Portrait
of Nelson

I would so like to be able to make the true portrait of Nelson. Were I to manage, I would reveal the secrets of an extraordinary love. I would tell of a magic. How a people gave its heart to this Nelson, as if it were all together but a single fiancée. And how confidently she waits, this fiancée, the people, for the freeing of a man held prisoner. As if they were all together but a single fiancée. How without a single shiver of hesitation she expects him to do the impossible, not doubting for an instant that the glorious day will come. How protected we all feel by the most powerless of human beings, this outcast, this extirpated, this caged-in-man, this man who seemingly can do nothing and yet who leads us to believe. Because he has the secret. This all-powerful man who can do nothing, if not absolutely everything. This is the secret. His powerlessness, his all-powerfulness. His too-powerfulness.

But I can tell another story while we wait.

It was a very rare day in the life of Zami. A day of personal blossoming. On this day, there were no human beings on earth, she had a date with the world and she had set out very early to meet it in the native brush. As though she had guessed that soon her youth would end, the age when one is still an animal among the animals and when one is still the earth's gardener, before the great separation. Crouched at the river's edge she was watching all that passes going past, and all that lives living. She living and going past with things and time. Activity reigned. The sky was rolling along the river's course, pushing its herds of big white clouds tinged with black along the black river beclouded with white herds. Time of ants and of lizards and of rustling leaves. Zami wasn't anyone. A day of source and of personal resurrection, day of plants of hands and of feet chafing the earth. And, coming from the Moon and Jupiter and from big uprooted cities, she was going down to the river to seek. To seek what? To seek. To seek confirmation, consolation, root maybe, she doesn't know what, a true, forgotten thing and one she's missing.

Rustling and crushing her way through the humming grasses she descends the length of the ladder of creation, from man to the river, clearing her whispering way through kingdoms and orders, in front of her lizards flee, serpents flee, a long time in front of me birds, insects, and butterflies flee, only the ants don't run away, advancing without looking back, behind them the monkeys in front the beetles, from cries to silent sounds, behind her forgetting and maturity, in front of her the earth regained, its red and black flour, the warm dry aroma of the world biscuit, and in the air, silence pierced only by the all-powerful metal of cicadas.

She was living inside herself in silence, feeling the slow activity of her organs in the heat. This was peace. Each according to its own program, each its own path, each according to its own species.

Suddenly the river's tender belly is torn by a frenzied hand. And through the shattered waters a little pink antelope shoots forth, surging up from the depths like a flying fish that can no longer fly. Her flight is caught in a crocodile's fangs.[31] What Zami sees: the river gutted, an antelope flapping her wings to regain the beach of air, but pinned. A palpitation pinned. And of the crocodile all she can see is his long immutable waiting snout. The crocodile has cast his net of teeth.

And now he does no more, he waits. Planted on the devil's fork, the antelope flaps with a thousand stifled wings. She utters a cry of horror, a cry of horrified surprise to destiny, a useless cry to god, to the stars, to the sky, to oneself. But if there is anyone more deaf than a stone beneath a mountain and more inhuman, it is the crocodile. The way the crocodile doesn't hear Zami's cries, doesn't hear the antelope's cries, causes her the worst despair: it is this absence of ears that makes Zami, the antelope, Africa, crazy with grief, it is this immutable deafness that drives the soul to despair too and not just the body. The crocodile's deafness bites the antelope's soul, no, it isn't dying that causes such suffering, it is discovering the calmness of the crocodile who is waiting patiently for all this noise to end.

So the antelope cannot refrain from weeping, for still alive she sees herself annulled and forgotten.

The teeth of ice plunge into the miracle of warmth without a sign. There is no sense. No. Nor delight, nor combat. Pure exercise of death. It is death itself that holds me in its lifeless teeth and all is useless. In vain the stones, in vain the cries and the club blows. How alone we are! And not even the grace of hate, not even the enraged joy of the witch at the stake.

In the middle of the horror that weeps and still has hope, Zami felt at a blow the pyre of hate burst with a blow into flames inside her chest. Such a need of hate, a thirst, a voracity of wanting to devour the crocodile's guts with huge teeth of flames. Such a need to one day kill the killer and devour his heart, and just as quickly such a violent resignation.

For I will never eat of the assassin's heart. I could never stand the pain this joy would cause me. I've already tried in dreams to get to the pitch of hatred, up to the summit of Table Mountain with my prey good and alive between my teeth and a stitch of hatred in my belly, but I never managed to reach it.[32] Having Voerster between my teeth is torture too foul.[33]

The antelope was the world's every entreaty, all the wings, all the prayers to no one. The crocodile was: Immobility.

So it's true, that there isn't anyone to hear us? It's true, nations, clouds, it's true, thrones and dominions, there is no mother, no one at the other end of the world to be awakened thanks to love by our cries, so it's true that hope is but the ultimate pitiful invention of our hopelessness? And that God is a man of whom we mustn't ask anything more? Of no one, no one?

Zami beheld the world. The antelope pinned inside the crocodile. And suddenly with all her might she didn't want. She didn't want to be the antelope. She didn't want to be the condemned without appeal. And with a frenzied jerk she detached herself from the beast. She rejected, denied, abandoned it to its destiny. This is only an animal story. It is not our story. She avails herself of language, and no more cries. And knowing she was in the process of lying to herself in order to bear life and death, she declared herself poor, helpless, and objective, for in any case the crocodile too must live, and murder has its place in the universe. Birds too were chirping for no reason. She had nothing left to do but run away, so as not to witness.

What stops her is the hippopotamus. Perhaps he's God? He's the incredible. Someone. The hippopotamus arrives. Whoever has beheld the hippopotamus come to the aid of the antelope will never again be able to forget this race. This race explains how the world can still exist in spite of hatred and in spite of death. Because life helps its own. The hippopotamus's race is total. From the farthest distance he heard the call he hastens at the strongest of his strength, the speediest of his speed, the heaviest of his heaviness, the earth trembles beneath the heavy pestle of his hooves and the river divides beneath his chest, the distance still separating him from the saurian is huge, he covers it and crushes it, and fells it under his thick hooves. He can't go any faster. The hippopotamus is epic. Nothing can divert it. He's coming. His entire life is thrown into this gallop. To embody a single will without second thoughts is the secret of invincibility. His Strength the hippopotamus knows no doubt. The hippopotamus is one. Up until the last second the crocodile doubted, or hoped, that the antelope would die between his teeth an instant before succor. But at the last second he leans over, spits the bit out, and disappears. The will of the hippopotamus is absolutely indisputable. Pure majesty.

What Zami saw next is true. The story becomes hard to tell now, because the characters have animal bodies, everything is taking place in the brush, on the butter-colored sand at the river's edge, but the limits of beings are indefinable. Behold: as if he had great round arms and heavy breasts softened by time, and as if there were in all his flesh the magic energy of a mother, the hippopotamus is fussing over the antelope.

And now all is mystery.

How the hippopotamus carries his antelope onto the sand, watching out for her sparrow-in-the-hand smallness, is a mystery. How he coos and moos and pleads for life, and how the antelope and Zami understand what he is saying mutely, with his enormous nostrils and his hooves for words, everything is said, received, and answered, mutely. The limits of this scene are our human limits, not those of the characters.

The antelope was lying helpless, like a pink rose with a slightly broken stem, her head weary, like a woman too young to be in childbed, and it is she herself who is the bloody baby of this event. And the hippopotamus, a mountain of tenderness and efficiency. Four tons of black intensity, on his belly an apron of mud, working, working at retying the threads of life. His huge garish pink muzzle works away skillfully like a hen on her hour-old chick. A tender ton weighs no more than a wing. The wing was fanning the little one. He promised her and informed her.

He told her: I cannot save you any more than this. I have restored you to the shore of life. Now it is you who must carry yourself on your own four feet toward the forest. Come on, be brave! Get up, away with you!

And the antelope said yes, a tremulous yes. And couldn't rise. Get up! insisted the huge cinnabar pink nostrils, standing he sniffed smelling the sweet smell of pink fur threatened by the smell of raw blood. And with the soft part of his huge muzzle he delicately dabs at her blood-ribboned flank. "Try to get up, lazarus, help me to help you my love, get up, you just have to try."

By surrendering to love, the antelope who could no longer rise, rose. And did not walk. Apologizing fell once more onto the sand, her eyes staring into the eyes of the hippopotamus. Zami was watching, her heart clenched with wonder. Everything the hippopotamus said she believed. You're going to heal. She believed it.

Call out to me again, mother, call back the life that wants to come.

The belly of the hippopotamus was dragging in the white sand tinged with red. Each of his tons' parts was enormous, and the whole was infinitely delicate.

His body was eternally bizarre and ugly. Zami had never seen such a big strangeness from so close up. And this big black ugliness shone with beauty.

Yes, the hippopotamus was beautiful like the incarnation of succor, handsome like the sweating warrior who sets his city free. All one saw in that moment was his body's soul, a simple heavy soul, blackish and stubborn. And the hippopotamus in all his wisdom was beautiful. He was smiling. He was the man with milk. The soul of her life. The man of her life.

The couple was alone in the world, absorbed in the cosmic task of resurrection. They were both doing everything they could to retain the life that in spite of him in spite of her was leaving with regret was leaving. In honor of the hippopotamus, the antelope was hoisting herself up onto her shadowy feet. Each attempt a shadowy birth.

"Then enter my mouth and take my soul from my throat, that is all I have left to give you," yawned the hippopotamus softly. And docilely, like laying one's head down to be cut off and the way a child lies down on the funeral-pyre, so the antelope plunged down to her frail shoulders into the gulf full of warm breath. What came to pass there in the world's mouth, what was it if not love, the very first, love with eyes closed, the one inside the other in intoxication, divine animal love, the one that does not ask what is your race but asks what is your need.

The birds were watching.

No one managed to go any farther. No one can give any further. Than the antelope in the heart of the hippopotamus. Everything had been given, returned, received; then exchanged. In the bottom of his gullet the hippopotamus came to know the trembling tenderness of a body woven from lightness. As if a rose had breathed into his mouth. And in the high cinnabar pink grotto, like a damp chapel, the antelope came to know the strong happiness of heaviness. Each one came to know its opposite and itself. Both were slight and gigantic for each other. And with all their hooves they trembled, heavily tenderly hoping to succeed. The antelope was in the bosom . . .

At that moment there was a pause in the pace of the things of this world, an abeyance of all that moves, the order given by God, the hand of the world clock stopped short in its stubbornness, and an absolute stillness of the scales.

It was a pure, a marvelous Maybe. Everything was possible on earth during this instant. Assassinations were held in check in all countries of the world. Hope was possible, like the song of a bird crazy with joy. Because the hippopotamus in a supreme effort had torn open all the ties attaching him to the interior of his condition, and with an invisible bound had leapt across all limits: those of tradition, of science, of what we think we know, about the animal and about the human. And there before Zami's eyes which were watching him, and without knowing whom she saw, his hooves placed at the four corners of the terrestrial heart sending him mute energies, with the antelope in the middle of nursing from the soul in his throat, he flew very high without moving above our disbeliefs, above our slender strengths and our innumerable mistrusts.

And yet, Zami divined, we too are capable of leaping over the walls of our skin, and of doing all we cannot do without running the risk of our perdition, I too, I feel it in the blood bewitched this instant in my arms, if love calls out to us, we will not hesitate to surpass the boundaries of our innate nature, if it were necessary in order to reach the lips where my life is laughing to fly and to brave the void, like a bird without wings I would brave it, I would barely fly a minute, turned into something lighter than myself I would be without myself, I would be pure life without death, I would be perfect and no one, for one brief moment set free from the fear of dying that makes of our living a common cage, and for an instant I would taste the joy that is born only beyond fear. But what the hippopotamus was doing, was this love? I do not know the name for what he was doing. It was a great mystery. As if he had found strengths beyond his strengths for drawing back his bow, and now an extraordinary desire flew forth.

Zami believed that the miracle was done. And in truth if the antelope had been able to live she would have lived, since she was trying. She was resting, but by resting she was dying without knowing it and no one knew it. The scales were absolutely motionless. For without knowing she was dying, she was living in safety. The weaning was done both softly and heavily. "Go now," gaped the hippopotamus, delicately laying his burden down. Yes, said the child, I'm going. And at this very instant the scales tipped, the beast was brutally broken on the ground, like a baby hurled from the plateau that is the sky. And already at this second she was no more than a relic, so far had she gone beyond herself in the effort to not disappoint the hippopotamus. During her brief resurrection she had already spent the drop of life that remains in the body at the beginning of death. And this was a miracle just the same.

The couple had done all that was humanly possible, and maybe even more than humanly.

Immediately animal life continued on. The birds took up their chirping again where they had left off. Traffic like in a city. And in this disorderly brouhaha brush business started up again, with each one running here and there haphazardly following smells, each for its own, and each according to its species.

Forgetting descended on the tragedy with the flock of vultures.

There had been no tragedy. Life was abuzz.

It is here that this story separates, each returns to its species. The hippopotamus mysteriously leaves. A white sweat pearling his black hide. Is he weeping with his skin?

The hippopotamus knew everything and yet he knew nothing. It was life that, wanting to live, had called on then forsaken him. Sadly, he searched a moment in his mind for the meaning of his presence here. Nothing. With a halo of solitude, he moved forward into the river.

Because of an urgent need to give life, he had invented. Each gesture invented and without making a mistake, as though he were born the antelope's mother. And up to the end, he had never stopped wanting the other's life. He was the mother of all wounded life.

On her way home she thought of him, of his slow rapidity, of his Maternity, and wholly charmed by his heaviness, by the beauty born of ugliness, by the strong softness of the strong, she felt love stirring in her womb, flesh awakened in her flesh, thousand-year-old root whose earth she was.

It was impossible for her not to be in love with Nelson: he was so much the man drawn on the walls of her rupestrine flesh. And not only the man, but the entire scene also, the breast itself, and the secret milk.

I don't know in what way this is the portrait of Nelson. But it is.

The ray of honey in the lion, this milk of the soul that doesn't ask what is your race, in order to give of itself.

The hippopotamus arrived neither too early nor too late in Zami's story. He is not an intrusion, not an accessory, not an exotic black passerby. He is the conductor of the orchestra perched on the edge of the musical gulf, the mute conductor of our intimate nostalgias. We barely look at him dancing for us, leading for us the huge herd of our passions. And yet, how to do without his familiar black back? Faceless water-diviner of our vital sonorities, he is here to help us beseech the woods, the trees, the strings, the waters, to render unto us our soul, to make our lost supernatural wisdom resound.

The Visit from the Ostrich

Starting the next night, when Zami once again found herself alone without him for the first time in the new life, she sensed she had married the terribly present body of absence too.

She was lying in bed with shapeless, tireless absence by her side, with absence courting her insistently, this ghostly love with its hollow caresses, this insomnia insinuated into the very bosom of sleep.

A night of terror followed the day with the lions. Everything is the opposite of the night before. The stars roared faintly in a mud-colored sky. The room is full of a strange smooth sadness preaching fear and apprehension to her. A black, false flesh bears down upon her flank.

When she finally falls asleep moaning it is to find herself face to face with the Governor General, who is waiting for her under the covers like a hidden hitler.[34] This white man has several heads, some parted in the middle, others parted on the side in greasily colorless hair, but all their little pink eyes are sewn outside, on top of their eyelids and of their teeth that stink of cigars. And what is horrible oh horrible is that he will not leave her, he hems her in like a hundred pigs, he trots on her feet like a bunch of pigs, he has a grudge against her beauty, he sticks to each one of her steps, he pursues her very closely like a herd of hogs, and recites to her belching a short letter in gibberish and gobbledygook. When she hears the filthy insult, the idiotic hailstorm of the accusation, this skin judgment he dares to place upon her like his hand on cattle, finally her sainthood explodes, finally she finds in her body the absolute, necessary arm, the generously bloodfilled Anger that in a second renders her superhuman. The battle against the demon lasts and will last a hundred years. With her own hands with furious fingers she saws away at evil stalk by stalk. Twists and saws, with a disgusted power. There is something dirty and immemorial in the limp persistence of the Old Man. As though he were obstinately persisting at deserving hatred throughout centuries of centuries because that is what he enjoys. Pig following upon pig interminably. Will I never see the end of them? And there are still some left when the dream expires.

If it were a man one could kill it; but the hitler is a numerous innumerable pig with an undiscoverable soul, if it even has one in it, and so we will have to stomp on it and saw away at it and carve it up and trample it down for hours maybe and for generations, for it is only at the price of this deadly digging that we can hope to arrive at the root of evil.

It is only in stories and for solace that heroes triumph in the end over evil.

But in reality, she knows very well she has dreamed true. The combat is ignoble and interminable. A grief for the beautiful combat that won't take place grips her heart. She feels like crying. She turns on a light to forget.

And there, seated at her feet, grandmother the Ostrich is waiting for her.

"You scared me, grandmother!" she says to make the old ouma happy, for the grand old mothers need to feel important.

Forthwith ouma the Ostrich takes the floor with gusto to

say what she had to say. And Zami as is fitting prepares to be pestered.

"Do you know that if you marry this Nelson you will be wed to fear? Yesterday you were taking care of children. The week before you were taking care of goats. Today here you are head of an army and keeper of the sun. You would do better to marry my brother's son. But you'll do what you want."

"With him I won't be afraid to be afraid."

"You think you know and don't know a thing. This fear you're going to marry you can't imagine it. Neither can I. The fires threatening this house don't give you any idea, the childhood illnesses, nothing. The police you see passing by with their dogs and their clubs don't give you any idea. The blood your sister died of, the death that ate your mother, the brigands who bashed in your brother's head, you have some idea of these. But no one has any idea of this fear. You may have had the nightmare about the monster with the one hundred teeth and each one of those teeth is a penis and from each penis flows a trickle of poison, you woke up so all that gave you was the impotent shadow of an idea. It seems a butcher from Bloemfontein[35] split his employee in two from head to toe exactly like a piece of meat, and I won't tell you the rest. This doesn't give you any idea. For all these fears were like a fire that flares up and then falls to ashes.

"But the fear you're going to marry is the sun: it will wake you every day of your life, shine a light on you and pursue you till you fall from fatigue, and it will be there before you wake up. Do you see what I mean?

"You are going to marry the fear of losing this Nelson."

Zami looked at the Ancient Ostrich to see what she meant. The Ancient Ostrich was smiling.

"But you're mad about him.

"But do you know who this Nelson is, the one who's going to bring you fear, hope, and solitude as a wedding gift?

Because he's going to bring you as much solitude as there can be in a woman's life, do you know that?"

"No, I don't know that."

"I was sure of it! That's why I came at once. If you take him, you take everything he is, everything he'll be, everything he doesn't know, everything he's hiding, everything he's hoping for and everything he fears. So me I'm telling you, you're also asking for cold, terror, hunger, solitude. And I'm warning you too you'll have to dread what is a woman's disgrace, I mean jealousy. Because you know, you'll always be first *after*. After his struggle. You'll be the first in second place. And the danger that is threatening you and threatening us all, your ancestors, is jealousy. This would be a disgrace for us, I prefer to warn you."

"I know I'm going to marry his white struggle and his black struggle."

"Nothing whatsoever, you know nothing. And you know, you'll be like a woman who must love and serve her husband's first wife. And don't delude yourself by thinking like I know you are that his struggle isn't a woman. Because it is woman *par excellence*. What's done is done. All that's left for you to do is be a mother to everything he has in his pouch. Without counting the fact he picks up anyone in need in the neighborhood. And if he brings you home a fat old white woman whose car has broken down to insult you under your own roof, you'll have asked for that too.

"I see everything and I know everything I do not know, so listen to me or don't listen to me.

"As for the meals?"

"I know."

"Good. So then I won't tell you that if he comes home, he won't have the time to eat. He won't come home and he won't eat. And you won't either. But if he has the time to eat, he'll bring you back ten people in his pouch, each one with a belly bigger than my stomach. And the chop, you'll have to invent it. If he starts to eat, he won't start. But if he does manage to eat once, he won't tell you how good it is.

"You don't want to believe me but you do believe me.

"I'll tell you about hope. Be careful of hope, it's bad. Hope for nothing, and you shall have perhaps.

"Wait for nothing and expect nothing. Because everything you'll have you have already. You have his love and nothing more. That's all you desire and for the rest you'll want.

"No flowers, no follies, no news."

"And letters?"

"There will be some letters. But that doesn't interest me. And never will a letter replace a good night spent with long, soft arms like a young girl's bottom. I know I don't know how to read, but if I had needed letters I would have known, don't contradict me.

"And as for the nights in any case, expect no night. You won't be spoiled with too many nights. Bits and pieces here and there, like birds you'll be inside the squall.

"And don't cry! Because a woman who loves knows how to turn an hour into a week.

"I'll give you a piece of good advice: you'll have bad feelings, don't chase them away. Honor yourself yourself. Everything you feel, feel it. If an anger comes to you, receive it. Listen to it with your right ear. Resentment, don't hate it, it has something to tell you. Give it your left ear. Mistrust false pride. We're bad, that's a part of our goodness.

"Everything you will be, be it befittingly, neither too little nor too much. Hold yourself upright like a young tree not like an old one. It's going to be difficult being the wife of Nelson Mandela. But not everybody sees an apple in the same way and not every woman sees a man with the same eye. For me this Nelson is too high up in the tree and anyway I don't need such a big one.

"And to end I'm going to tell you the gravest part of this story:

"This life will be your sacrifice.

"But the problem with sacrifice is that nobody knows what it is. Who sacrifices who is sacrificed to what by whom no one's going to tell you.

"The laws of sacrifice exist but no woman and no man can explain them. All we see is the blood. But whose? As soon as there's blood it's mine, as soon as there's blood it's yours.

"If you can't understand me that's because I'm talking to you about the incomprehensible. Do you understand?"

Obscurely and without understanding Zami could feel the blood pouring out like her body's tears without being able to stop it.

"We women we're against our own sacrifice, but how to avoid it? We women who are a mix of mother and son?

"So now tell me one thing," she leaned toward Zami, her face all lit up with ignorance. "Do you get along with him in the pleasure department?"

She asked with eternal gluttony.

"Because you know me, with my husband, I had to make jokes so as not to shock him. For my relief, my child, I had to go a good ways away from my home, for fear he hear that just like him, I too suckled at my mother, and that the beast stirs in my bag.

"I pity the wife of a man who can't stomach women and can't stand their smell."

The Ostrich seemed less ancient to Zami and less inspired, except from hearsay.

"And tell me now, how do you get inside to love him, he who is like a golden-ramparted city? By which door do you enter the fortress? Through which weak point?"

Zami saw that the Great Old Mother was losing years and no longer hiding the fact that it was from hunger for life, and not for death, that she was dying.

Then she told her Nelson's dream: it is a day the world like a Sunday morning at the Ocean's shore, with children, women, herds, a day like a meadow of green grasses, of corn, of river, of pale golden sand. This meadow would take place in about thirty years. How radiant and satisfied is the year eighty-eight! It parades past with its herds of goats and its children brimful of childhood, and its boats riding its big fish like horses, and I am there, old Mandela a little tired, but content, contemplating our present.

At a depth of one century the past lies buried in my memory.

Do you remember the year '48? and '58? And '68? They are in the past and cannot hurt me anymore.

And there is nothing, not a dread, not a humiliation, not a howl of hate, that time hasn't changed into a strange jewel.

Prisons, torture, slavery, can the year '58 imagine a beach, in thirty years at our ocean's shore, and will we tell the Story become unimaginable?

"Who will see it, this dream?" said the Ostrich. "Me, in '88 I'll have already returned home to the ancestors many great years before."

Night's end approaches, the year '58 is in the street, and the future has once again become unbelievable as usual, far away and forbidden. Thinking about '88 was a sort of shamelessness.

The two women fell silent and they were right to do so. Enough dreaming.

"You won't forget my piece of cake?" said the Ostrich going off toward death.

And yet Zami saw how ouma the Ostrich looked beautiful upon leaving, going off beautiful and without skinniness on her long forever graceful legs, as if a favorable eye had looked on her, but there had never been any look, as if everything that had never been given to her had been unable to pale her luster, for her life's lamp was interior, and hence her whole life she had been radiant for no one. What good is it to ask the sky to rain and the white man to be black, and conversely for the black man, and for men to thank their mothers? It is women who understand women and men are born to not understand each other. This is why she had come to visit Zami, for the pleasure of the echo.

Just before she disappeared the Ostrich shouted:

"And the weak point? You'll tell me?"

And the curtains of a rising sun, shining like honey, closed upon her.

"You didn't tell me your weak point my beloved, it is this silence that estranges me from and scares me about you, I am standing before your smile, I adore you and I am exiled, I want to enter into your heart of hearts, your strength leaves me outside,

"You watch me from everywhere, I am dazzled by your spears, douse your glory for a brief instant and speak to me in the tender dark. Tell me where you are one-eyed, where you stammer and where you limp, where I can strike you and yet will not strike you, where to climb higher than your heights and I will not bring you down, where I can give you all the forgiveness I have for you.

"Don't answer, laugh at me, look at me sniffling, lay on my shoulder the delicacy of your face, I will caress each inch of skin, in the end I will find the flaw. The white stain on your left shoulder. Something too ancient, a nothing you have on your back and where I will manage to root my love."

At the first breath of day they came to fetch her to take her to the dressmaker's. Misery, filth, fury were still veiled. And not a fear, not a flame of revolt, not a pang this sweetened dawn didn't change into an ephemeral hosanna.

"I am jealous of this passing Zami, oh why don't I have another life next to mine for spying on and enjoying myself," suffers Zami the blessed in the year 1958, on the way to the wedding dressmaker's.

During the week of fittings, Zami tried to live the same reality. The dressmaker's mirror helped her a little. What was happening to her was happening to Zami in the mirror, a young woman she was watching.

"And no one to complain to, mother I am struck with perfection and I cannot bear it, life as it is happening to me escapes me, I want to kiss it, it knocks me to the ground it jumps me like a giant, it is too grand, it is too grand,

"I barely have the time to want, what I want comes crashing over me

"Like a wave of joy, I am swept along and taken in, lost, I would like to swim in it I am drowning in joy, I would want I don't want

"Receiving resembles dying which I do not know, like two tidal waves

"God is filling me to overflowing with blessings, I am fattened like a goose, I am stuffed, I am white,

"And no one to tell that I wish God would bite into me and break my jaw anew, may he say No to my desire

"May he make me languish and grow thin, instead of running around in front of me with a dancing tail and barking with joy.

"What I'm missing is the time to pray and to not possess,

"The time to tender my arms, the tender imperfect trembling time of soons and not yets, the twilight of birdlike terrors,

"I'm committing a sin, mother, I know it, but it's all I have left to protect me from the too clear day, to save me from the too strong grace of having seen the sun Mandela rising too beautiful for me."

Not too much, not everything, Zami was begging softly.

If Nelson had been there that week she would have thrown herself against his hardness, she would have rubbed her head against the rock, she would have assailed him with whims, until he lifts an annoyed hand and says to her: ah, enough already!

And she would have fallen like a crushed fly and finally at rest in the crash. But she could flap in the air with thousands of permitted wings. The flight was exhausting.

She persists in taking two superimposed paths.

On one she walks eyes wide open and multiplied, passing amid the bushes full of cops, the air is full of men with viscous eyes inside carapaces of steel, she walks along quickly, disgusted, proud, dazzling with beauty, twice as big as herself, and at each moment it is time for a death to be unmasked. At the end of the path black Jerusalem awaits her, doors proffered, fists clenched, and it is in extremis that she takes the plunge, shins foaming, between her breasts a river of sweat.

On the other, which slowly runs beneath the path of steel, she walks along as if there were only one road all twisted with love, as if she believed it, as if she were forgetting the unforgettable African hell, and subterraneously down to fatality she makes her way in the lost garden, step by step remaking paradise complete with its roses and its thorns, with its deliciously intestine wars, and the beloved for only enemy. Her mission is to recompose the promise. At night she replants dream by dream the earth the white years have uprooted.

It is a work of madness. To accomplish this madness you must have two souls that agree to live contrarily in a single body. Luckily, this woman has two names for disentangling herself a bit. To go to Johannesburg she wears the name Winnifred with which her father barded her not knowing what he was doing, but the gods knew, a name of German iron made to consternate the adversary and proclaim that this woman fears neither dying nor killing. By her bearing, by her nerve, an inner but real invincibility is proclaimed.

The man who could make Winnie falter has not been born. All he can do is murder her. He'd have to fear the immediate return of the name Winnie, wholly armed, and definitively unbeatable.

To go to Jerusalem she wears her Xhosa woman's name, and her eyes are fountains for the birds made mute by the heat.

———————

Nelson loves Zami and it is Winnie he adores and he fights. In general names know very well what they're up to in this story. And more than once it is the name that knows before the body.

Sometimes Zami starts loving Nelson and it is Winnie who finishes.

He is the pillar of my temple, I make my nest on his cornice, around his trunk I fling my voluble stalks, at his foot my helmet my spear and my shield.

Next Saturday at 1 P.M., the pillar is in his office. On Saturday at one o'clock Zami enters the office, it is the office but it's not the same Saturday, the waiting in the office says so, Zami enters and hears it, she doesn't see her pillar she sees a gentleman waiting, Saturday turns around, worried. She sees an invisible wall, she enters and the not-waiting for Zami rises up before her, she flings herself against it and bumps her wing. For if one cannot see one's own absence one can feel it. She can see fine and thinks she sees he's waiting for a not-her since it is not for her he's waiting, but behind her, who? no one she knows, no one more than her, what secret secretary?

So then with her all-powerful hands, she takes Nelson by the skin of his neck and without explanation, she takes the pillar by the neck, like a rabbit she holds him and shakes him, and before the world assembly planted thick and fast in prayer, she grabs him, like a carrot she pulls him up unearths him, and drags him roughly outside the temple, outside the City, and up to the Gates of Creation. Leaving the office to stand on its own without a pillar as best it can. Before the eyes of an extraordinarily beautiful and strangely foreign secretary.

"How harsh you are, Zami, my fiancée, my fawn, what sharp teeth you have, how yellow are your irises around the scarlet almond."

One could wonder if Winnie hadn't slipped her hand into Zami's hand. But it was definitely Nelson Mandela the young woman was seen dragging at 1 P.M. by the skin of his name.

This is how they spent the night of Saturday to Sunday: very far from the cities and offices, at the exit to time, lying down, and sometimes on their knees, enveloped in a violent admiration for one another. They both acknowledged themselves vanquished, and each rejoiced for the other's victory. Zami was vanquished and beaten by her own victory, and Nelson was exulting from his crushing defeat.

The wind of victory is blowing now on one, now on the other, and they marvel beholding themselves endlessly knocked down and picked up to be knocked down and picked back up again.

Stars at their feet, like two generals enlisted by legend, here they are surveying the solemn hours before the sun comes up, talking nonstop.

There is so much to say to each other during the last night before the beginning. There is so much to enjoy before the irremediable union. It is during this vigil the night before that we reproach and divide ourselves and each other, blessed be reproach and division, and lodge against ourselves and each other complaint after complaint. The gifts are numerous and refined. How strangely foreign they both still are, and marvelously entrenched behind their shields. Regretfully they parry their last blows before the sun comes up. And in haste, with fervor, swear to each other hour after hour that even when they are married and mingled, they will never forget this Night filled with shocks and dissensions.

The moon is pouring her silver milk onto the earth. A nostalgia for this same moment follows the scene like its milky shadow. And they prepare themselves for the upcoming marriage as though for the most subtle of separations.

They may never again feel as mysteriously close. For there is a hidden avowal in the reproach. I love you so much I'm almost not myself anymore.

At the end of the Night they struggle feebly, barely. — Will you grab me again by the neck someday? — I will want to, I want to.

The sun rose with a bound. And like two generals turned toward the enemy they watch the enormous aster climb. Events will come from the front.

———

And it is with Winnie's hands that on another day in Orlando she is going to take Sergeant Fourie[36] by the shoulders and, without wanting to kill him, she hurls him surprised across space into the mire he merits. He falls head first into the slough he desired, and thereupon the dressing-stand falls over on top of him, like a mountain falls over on top of a rat.

I hadn't meant for him to break his neck, but I say to him, "Stay there with your cries and your pain, and may the mire you are made of eat you with your own teeth, for I would be happy to see you boil and boil again in the mud."

Zami means "test" in Xhosa.

A clear face, with eyes that think of he who isn't here, who isn't in the street, who isn't in the town, who isn't in the province, and her gaze departs, and travels, travels, her immense eyelids batting slowly, for a long time, arrives at the edge of the earth, the sea is somber, it scolds and her gaze flies trembling, above the foaming, barking waves, arrives before a wall, and seeks by where to enter, by where to enter . . .

All her faces have big eyes that travel over there, so far away.

A woman so full and round and padded, she always seems to be expecting a child. And in truth she is expecting one.

She wears the traditional African long green and black dress.

Nelson already had a hundred years behind him and before him still seventy-seven to race through.

He agent of the promise and the urgency to go straight to the goal.

He representative of the wind. He never looks at the earth beneath his feet. His hour is always the next one.

Zami was his unexpected. The dream we haven't had for twenty years that comes one night we know not whence.

She enters my office, like a woman I've often thought about without approaching, like a woman never imagined as being here, in this office, like the adored woman of my reveries, the never expected, never hoped for stranger, inhabitant of another time and of another continent. She enters haloed by this long incredulity, coming from the end of the world, and sits on my sofa, in reality. A great rending of meaning. At her entry, the entire world became strangely foreign to me. Reality took one step forward. Gestures were made in spite of me but not without my submission.

"No," I say, "I cannot." And I accepted what I was refusing. For all was irresistible.

"As you wish," she says to me, eyes lowered, but the light was everywhere. I was without door, without eyelids, I was open, at the mercy of the light.

And at once, everything that is within my walls and within my body feels itself being delivered up to an unprecedented tyranny. It isn't her fault, it is her power it is something in her flesh or in her body's dough, something invisible that strikes my reason and brings it to its knees. An all-powerful flameless foreignness is burning up the atmosphere. She sits down on the sofa, I am seated next to this woman from forever who is shattering my earth and whom I'll never understand. It is her soul I dreamt of it is her body that came in.

In my fables I used to venerate her wild, savage genius, with my words I used to invoke the spirit of struggle, her impalpable divinity, my imagined muse.

The unexpected of this visitation is this incarnation. As if divine matter were emerging living and knowable from the land of the dead.

Her body's presence is an army that knocks me to the ground and holds me prisoner. As though bent by a nonexistent wind I am held within her walls, I am adapted as close as possible to her forms, I am broken and fastened as close as possible to her proximity. So as not to touch her I break my fingers. So as not to take, with full and destructive hands, the object the mother holds out to him, what does the child do?

— He takes what comes his way. For he desires before the law, he is still a fish in water and whenever he's hungry he devours.

But me, I mustn't, I was weaned a long time ago, my marrow turned to wood a long time ago, my years are adding up, my body has been made more of will than of yeast-filled dough for a long time. What makes me rise is tomorrow, is the crowd to be made to rise up, the severe song of the ANC,[37] the battle to be calculated, the incessant and bitter speculation about what it is that thinks basely, powerfully, in the brain of whites, the lookout for the enemy with the greasy heart.

For quite a long time, my proud and faithful body has served me merely as friend, as horse, as loyal companion. There is no more child, no more furious cry, no more naive, capricious inhabitant in my house. And for so many years, no fruit, no female, no spicy food has passed through my dreams.

Immortal like all warriors haunted by the flag I was living without life and without today. I am telling the truth that on this day in the year 1958 was denied, undone, and dismissed.

This was the day of my dissolution.

She sat down next to me. Meeting with my friends in half an hour, I proclaimed, clutching at this memory, letting go. A passionate forgetting encircled the scene. The outside became distant and muted like a conversation past.

Her body became my world, a low mountain is all I see, I see the world and I have only this mad look of a navigator whose prayers have been granted, who sees the end of his blind migration, sees and sees with all his eyes the earth's form taking shape over there, who wants to run across the water and does not run, who wants to die of impatience and does not die.

I see that the blouse of slightly ruffled white voile is full. The way a cotton cloth spread out to dry on a meadow hides and hides nothing. And because they are so close, so nearly visible, so delicately invisible, a poignant fascination grabs me in the gut. I can already see they'll be large and juicy, and they'll surprise me by their heaviness of woman yet virgin and already ripe, and already I'm surprised and stricken with intoxication.

My face feels like fainting in contemplation,

And like a tearful cry desire gushes forth in my breast like an ache. From the bottom of the resigned earth I cry out toward you. Ah! The return of a rain. I wasn't even thirsty anymore. Your softness struck my heart two times and my need explodes into a sob. I had forgotten this thirst.

The sun climbs slowly back up toward the surface of the plump perfumed earth, leaving behind me absences, disbeliefs, patiences.

The ripened flesh emits the mute message that makes the wise man go mad. I had forgotten that genius could reside in flesh. In one night of shyness he touches genius with his fingers, at first still anguishing over the impossible, fearing sacrilege, until chastity finally grows softer and is assuaged.

As when I was keeper of our beasts, and used to caress the heifer all over to get to know her and to give her her own body to enjoy, so that the heifer would not be denied either the firm form of her flanks or the delicious indolence of her blond udders,

he races over her entirely and without unveiling her, for there is an order in creation, and following the order is a joy. He tastes the growing pleasure of the stations. And one morning he touches flesh. Her legs are nude.

Her skin, such silk! Whoever feels it this smooth, this fine beneath his palm, weeps. There is something in the silkiness of this fabric, such a fineness clothes this so strong strength, one could die of it. And for a few minutes I do die, I become merely this enchanted dying man, and I receive the silk's violence like a grace.

Suffering came back to me. I would never have imagined it. And I no longer knew in this breaking of birth if I was still losing death or if it was already the other life I was reaching.

I crashed saved onto the shores of the New World I no longer knew anything I was ignorant of all that was to come I wanted all that would occur, to live it all from now on with the skin of my self as sensitive as a flower and by the light of her skin I needed it at last, eternally.

———————

Nelson didn't ask her to marry him.

He asked her to remain for him forever strange and painful and familiar, and to enter his office like a resurrection.

Forthwith began the fatality. And it was prodigious in events. So many stories began. Among all the stories from which the marriage is woven, there is the story of the cake.

What is beautiful about this story is precisely that it isn't over.

Certain stories are beautiful by their ending. Others are beautiful by the promise of their ending. Others are beautiful because they leave us hungry and hanging.

And each story told to us is bread for our hunger. With big or small bites we are there to devour it.

Among the Xhosa one eats stories all night long, taking small bites, for one knows the price of goat and of bread.

In societies without hunger one almost doesn't read at all anymore. The loss of hunger is also an unhappiness and a poverty.

———————

After Nelson's arrest, Zami no longer knew what Nelson was eating. He was eating. But the question mothers nourish their worry with was forbidden: "So, what did you eat over there, my child?"

For eighteen years Zami wasn't able to share a single dreamt-of dish with Nelson. Not sharing increases separation, adding to it a strange, hungry substance that has no taste, and plates of blind, unappeasable food. Mute meals.

Akhmatova's Egg

It is the story of an egg that was the last supper of three inseparable souls between whom the evil Russian century would pass its time fashioning abysses, stone hedges, barbed wire belts. But between friends everything becomes bridge, tie, letter, telephone, and with barbed wire one tresses crowns.

A poet is never short of metamorphoses. Nothing could have separated Osip Mandelstam, Nadezhda, and Akhmatova. Nothing and no one, not even distance. The space between them unceasingly murmuring with the mysterious silk of splendid recitations. "Listen, Nadezhda, do you hear, on Tver Street, those heavy accents of feminine organ, that pronunciation of ancient gold? It must be Akhmatova arriving. It is her pride, in St. Petersburg, our granite cradle, flaring up in arrogant lieder above the century's passport barriers, and already Moscow with its inebriated ears can hear her. I sense Russian Cassandra aboard a white night, setting sail on a squall over to our black night. Let them try then to throw three oceans between us, we will make their accents roar in three harmonizing languages."

The ladders the shadows the stars strewn about the dreams with their countless wings are their signals their messengers, and everything sounding like Schubert and Brahms that they hear in the winds.

And yet the pest with its black claws and scratchy chords is threatening to cut their thread, to crack their voices, to scratch their ears with ignoble ululations, to pour delirium-causing poison into the cups where their wormlike verses fizz.

One day Mandelstam writes the truth: "My friends, it is all well and good to say that love has wings, this century has plucked them, already my body is no more than a breathless rock, I proclaim to you by all the heavy bells of Moscow, it is death that is leading my flights. This is my truth." Signed: what remains of the poet in 1917. His ailing truth, his tocsin, the first death rattle of his soul intoxicated by the general drunkenness. We must be clear: the poet is made of the frail flesh and pink blood of children, and of nerves thirsty for song, he has such a need of everything so much, to inhale of the earth's armpit, to roll around in its lap, to lick the salts of skies and seas, to share time's banquet with Dante, Pushkin, Akhmatova, you, and thou. But in this century, there is no one at the poet's table except the dead and Akhmatova. They have all fled, the You's, the Them, they are all feasting roaring with laughter at the next table. How sad he is under a sky so proud to be modern, to be taking his eternal meal all alone almost entirely alone, with the whole country toasting, roaring with laughter under my sky, and shouting at me: idiot, it's mine now, this sky and all the other skies, we are the ones who have won it, conquered it, and tied it fast. Come up on board our universal ship or sink swimming.

Yes, I must make myself clear to you, my friends, my sisters, I have the longing of men in my blood, I am cold, I am living here all alone in the deforestation, how many years can the bird wait for the forest to grow back in order to remake its nest? All my might and all my memories will never be enough to conserve the life in my last egg.

By dint of writing and wanting to write poems on frozen ground, Osip was all worn out, soles worn out, leather worn out, heart worn out, courage full of holes, eyes worn out for trying to see if a day would exist behind the century's time, a world where forests of symbols would grow again, where, from the ashes, marvelous languages would be reborn, where the airways would no longer be forbidden to magic musics, to metaphors, to ageless travelers.

What's the use of waiting for the posthumous and perhaps never time. Have I walked onto the wrong stage? I should have been born three centuries earlier or later. Too bad, now let's be from this one. I have missed the prophetic chariot. Let's hoist ourselves up onto the back of the wolf and pretend this iron fur is our velvet.

Tomorrow, Mandelstam was telling himself, I'll caress its spine, if not tomorrow next week, and if not next week, as soon as I have removed from my resisting fingers all reminiscence of Dante and Mozart.

I was bird, tomorrow cockroach. Isn't the flea happy nesting in the wolf's crease?

But the bird beneath the crust of ice is no more than a pebble past. Thus Osip strives to extricate himself from Mandelstam's destiny. Yet the two women remain, like two inexhaustible oil lamps, keeping vigil, flickering in the shabby Temple that serves as kitchen, cave, chamber, palace, as synagogue, hive, boat, as voyage. Two uneasy but transparent flames. One of them, Akhmatova, royal visitor dressed like a deep-sea diver: to go from St. Petersburg to Moscow, she had to traverse tempests and years. In her honor: the egg.

There was nothing to eat in the temple of May 14. That evening they ran through the streets to find something to celebrate the friend's coming. It was the egg. The only egg in the neighborhood. So it was everything. An egg for Akhmatova. With an egg she can make miracles. Egg rhymes with fire, with child, with mother and in every language, as we know, with creation.

An egg is enough to make the world come into being.

An egg for three, Tver Boulevard, and all the century's music is brooded and hatched. An egg. Cosmic kernel.

But no. We know only too well and not enough that in the so very starry sky amid all the good sparks is the blind aster Azraël,[38] a star of prey with scaly eyelids and a horribly fascinating hiss. On this night, Azraël hisses to Osip.

Combat in the shadows between the egg and the cold aster. The egg says nothing. Azraël hisses:

"The day has come for you, Osip, to renounce Mandelstam. Enough of singing behind the wall with the grains of sand for an audience. The day has come for you to howl with the wolves. Are you then of the race of rocks? Who can hear today the dust of prayers you mutter with your purple lips? Don't you see you are alone? Alone with Akhmatova. And with Nadezhda that bit of straw, for roof and for you. Alone and two times more alone to be only two or three in this shell of straw, three dried up fetuses past,

"Fool that you are, what are you doing there, frittering away beneath our feet? Above you life passes by at a gallop, howling with joy, her[39] claws firmly planted in the panting flanks of time, she sits astride the country's frothing shoulders, all that smells of sweat and blood is reveling above you, she is moving up, you are moving down, to us the century to you the hole, and after us, make no mistake, there will be us again, to us truth with a snarl in its throat, to you madness with its untranslatable chirping.

"Rise up howling from among the larvae and the worms, from among the spineless and the poems, Osip, and call us brothers, it is time to betray Mandelstam and Akhmatova, to spit out the word sister and the word woman.

"Let the egg be for these beggar women, for you the swarming space of the veritable species."

Temptation tempts Osip. Such a desire to stop inhabiting the brazier. To drink wine at everyone's table. To have one's ears bothered by sounds other than these defunct murmurs.

To have friends in the flesh, with close-shaven mustaches and blank unanxious eyes. To live like Them, with electricity, to admit his inner light obscurity, to forget this fool Mandelstam, to kill him and be restored to life with four paws, with his fur bristling and his brain set to the time of this time period, without memory and without ulterior motive.

The egg glows no bigger than a glowworm at the heart of a Universe of foaming Them.

It is then, in the middle of a night in May, that the Arrest comes. It arrests all of Osip. And with the same blow cuts off the hiss of Azraël. One minute before despair.

Enter some faceless sneaky-bodied Them. Seize the poet's shadow and accuse him of still being Mandelstam. Thus, everything is accomplished according to the destiny of he who writes, and he who was going to howl will never have existed.

"I wanted to flee, my God, but where to go, my life is before me, its pages of virgin snow are spread before my sill, waiting for each one of my steps. I am cold, I would have liked to envelop myself in a wolf's fur-lined coat, but a might mightier than I took possession of me, and is bearing my breath, shivering and safe, far from the warm arms of flight, far from the suffocating furs, amidst the winds no lie will ever bridle. In vain I have tried to cover Mandelstam with the lion's share of prestigious coverings, it is written by my own hand that for taking cover I will only have the old Scottish plaid or the earth God lends me."

On this morning, exile opens wide before Osip like a golden eternity. Is it possible to dream of a country more vast and more strangely free? Here no one will ask you what right you have, where your passport is, what your birth date is, what is the date of your death.

On the table shines Akhmatova's egg. "You should eat this egg, you, my brother and my pain, you who are leaving now for the country I come from and where I have never gone." He salted the egg and ate it. Them, they were felling the trees around him. And on the earth, branches, trunks, poems were being put into piles and readied for the brazier. God had reentered the temple where the two lamps never tire. I mean to say God, the inextinguishable truth. This was the last egg in Osip's story.

There were at least a hundred reasons for arresting Osip Mandelstam and a hundred more without reasons and a thousand times a hundred no reasons.

For each line, for each joy, for each temptation, for each death and each resurrection.

"Over there behind the barbed wire they are leading Dante's shadow away to be interrogated."

Akhmatova and Nadezhda sitting face to face, for them alone the whole world.

For what reason did they arrest him? For poems.

For poems on the river. Rivers aren't arrestable.

Rivers are flowing now behind the barbed wire.

And also for sisters.

———————

Blessed be the blackness of black skin. Because he who has white skin like Them may one day be assailed by the temptation to howl with Them. Life is so short and exile is so long.

———————

Three months later Osip blooms from the first tomb, his gray body seventy-five years old. New address: banishment.

And as if she had been struck down by the same exile, Akhmatova too had aged terribly. But this is nothing.

Spring is taken from them, they are covered with ashes, and a winter skin is thrown upon their bodies. Broken old people in the fullness of youth. But this is nothing.

There was worse.

The worst was the voice's arrest. The long and dry arrest of the poem, and for four years this desert sky, these completely birdless springs, neither at Moscow nor at St. Petersburg, neither at Osip's nor at Akhmatova's, from 1926 to 1930 not a trace of wing.

Exile is nothing next to these sterile roofs. Empty nests. The violin dies in the absence of the bow. Cage of mute wood. There must be something in the air. That doesn't arrive.

And waiting for the poem to want, the bewildered poets prose. Why such an arrest? Don't they want us anymore? There must be something missing in the air. An arrest of the air inside the air. Lord poet has fallen, poor devil without Virgil to pick him up, without ground, without staff without help, and more dead than the dead. A lack of earth upon the earth. And time is lacking in present and in all future times. The poems were. The past is extremely past. In vain Akhmatova strains her entire body like an ear. Not a single breath of inspiration.

Is it possible to survive life itself? To be posthumous to all Poetry? And for the pest to have truly struck at music in its invisible sources?

Where now the saline sonatas with cavalries born of cosmic insomnias? Where the picking of fruits and leaves by entire concerts?

For four fleshless years, come poems without air without wing, without love without o without m without l without o,[40]

Poems with broken breath, come poems without skin, with nothing but beak and bones, to expire with one last gasp on the tip of a tongue turned blue.

Osip was breathing with great difficulty, his chest tight as a net, was it poet or poem the era lacked?

The worst was this abandonment of who knows who by whom, this desertion by the strings, this orchestral stillness, silent carcasses of buffalo beneath the moon. As though the air were no longer of this planet.

Until in a noise the same as the humming of hives an anger rises in forsaken throats and frees the lips from asphyxiation, in the year 1930. And never again this asthma of the soul, amen!

Old people, but of what old age, that of Christopher Columbus, of Ulysses, of Rimbaud,

We go around the world and we arrive still young at the setting of life.

At twenty we saw the bridge between the world's two parts, the entryway of the earth still virgin with humanity, and the single cord uniting Good and Evil to the same celestial placenta.

For Mandelstam and Akhmatova old age is, in the middle of life, having made the trip beyond.

And they'd like to take from these travelers the warm seas, Africa, the magic mountain passes?

Let them try! The chariot, the mount, the helicopter, all is imaginary.

From Voronezh to the hills of Transkei[41] there is but a visionary glance. On this page is Florence. The next page: Territory of the Issas and the Afars.[42]

To take from them the colored faces of the universe, one would have to uproot their eyes.

The Parting of
the Cake

In June of 1958, Zami and Nelson began to marry. This would be a perfect marriage, the marriage of the future: at once traditional and modern, it would unite East and West, heaven and earth, Xhosa kin and Tembu kin, ancestors and descendants, rain and fire, salt from tears and sugar from saliva, hope and certainty, ostrich and hunter, faith and science, black knowledge and white knowledge.

All these vows had been incorporated into the wedding cake's dough.

The cake demands that the first half be eaten with the family of the bride, the second half with the family of the groom.

Zami and Nelson had barely begun to eat the Pondo[43] half of the cake, in Bizana, when the telephone rang, they weren't able to finish, whisked back to Johannesburg in a gust of wind, everything was interrupted, the celebration, the cake, the dough, the desires, parted, the reality of the other side, the dance, cut, the cake cried out, the wind blew, the telephone roared, the sentence was handed down. Happily the parting did not take place between them, but in them, in the soft part of their flesh. Both of them felt the pain gash their bodies and, while a dry dust storm accompanied them back to town, each nearly wept with pity for the body of the other. In the plane they smiled at one another, their gazes mingled, a soul cake was being made. Each their eyes swollen with tenderness silently showed: I am hungry for you, my love. Zami's eyes were round and large, like the eyes of a blue antelope in summer. Your hunger is sweet to me, it assuages my hunger, said the narrower and ancient eyes of Nelson. The two hungers were wed. Their eyes made love, from their lashes down to the humid night.

And the cake? The cake is made from the same dough as their love. It is a cake of superhuman resistance. It had all their good qualities.

It is still alive, at least what's left of it.

Since the month of June, 1958, it has held up, it has waited. Nelson's part intact and patient. Zami never parted from his Tembu half. The half a cake is twenty-nine years old today. Zami took it to Johannesburg, then to Orlando, Soweto, then to Johannesburg. Then they were at the Cape. Then in Soweto. The traveling was endless and perilous. The cake didn't suffer. When Zami was in prison, Zeni and Zindzi[44] cared for it and didn't touch it. The cake was their papa, their little brother, and their baby.

But then there was the night of May 16, 1977. And I wasn't ready. The things that happen when we think the worst has already happened are the worst.

I shall never forget Zindzi's sobs in the room rent asunder, still crying as only children cry, like a vain prayer to the demon, and all the misfortune that struck me struck her. Even dead, even queen, even freed, I don't ever want to forget the army's terrible fracas, and the terrifying absence of pupil in their blond army eyes. It was a disemboweling, and the butcher gutted the beast clumsily, without thinking. The disemboweled house, the crying child, outside the truck roaring like a funeral-pyre

all of a sudden the cake cracked.

By dint of not surrendering to the persecutions, and of holding fast, and of being persecuted, and saying no, of being thrown in prison and forbidden to speak to three people, to two people, to one person, from leaving her home after 8 P.M., after 7 P.M., after 6 P.M., after 5 P.M., forbidden from accompanying Zindzi to school and from going into a shop to buy bread and from receiving Reverend Father Rakale[45] under her roof, and from going into a church and from going into any human construction, and from going down a road, in a car, in a bus, in a train, in an airplane,

and by dint of not having touched with her hand a single finger's breadth of Nelson's skin for thirteen years

and by dint of having erected the world in ruins every morning, and by dint of having thanked God five thousand seven hundred forty-five times for the grace of knowing that Nelson is still standing on the same terrestrial globe as Zami, and by dint of having admitted that all was well since all could have been so much worse,

she who had a Zeni and a Zindzi to warm her right side and her left side, she who had for spouse the most just, the most grand, the most tender, the most cruelly desirable man in the country, and what else did she have? so much luck, so much strength, anger, certainty, pride, hate, so many people to shake up, she who had everything and wasn't wanting for anything except her own life,

see how suddenly, on May 16, 1977, when armed men came at four o'clock in the morning to seize her

when they invaded her house in Orlando, they threw her with Zindzi into a truck, and deported her to Brandfort,[46] a small town that exists on no terrestrial map, for it is one of the infernal villages,

on that day the crumbling of the cake began.

It was at the moment when Zami and Zindzi were thrown like garbage onto a pile of trash.

There was Zami lying helpless in the dust, her face stuck to the wretched skin of Africa, face to face with this land of pain, her lips on the maternal leprosy, and news of the Crime went rumbling off, misfortune rolls over the great humiliated imploring body of Africa, misfortune with its army its trucks its machine guns its empty eyes its cadaverous cheeks, the terrifying misfortune of idiocy moves away on its wheels, causing its engines to whir in the sad African silence, then news of the Crime disappeared, the poor night fell trembling back onto its tatters and its godforsaken children, and there was Zindzi, clutching Zami with all her hands, with her dozens of little arms in distress, like ten desperate children, like the little girl, wanting nothing more to do with the universe, who knocks at her mother's womb and wants to go back in, clutching as only human children do who hope to scale walls, cross borders, and flee life, by retiring into the mother's night, by way of love. And if Zami had been able to open herself up and take Zindzi back into the nest, oh how relieved she would have been of a part of her pain.

Silence fell upon her like a sheet of tears, at that moment such a solitude encircled them, they were the only living creature in the deserted night after the end of the world.

Is this her, the native land,

This dirty weary dust that no longer recognizes her children's voices,

This brutal boorish dust

Is this our mother to whom we must return when we have finished clenching our teeth and grilling our tongues on burning coals,

When we have had enough of stuttering with rage

Is this her, this dust without might without memory, that cannot distinguish the enemy's boots from our poor black palms

Is this really her, the mother who's expecting us?

Yes, this is her.

Zami was crying on the dust that can do nothing for us

On the lost mother, bought and sold so often she no longer knows how many children she has carried and forgotten

The ill, mute, paralyzed, destitute mother,

On whom the aged infants fall, reduced, humiliated, impoverished,

Light as dead leaves

For whom as sole good only a wrath remains[47]

At least it is immense.

Zami wept for the helplessness of the dust that couldn't even remain collected upon itself anymore. Almost dead of scorn.

The dust smelled of the tomb and shit. Then Zami's body split open, the earth split open, and, from the barysphere, all the world's indignation has gathered into a lava of blood that is trying to spurt up into the sky, up to the impassive face of God, up to the dry eyes of God and behold: with all her might, with every sinew in her body, Zami hurls a long powerful heart-rending holler in the direction of God's deafness!

And there, as if she had been thrown from the other side of the border, as if she had suddenly seen the truth she had never ceased perceiving, as if the absolutely empty sky had suddenly lowered a veil and revealed the unbearable grimace of this very emptiness itself, suddenly she saw the true face of the age bent over her without expression, its mask made of stone, without a trace of emotion, its human eyes choked down far behind its eyelids. It was obvious, one could agonize in the most wrenching torments, one after the other, one after the other, without an eyelash of this pale era ever quivering.

How do you manage, triumphant beast,

If you are beast of the human species

How do you manage to keep your eyes so firmly closed, night and day, night and day

How do you make, at night, amid our cries, the silence?

113

With plugs of mud and blood in your ears
With eyelids of iron atop your eyelids of flesh
With deaf feet you tread on my children
Munching and masticating big morsels of my flesh
How do you manage to munch my entrails like chewing gum?

Do not listen to me, do not hear me, stay behind your seven thicknesses of stone,
Your stone will not shield you
Your cecity will not blind you
You will see me enter your brain's lair
Through dream's window like a black she-goat,
With a bound I will clear each one of your walls, You will see me
My paws are all-powerful, my voice inside your lying night is stronger than all your lies, You will hear it
And from muddy step to miry step I'll descend by bounds, with the poet for lamp and friend, down to the stinking marsh where your heart jerks convulsively. Don't think, master of cruelties,
I'll let you calmly stew in your dung hill
I'll howl and I'll howl for as many centuries as it takes
And I'll find the holler that will crush your heart.

There was absolutely no one in that Brandfort night. No sister. No poem. Only the hollering. Which is the last dignity of the human species. Only the cake heard, and for the very first time it fell to pieces. The cake was going to be thirteen years old.

There was no one in this night to give to Zami the May egg. In Africa, even sisters are forbidden and everything is wholly separated. Hand from hand. Sister from sister. Earth from earth. Human from the human species. The tree mustn't speak to its branches.

And more than one person at Zami's side is already a country, it is forbidden. So if Zami is with Zindzi when the grocer passes, and if the grocer says: do you want some eggs?, prison arrives at a gallop, and throws them both into its dust.

Dust lying in the dust, Zami had had enough that night of reviving only in order to lose everything except despair. In a deathlike sleep, she lost even despair. For one hour, she became her mother of the scattered word. Without echo.

The landscape of this chapter is an erg of scalding silences.

And yet it is the most beautiful country in the world

The white days gnaw at our skulls and spit our desires out onto the sand, the light is pulverized even into my eyelids

And yet, I'll say it: it is the most beautiful country in the world

The earth of centuries ago the earth with short dark yellow hair the color of honey. And in our ears, the ancient song of crickets.

The moon is seated atop the world's table. Herself the hen and the egg.[48]

It looks like the very first pages of the book of the earth. No one can tear them out.

Yesterday the brilliant nails of great cities were hammered into our flanks, with febrile hammer blows. And now the nails are shooting up, hard forests of nails. Between the iron shafts, young automobiles with blind tires crop up night and day, they run to crush the veldt on every day of the calendar except eternity.

But the moon atop the table rejuvenates by brooding. Our dancers dance for her. Time dances for us.

Without a single doubt, it is the most beautiful country in the world.

If only there had been an egg. In the world that night there were no more dry and empty eyes than those of this town.

Dust in the dust, before my buried eyes I no longer manage to grow the humid future earth in which to root myself. With the past for tomorrow, how to revive?

I am dying from not killing death. From beneath my bones I cry out, I burn my soul on my anger.

May I be given the keys to hell, I want my rights, and may I descend one day with Zindzi on my back, to make a long visit to the zoo in flames. I shall walk without hurrying along the red rivers, parting with an elegantly annoyed gesture the thick smoke that from time to time keeps me from seeing clearly your cooked and peeled miens, o tyrants who have taken from us our blood.

With what offhand and gracious scorn shall I watch you boil in the red broth, eternally coriaceous brood, admiring how the purulent skin always sticks to your flesh, flesh so hard that even boiling blood does not manage to remove it.

I shall blink my eyes at you, like a slightly nearsighted lady stopped before a display window, who assures herself she really sees what she sees.

And it is really you that I shall see, it is really you beneath the grimaces of your masks melted by horror that I shall see, my old acquaintances.

Then I shall look at my gold watch, bored, and without casting a last look your way, I shall leave, I shall go up toward the light with the air of a woman grown weary and a bustling step, with my Zindzi on my back, and that movement of the hips that is the charm of the young Xhosa woman.

The End of the Unfinished Poem

The last poem before the 1934 arrest did not see the light of day.[49] It isn't that it wasn't there, Osip's last poem, the last poem before the first step on the wrong way.

The poem was in Osip's breast, detained inside the red night, sob retained, stone of tears, in spite of him, in spite of him. Waiting for the way out. He simply could not write its end. The poem clutched at his heart, nails, beaks, teeth, hooks, talons, one causing the other to beat, one causing the other to shout, neither the poem nor the heart could get away, this poem was perhaps his heart, his very pain itself, which he wasn't managing to pour out and which was remaining clustered bitter drop of blood under the black blue that was filling up the sky and the world that year.

A tear was ripening on Osip's lashes and was not falling.

It was a poem for the death of Andrei Bely, for death, on the death of the poet his brother.[50] There was abandonment, solace, and solitude. Why weep? How not to weep? It began thus: "I think he feared death."

Then he cleared, running, the first eight steps toward the light and at the ninth, as if he had perceived a cage of clouds, or a net, or the archer up there waiting for him, he dropped everything and fell back down in a tangle, into obscurity.

He was a tear.

And Mandelstam and Bely, one suspended on the other. Lash and tear.

I think he feared death. Who feared death? I think they feared death. I think the dead man feared death had feared and still feared death and the police. But he who feared for the dead man was the still living man, it was Mandelstam I think who feared death, feared the dead man's death, the one that still kills even after death, and feared his own death for how not to fear dying a little in each death that comes next. This is why the poem spurned its own end. For this, I think, and for other fears as well.

January Tenth 1934 simply could not end.[51] It was a relentless poem, it was a day, that fought against the end. Would face up to, begin, turn its cheek and refuse, and at the halfway mark turn back toward dawn, clambering noisily back up the slope of time. There were at least a hundred versions of the beginning. January Tenth 1934 had seen a hundred sunrises, the prophetic staff ploughs the silence a hundred times, a hundred mornings go past, trailing in their course the Caucasus massifs and the alpine paths all trembling with the footsteps of a hundred poets, and with each fertile step fifty years celebrated in song spring forth at the magic clash of five words. And then: nothing. A rock. In front of the rock the same feet tread in vain, wearing themselves out in merely marking time. I won't go any farther, the poem does not say. A hundred beginnings and no end. I'm not writing, I'm being born — not writing — I'm being born and born,[52] but I have barely taken a few luminous steps when a darkness falls before me, suddenly I no longer know if I am me or if I am this you that I am, following,[53] yes, that I am and follow and have followed and accompanied, my staff listening to your staff, my brother, for a sweet hundred seasons or so, suddenly I am afraid to follow you and to accompany you too far, you who were my older brother up till now, and from now on my brother feared and become a stranger. Beyond this quatrain, no, I cannot not untangle myself from you.

Here begins what I do not know, how to write, or feel, or even understand, or even how to follow not even from very far away, or even believe, or even mimic, and what I only know how to fear.

Here begins what I can neither forget nor not forget. This death of you who declares me living and keeps me from living. You, Andrei Bely, my brother and my elder on the mountain and in death. It is you I am following as far as January 10, ascending and resounding with your resoundings, you echoing my foreign storms, me echoing your kicks in the ice, slipping and sputtering and traveling together, our lips naked, up to the summit.

But no farther. Go now, Andrei, go, descend into your silence, your finger on your lips not on mine, your eye light blue, mine very black, go on ahead and far away from me who am not, following, you, go on with your silence from now on and let me sing. I want to finish writing from my own side.

I want to weep. I want to take note of this tear.

Yes I think it is he, the not dead yet, who feared the dead man upon leaving would deport him, feared the dead man with whom just yesterday he was carrying on a rich life of friendship.

We is dead, wanting to resume his I.

No it isn't you my brother, my bird at the head, who will make me fall into your downfall. It is I who shall scatter you in my poem, bury you and rock you and call you by your name, hold you back between the centuries by the hairs of your name and announce you, you and all your titles and merits, to the beings to come. Not I with you in your earth and your silence. It is I in my sky and my light and starry song who will reweave for you after death another life, I who will recompense you for your musics, and carry you upon my breath till the end . . .

Till the end of what? Till the end of breath? Till Mandelstam's last breath? No this Osip could not write, this 1934, without suffocating. The poem was running out of breath before the end.

He didn't want to hear himself saying. That's why. He didn't want to hear himself saying: death. To hear himself saying the word, and to hear himself saying: you too. To hear himself saying: "Who is dead? Who is it?" Isn't it you, you too? They would say me. And if it were me? Who arrived at the destination? Wanting to write what he did not want to write not wanting to write what he wanted to write.

That's why, I think.

The poem had a strange voice. As though it had a teardrop on its tongue. Or else an accent.

Difficult to say death in his own tongue. Bely should say it. And maybe he is doing so in this very moment, with mute words, with impalpable steps.

But how to disentangle me from you this January tenth, yours, your day of farewell, you all farewell, and me not knowing any longer how to tell you "farewell and stay."

Who can say: I, when I speak of you? And who can say of whom I speak when I speak of you? You first-born and first-dead too.

Sometimes it seemed to him it was Bely who kept him from finishing this poem, and sometimes it was true. Yes sometimes it was Bely. This *January Tenth 1934*. But how can a dead man speak of death? But how can a living man speak of death?

The poem pulled up its lines and fled. It was deadly.

But behold the end doesn't come. As though it were the dead man who had it. Perhaps it was *their* poem, the poem by the dead man and the living, the same pang of the heart, but each one writing from his own side. Death was missing nonetheless. Only fear was throbbing. The poem has two tongues. One tongue mute, frozen oyster.

January Tenth 1934 was panting, clinging to its own edge, almost dead of impatience and temptation. And nothing was happening. The bird darts forth and there is no air, not a breath, not a void, not a space. Who can imagine what follows? Neither movement nor immobility. It was a poem about Andrei Bely's fear of dying. Mandelstam's fear. A poem about desire and the height of desire which is jealousy. It was the strange jealousy of the living for the dead. The desire to know me too the impossible, the impossible desire to die from here, to die without dying,

the marvelous desire of the human being for the stars and for the stars' roots and for the world's ovaries and the curiosity of the child for the seeds and for the blood, and our nostalgia for the absolutely foreign fatherland, when I was a drop of dust.

Osip's me too. It began thus: "I think he feared death." Who feared, who thought, who began, death, it was one and it was the other, one already and the other not yet, one thinking behind the other, the other fearing before the other, Dante trembling and vacillating behind already-Virgil and yet trembling still. And sometimes, from brushing past so many out-of-breath disappearances, Dante would fade for an instant, mimicking death one time, leaving the canto bereft of an end wandering above his lifeless body like the shadow of a bird. But while Dante is no more, Virgil is vigilant and the canto continues. One must be two to die.

January 10, 1934, Mandelstam went to ask Andrei Bely what he might already and not yet know of what none know.

Went to ask the dead man the secret of the end.

Dead who will I be, Osip wondered. And will you still be able to see on my unfathomable face that I saw, in a flash of lightning, the door of the last poem swing slightly open? Will I still be poet or already skeleton?

The dead man was very white that day, all in sharp accents and circumflex accents. Only his lips had a roundness. The whole very underlined and very accentuated. But all these features did not make a man. This is what held *January Tenth 1934* back on the verge of itself. How to say? To what degree this dead man was a dead dead man, as dead as Bely had been alive. This wasn't the same man. Only a cardboard copy. That is why there was nothing to say about the last moment. There was no truth. Truth has a fever, her temples are throbbing with nervous irritation, she wishes to say, and she clears a hundred passageways among the forests of words, slicing and gathering, reassembling and rejecting.[54] The real Bely was the one who spoke endlessly, seeking, seeking, in a wake of contradictory flashes and all of them dazzling.

This dead man really had nothing to say.

In the end there was no end. There was nothing to say about this dead man. About the living man everything. To such a degree was the dead man foreign, he was empty and no one and nothing to do with Bely.

And not even a mysterious absence. A little cardboard door leading nowhere. It was: the opposite. Osip believed in immortality. The dead man was there for nothing. On the bed one would have thought there was a bone, not Bely.

In the room there was on one side this very white skeleton wearing a man's suit. This moulting man. On the other the uproar of the blood in Osip's veins and the panting of the poem that was living with all its might, clutching at the warm flesh that was one foot away from the dead man.

What was happening in the room: Osip living himself living. Breathing and sweating, and galloping in his alleyways, and walking in the streets of a city full of people and biting on a bit of bread, the wind is blowing and everything is in his body, blood, fields, winter woods, the roads that run behind my heels, the mountains of Simbirsk[55] and the bridges of Leningrad, everything but the unbearably endless steppes. The world was inside Osip with its languages, its rivers, its landscapes, its italian cities, its armenias, its crimeas, its birds, its collections of pebbles, of shells, and of bursts of wormy verse,

his face dedicated to the stars, his neck, his arms, his legs down to his febrile feet, he was all this, and his thighs in his only pair of trousers, the trousers accorded by Gorki, his due and his right, trousers, shirtless and shoeless, and his chest signed Osip where the poem beats, his lips trembling and his eyes motionless, to better hear the words come.

There's nothing to make of the body. Except phosphorus, calcium, magnesium. Hence it was a poem that could not end in words. Only slowly fall to dust, like a very ancient city that crumbles for centuries.

And me, Osip, next year I shall descend down to the clay, down to the chalk, down to the yellow sand, down to the silence. And what I would want to become, if it were still possible to want, is a stratum of striated feldspar.

The day was descending toward its last hour. Osip dedicated the poem without end to all those who are going to die tomorrow. At the end, just before the end, he stood back up with a bound, more alive than ever, alive to be alive and to not yet be dead, alive in flesh and in blood and in future feldspar, and he withdrew from nothingness and from the mew, like a dreamer from a bad dream, flinging back the covers of earth.

A poem was rising in a boiling of wings, like birds awakening at the end of night. The silence was dissipated.

From all his gorges of copper and crystal and all his underbrush Dante is rising again, crying out toward the light like a flight of wild geese. You Virgil, wherever you are, gather together your hymns and follow him. The most beautiful poem of the year was sprouting with the dawn, how the fear of death falls silent, and how the earth with its innumerable blue-black breasts snorts as it shoots up above the skulls and skeletons. In the middle of the tillage as of the Ocean advances, sowing to the right and harvesting to the left, Osip the fabulous gardener, risen this very morning from the chalky ground of our tombs. A young tree of sparks was sprouting before his eyes, in a sputtering of consonants, in a shower of vowels.

The poem began thus: "And for all that I am alive!" And remembering the underwater origin of the mountains whose pasture is the sky, it set sail full of wind like a drunken traveler, slipping away despite the mustached age, from era to era in the direction of the desired Ararat.[56] Up there an ark would be waiting for it . . . Right here, at this very comma, at this tear, at this hybrid crossing of threat and space: +,

The police knock. The poem falls.

Here in full flight above the cage, the arrow reaches him. Enter the police. Like plumes' wax beneath the sun, the metaphors are melting. Osip is lying helpless on the ground like a pebble without qualities.

Where were their eyes, those who turned up the floorboards' fingernails, and did not see the wings of paper shrivel beneath their boots?

After the house search, Nadezhda entrusted the surviving slip of paper to Emma Gerstein.[57] The poem was nearly finished. It is Emma G. who put an end to this story. In a fit of panic Emma burned the lively survivor.

It was during their exile. Now everything was finished, life, death, the passage. The tree was charred to the roots, not a single atom of the Ararat is still breathing.

Death comes from without.

Nadezhda doesn't know why she wants to slap Emma. What revolts her is the candle. I cannot bear the idea that instead of throwing the slip of paper into the fire, Emma gave it to be gobbled up by the candle's flame. Hence someone I'm pursuing with my hate enjoyed the bird's agony. Someone with an unspeakable greediness watched it die, contemplated its death. With her little rat's trap.

But all this is the fault of these poems. They were too beautiful and too brilliant with tears and desirable. One day or other, someone's going to kill them.

Hence it isn't even the fire of History with its heavy boots that devoured the phoenix down to its egg, only a half-friendly soul led astray by a fatal appetite.

It takes ashes in order for the spark to shoot forth.

There were no more ashes at all.

One has never seen so many borders inside a country, so many hedges, bars, barriers, palisades, barbed wires, so many customhouses, and no's

No, you may not pass, oh, you may not pass.

My country is not my country. There was no barrier before my door yesterday. Today I open the door and I'm a stranger.

Oh you won't move forward, no you won't cross over. If you want to take a step, bend down and descend below the earth.

A barrier, a slight barrier of wooden boards painted white cuts time and the earth from top to bottom like a knife slices flesh. A blow from a barrier of white wood, I stood on my own two feet, I spoke four languages, behold me lying here legs and languages cut off, what remains of a butterfly with its wings torn off. I am descending now, writhing, the ladder of living worms of verse, from anger to anger.

The most beautiful country in the world has the plague of the soul. Who has the plague who doesn't have it? Whoever has the plague flees whoever doesn't have it like the plague. Even the sparrow must show a pass. And even the blood in our veins. Whoever has a heart must place it in quarantine. The whole country has the hatred.

If murder were wheat what beautiful harvests this would make. There isn't a sane person on this earth bristling with harrows who hasn't dreamed of slowly cutting a throat. It is a need, it is a vital, vital thirst. Cutting a throat from top to bottom, cutting through the law's heavy barking, axing the ax, barring the barrier, is such a need, it is a dream.

At night Zami resumes her loud breathing.

During the day, the entire country is on the cross.

On the Move . . .

In the train that was leading them from station to station, one day, one night, one day, one night, one day, moving from step to step, on the endless, lightless map of the land of exile, there are no more cities, no more countrysides, no more forests, it is in the train carrying them toward the country where neither the sun nor a gaze rises to meet the gaze, that Nadezhda and Osip Mandelstam were thrown into exile well before the journey's end, one day, one night, one day before exile. Standing with their two faces pressed up against the car window, turned into transparent ghosts. Everybody passed in front of them without seeing them: men, women, old people. An invisibility envelops them. Look at us! Not a look. And passing before them always the same face with its unseeing eyes. As if you could catch exile through the eyes. What is forbidden is forbidden. What is banished belongs goods and blood to banishment. With their four eyes still alive, to see themselves effaced, in mid-train, from this earth. To see the world with deserted eyes, the water that no longer reflects any images. To see oneself become no one and yet not dead, and yet not of this world. Eyes that see this are widowed of all humanity. And we no longer know for which death we are weeping with our tears, is it you or me who has lost the day, is it me or you who has gone down into the abyss? We no longer know which eyes to punish, which eyes to close. Eyes that see want to close soon so as not to see the crime. But they want to remain open wide open to see if perchance one time a look will be returned. Would not be returned. If perchance the eyeless age had one weakness, one eye at least in a million that would dare to lift itself up to the rejected face. One eye would suffice to save the sun. But there were none. As far as Cherdyn[58] there were none. The sun rises in vain, no one leads the exiled back to the pitiful human light.

"See how by decree we have become past.

"By decree we have become feared: you the thunder and I the plague.

"By decree disappeared and undone: you the cinder and I the sand.

"Time has spilled itself into my glass. There is nothing left for us to live save the scooping out."

Face to face and one against the other Osip and Nadezhda, they were caressing each other with their eyes, they were seeing each other and giving themselves to the other to be seen, in a clear pity surrounded by black. The train tolls like a knell.

Exile is inside the train. In the train, terrified eyes are being taken away: they have seen the invisible assassination. There are four eyes too many in this car.

It is the train that is too much. This train that isn't of the living or the dead, neither from one country nor the other, this train that is a flying country, that obeys neither one law nor the other, this blind and pitiful train that would do better to pass into the ether far above the earth gone mad, this earth that pretends to be without sin and without knowledge, as if it had never heard of Adam and Eve.

Osip feels effacement falling on the car like an eternal snow, with an interminable abundance. Or maybe I'm a dead man who is dreaming he's alive? A crazy and conceited dead man? Maybe I am merely the dream of Mandelstam the

dead man? And you, don't you hear already this silence behind the windowpane, Nadezhda?

But in Russian Nadezhda's name means hope.

In Russia, towns are closed to them forever by the score.
All the towns are encircled by walls of fire, at their doors the
archangels have cockroaches for mustaches.

— You will not enter oh you will not enter, no you will
never again enter either Leningrad or Moscow or Kiev or
Nijni Novgorod, or. You will never again throw yourself into
your beloved's arms.

The exiled run from one town to the other, closed closed,
still happy that there is, between the circles of fire, a narrow
passageway through which to pass, till hope expires.

Neither Leningrad, nor Kiev, nor, but we still have the
shadow of Moscow, the shadow of Kiev in which to reside,
the purlieus, the forests. Till the day when they are banished
from the shadow and from the forests too.

And alive I remember the lively villages of my childhoods
like an old man remembers, with farewell and torment. Exile
has suddenly sent me to the end of my life, fifty years from here.

Under the same sky, I am no longer myself, I am no
longer in my homeland, I am in the train,

one month away from myself, one month and three generations, I lean over my own memory like a foreign traveler,
and I listen to the tender reminder of what is no longer mine,
you remember,

it was last year, or one of my other years,

it was last winter, another winter in an altogether other
time

I was at home in my homeland, such a long time ago yesterday, and I was going back up the Neva on skis, me on the Neva without exile the same Neva and without a pass, remember?,[59] I remember, someone in me remembers with a voice I knew well, and now I remember the free voice I had in an entirely other century, me today with my foreign voice,

in this century, under the same sky an entirely other voice. You remember yes I remember in another memory.

I remember my homeland every day and from top to bottom and each year we would go to Nijni Novgorod, and we would descend the Volga in seven days to Astrakhan,[60] when I was still me

Oh how to forget you now without forgetting me, you who are no more my homeland, how to forget you without forgetting you, you my homeland my strange foreigner my tomb of familiar shores.

I am standing in the train, following Russia with my eyes, Russia is passing by

Without looking at me

I follow with my eyes. Only my eyes . . .

Eyes that are looking at Russia not looking at me,

This is what I am: abandoned eyes.

―――――――

If Osip did not die in this train, it is because there was the miracle of the chocolate candy. This candy is a much shorter, more humble story than the story of the cake but it is perhaps the same one in the snow, the same one in the dust. And this one seems to have an ending.

The candy came in through the car window like a rock, like a bird, like a messenger from on high, like an anonymous letter. From pity.

The train had just left the station, exile was enveloping Osip with its sad magic coat. A chocolate candy falls at his feet of footsteps effaced. Someone we do not know has trudged through the countryside, outwitting the cold and the station guard, to the railway tracks. Walked under the cover of darkness carrying in his or her magnificent hand a chocolate candy of very great worth. There was surely but one chocolate candy in this unknown town.

Someone unknown and who knows. Who knows about exile, the circle of emptied eyes, night that falls upon day like a knife, and that there are creatures in the cars who only yesterday were like others, today like dirt.

Someone reaches the track without anyone seeing him or her. But man or woman it was surely a mother who cast this candy into the night into the passing train, this candy for someone unknown, this candy for me or for you for all persons deprived of past, of future, of true death and sepulcher, and condemned without judgment by almost all humanity. The grief of this person in the train is so very great: she, or he, has lost everyone. The candy is destined for this excessively stripped and saddened being.

This means: you whom I do not know, I know you. We are from the same slime and from the same water. You who are right to despair, I send you a reason to not despair. To you who is right to not send any doves through the window, you who do not even think of doing so, I send you a dove.

You in exchange, do not, this candy, eat it without lighting a candle for me, without burning for me as I do for you, the candle of a thought.

It was a mouthful of bittersweet chocolate. Who knows what next befell this mother? The candy was unsigned.

In the past God it is said would save cities for a candy such as this. Who would dare to tell of this, above the earth or below, in this century scarred with camps?

Who knows what befell the knight of faith, who doubtless was a dressmaker in a Taiga village?[61]

This might be the end of the story: once upon a time there was a woman who was condemned and banished for a candy. Or else it is by the candy she was saved forever. For in any case, one could not exile her heart from her.

"At that time" God became the unknown woman trudging along in the frozen night, toward the train full of the forsaken, with a star in her hand.

———————

When will one say "at that time" in Zami's house? Her lips are saying: Soon. Next year. Her heart wants to believe what her lips are saying. It is too early to believe.

There was something deadly in the banishment to Brandfort. Zami's body started to crumble, to abandon itself to ulcers and gangrene, and to disgust for God.

But in the end, the cake had the upper hand. The pastry turned out to be stronger than all the forces of decomposition and dispersion. Not a single crumb of the cake was lost.

And one morning Zami was awakened by the desire to plant. The debris and deadly dust have receded. A bit of immortal earth has collected. Zami disinfected a little patch of Africa. Helping hell to bear fruit was in the end a victory over herself. Because forgiving Brandfort for existing demanded of her a superhuman effort. Nonetheless she managed to go as far as to plant a willow tree. Zami's willow in Brandfort immediately became her green standard, her crown of laurels, her panache, her ostrich coat. The willow tree was the triumph of the cake.

Today the cake is 29 years old. All its crumbs are now safely in Orlando. Nelson has been in the Pollsmoor prison on the Cape since April 1982. I am writing this in April 1986. All of Mandela's crumbs are alive. The cake has even begun to multiply. I am writing this in December 1987.

What is a 30-year-old cake? What will its flesh taste like when Nelson and Zami finish marrying? Ah, this entire story will have been but the longest, most painful of marriage ceremonies.

And in the meantime, it is the past that continues to serve as present.

It was in 1960. He had not come home for ten days. During these ten days time almost stopped passing. Without air how to breathe. The air no longer comes, Zami has lived for a hundred days by day clumsily pushing before her the millstone of time.

Neither crying, nor praying, at each instant of the day, struggling hand to hand with terror, at each ring of the telephone a joy that dies.

She wasn't there where she was nailed she was suffering in a hundred other places, she wasn't in the house where underneath the waiting she was waiting, nor in the kitchen where her strangely foreign hands were cooking, nor in her body rooted to the spot beneath an enormous absence, her soul is running through the neighborhood, night and day at each door, at each crossing, in a watchfulness cradled by illusions and supplications. And for these ten days suffered and counted a thousand times, so many assaults painted in blood.

She saw Nelson's ghosts by the thousands, a thousand times arrested, a thousand times dead, assassinated, hanged, throat slit, castrated, disappeared forever, there is not a single death she hasn't lived and relived, and one after the other wrenched from her moaning, their fangs gripping her forehead, their long claws in her hair, it is true one can live an entire death in a second, thus she sees her beloved cast naked from atop the world, without being able to prevent the plunge, sees him falling to the utmost ends of the earth and it is in vain that she attempts to hold him back by the jacket arms that no longer clothe him and which she is clutching, supplicating the sky in the kitchen. He is falling and she sees how she is bathing his adored body in long streams of tears as though all the earth's rivers were hurrying into her chest to fill her need to pour out her inexhaustible chagrin. The ten nights are full of jumps and starts, of rapts, of false burials, and sometimes a bee alights on all this panting earth, a clear vision from another time, it is the stroll in the veldt, before death, the familiar heat, the footsteps that graze the maternal ground, a tribe of ostriches that plunges over there into the immense kingdom as fast as their legs can carry them, it was during Life before the fall, and immobilized breathing softly so as not to scare away the visitation, Zami drinks the light of what was and now who will tell of our short immortality?

Herself the scene of separations, the scene of consolations, she leans over herself as if over a chalice of grief and jubilation.

What every woman who loves in fear does, she does. Enters the deserted house saying: for a long time, wasn't I expecting this day so pure of all hope?

Till the moment when she began to believe he was dead merely because she no longer had the strength to believe he was alive.

In the eleventh century of the disaster, Nelson, who was coming home in the middle of the night from one of his late meetings, saw the lights on at Adelaide Joseph's house.[62] Stopped to make sure that everything was going well with her people, Paul too? the little one, too? then he went to find his Lady, his luck, his eternity.

She did not tell him about the nights with vulture eyes, the days with arms ablaze. Nor how this day was the feast of the resurrection, and each thing had the sharp excited taste of childhood's grand adventures.

But when Zami found out from Adelaide that Nelson had stopped off at her place, as predicted by the ouma, this time she didn't say anything. She mused all day long on the mysterious ways of love. On the cost of generosity, on the bitter flavor of self-sacrifice. And also on the just measure of heroism.

— Was it necessary, Nelson's station at the Josephs'? For during this time who was nailed to the cross, you or me? But Nelson didn't know she had gone and made this cross and this bouquet of thorns. Something any woman would know. But Nelson had said to her: don't worry, nothing can happen to us. And who had broken faith?

Nelson did a good thing by stopping off at the Josephs', it was impossible to do otherwise in this street, I'm sure of this but I don't agree. There was no obligation, only this destiny that does not doubt, is not divided, and all paths follow in his footsteps. The entire world follows him and resembles him and it is I who loving him do not resemble him, loving him do not want to cling to him like an iron filing to a magnet, so as to go on loving him, from out of me, outside of him. Taken by me the street would have led straight ahead hands full of roses and carnations to the bedroom door. While accepting the stop, I refuse, if I didn't refuse I would follow him, there would only be a retinue, a life without encounter without fury without noise.

In the Beginning he wasn't expecting me. It is I who came to him. The one who arrives is I.

The river doesn't change its course. It is the stream that rises and with her two hands gathering around her the brilliant folds of her waters, throws herself entirely into another bed. He should have been expecting me. And if I hadn't been expecting him? If I wasn't expecting him? If I wasn't dying while he isn't here, while time goes by with a lively but even step, if I wasn't sowing absence with my tears? Without expecting, no arrival, no birth. There would only be destiny, and

135

no one to invent the disasters and the miracles that are the life of life.

———————

It was June 12, 1960. And miraculously, Nelson has returned. But for Nelson this was nothing.

In 4 years Nelson will be condemned to prison for life. Still four years. None know it. Who knows how one knows what one does not know.

Still four times three hundred and sixty-five days. One must write the numbers out in longhand. This is how I live, letter by letter, holding back the present by all its hands, by each one of its fingers as though I knew what I do not know, it is fear that is my law. Prudently, deliciously, Zami lives in a delicate avarice. She, she has all the time. It is destiny who has less. And this Zami fears in a low voice.

Still one thousand four hundred and sixty days minus one thousand days minus thousands of hours minus thousands of centuries, and all this minus is nonetheless a plus, but unbearable, still one thousand four hundred and sixty days light as birds, only minutes, real days but that burn up suddenly, still one thousand four hundred and sixty births, one thousand four hundred and sixty brief feasts broken up by death's agonies.

Zami lives. Had she been told that the nights with vulture eyes would equal one day in another life, nights to which she would dedicate her most quivering regrets, these deaths that would end up dying, had she been told that in another life she would relive them as one relives the crowned hours, days of fire among the days,

We never see the true face of the days that wrench from us cries of anger. And the day comes when I love what I used to hate.

Had she been told, she wouldn't have listened. For she wanted to live day by day whatever came along. She wanted everything and to not deprive herself of anything, and to live like a woman who loves a man on this earth and doesn't renounce any of the terrestrial rights of women.

June 12, 1960, she raised a weak protest like a woman who has the right to disagree.

He may have the duty but I have the right, and I have the duty to have the right. If he's still a man. But maybe he's right to conduct himself already in spite of still, and in spite of their terrestrial and innocent bodies, as though he weren't altogether a man anymore, and maybe he was wrong.

Maybe the streets had really already changed, and the country was just a little farther away than Zami's homeland? Or maybe Nelson was steering with a firm and slightly impatient hand?

Like a new Just one, a little proud in utter humility, and in utter tenderness a little hard.

But what is a Just man? I don't know how to define this. It is nonetheless a kind of man. All I can say is that Nelson, by stopping off at the Josephs', steered his body with a just hand and not with a lover's hand. And immediately afterward, in truth, he drove at full speed and like a lover.

The meridian separating the region of just justness from that of unjust justness is so invisible.

It can happen that the Just man, carried away by the ardor that leads to justness, is a little too just, and passes imperceptibly by a single breath into the region of the unjust.

What is beautiful in the Just man is this possibility for error. This is his grace.

Nelson thought he was being just by what he was accomplishing. It is into what he did not do that error slips. He stopped off at Adelaide's, and this is good. He didn't head straight for home, and this is not good. Of this is Nelson's strange virtue made: of an addition. And in the end it was good.

———————

At first Zami was madly in love with Nelson, the greatest, gayest, most elegant, most distinguished, most radiant man. And in his voice, the secret. His voice: Samson's thick head of hair. Force that no one can resist, not even the court judge, song that recalls an ecstasy one will never feel

The Voice. She resounded in the garden where we have never been.[63]

Voice come from the Promised Land. I didn't know her I recognize her. That is how I recognize her. By this unheard of recognition. Nelson has a voice that makes men nostalgic for the absolute garden. Had. This is the voice that has been shorn, close-cropped unheard for twenty-five years.

For Her, origin and music of the origin, for Her and for him, Zami would have done anything,

But then Nelson became Nelson Mandela, a Just man, neither altogether a man, nor altogether human, nor altogether from this street, nor only from this era.

But Zami yes: altogether from this earth and from this dust. Until June 1964 she was mad about him and hanging on his breast like a child on its mother.

It is in the evening of June 12, 1964, or perhaps a little later that the other love begins. The saint of saints. Zami entered it. Rare are those who experience this love. It takes a prison.

No one can know from the outside what happens in the heart of the saint of saints, we can only try to imagine it.

It takes a prison. It is of prison I am bereft, and that I regret.

But the other love began perhaps a little earlier, it was

138

germinating like a divine seed under the ash waiting only for a spark to explode. Prison lets it loose.

He who sees the end coming in the middle of the path of life and not at the end, with what step does he move forward?

Nelson's shoes were chosen with care. So many things secretly depend on the shoe and the foot. The soundness of the step has the exact same measurements as the soul's size.

Always on the move, always afoot.

Even when he stops off at the Josephs', he is racing through the years. Even the stop is full of movement.

We are engaged now on the narrow footpath between the high walls of rocky time and the pits of damnation. The earth is shrinking. Soon there will be only the airways for walking.

Moving forward, moving forward, there is still the earth, there is still time, vision, and will. Less and less time. More and more vision and will.

To really travel well all the roads of this century's Hell, how many shoes will I have to use, Osip wondered, advancing just behind Alighieri, not letting a sole come between him and the master, now that he had a passport for the Doleful City.

How many ox hides for a Voronezh notebook? How many steps for a poem? The steps are countless, one must look for each line abroad, in an ancient, eternal Italy or at the edge of a Crimean beach covered with musical shells. One must go to Koktebel[64] yet another and last time, and say one's farewells to the shells and travels, one last time for contemplating the sea one will never cross, the journey is coming to pass over there, without me, and leaving me the world's orphan and without dreams. No more sea, no more earth. Remains the garden of Hell, the inexhaustible well of wails. Tomorrow I will put on the yellow shoes and I will enter full of life into the throats of the polyglot organ. With my yellow shoes, it is I who will compel you to sing until the steps are worn away.

———————

But the day Osip wrote the famous Poem without music and without Poetry, the only Poem molded with trembling fingers from stinking mud, the dirty, detestable Poem, he was wearing, to write, big boots of black leather indifferent to excrement. He had shod himself deaf and dull for going to kick at the Kremlin door.[65]

He had borrowed the pathway all dirtied with dung and bones by which in the evening those who dwell in Hell before their death return home. The body with its fatty fingers is still well installed up there in the shelter of the famous Kremlin mountains. And seated at the table in the dining room, the damned, so very alive, wipes his enormous cockroach mustache with hairs from his head that he's just been gnawing on.

At this dense door the poet comes knocking, with boot kicks big enough for the world's deafest to hear his foot crack. The poem is almost as heavy as the big coarse curse words that fall from beneath the enormous mustache. The illiterate can read it, so thick and fat is it written.

With sixteen heavy-footed lines, Osip has drawn a dance of death around the broad-chested Osset.[66]

Che fai? What are you doing there? Crazy fool that you are.

Isn't this a poem you're making, you who were clarinet and oboe, voice of honey and of silk? A poem? No, an enormous, rhyming fart. No. Eight double farts fired into thick ears. For just as Dante plunges with the perverse instinct of the impolite poet into disgusting interviews that end discourteously, and like the idiot prince who rushes over to the devil's as though he were hastening toward God,[67] thus goes Osip like a headstrong fool, and invites himself to the executioner's table.

The white goose asks to be served up. She is stuffed with maggots and with worms of verse.

This was a poem with a pasty rancid tongue. Graceless. With big round eyes under the enormous mustache.

This was not a poem. It was Zami's howling in the dust. The surest way of giving death one's address. Into the right clean hands, with their thick, notoriously fatty fingers.

You won't crush me, chirps the worm wearing boots of black leather. It is I who with all my infinitesimal strength have come to mash myself on your molars.

All of Mandelstam's friends beg him to forget this piece of shit unworthy of such a sublime swan, to bury it beneath ten sands, to wash his fingers in ten pure streams, to remain standing head bent, barefoot and innocent, to not have written this howling, to not have knocked with a weak, idiotic hand at the hairy chest, to burn the boots and at the same time this Quixotic soul.

Crazy fool that you are! What are you doing there! Man nothing less than clever. You'd have to be a mole not to notice that Mandelstam doesn't know how to behave in this mustached century.

Nor how to say, nor how to greet, nor which words to paste onto the poems so they will seem well dressed.

All the moles begged Mandelstam to watch where he was putting his feet.

Only Akhmatova hears the poet fart and laughs. And transformed into a goat with headstrong hooves she belches too, and dances with Osip a few feet from the end, on the narrow footpath that worms its way between prison and the tomb.

Nelson was moving toward the Arrest. The Arrest is looking for him. It will take place. It is expecting him. The wall was rising up, eating up the earth, eating up the sky. It would stop his body, his voice, maybe, maybe not. It wouldn't stop his will. And wending his way he moves forward without slowing down and without hurrying, as if he had all the time and still almost all the earth and all the sky. He lives like a great Lord, time galore.

The wall was eating up the stars. He still has the time. Until the last minute, all the time. So he stopped off at the Josephs'.

The witnesses witness: the poet was firmly conducting his life toward the death he desired. Not just any death. The one that by this century, by birth and by his art, he should have deserved. He drew her age and her face a long time ago.[68] She will be still young and violent and oriental. And it is in some train station or other under an icy sky that she will take his outstretched hand.

And I in the flower of my rage, pale, resolved, I will pour my last fiery tears onto a snow.

In this century of the condemned to death caught without breath in the net, he at least he wants her poetically and quickly. He never leaves her. He calls after her with stars, he attracts her with poisoned poems, he wants to live her and to kill her at the same hour. But since he still dwells among us, from time to time he is touched by the ancient fear of those who die reluctantly. Nonetheless, impossible to cancel the

142

scheduled appointment. She's coming, it's as if she were already here. The train does not retreat. What remains to be done is to pretend to be yesterday, to pretend to be one of the living, to be.

But there are the poems, and everything is made with his own hands.

Thus, by moving toward the one he believes in by not believing, Osip leads his life at a gallop, astride his cross.

He falls a little from time to time but not here. So be it. Let us stagger on a little farther. Not at Cherdyn. Not at Voronezh. Isn't she going to run from him?

At Voronezh everything is a long time coming: the poems, winter, death, the trials, everything that is announced. As though History had suddenly hesitated in a funny sort of way. By keeping them waiting perfidiously, everything is making itself darkly desirous. Everything will come, next year, in order: the poems, winter, the trials, death.

In the meantime they must eat. And Nadezhda goes to the market, for they must eat whatever comes along.

In the desert it is the crows that nourish the deserted.

Here it is the typographers. The typographers remained, on the steppe stopped between seasons. Only the typographers remained to lend an ear to the comrade poet.

Earless the voice is a nestless swallow. Osip goes to the typographers who will never print his poems again. He arrives with his lips moving, and his soul that wants to break away.

They no longer possess the paper, nor the ink, nor the right. But they still possess the attention. In silence they listen to the poem rise, turn, and disappear. The poem passes. Osip's step weighs heavily upon their aged hearts. The oldest says: "again" and weeps. Meanwhile, the least old runs to buy a scrap of bread. And he stuffs it into the wretch's hand, bowing very low like a beggar before the Lord of mercy. Lord of misery yes! There were still the typographers for giving alms as though they were receiving them themselves. And for acting as though they would die of thirst if the fountain didn't gush forth. But perhaps they really would die of thirst without poems?

They too were the shadows of those who used to print.

Each one of them goes to warm himself at the hands and at the bread of ancient witnesses. Who can say who asks for alms who gives a scrap of scraps? Receiving, asking, begging, giving, are synonyms between two shadows with memory in common like a dead mother whom one evokes in vain, begging, receiving, thanking, it is the same smile between shadows who remember having played together.

Waiting for death, his crown of thorns planted on his head by his own hands. What he had earned, he who has nothing, pushed toward the end of the earth, what he had deserved and paid for in cash, he who has vomited into the world its only lead-footed poem.

Always on the move, with long, light steps, as though the wall's teeth were not piercing the sky, the threat isn't threatening him, as though he were absolutely not expecting Mandela's chaining, he moves forward, feeling his homeland beneath his feet inseparably.

Never in front of such an unflagging step has there been a deafer, more unbreakable wall.

Never a stiffer, more unfeeling mustache.

The people at the table over there in the back, in front of the beer, if the wall were suddenly to tremble on its fatty foot they wouldn't even feel it: they have mountains on their ears and an embalmed cockroach in place of a heart. The wall isn't trembling, not yet. Nelson walks toward it, a song on his lips, in his hand a pebble. It is certain he will make the wall fold and the giant fall down on his knees of brick. At daybreak. Night stretches. May day break. Is there a single wall in memory which, once ripe for death, did not succumb? May the century come.

Osip's Last Letter

She isn't running from him. She's calling to him. Never have so many poems come as in Voronezh. Cranes or crows, or this confusion of rooks. Just as the goldfinch all alone like the poet amongst so many phalanxes of poems. Or as if one had to live ten springtimes at once. And the red robins.

Two lips are not enough. His hands are running. His soles are falling to pieces. There are not enough doors, roofs, not enough windows.

One alights where one can, on a slip of paper, a turned up envelope.

Birds see from all sides. See past tomorrow. See above the walls and below the earths. See the blind skulls wandering for a hundred years along the walls. And see the sky fill up with hazelnut eyes and candles, in a few dozen generations. Too many poems? in the room next door the neighbor calls the police and stamps his fiendish foot.

Never so many murmuring arrivals. Emergencies of every color, blue, yellow, red, green, black, brighter than ever.

And they all come to him from her, from death.

She shows him everything he still has and will have no longer. He sees what he will see and he will see no longer. And sees too what he will be when he will be no more. What comes to him in a worldwide scintillation is a presumption of survival: you're still here, you're not alone yet. And sees how vast and splendid is all he will lose and he will lose no longer. The world is too much for one man alone. The dictation goes too fast too richly. Roaming creation he wears out ten pairs of shoes.

He can no longer stop living. Beneath each poem he draws the letter *V*. Why do you do that?

Death will know very well why. Each poem signed *Vivant*. Signed *Viens*.[69]

Will he arrive? When will she arrive? What, who? We do not know. We have all we will have, and all that is, is ours according to our desires.

Poems arrive flying in a very very low V, in tight Vs — as if they were all of them made up of but a single bird with slightly closed wings, gliding in black, regular flight, belly to belly with the icy earth. The black sky descends like a printing press onto the earth.

And for paper the spindleless ream from the plain to the painting's background and much more than is necessary.

Too much plain! Enough! But can one complain of too much? At least we see the space if not the race, the space so similar to the future which we will not enter. At least we see the white future without us before us. So much future before us. A flight in a V alights, over there.

The inaccessible is before us so beautiful, so cold, so near. What rich poverty. And all our senses illuminated at the window.

Our mouth full of words. We don't want for much to be happy.

And maybe we are happy, in the inaccessible secret of our interior pockets; maybe it is being written in secret, the letter. The V-shaped letter that will tell of our voyage to Voronezh, when we were alive and rich, maybe the last will and testament is being written behind our jacket, a wonder-filled

Letter that is counting our infinitesimal riches on ten thousand fingers: we have here an immense sky with from time to time some heavy barges of clouds—our cinema is this celestial string.

And down below we're not counting the earthworms, the dragonflies, or the shining memory of snails, or the spiders from towns and attics. And not counting the sciences, crystallography, biology, mineralogy, archaeology, chemistry, the sciences our manifold dukedoms we shall bequeath to no one. At Voronezh we have everything we'll have no more, and our mouth full of words, for talking of nothing else.

There will be a day of empty mouths, and not even words anymore to weep for the marvelous scrapbook from Voronezh.

———————

V? If it's not at Voronezh, then at Vladivostok? Are you coming?

Could this be Her, at the door to barrack #11 at USVITL, in Vladivostok?[70] December 27, 1938?

Skinny, exhausted, unrecognizable, oh this is not the one I was expecting. I would have thought her taller and more majestic, in her threadbare clothes, with Akhmatova's blue sparkle in her eyes, and I thought she would tell me the last words, although the world was so somber, I thought . . .

—In truth you have just said the last words, and with your eyes watching from both sides, you can clearly see that I've just arrived.

So Osip quickly writes the last letter to his brother:

"Choura, I'd like to ask you to send me a pair of shoes, but I don't know if there's any sense in this. Here I am almost beyond recognition . . . "

In order to send a last letter. The words wouldn't come.

"P.S. Nadezhda my beloved, are you alive, my darling? Choura, write me about this at once."

Are you alive? Here I do not know where I am anymore. I am almost beyond recognition. Osip really wrote this. Alive or dead who can answer this in truth, who can answer for whom, in this time when to be alive is to be not as dead as the dead?

Me, I am a little dead I think, but not completely. My lips are still here.

But once the letter left, a great anger took hold of Osip. Don't think I'll let myself be had by a strange and foreign death. I wasn't waiting for you.

He takes up his staff and he fires. And everything became uncertain.

Not this aquiline nose, and this bitter mouth. And these eyes like black waters. No, I wrote it four years ago: mine is black and she has blue eyes, my dragonfly of death, I described this ten times and I haven't ceased affirming it: My dragonfly has blue eyes. You, come up from black waters, you are a mistake.

He takes up his pencil and he strikes.

None was there in the barracks to say who carried the day, who took him away.

—I defy you to say, hypocrite, which one of the two of us is scared of the other. Where is the truth, liar, I defy you to say who has won, who is going to die, who is carrying the other on her back, who is dead? Where is the limit between us? Who is on her knees now?

—My head hung over a pail, I see a world in the black water. I saw this world on another journey. It is altogether Africa. Hey! I wasn't expecting this.

To pass through, my mouth still full of white flakes, my white eyes full of snow, into this other hemisphere.

—Did you not write that dead you would return from among the dead to tell the children: listen, the sun is shining?[71]

He did write this. It's the pail that makes the plane.

And before the pail-plane, there had been Geryon the propeller-operated dragon.[72]

—I had nonetheless clearly written that Dante Alighieri would be waiting for me at the end of the steppe, the keeper in a kepi. We never believe what we ourselves predict.

———————

On one of those last days of the year 1938, Osip went in a whisper. There wasn't anyone to take the message, in barrack #11. No one except Alighieri.

There was no light. Or darkness. There was a purity.

"I'm going. Quick a camel and some sandals.

"My soul's sole is worn away, but I am still young and a traveler. Let a passerby pass by, with a hurried air, pity painted on his face, and I will dog his footsteps. Ten years, Alighieri, I carried you around in my jacket pocket, ten years and not a day without you and your Hell in my pocket.[73] You were reborn through me each day. I introduced you to obsequious Moscow of the yielding spine, the shy, musical Armenian sky, the universe of metal departures in the forests of tall train stations, I showed you the trams and the trains. I helped you cross unencumbered the chasms of time. I was your camel, your calèche, your taxi. I introduced you to my friends. I lent my breath and that of Akhmatova, her modulations of precious shawl, to each of your anxieties.

"We carried you around for so many years clinging to our loud voices' necks. Dante stuffed letter by letter into Mandelstam, eh?

"It's your turn to carry me in your pocket now, your turn

149

to make me traverse time, me with my Hell of leaves dispersed by the wind.

"Take my hand, keeper of restfulness and of the backwaters of the dead, take what remains of my hand, and lead my trusting corpse across this story's winter till the too hot day when, under the storm, run the cohorts of falcon-feathered ostriches.

"The keeper takes the pail with a firm hand. From where I am I cannot read what is in his gaze without warmth. Inside the pail, like, in the vanishing of limits, beasts transpose themselves and trifle with forms, like flakes make the ostrich and the pail makes the plane, me I am molting into icicles and crystallized ash. The keeper of the passageways takes the pail from before my very eyes. Master, what are you going to do? Pass my being from cold to hot, from nothingness to the cradle?

"Ah! If I could no longer see with my eyes life turning over into death, and human desires endlessly changing state, now melting, now freezing. Nothing, not even death, arrests our torments.

"But behold: I feel my black pail swinging in my hand that is sowing hope and panic amidst the rows of shadows. I want to cry out: stop! stop! What remains of the poet? A wingless vertigo.

"And when Alighieri says no, it's no.

"But suddenly, as if he were obeying an order from Above, he makes the pail gape, and spills me all bewildered onto the yellow grass of this other world.

"I had written it clearly: this earth that suddenly rises like a lion. The musky air is sparkling. I rise from among the sands and stones to say: 'The sun is shining on the bound continent.'

"I am speaking in the name of Dante Mandelstam and the others, with enough breath deployed to make my Russian Italian soul effortlessly reach the austral ears.

"Haven't I always had two lips?

"I knew very well that the Neva, my river, my tomb of water had two banks.

"One I left behind me, shivering with cold.

"And behold how today, my breathing a little weary, I arrive at the other lip, trembling all over with fever.

"A flight of mosquitoes receives me in an electric fanfare. Paludicole Talmud. Welcome, Mandelstam's atoms, here Africa adopts you.

"No one sees me, but there is no one who doesn't hear me. I can see it, here too the century continues to metamorphose into a monster. Here too one bursts the stars.

"Choura, quickly, send me some shoes. I'm going to be on the move again."

———————

Who saw him go? No one. Who can say where? Legends roam the country and return unsure. He might return. No one saw him return. But no one saw him leave.

The last time he was alive he was wending his way with Dante, one reciting the other's song, followed by a confusion of birds.

———————

From the same time are we, from the same Osip's century, but separated by centuries, so close, so remote so remotely close, remotely, closely.

Far from my right hand

An unfolding of black fields, of white fields, and in the grooves the enraged gallopings of poets beating the snows, lifting up the waves of the black earths with their truffled breath.

To the east of my shoulder, far from my right hand roaming the long unknown versts, even the blackness of their blackness is unknown to me. A high hedge of thorns encircles this century.

What does the word *contemporary* mean today?

Who is the contemporary of those who have lost all address on earth?[74]

And yet no one is more of a traveler than these travelers of travels enclosed.

The Song of Paths

From 1958 to 1964, every day it was the Song of Paths, the song of Nelson and the Bizana rose, of panting early mornings, arise my love, from Orlando, from Pretoria, he shall come, of nights without him by my side with him in my heart, of nights filled with comingness[75]

humid with the hope of him, the nights do not sleep, they search for him, they hear him coming across mountains, over hills, through police nets, and he never stops coming, he's arriving, he's only a few centuries, a few kilometers from my arms a few moments from my lips, a few walls away, this was the song of moist flesh, of bunches of grapes, of apples and fig leaves on the wire-covered windowpane, ah! everything knocks at the sacred window, all the fingers that are not yours, the fingers of the wind and rain, the fingers of the jacaranda, until finally his fingers his moonvoice tap in the dark, for this winter has just passed, come, it is the hour of flowers and of doves, the hour of hiding-places in the staircase, of cracks in the rock of time, I never knew when,

when one never knows which when, each when is called soon, now,

always, at every moment he is coming, the air is full of his footsteps, over there love is pushing open night's damp door,

The soldiers guarding the neighborhood found me, they ransacked my house, my drawers, my bed full of traces of him, oh love of my soul do not come do not knock at the pane, my friends, my Bizana sisters by the gazelles and the zebras of the veldt I beseech you, may he not appear, may he not loom up out of the desert like the tamed lion scented with myrrh and incense,

come don't come I call to you but do not answer, I want you to flee but I want you to come, through fire and firearms one more time again, for I am sick with need.

Never before a pane were there so many prayers and so many tears held back and so much abandon, so many deathly agonies and so many resurrections. Dawn stops breathing. Not a breath between life and death, the sky listens and moves no more.

All this when Nelson was only accused of treason and still so divinely possible, around him no bar, only men and mobs, and while it was possible that he might come, that he might truly arrive one day or another day and no matter when.

This is why each gesture was so fateful, Zami was no longer breathing, and each hour was the angel she wrestled hand to hand with in the dark, until wounding until victory. The miracle prowls behind the wall, it paces up and down the immense night with its magnificent and tranquil footsteps. Motionless, its ear to the pane, so as not to lose the most far-off footstep, the last footstep, the first footstep.

"Peekaboo!"

Life plays with terror. "Peekaboo!" and all the fears are carried off. For one hour sometimes even two they take pleasure in immortality. So many bursts of laughter, so many roars, so much proud, frenetic liberty. For one hour and sometimes two and even once or twice for four hours,

Love carries them up to the peak of time. And there, from the top of the world that resembles the table of the gods, they see the promise, and for one hour they have all. All they will have. Hills, rivers, plateaus, winds, spices, fields of corn, oceans, herds, fruits and vines, all is liberated, returned, distributed. All will be. Will be is already.

So many visions and certainties, and so much space smelling of fresh thyme — in such a narrow bed. Life climbs so high, so strong, that way up there it grazes death. Oftentimes one dies upon the other during an embrace. And without a doubt, passing through death they arrive at eternal Africa.

He departs: mortal life takes up again. He departs and all is sacred. All that touched him silently resounds. Everything hurts. The chair hurts. The door burns. Zami closes her eyes and sees him as he was just now, he is still inside her eyes, she sees the bed full of his big black body, the bed is still alive. Cake of life. First flesh. In her hands, the intoxicated joy of God when he felt in his nonhands the downy firm warm limbs of the human being. From her hands, joy recedes.

The bed is going to empty. Empties. Nelson recedes. Everywhere are huge invisible panting holes. Then come his ghosts. His ghosts are big and strong. His Absence is stretched out now on the sofa. The bungalow is full of his Absences. But finally Absence too begins to fade, to fall silent.

It's the dirty shirt that holds out the longest.

But at the end of two weeks, Zami resigns herself to washing it. Because she is his wife and because he is alive. In the hope it will soon be dirty and very alive again.

Our human misfortune is that our immortalities are so brief. They don't hold onto time. We regain the huge house called Paradise only to soon misplace its keys. We enter, we exit. At the cost of great sorrow we lose the door. Fortunately the sorrow is a consolation.

But then behold: from hour to hour we lose the powerful memory of the house. Paradise pales, have we ever been there, kings and ardent with joy? Behold us pale and chilled. Only now do we truly lose paradise, whereas from hour to hour it is loss we lose, and sadly sorrow retreats. We are no longer bitten and bloody. The wounds fall silent. And at the end of a few weeks, the shirt is like new.

But this fading, this force, is also our human chance. It repairs everything, good fortune, bad fortune. And just as we lose one day the taste of the bread of joy and the memory of joy, so also will we be able to lose one day the tenacious taste of sorrow. The earth forgets. This is its strange privilege. It is Hell that is a prey to memory.

And this Zami knows in the wisdom of hope, and in the madness of hoping exaggeratedly, which is our secret wisdom. Hoping is an exaggeration of life.

Washing the shirt, Zami acted as if she feared neither separation, nor loss, nor fading. We will return to the huge house at the summit of Mount Ararat. It is the future that must be preserved, not the past. As if she had nothing to fear, or to regret. Would iron, fade, tidy, sweep, fade. As if. This woman is sure of having to start again tomorrow. Since he'll be alive, free, and untidy again.

Something is stuck in my chest. A breath. A key that won't turn. I can't open the door. I'm standing in front of the door. The world around me is terribly clean. It looks like snow.

And the Absence of your voice deafens me.

But on the tenth day noise returns, with untidiness, shoe prints in the kitchen, grass breaks through, immortality is going to sprout again.

But not a single immortality for twenty-four years.

The shirts are in the closet, because he is alive.

But during these twenty-four years life has been desired day by day with such determination, each day contested, beset by anguish, rescued and released, and finally conquered and counted. Twenty-four armies defeated and routed.

And sometimes it's Zami who is a bit defeated.

It is January 1, 1970. I have to live. One more time. Even though I've pushed the army back six times already. The year is camped out again before me, its three hundred and sixty mountains pitched before my door one by one to be clambered up and started over. I don't get up.

An enormous moon watches me lying here helpless. This woman is in distress and trouble. The year arrives before me with its three hundred and sixty fortresses to dismantle.

This January I don't get up. An enormous sadness is lying on top of me, I cannot lift it.

This woman doesn't get up. She doesn't want to see the army of mountains standing in front of her face. She doesn't want to see the pack of faceless rocks planted in front of her door.

This woman woke up too alone. She alone is this alone on the entire planet. She alone walks barefoot on the burning sands with a mountain on her back. She alone scoops out time with a spoon.

The circus is full to bursting. With its millions of curious eyes it watches the ant confront the tigers in the arena.

The ant is black and golden. She sees the millions of eyes watching her prepare. What interests them is her cry. The cry that startles the tigers.

If one could live like dying sleeping dreaming perhaps from one short year like a shirt, from a flat, brief earth, without mountains, without war, without a hundred thousand kilometers to cross feet bloody upon the path of shards in order to take one step, only one big step toward freedom.

I've fallen into the trap, this January has pushed me.

—I know it is a trap, but no strength to flee it. I no longer manage to think above the mountains. I no longer manage to invent the present that is going to come later and I know not when, I no longer manage to fling my life forward. Falls upon me all the weight of the present to get past, of the present pressing its heavy weight of presence, of test and iniquity. And on this day I don't manage to decompose it.

Nestled in regret, she considers the life she could have had, all the life she will never have had, and which above all one must not regret, and that's precisely what she regrets. Does one regret the unborn child? And that's precisely what she regrets. Nestled in what is not, she is lying helpless beneath lost time, like the dead man who attempts to lament beneath the pyramid and is not born.

I'm terribly tired. So, isn't there anyone to help me raise this sadness so much stronger than my strength, so, isn't there anyone, so, isn't there anyone?

It would take a rose. A rose from his hand. The rose that will not come.

There's the massive moon that can't do a thing.

Comes the Ostrich who can't do much.

"It's the date that pushed me. Every number claws at me, every number knocks me to the ground. It's the year's name that has wounded the bravery within my breast. At the calling of their names the years grow and multiply. I hear the years galloping toward me one after the other, the tournament list is interminable and I run away."

"One must fly very high in the nameless numberless time up above the time of nations and condemnations.

"The birds know only a single terrestrial country and a thousand landscapes, and all the landscapes are good.

"Arise and fly straight ahead of you, till the day of the return. Without ever looking down. Here there are no years. Here are only patience and promise.

"And there is only one time that interests you. The one that starts with Mandela. The rest is space."

I rise. One leap into the light and I find my way again. I'm going that way. Alone but in the direction of him. Without him by my side, but not without him, since it is toward him that I go.

What is it called, this powerful and pointed flight, this answer to the sole Voice whose sound I do not hear, this joy without happiness? I have a wound in my side, which is Him. Alone I am not alone. Torture doesn't hurt me, thirst intoxicates but doesn't parch me.

Time around me passes very quickly very slowly. I say "time," without knowing very well how many mysteries and contraries this word contains.

Down below crawl some seven-headed snake-years, the roads get tangled up like octopi.

Up above the path is panting at my heels, no one stops my racing, the air is so pure, nothing will prevent me from catching sight of Nelson at the very first second.

And while waiting to be born, I live toward him.

I think of the Day when after all this All and all this Nothing, Nelson and Zami will be together together.

This story will have begun with the last days and ended with the first.

The turn of a key will be enough to make years of exile disappear at a blow, as irreality is exiled.

This key is the one from the Moscow apartment, to which Nadezhda and Osip returned, showing up after exile expired in Voronezh at the end of the year, 1937. Oh, who will tell of the other train, the train of things, with its head on fire, its thoughts up in smoke and sleeping not a single minute, for fear of waking up on the other side; for fear of waking up.

There they are before the door, and that's the key. The very key. Nadezhda places the proper key in the lock of the very door, and behold: the door swings open.

And before their eyes, the very apartment itself, and the very same apartment. Here ends exile and memory. Under the power of the apartment they thought that once night was over day would return. They forget where they were born and that they've died of it, they forget the date and the enormous mustache, because it's the very same apartment. It's really the bed, the very same curtains, the very same pots and pans, hence it's really their very same selves coming back into their very same selves on the bright side. Nadezhda feels the floor, the house is rolling in poems. Everything is really here, it's me over there who was someone else I've now forgotten. Nothingness reverts to nothingness. And the *Fourth Prose* springs, tapping its foot, from the big cushion's feathered breast.[76]

Behold: Osip recognizes the shelves and the shelves recognize him. He runs straight away to the Museum. And all the French ones recognize him.

The day of their arrival in Moscow, even though it was still so dark, they crossed the unbelievable with the turn of a key, and they believed.

—This is why all the poems that arrived in Voronezh came with 7 lines or 14. It is 7 that is the key.

How could they have not believed everything and anything? This was the huge House. And believing they were born, they were born. There was a first day. Like those who climb up from among the dead, they had never been as fresh and luminous. With each step the world is good, women and men are good, and tomorrow we shall forgive.

The lips of the enormous wound shut, crooning, of their own accord.

And yet the poems from Voronezh had clearly said: dying? Yes but they would come in sevens.

And perhaps they said dying for fear we no longer loved enough a life so poor?

And sometimes I would say dying, I am dead, for I couldn't see clearly on which side of my breath I was writing. And dying isn't that living too but very low, in a very low voice.

The House remained huge for several days. The trams were running. Akhmatova, unable to board the tram, came on foot. Everything was happening unbelievably, in reality.

They wanted to believe and were happy to believe, until the end of belief. What's the use of not living, in truth?

In the beginning then will be The Day. This day, the day when Zami will be together with Nelson together with her, married and reunited like wife and husband, this day (if it comes) will be an ordinary day. This is what Zami wants above all: a day of man and woman together all day long.

It will be a day with ordinary rising and retiring. Including jogging and a little massage. The massage will be done with slight boredom, for everything in this day will be exactly ordinary. So she will massage him and he won't think of massaging her. The word *peace* will be lived simply by the blood in their veins.

Breathing will be regular. Time will flow as it likes. One of them will find it fast. The other one will find it normal.

If all goes well there will be the wing of a quarrel, teasing, and small worries. As for the table, it will be perfectly set, as usual. Each thing will be in its place according to its destiny. If the spicy chicken is ruined . . . No. Zami couldn't stand that. She places certain limits on the ordinary. Let this be a perfect ordinary day. This is what she wants.

And of course without fear on every side and without the pit and the net, and without the bitter waiting, for weeks, for the coming of a day for which she has ruined herself ten times with love so much so that when it arrives, it is smaller than hope and hopelessness.

And just the two of them without the whole world. Is this ordinary?

Zami has no notion of the ordinary, since this will be the first time. She invents it, with nuances.

For part of the time we won't think about a thing. We will be. It's very difficult to imagine this day because it won't have anything remarkable about it. It will be uneventful. But the light will be beautiful. Time will be the time for living. And also each one in herself and for herself. That is what is most difficult, because of the jealousy that is in us. It will be the time for leaving each other in peace. And of being there without losing one's head over such a simple presence, without feeling obliged to assure oneself that you are really here, without demanding, without touching, without patting each other's arm, without rushing into each other, without fleeing oneself in the other.

Thoughtfully Zami will prepare the coffee. Thinking about what? About the coffee. About life, which is so delicate to prepare. The coffee will be excellent. Nelson will drink it thinking. Thinking about what? Zami would like him to think about her. But without asking him. What are you thinking about? there, behind that silence?

It will be a very difficult day to pull off because they will have to live it right away and now, they who have become accustomed to putting off living for later.

Now they are sitting on the sofa. Then he will put his arm around her shoulders and the world will be revived. And thus, leaning against the cross turned back into a tree, she will turn perhaps for an instant toward the old years gone past, and with a mixture of astonishment and nostalgia she will dream of all that pain whose mother she was until last night, and of the punishment of every day and every night of this era still very close and yet gone forever, of the punishment that was starting up again yesterday all new every morning and that today is already a part of yesterday, and softly, without shouting, for a long time she will listen to it leaving, going very far away, very fast, as the horses of pain withdraw from our bodies. One bound, it's over. But for a long time we hear the last notes of the plaintive music resounding. Seated under the tree of life, she will listen to the past taking shape, like a country turning strangely foreign. Where I shall never again return.

And this day shall pass.

Then on the day after the ordinary day a very sweet, slightly surprised joy is born: this day, they discover the next day, by dint of being ordinary, will have been very beautiful. Without heroism they will have accomplished the feat of having lived together for one day without fuss or glamour. For Zami there is no greater intimacy imaginable: to be sitting on the sofa, sweetly side by side, with between them, like an imperceptible veil, the sensation, too refined to be really felt, of a very slight difference. It is this nonseparating separation that reunites the togetherness. Not being alone. And not being him.

Because, what can one do of more ordinary on an ordinary day? We become different from each other and that is all. And we forget each other a little. And it is in this way, in the shelter of a slight forgetfulness, that one meets the other the most delicately. Are you there? Yes I'm here.

This will come to pass like this, with this tranquillity. If this day comes. If it will come, no one can say, can say when, no one. But is all this ordinary? I do not know. But what I do know is that this Day already comes every day to comfort Zami with its menus, its numerous, slightly different versions. And it is of an extraordinary slowness. It is from this dateless, faceless Day that she feeds her huge hunger

From the crumbs of this day. Every day of dearth she regales her starving soul with this dream of the first sabbath.

Come, o day, you'll see how I shall live you, as if you were a lifetime.

But sometimes a wild hunger rises, a scandal, a squall that shatters everything in its path, and pulls the ordinary day to pieces. Shouting: if there's only one day, then let it be fire! And right away, throwing oneself into this day as if into the fire of love, one drinks the fire, is killed, dies, loses one's skin, one's thought, one's bones, and yet suffers from losing oneself and only ceases suffering when all is consumed. This day too is beautiful, but all it leaves behind in the memory from which to take bliss is a brief incendiary trace.

No, it is living she wants, living at the slow pace of the she-ass.

———————

One day there will be the first Sunday. And on the second Sunday, the first Sunday will have already passed. On the third Sunday, the second Sunday will slightly obscure the first. Forgetfulness will have started.

This is what Zami wants most in the world: to forget one day ordinarily, without fear, without regret, and without even noticing. One day to be delivered of her starving avarice and to waste, waste, waste.

———————

How did exile, in order to go from Voronezh to Vladivostok, pass through Moscow? Thanks to hope. This detour was a marvelous stroke of strength stronger than reality. To make this stroke, hope used everything: chance, illusion, hallucination, desire, all the artfully innocent odds that are the rungs by which the dying climb the slopes of the somber forest, with a suddenly incredibly lively step, and regain the other side. And lighter than squirrels, they cross the threshold and clear the pit, the net, the bars of black fingernails, and fall for several days toward the sky which is their natural bent, fall toward the Golden Age, and for a few days there really is no one to stop them.

How could they be in Moscow instead of in Vladivostok? By illusion. Behold how they successfully carried out this illusion: by a spontaneous error on their part. Because they didn't know they were impossible. Because they thought evil would end up ending, whereas it only ends to start again.

Because miracles exist: they are made of a mix of hope, illusion, and charity. Being is the author of all its dwellings, its falls, its transports. *Le Paradis c'est moi.* The laughing face of Moscow regained, *c'est Osip.*[77]

By dint of wanting to fly one ends up managing. All it takes is wanting to and time. Dante wanted to, then da Vinci wanted to, then came another man who really wanted to fly, and three hundred years before the airplane these desires had visited the moon. And in the end truly flying man came into existence.

And by dint of wanting to live one ends up finding a way not to hear death's call.

In truth the secret is in the wanting. It takes a Dantean audacity to clear the hurdle of one's own human limit. And to be able to say without pride and without humility: why not? And why not me?

For whoever allows herself to say this with superhuman dignity and without pride, the door to heaven opens twice.

It has to be possible to discover America, Hell, Purgatory.

And it is Mandelstam accompanied by Hope who sees the door to celestial Moscow open yet again before him, although it is already locked and rusted for all eternity. This was a sublime and provisory conquest. Enough of dying! Living now!

Osia lowers his long lashes and straight away, everything one mustn't see so as to survive until the terminus he sees no more. For an entire season of cecity I do not see my friends turn away from me in fear and shame and in fear stronger than shame, I do not see what I see, I do not read what I read, an entire season of clairvoyant blindness on board a tram, I alight amongst the strangest of strangers, my brothers become strangers, my friends become enemies, but I do not see them. The illusion was perfectly clear.

The illusion that exile had been exiled and that the exiled from now on ex-exiles were themselves the mothers of their own destinies was perfect. It wasn't an illusion. There was no difference between what they believed and the Truth. For a long time, for some time they invent Time and Truth. Truth changed masters, it is Osip who commands and Nadezhda obeys easily, for what the poet recounts is too good to not be true.

The sky is by Michelangelo. The music is by Vivaldi. The Mustache is forgotten behind a wall. Us here, them there. Fools here, wolves there.

World of two worlds. One of the two has only a sky. And in this sky the sun and its train of stars. The other one has all the mire, the cracks filled with blood and the wells with mud.

The streets of one glide between blind jaws. At the corner of Tolstaya Street Akhmatova comes running, her pale queenly cheeks reddened by the child's game, and the supply sack filled with all one would wish to invent. At the corner of time and eternity, behold the woman contemporary of the man without a single contemporary.[78] They exchange their crowns made from ears of wheat, their precious stones in seven languages, everything that comes into their minds they bring to life, everything that comes into their voices is saved. In the streets Akhmatova and Mandelstam play at whoever dies lives, and weave, with skeins of Turkish and Tartar colored silk, rutilant ladders for tomorrow's dying. This city removed for a time from terror, is Moscow forgiven and signed A and M.

Take the A tram I'll take the M, and let's meet up again alive at the century's terminus.

What are they for one another? Two slightly damaged Dantes.

And all this because they did not know that exile was following them everywhere, and that it was impossible for a man condemned to death not to die, absolutely impossible, impossible not to lose paradise, they did not know this because they were naked and not suffering either from heat or from cold, or from seeing each other as they really are, without mistake, without makeup, without masks on their tongues and condemned to deportation for it. They were inventing Truth but the lie was stronger.

And the shoes? Without which no path and no poems? Osip had yellow shoes. The shoes had been cut from the leather of a yellow suitcase. As indicated by its sticker-spotted skin, this suitcase has traveled far and wide. So Osip was shod in shoes of seven leagues which had traveled in advance of him everywhere he would have liked to go.

And all these travels on foot carried him without effort beyond borders. And without a passport. The pilgrim instinct is in the skin. He puts on these yellow Alighieri shoes, and right away, he is on his way to the travels that don't start on earth, and on which Moscow cannot put its ankle-breaking stamp.

Illusion the travels on yellow wings. Illusion the end of the Age of Wolves. Illusion the Victory of the Greyhound.[79] Chance the huge house that responds to the key. They believed for a time they were at our place, but the house was already Their place, and one morning it closes again around their flanks like a mouth.

As long as the lamb does not see the teeth descending on its neck, it sees the world as a prairie where come and go ewes, and wolves that look like shaggy ewes. Illusion has an ancient charm. Illusion is a gift from hope. And it was good for a time.

If they hadn't had to eat to live. If Akhmatova's basket had been inexhaustible. Because when they begin to knock on doors, beneath the gaze of the inhabitants of a world without sky, they lose their colors, the blood drains out of their cheeks. And they become what they are seen to be: the shadows of birds of ill omen.

How lucky they were to believe for one last hour beyond this century, to believe for yesterday and for much later, and what strength in the dark! Because they couldn't accept that Dante be no longer of this world, they couldn't open the door to such a thought without being immediately blown out by an icy breath. And with all their extenuated might, with their memories weary, their throats throttled, they never stop remaking for him remains of a universe, a village, a kitchen, a foyer where he can reign forever.

The time for the extinction of certain species having arrived . . . Who could have believed that in climbing up the generations men would end up climbing down earless into the dark, letting their works, their musics, their eyes brilliant with tears, their own hearts, drop behind them like excrements?

———————

To return to the time of the trial for treason. Everything happened vertically. The moment fell like a stone and disappeared like a falcon.

—Someone came to fetch me in an old pickup truck, a tall fellow in a white dustcoat. When I was seated beside this man, it was Him. He drove the crock of a truck to the city center, while he was speaking to me very fast I didn't cry out with love, I placed my hand up on my life's knee, and down into the depths of my body I drew life, I lived. In the center of the city, at a red light, he told me I'll be back, take care, my beloved disappeared, it was at the corner of Sauer Street, I didn't have time to cry out I'm dying, this life is killing me, I slipped over onto his seat, my buttocks in the imprint of his buttocks my hands on his hands his hands beneath my hands, I felt his blood pass over into my blood, hundreds of Whites crossed the street.

At the wheel of solitude in Johannesburg my lungs are full of groans, there isn't enough room in my chest for the storm. The truck would like to explode. Into howling, into a howled no. Ah! To be a bitch, a female ass, to bray with grief up to the clouds! To let the cry cry out down to the last rattle! In the middle of town. That's impossible! My mouth is not enough. It takes a snout to suffer.

But all this deathly agony, this shattered joy, what happiness.

Life was dying of the fear of losing this moment of caress, this minute of nourished hands, in this moment I touch the warm, undeniable chest of he who is my life and already in this moment I think cruelly "in this moment I still feel your chest alive beneath my fingers in this perfect full finishing moment I am still alive, I don't remember yet but soon I shall caress with my famished fingers the memory of this happiness."

And sometimes for a quarter of a day, existence was almost normal. The children would go out and come back like birds. Whenever this occurred Zami got a migraine from stupefaction: being normal was abnormal. She would run to check herself in the mirror. The abnormal had become normal. Peace would vaguely worry her. But it never lasted.

All the Things
They Couldn't Do

All the things she couldn't do:

Do the shopping with him,

Do the shopping without him, not giving him a moment's thought, like a woman alone on a Saturday morning in Spring she is queen of the universe, all the things she buys and all the things she doesn't buy are equally hers, she does exactly what she wants. And to thus discover the secret of freedom which isn't doing what I want but: escape.

Go off leaving him still in bed at home, and find him at home when she gets back,

Not let him know she wouldn't be coming home tonight because she was going to a meeting of the Federation of Women.[80]

Set the table for him and the children and then see themselves truly seated at this table all four of them,

Hesitate in the morning between three dresses and ask him which one to wear. And then wear one of the ones he didn't choose. Because I can choose freely only if first you give me your advice.

Otherwise now when she dresses alone and without advice, she only obeys herself. And there is neither choice nor pleasure.

All the things one can only do for oneself if there is the

other with whom not to do them, the other one loves so much. And too often today if she happens to put on a sumptuous dress, it isn't only for him, it's above all against Them. This is her superb way of displeasing them by all that should please human men. She puts on war robes. And with a stroke of shimmering cotton, she kills them.

And all these slight sacrifices without which independence is but a vain word, and all the skirmishes that are the pride of a Great Love:

One day, refuse to do what he wanted. Once at least. She would have liked to say no. And for him to say: Oh. But that was really impossible. In this life there wasn't one minute for disagreeing.

So life has always had a skeleton's purity. But this was not at all from preference.

Ask him why he chose the smallest house in Orlando, number 8115, a bungalow with only a kitchen a bedroom and the front room, whereas he could have chosen the four room bungalow next door, since in these 1940s he had the right to do so and the chance too and there was no harm in that. Not that she doesn't know the answer, but to let him know that whenever she thinks about the children's lives, just the same she's sorry.

Make him realize she's not a saint, otherwise what merit would there be in her loving him as she loves him, and in her bearing so many unbearable things.

Make a scene in front of him, which she would have had to do more than once, for a woman living in Africa, even if she has the privilege of being the wife of such an admirable man, sometimes finds herself in an unpleasantly ancient situation, of which a man doesn't even suspect the causes or the existence.

Besides wherever she is a woman has to make a scene from time to time.

172

For example when he would come home from the court-house for dinner with the ten invited guests although there's only one cutlet in the refrigerator and he knows it and has forgotten, and he shouts you're going to see what a great cook my wife is, this was something she really couldn't stand. But she could never bring herself to tell him. He was already on trial for treason. And he was the most just most innocent man in the whole country.

This is what made life so athletic.

For it is much more difficult to love an innocent person than one who blunders.

―――――――――

Once Nelson came to listen to Zami speak before a national congress of the Federation of Women. Nelson was seated at the very back of the room. It was the first time he had come to a place where it wasn't he, it was she who was speaking.

Whoever has seen Zami with her May 1 hat cannot imagine to what extent she has always been afraid of exams. Nonetheless, one of the reasons Zami insists on always having a hat is also her fear of exams, and the fear her fear be seen.

That day at the Federation she had a superb Pondo coif but finery did nothing for the fear.

She was before the hall as if before a court of angels. From the big tall woman she usually is she had shrunk to the size of the nine-year-old child she once was. And although spending the night trying to nourish her little three-month-old brother, all the while she was also learning the legend of Bismarck for her history professor.[81] But the baby despite her efforts was on the verge of dying.

There in the back Nelson looked like the History Professor and on his jacket he wore an examinator's badge.

This was the exam of all exams. She opened her mouth, and at her first words a sparkling cecity fell over the room. Before her, at her feet, was spread a sea she had never seen, a sea that was unrolling to the far end of the world a surface of black silk so smooth, so perfectly brilliant she could no longer see any color other than this milky brilliance, dense and light and quivering. She was sitting on the back of a golden hill, very high above this silk undulating under her words, and with each phrase flung toward this infinite face, the face would fling golden sparks, as if it were the sea showering stars toward the sky. And see, the sea was so crackling with gold—it was flinging fistfuls of glittering gazes—that Zami took the plunge, and as she was falling she flung fistfuls of words at the face of the sea, she spoke faster and faster, carried away by the wind by the beauty by the intoxication of the fall into this starry mirror, and she addressed the story of her life to the eyes in the water, to the smiles, the sands, the clouds, the women, she heard herself tell pell-mell everything she knew, all the stories of all her country's women, dancing story of all the destinies here assembled, she put everything into this headlong fall, everything women don't understand everything they know everything they do well everything they dream of doing, all their shames and all their courages, the sea wept spurts of sparks, the room was but a sole memory, a sole regret, a sole exclamation.

And beyond this unanimous sea, Zami perceived a single face, round and motionless, Nelson was the only fixed unrousable thing in this upside-down world. He anchored the entire sea.

When Zami landed there was calm. Then the women began to sing of Zami's exploit.

And he? He was a man before women, and one of them was his. He, father and buyer, sees his little girl being sold at the village merchant's. He doesn't see the sea.

And says: "Next time, see to your hands my love. You didn't stop tapping your papers."

He really didn't have the time to tell her anything else, for the women of the Federation surrounded her on all sides, all wanting to touch her hand.

This was the last time he had the chance to see Zami deploy her secret voice like a standard. He didn't see the voice, or the army. The time not having come yet for him to think of seeing what a woman can do with her voice.

"Next time, husband, you will accompany me as squire and not as master. Next time or the time after." This retort could not be uttered. It expressed exactly the inexpressible revolt of Zami.

I am not your carbon copy.

Only the poet can picture the country where one fine morning would reign a king and a queen or two kings or two queens or a superb man and a superb woman, who would shout with laughter on the public square. And this would last a whole morning long.

But here's the surprise: from Robben Island, one time Nelson writes: "My love, I want you to be queen." It's from up close that he hadn't seen her. From far away he sees her with the eyes of the dead, of birds of prey, and of deported poets, and he sees clearly that while she waits for him she reigns, and resembles him not.

"And I great king stripped of everything, of earth, of voice, of appearance, king made of pure royalty, one day my love will be so assured so serenely great, that I will lead you toward the palm gardens and give you counsel."

In March of 1961 at the end of the trial for treason in which the fatal trial was already being hatched, Nelson stops by the house, accompanied by Walter Sisulu.[82] They are standing in front of the door. In the street. She standing out-side the street.

"My love, pack some clothes in my case I'll be back, when we never know." He stays in front of the door, I can still see him, I hear him, I cannot touch him, an enormous crowd surrounds him wanting to wish him well, their wishes not mine, the crowd takes him in its wide mouth, I am standing at the world's edge without wishes, and already widowed again. My hands quickly pack his suitcase. When I want to give it to him he isn't there anymore. He has gone behind my back. He took his leave, didn't give it to me. I didn't see him go, I wasn't able with my eyes to eat each second of less and each second of still, I wasn't able to feed my eyes with tears and my palms with skin and clay, a violent emptiness gnaws at my breasts and arms, my sorrow worse than sorrow, my sorrow no longer knows how to suffer, I miss my sorrow and it mocks me, I didn't kiss him, I didn't eat the last morsel, I didn't fill myself hastily with hot touching with farewell flesh, I didn't mingle my breath with your breath, your sorrow didn't wed my sorrow, I am completely widowed, deserted and disinher-ited by my body. If everything is taken from me and nothing returned, how will I live this absence? You didn't fashion me, my arms for your absence, with your hands you didn't mold them, you didn't put the tongue in my mouth for pronouncing your name in the night.

the lips in my face whimper like deserted dogs, and not one word from you to rock me, not one echo to assuage my ear's hunger, clothes in the suitcase and not one voice inflec-tion for my need,

no, one cannot live without the words that celebrate pain, and without the rituals, without the partings that say they're sorry,

there was no scene, even the earth underfoot was refused me, I didn't take toward you the steps that show the starting, separation hasn't started, when I wanted to hold out the suitcase it was already over, I wasn't there, I didn't live that, when I came back, no more earth and no one to help me cross the abyss.

There was no parting, there was rapt and irreparable damage.

Someone came to fetch his case an hour later. A hand that isn't mine holds out to him what he needs.

Separation stayed before the door. The threshold was the place of the accident. It is here he disappeared. Zami's soul roamed for a hundred days before the door, her eyes empty, desolate. And every day the sore that was her body would re-open.

One day I'll make a scene. I'll make it before God.

The next day he was in the papers, in Pietermaritzburg.[83] He spoke before a huge crowd. Zami's soul roams before the tent, I am not admitted to the banquet. 600 kilometers from my heart he's addressing his people. He is giving himself, without my consent. I wanted to give him my consent. I wanted to give him. And for him to grant me leave to give him this gift. There's nothing left me to give him but this, this giving up of giving, this nothing left me, this absolute abnegation. Walk on me my love, walk, with hurried step, and hasten toward your beloved people. And give them your comings and goings, from me without voice without arms.

———————

But what is uniquely and forever hers and was never anyone else's in the world is his Rolihlahla voice, his little boy's voice in the village morning, before the sun, his voice before Nelson Mandela.

He gives her this voice whenever he is there, it is the most precious thing he has to give her and the thing he wouldn't entrust to anyone. And in this voice is hidden his entire childhood, barefoot among the lambs, and his bath in the black water of the Kei,[84] where one feels the dead passing alongside one's body but the child doesn't fear death so close it is no more than a damp and silent sweat from swimming. And hidden in his voice there is his first love: the love of antelopes, for it is believed they are already and not yet women.

And also the thought that basically I'm not as big as all that, and the fact that you, you know this, refreshes and rocks me.

4 o'clock in the morning, when the sky rises in bluish vapors from the crests of hills, is the hour of this voice. Behold how it springs bushy-eyed from below the enormous body still royally wallowing in its right to the night and tenders tiny ringing fingers, like a joyous joke. No one would believe that in the wee hours of the morning, beneath the somber, vast voice of Mandela, a sort of elf stirs. This is why Zami adores him. His tiny-fingered voice is her treasure and her secret. And her hostage too.

It is to this voice she sings all her songs in Xhosa. It is to this voice she calls in the hours when she loves her love the most, before the beginning, when he is still a little soft and a little milky. And even in the nights of the trial for treason, in the most inflexible, the most ironclad of times, it was always there, tendered in the dark, arise my beloved my littlion,[85] the battle is going to begin again, the trucks are rumbling in the forest, the world clenched around their hiding place, only the trees breathe and sway come rise and right away it's there, the unexpected, with its fluty silver accents, coming by river and by blood, coming by boat and by the Tembu initiation trails, from time's source all the way to the bed.

And to her alone it shows itself in its nudity, in its modesty and its immodesty, its charm and its vanity, and lets her hear all its tones, its calf mooing and its wood pigeon cooing.

Night is a creation of the ear drum.

At night Nelson doesn't hide from her the secret child stirring among the bamboos. And sometimes it is a young woman's voice one thinks one hears laughing in the copse but one can't really believe it. It seems impossible.

It is still the hour before the war, Zami calls him by all the nursery animal names she knows, my little buffalo of milk my lamb of fire my tigger, and lying nose to nose behind the night they commit all the sacrileges, marriages, incests, crossings, and metamorphoses. O fecundity of bodies, genius of nomination and of voice. In one hour they are everything and gaze by gaze they take the tour of all their natures. In its cradle the vast Universe is playing with its toes.

And she will surely have been the only woman in the world to have called Nelson Mandela a ladybird.

And you, like an enormous pumpkin in which the moon candle rocks.

But when the sun's wings open wide, childhood instantaneously retreats into the ancients' cave, with its flights of birds and stones. Everything gets dressed and grows up. Nelson puts on a shoe. The telephone rings, and it is Mandela who answers. End of the voices' voyage. Day.

———

So many gestures Nelson hasn't made, he who did not have eternity, only time made shorter, the collapse of time beneath his feet, not enough time to come and go around a thought, not enough time to make the herbarium of thoughts, barely the time to change shirts and always the same skin, not enough time to do nothing with ears cocked, not enough time to meander, the deep, motionless time of the eye guided by smoke, by the butterfly, by fish, quick time to change voices with a start,

Everything he didn't have the time to think of thinking of or to think of doing, long distances raced around the goal he has never been able to allow himself to outline.

Without hesitations, without metaphor, without sketch, only feverish rough drafts of the action. Standing at the bow of the caravel, to see if Africa would break into view. At the bow and with two eyes only. A colossus of a great purity. As for ulterior motives there are none, luckily. No, this was a prow and a poitrel, an all-powerful prow knight facing front, his gaze is unbridled, and on his back a thousand easily transpierced points.

Sitting two steps away from him the earth is full like a ripe watermelon, inside the future Zindzi is rolled up into a ball.

This is how Zami was in her eighth month, her toes so very far away from her fingers. And if Nelson hadn't only had his back toward her, he could have thought of cutting her toenails for her himself. But he wasn't where he was. And while he's slipping on his socks in Orlando, his soul is starting the meeting that will start in an hour somewhere in Johannesburg. From the corner of his beautiful moiré eye he could see Zami lifting her foot toward the stool. In this position she looks like a gigantic orange. But although still here, he is over there, he is gone, without really realizing it, without see you soon and without seeing.

––––––––––––

Until one day life too rapid life without ritual stops short. In the middle of the race the arrest, hamstrung, the dark gray dust bites him in the face.

And in prison time is waiting for him. The too much, the enough, all the time he used to skip over yesterday, all the past that had no present, all this lost and saved time is waiting for him in prison like a belated, unexpected gift. Among all the evils one good at least is returned to him. They take movement from him, they give him time.

Rivers are flowing, birds are flying, clouds are sailing by, cars are coasting past, pathways are walking beneath our feet, roads are crawling. In this moment while I write with only my hand and my imagination coming and going, I'm looking at the walls of the small room where in this moment I'm only moving my hand. And I invoke the truth of prison. I invoke the impossibility of leaving this room. I invoke the possibility of leaving this room. I invoke the impossibility of desiring. An ax spins close to me and severs my knees, severs close to my forehead the images of the steps I was going to make. I am severed alive. For one instant I feel that prison is an ax that every day begins again to cut up the bodies reborn from my body and severs the space before my window that is my body, and takes from me the path that is my body and wrenches from me the country that is my flesh, and cuts from me the rivers that are my veins and the sky in my chest that is my root, and the seas' shore without which I cannot speak. For one instant I feel my body entirely surrounded by active knives. My entrails knotted, my flesh curled up on my bones before the blades, my eyes close in terror, myself I reduce to a bundle of nerves, which only want to run away and die at these walls that are biting me and devouring each one of my extensions. I have to be a rock.

I die for one instant and forthwith my life resumes.

But twenty-four years of this retrenchment I cannot imagine. I am submerged by the infinite, twenty-four, ten, a thousand, everything gets mixed up, I can't, the endless torment, the freshness of the ax, the repeated newness of the wrenching, I can't and I want to imagine, the immurement, I can't and I want to approach this exile in a coffin, with a window for suffering.

"I can" is not forbidden to me. I have the right to want. I want. I have everything.

And yet sometimes I am struck with poverty. I am covered with ashes. But this is a bizarre, luxurious grace. Sometimes I feel poor in terms of poverty. And perhaps this is an unavowable poverty, a lie of the rich, an attempt at humility. Unless it is the ancient maternal desire to taste everything, the good salted with the bad, the bad that has no taste except accompanied by the good.

For if we eat nothing but the good, the good has no particular taste.

Eight hundred kilometers from the penal colony, in the kitchen, Zami is having a talk with the Ostrich.

"Don't you think that if we aren't familiar with poverty, we don't know how good the world is?"

The Ostrich who is chopping tomatoes says:

"I don't know, maybe. But there are poor people who become rich and they are perfectly happy. But maybe the ones who are up there in opulence don't know anything anymore? Me, I don't need to be poor. Do you have to have an answer?"

"Yes."

"By what time?"

Whoever doesn't lose what he has, doesn't have what he has. And so it was for Nelson. Once his knees were broken on the concrete and his hands separated from Zami's feet, he knew all that he had.

He took time and blessed it. He had the time to think that he hadn't had the time to think. And he didn't give up anything. Nothing of what he hadn't done and nothing of what he doesn't do.

So he began to create an earthless, pathless, almost perfect world. He began to make regained, rekindled presents of all those moments that hadn't had their chance.

What hadn't been given was offered in humble pomp and ceremony, according to the means of the poorest of the poor, which are intention and attention. And according to the prisoner's means: nostalgia, regret, desire, hallucination, the letter.

He wanted for her what she wanted, softly and slowly, knowing that all he had in this world was wanting.

He would have liked for her to have a big kitchen. A low-cut dress of black silk, its straps embroidered with pearls. For a birthday present. Hers. Low-cut in front and in back. A little French car, but of good quality. The time to study medicine. A honeymoon. Wherever she'd like? Wherever she would really like.

And who says this wanting has no power? Am I not an inventor of worlds? Such wanting is a power. And even if I were dead my will would be accomplished. I send you the flowers and then the fruits. And myself in flesh and blood: the first winged creature you see will be me. No, not the wild duck, the gray-breasted pigeon that can't take its eyes off you.

———————

And by letter she had what she hadn't had.

If the walls had stopped his desire, and if the walls had stopped the gift, they would have died.

But they've already stopped all they could stop and they can't stop anything more. The air of Africa is now streaked with messages, levied with armies, ploughed and sowed with gardens of colors.

They camp freely on the other earth, several-bodied creatures. Only one of their bodies is captive. The other, their poetic body, leaves far beneath itself the walls fixed down below.

In vain the citadel raises its arms of stone to try and catch their flight.

The letter became an alchemical airplane, the vessel that in midflight fabricates what it is transporting, the voyage, the dress, the music of passions. It is there, in a letter, that he cut her toenails for her, and for the first time in eighteen years of marriage he languorously kissed her toes, because now he'd thought of it. What hasn't been takes place. Almost everything is bandaged and consoled.

And Zami discovered that Nelson was a poet in this other story. There was really another kind of story being made and in which they are living another royalty.

He is so near, leaning over her so close to her, thinking of her so, he who in the time without time was sometimes elsewhere in her arms, that sometimes she almost feels the gentle fire of happiness warm her skin through the walls.

Several times they were even almost happy. They weren't far. One minute away. Thirty seconds. Twenty seconds hand on hand, an instant of skin, and the desert would have been broken. If they could have, for thirty seconds, twenty, touched each other. The walls would have collapsed on the spot, obviously. And by way of Zami's body, the universe would have been given back to Nelson, the universe with its paths, its legs, its races, its turns, and all its shores.

This is why, to forestall all healing, skin was not permitted them, not a second of touching for twenty years. So that they will always miss the world and all its inhabitants, so that the trunk will be shorn of all new shoots, the palm eaten by crows. So that their bodies will remain widowed and frozen, and though Zami was able to place babies on her breasts and on her dried-up lips, Nelson for his part has never had any flesh to fool his famishment, not even a hen, nothing warm nothing trembling nothing silky. But sometimes with Walter Sisulu, sitting side by side in the glacial, somber nave where their burial is being rehearsed, they take each other's hand,

and fingers wedding fingers without a word the two men deny their death, each one proving for the other, each one giving back to the other warmth, flesh, and human form. Thus: from one hand to the other, they rekindle the world with the agony of death.

"Love me for the love of God. I need human flesh."

More than once there was this wedding of hands this unheard of marriage this resurrection of the flesh. They never said a thing to each other.

If Nelson Mandela is kept in such an absolute prison it isn't only to prevent his magic voice from speaking to his people

It is also to prevent him from being so happy.

How does one know they are so close to happiness inside the enormous enclosure of separation? You can see it. Everyone can see Zami's new hat. The golden sheen of anger on her cheeks. Everyone can see she is beautiful without abatement. And there is no law that can hide that.

And the day she testified in court about the last accusation, in spite of the obligatorily Western dress,[86] one saw clearly that her body is lit from within by the sun itself.

They are happy.

Do we have the right to say this?

We don't have the right to not think it.

Nothing separates them except this prison.

He knows he is present outside.

She knows what starvation is.

Starvation is all she knows.

They are alive.

She thinks: I am free but I am not free. I am not free but I am free.

The Without Farewell of the First of May

On May 1, 1919, Osip and Nadezhda addressed their first words to each other. And it was on May 1 in the year 1938 that they didn't address their last words to each other.

May 1, 1938, not a last smile, not a last conversation, not a last oath, not a last sentence, on the last first of May there was not a single last, not a look, not a word, not the smallest seed to plant so that memory could sprout above the void.

This not smothers the voice in my throat. I want to tell about this day, I advance, the words stop some time from here, a few kilometers away. Too much snow, too much silence, too much absence, twenty times I start anew, once again I take the icy path that leads to Samatikha on this first of May,[87] before me all is obliterated, there is not a space not a landscape, only the snows, and beyond neither village, nor train station, nor beyond, only a nameless wayside station, a very strange and calm abandon, without sudden starts, without nerves, perhaps just simply winter. The without. The too great absence of birds. It looks like a cavern. Night clings to the corner of the eyelids. Sometimes Nadezhda huddles up hard against Osip, and a spark of presentness shoots forth like a flash. I see them by the brief light of these seconds. As though asleep beside themselves. Sometimes a frightening dream awakes her, but it was only a dream and the snow covers over the fear once more.

But can't you see what's coming! No one to shout this. Things were not what they were. They're not happening in the time or the tense they are happening. There was a gap. It was already after, how to tell of this? Time was an icy present conserved like an illusion of presentness. What was passing between them was what wasn't passed, what wasn't thought, what wasn't worried.

It isn't words I would need to tell of the lightless whiteness of this year, but the violoncello with its heavy notes held back in the chest's rays, but the violoncello whose voice wells up so slowly from beneath the earth of our anxiety, cantor of our difficulties breathing with the mountain on our shoulders, to sing this slowing down of the heart, this suffering without grief, this burying of the song in the throat of the biggest crooner of all, all this without that little by little is gaining on these still living bodies, this impatience that cools off as it goes along, this breath that is flowing now like a blood, the powerful lamentation of the violoncello, and no one to break the spell.

They who had always been alarms and trumpets. Where now the cymbals and clarinets, where the mouths of copper and of gold, where the cracklings, the slightest creakings of the pines, the rains of multicolored sounds, the handfuls of sands at the windows, the cooings of conchs in the tympana, where the drums and hammers of trains, and the chirpings of birds? Where the normal world, world of beignets, Chinese laundry, itinerant photographer, seeds of fat grapes plump as pigeon eggs, between the curtain of the eyelashes of Armenian women so simply beautiful, the abnormally normal world, where?

They had hardly had any words anyway for several weeks or else breath too short to clothe the tongue. Only sentence pieces bits of words made it up to their teeth, an absolute and impersonal misery: "one should . . . it would be good . . . it would be better . . . it doesn't matter . . . " and no more you, no more me, no more appeal.

They both remained hungry. And no more endings ever: there weren't any more for them that year. And impossible to go on. Life was of a leprous incompletion. We'll see they said. Not seeing and not managing to see what they would see. Seeing pushed back to later and later pushed back to much later. They had truly become beggars, and their hands in vain. The true beggar: the one who receives no alms.

Do they know it? They know nothing. They were extremely cold, that's all.

And dozing without form, without image.

Do they fear? They fear nothing. To fear they would have to be able to hope. They were suffering from a faceless fear.

This was not a life, but one couldn't say they were dying.

The days passed. They passed. Days were merely the paths they didn't take. We'll go. They didn't go. There was no going. Only a coming foretold, by fading. By loss of fear, by loss of alarm, by loss of loss, this is how we let life, death, the moment pass us by.

Osip had always said: "We are lost." Until the day in 1938 when these words left his cold lips like birds bolting off to the warmth. The sentence never returned. They never spoke of it again. It faded away.

And if May 1 arrived, it's because in the end they were afraid of nothing else. They no longer believed in the sentence, that's when it arrives, its chariot is white, its four black horses are in a hurry, its officers are impatient, enough time lost, they cut across field, they cut across flesh.

Arrested for having been arrested.

Suddenly not a minute more, not a second. The men took time from them. They didn't kiss. Nadezhda said: "I . . . you . . . " Took their breath away.

The arrest lasts for twenty minutes. The twenty minutes last for one minute. This minute had the infinite depth of Hell. Neither Osip nor Nadezhda was able to live a single drop of this time. Suddenly thrown out of here out of now out of all time and yet maintained between four walls, twenty empty unbreathable minutes, without living and without dying. There was absolutely nothing to live except the unlivable, not even pity.

What happened didn't even happen to them. Wasn't given to them to live, to doubt, to howl.

Unfortunately they had succeeded, I don't know when, in thinking that soon they would exist no more. This thought had made its entrance long before the hurried officers.

This thought that I cannot think, that I can only imagine, that I've barely grazed in moments of extreme horror, was inside them both, between, them. May 1 they were already full of nonexistence already. Only they hadn't noticed it until then.

The thing is, one can die without feeling it and without incident. Like dropping a flower plucked along the way, distractedly. We picked it instinctively an hour ago, out of necessity, for its beauty, for its very life. It is no longer alive in our hand or anything, and our hand opens of its own accord without thinking. We killed it without killing it. They had been dropped upon a pathway, somewhere, some day.

In the room, the arrest was happening in their very absence. There was an enormous suffering in the air, which they were not managing to breathe. Their lungs dry, their stem snapped since yesterday.

It was a brutally exhibited rehearsal of their secret arrest. A dreadful imitation of the plague. They were already so arrested. Being arrested had become their definition, their chemical formula. Arrest had spread throughout their limbs, in their blood was incubating the unknown, familiar poison that had been halfway eating up their sentences for weeks.

And then on this day in 1938 the arrest exploded. Disguised as police officers disguised as nurses disguised as men. Like one shows the phthisical a radiography of his caverns. The progression of the end. The inside outside.

If they had been able to live this, if they had been able to take fright, to contest the sentence, to fight against it like fanatics. An absence stopped them from doing so.

One is mistaken to think that Hell is only this huge iron building where one suffers from sufferings. Suffering is still a pleasure, a memory, a link, a comfort, and it's mine. Inside the four-walled room like in the inside of a die cast, there was the Hell of being the gagged witness of one's own expulsion from the world. Being the object, the place, the ground trampled upon again, but not Osip, not Nadezhda. The present horror of being this-is-not-me. And living what cannot be lived. Exactly like the poor dead man standing in the train full of the living and who devours all these faces, prey to an infernal nostalgia. He has lost the secret. So Hell is this place without space just at the door to Paradise, the very embrasure itself and the door too, this threshold where is made the lightning quick but interminable exit, the absolute, flamboyant loss, the conflagration of all goods up to the lowliest last one, the emaciation down to being's bone, the threshold without place without time, where one sees oneself with nothing left, all is annihilated, including the terror that was a desire, including the memory that was our consolation, and the dignity, my god, the dignity, this kingdom, oh how we are no longer real, no longer man, no longer woman, no longer Russian, no longer husband, no longer wife, how we are repudiated and forgotten not even, flung our heads crushed, I am I-was-Mandelstam, and yet in the absolute darkness of consciousness where *I was* is thrown and immured, a fissure is fitted up through which the eye-splitting light of lost goods strikes. All rights are lost except the right to see oneself lost.

The worst of May 1 wasn't even the arrest: it was the without farewell. They were already so separated, so stricken with the plague of separation, so impregnated with impotence, both so separated from themselves with thirty kilometers of snow and ice between the room and the door and not a single means of transportation, so sunk into the last icy step, they didn't manage to make of the moment of separation their last bitter good.

I am sitting at the end of the world. The door opens. Here begins our obliteration. They let themselves drop into the pit. Tired. Like those who have just been subjected to the ablation of life.

They who had always been stronger than their feeble bodies, more courageous than their profound timidity, they who had invented the one hundred temerities, where now are the races without tickets and without shields, down the streets of irritated eyes, David's combat a poem in his hand inside the enraged arena, the indefatigable circulation of carrier doves, where the goldfinch's flight at the storming of the Urals, where the young cock's beak attacking the tanks and the greasy-haired Kremlin billy-goats, where the cavalier gnat of the dragon century perched between two vertebrae, the downy babe striking with its feet and with its staff at the immobile doors of big besotted cities?

They didn't have the strength to suffer. Their hearts fleeced and fettered. Suffering short of breath. The room absolutely airless.

There is no more water in the ocean. One hears not a psalm under the sun. Can this happen? May 1, 1938, has arrived. There was neither light nor darkness nor music.

This last day didn't take place. It had already come to pass so often before.

May 1, 1938, they went and were below life-level. And like the dead and buried they saw their supreme misfortune going past over there, passing them by far above their bodies in a squeal of wheels.

The last good fortune escaped them. They didn't have the dazzling misfortune of Paolo and Francesca,[88] the blessed misfortune of losing themselves in each other, with each other, in a selfsame fall. Not the joy of enjoying a similar misfortune. Not this first of May.

Neither of them was at the surface. They missed all the trains in the world. They didn't shout. They were in an unknown state. They were taken away on the spot.

Nadezhda watched Osip go. She was watching what cannot be seen. In this second, having been born was useless.

Had she been able to think about what she was feeling, she would have been the innocent author of a crime. But there was no thought. Only this feeling oneself feeling born arrested born chased born denied.

There was no sign. I do not know what she saw. Two soldiers were pushing Osip from behind. But that wasn't it. She didn't dare to see what she was seeing. She was seeing Osip being pushed into eternity. Impossible to see that.

And all this impossibility because in order not to make any noise everything in the room was lying.

And Osip hadn't said "We are lost" for such a long time. When they wanted to say to each other "farewell we are lost, lost that's what we are," there was no one there anymore and not one second more. She didn't scream like an animal.

She did nothing of what a human being can do. She didn't jump out the window. Osip didn't run toward the forest. There were no more windows. They had lost the forest, the force, the faith.

There was no more world to run toward in this year of 1938. No more magic slippers.

And this they had known without knowing it like we know something is bad even while we lie to ourselves about it. This is why the sentences would come, turn around, and not finish. They had nothing more to say. For a month they had seen nothing but backs being turned.

The last time they had run, talked, discussed, lived, when was it then? The last time they had feared, where was it?

Where had the living end happened to them, they to whom later on the dead end just happened?

It might have been on the Kalinin bridge,[89] the last fight. The last time they had been in Moscow, the forbidden city.

And this last return trip in the last train at the last minute. For one didn't let go of life for a minute, nor of the city of Moscow, nor of anything that was forbidden. And if there had been a single crumb on the round Red Square it wouldn't have escaped the greedy eye of the swallow.

The fight began in the train.

It was about the fiacre, to take it or not to take it.[90] The fiacre was their vision of the world. Because of a fiacre anything can happen, hatred, war, repudiation. Across the fiacre they beheld each other through a magnifying glass, each feature of their souls enlarged, across the fiacre they judged each other and hurled thunderbolts at one another. And like aging prophets they uttered calamitous warnings, beard to beard. The consequences of the fiacre formed various apocalypses.

At the station there was no fiacre. Both of them lost their chance to win. Like two conquered conquerors, furious without reconciliation, they went on their way. The fact there was no fiacre was neither their fault nor their luck. The ultimate duel that hadn't taken place was flying over their footsteps. And now there was the bridge to cross.

The bridge: the cause, the source, the violent metaphor of their destiny. The bridge was never-ending, multiplied by the whipping wind it was easily worth a hundred bridges.

The bridge made their hearts ache. It was so much like poverty exile, all the distances, and on top of everything the cruel and meager landscape of their separation. Something evil made it impassable. In canto XI under the sway of anger, Dante is moving forward quickly. He is tortured by a thirst for flight, gripped by a hunger for hell traversed, and in his heart he's blaming Virgil for his pains. We can't see a thing, we can't move forward, this bridge has at least five heads, we should have taken Geryon along instead of sending him away,[91] we are living contrary to life, we are saving the silver money, we are losing the gold, our blood, our breath,

Swords fly above their sopping heads.

"It's not my fault there wasn't a fiacre. Are you angry?"

" . . . "

"(Go to hell.)" ("I'm going but not without you.")

And this last time Virgil has had enough of her insurgent protégé. She lets her Osip take one forward step with a feigned firmness feebly cleaving the cold air that whips their faces, spitefully beating back the black night with his absence of wings like a beaconless sea.

Beneath the bridge the Volga doesn't matter to them at all. They have eyes for nothing but the narrow scene of combat. Distance rises like the sea, the bridge stretches out.

Beneath the Volga's black water the irascible their gullets stuck in the mud are making bubbles, but those above have not a glance for them, the dead.

It was a bridge for lovers. A bridge for tearing each other apart, for making oneself feel the length of solitude, the too salty taste of mourning, and all those luxuries of fury and divergence that one can allow oneself if one is very sure the web will resist all wounds. A bridge for playing at dying, at hating each other and at dropping each other. And they could go to the end of their hungers and of their thirsts for in the time of the bridge on the Volga their existence hadn't deserted them.

How happy they were on the bridge, separated by anger, the cold, despair, the fiacre, the bridge, and everything that separated them united them strongly, unhappiness was an awry joy, the cold a warmth, they were still on the side of the living, suffering and perishing and cursing in the wind, so full still of terror and of calculation.

They used to fight a lot, in a marvelous way, when they were living mercilessly against each other. Still in opulence in the month of March last. Shortly afterward they ceased fighting and reconciling and kissing like the living do for whom everything counts and who don't count time.

Life stopped on this last crossing.

After the bridge, death began. At first they don't even notice. Dying isn't what we believe. And living is fighting for each gesture from its opposite.

The bridge came back to Nadezhda in waves on May 1, after the exhaustion. Always full of energy and ill humor. By way of the bridge the world and almost all the time since May 1, 1919, came back to her. Nadezhda alone in the gaping room suddenly became the mother of their Universe. Immense, dilated, overrun with carioles, trams, and trains, with Osip trailing his soles over plains and strands, young memory in the flesh, bigger than Russia, more populated and more deserted, with Dante and his herd of Italian cities moreover and the century in her chest, she rose suddenly, heavy and disenchanted. Everyone had boarded her breast except the poems. The poems were outside. One stone's blow and he's dead. She began to run here and there, whistling and crowing to try to call them back, the birds.

There was a good long way to go, with and without Osia. She had to stop being dead.

Although dead from both their deaths, she had to rise and race the forbidden cities again, gathering up those leaves filigreed with secret life.

Osia was a hybrid now, a paper Osiris,[92] granular and airy, who couldn't still be killed. He came back into her hands by letters, by lips that stir, sometimes fitting briefly, wholly, on the membrane of a single wing.

Guardian of breathing and of visions, I am descending time with slow steps leading my herds of poems, bending down a hundred times a day to pick up a flash of wormlike verse, a flake, a seed, a bit of gravel, a shudder, an echo, the entire world is imprinted with his caresses, not one tree not one sea not one piece of clay not one musical instrument, not one shore, not one creek, not one river ploughed by oars that can't bear witness to having felt and heard him passing. We cannot separate him from the world.

In this moment he is bringing to his lips a cup of earth he was studying yesterday word by word and name by name was singing. We can't stop him from tasting everything, from enjoying everything, from feeling and sucking everything, and burying himself and sprouting back in spring. Carving out his path among the blues the reds and the sulphurs. He has no more hands. Only desire now. And the imprint of lips, earth color, hers.

———————

Fifty years later, Nadezhda will think: what united us on May 1, 1919, was chance, the marvelous, the human sprite. Absolutely no reason. A day red with youth. Nothing tied us, that's what tied us. And then each line of each book. What united us across youth, desert, and icy old age was the abduction of May 1, 1938. Time passing snaps there. Then eternity expands. Between him and me separation has established an indissoluble link of stone. Would he have abandoned me one ordinary day do you think?

"Naturally," said Akhmatova. "One white night in Saint Petersburg love with emptied hands would have written an ending. The old man goes off with a young, youthful girl. The old woman remains. On the table, a last letter.

"What good fortune, if I had found this letter, if he had betrayed and abandoned me, if he had destroyed fifty years of life on earth in one night with a single letter! What a desirable misfortune."

They are drinking very black tea. Pell-mell good fortune-misfortune. This era is Greek to everyone, no one understands it. We are walking on our heads with the prophetic staff behind us, blindly, good is bad, black tea is our only certainty, at the corner of time luck is waiting for us with its gilt-worn crosier, ready to cosh us.

The Day of Condemnation

She just barely had the time to nitpick him. It is by nit-picking that we enter our loved one's private depths.

Sitting with the old woman in the evening in the cool, with one old woman or the other, the Ostrich or Helen Joseph,[93] and waiting for him, drinking orange juice and complaining sharply and plainly about the one who's late, is a woman's pleasure. Riding on the night wind, the odors of the earth and of the prickly plants climb with the plaint in the dark, it is the hour of complaint for the whole world. God is but an everyman, there are imperfections in his perfection, this is why she loves him so much. The more one loves, the more one loves to complain. It is a sexual delight to have grievances against god, to minimize him, accuse him, contradict him, to spank him and forgive him. Flaws are hands held out. Luckily Nelson wasn't lacking in them. By your flaws I hold you by your hair I bow your head. Flaws are one of man's proper properties, and one of his sloppy properties too, are his offering to woman, his humble way of redeeming himself. Accompanied by the smell of jasmine that rose above the swill's slight stench, Zami was bragging about her man.

For being late he has no equal. Except for ANC meetings, there isn't anything in the world he fails to forget. And for spending, a crazy fool. He lives like a penniless saint extremely rich. What he hasn't earned, he gives away. Invisible pieces of gold flow through his hands. Praises all that. Explaining in detail all these bad qualities he possessed was almost Paradise. Paradise is the theater of authority, of disobedience ripening in the garden like a fruit in the warmth of innocence, and of the strange pleasures of falling, of being helped back up, of helping up. One plays school, there is the teacher, there is the student. And what is most intoxicating isn't changing roles, it is that each one, from his or her place plays the other.

Under the moon, Zami the student was playing schoolmistress. She was scolding and promising herself to really thrash the schoolmaster as soon as she could get her hands on him. One day. On this day the schoolmaster's voice quakes, and maybe even quavers slightly, and his eyes are big and round like a little child's. And she will reign over the king, at least once a month.

But there are some women who don't complain and don't even have anything to complain about. Women who can't get anything out of their poverty, neither a song, nor an accent, nor a chance for pride.

No one called out to anyone for help on April 4, 1964, deaf day, dull wooden day, and no one cried out, day without throat and day without you.

There was no one under the entire sky. There were only the three police officers, Karel de Wet, Burger, and Brits, three creatures three mistakes. En route they caught a Bush couple.[94] They wanted to have some fun by seeing how Bush people do it, ignorant beasts that they are, beasts like the mustaches, like the giant cats, like the jaws of crocodiles, beasts like the red cavalry, beasts like the white cavalry, beasts like the blue cavalry. The Bush man didn't want to. So they attach the male to the female and they whip. But all he pissed was blood; and not a word. So they throw his body over the hedge.

Next they rammed the bitch. There was injustice in this, for even though it was Karel's idea, it was he who took his turn last.

What made them laugh the most was when it was Burger's turn, because his member's reputation isn't overrated and it only barely didn't pass through and out the other side. As for Burger, for whom it was the first time he tried it on such a small mouse, he said it made him neither hot nor cold, and that it was better with the fat ones.

Karel stifled his fury and laughed. It was his idea, but Burger was his sergeant. Karel had been dreaming of a Bush woman for a long time. When he was five years old, sitting behind his house cutting open kittens' bottoms with scissors to see what they had in their eyes, he was already thinking of her. Of eyes great like the world, invaded by a violent sky.

In spite of everything he held himself back during two tours of duty, like a man who knows how to contain his dreams. Moreover, for nothing on earth would he have told the sergeants that for him it was a sky.

And behold where love shall build its nest: in the devil's tail

He didn't ask for a moment of silence either when the sergeants spread her paws like a butcher's rabbit. If this had been his dream that's what he'd have done: a moment of silence before the entry. A moment of silence for thinking.

For thinking of what? Of the mystery of the entrails, of the Earth's trembling womb, of the forbidden torment of maternity. Karel's thought is incredibly rich and fatty and ramified, like a field swollen with seeds in Spring. But it was useless to want to share such intoxications with these dull-brained imaginationless men. Karel was in self-denial.

So he merely proposed holding the two tiny wrists in his hand while the others were going for it, because at least like this he could feel the fluttering.

It was Sergeant Burger who went for it first, but like the idiot he is without merit, without grace, and he couldn't tell the difference between a cow and a chick.

Under the shock the little one closed her eyes as though she had swallowed them but she didn't let out a sound. Moreover, she was so small and so mute they didn't even notice she had died. It was Karel who saw it. Because he wanted an answer so badly. The others didn't notice any difference.

To finish each one was found equally guilty and condemned to pay a fine of 3 pounds. For Karel this was the final blow.

Three pounds, just like for a Negress. He who had set his sights on the Virgin and the stars. Reality suddenly appeared to him such as it must have always been behind his dream: vulgar, tasteless, heartless, without ambition, without poetry. This is why we damn ourselves, and nothing is worth it. This is what he confided to whoever would listen, but no one understood him.

The trial took place in the same way. It didn't take more than an hour one morning in June 1964.[95] No one understood anyone under this sky.

All was irrelevant. Clouds were traveling by in the sky, like strange and magnificent giants, just as indifference itself passes by above us. And we here on earth, seeing them pass, slowly rapid and regular, we live the surrender of those who go unnoticed, ants crushed behind hedges, all the little people without last hour.

When Zami and Nelson received the Life Sentence, they accepted this glory with humility. Thinking of all those who haven't had the right to the crown of thorns, only to torture and the garbage pail.

———————

The day of condemnation was a day of three days at a single breath and no night, a motionless trudging between the nevermore and the nevermore.

The people are climbing toward a nowhere. The air in the courtroom is heavy with accumulated tears, and hope is wandering from heart to heart, so intermingled with hopelessness that none can still receive it. All thoughts arrested before the unthinkable. A people of birds turned into stones. And inside the stone a tear of blood is collecting for tomorrow.

But their ears have become so keen, a people of ears.

Do you hear? Zami hears everything, she hears the sun rise, time's shuttle, the wood creaking, hears everything, what will be, hears the judge's hoarse bark in the language of iron scales, the soft buzzing of sister griefs, sometimes the world with its choking throats falls so silent, she can clearly hear what Nelson's heart is thinking.

Nothing is as we believe it to be: neither hoping, nor dying, nor hell, nor mourning, nor the day of condemnation, June 12, 1964.

It was a space with two sides: on one side the courtroom, on the other the temple. One time with its two masters, one descending the other ascending.

Condemnation was coming. From somewhere else an act of grace was coming.

This was a long day of sacrament, psalm, and ascension. And on Friday Zami was no longer on this earth.

Nelson's voice rose very high, for a very long time, above the dirty waters of the courtroom to the sky of the future century, a pillar of transparent gold sprouts up across the ages, nothing but the target can stop the arrow, and perched on his shoulder, caught on the capital, Zami's soul is a drunken dove.

During the entire day of three days she didn't leave her post of exaltation. Upright, immense, absent from here below, Zami seemed to be standing on the square in front of the Courthouse. In truth beside herself, perched on the golden tree and hidden in the vine, but nowhere to be found here below, this is how she traversed the unlivable.

Nothing happens to her, nothing touches her, nothing pierces her chest, misfortune rolls out far before her its rivers of ashes and salt. Never was Zami nevermore will be in such pure submission to the Mandela destiny. Day without me and without you. She opened her hands. No more mine no more yours. She forgot herself, as a poet forgets herself under the poem's blow. Alone is the poem. Alone is the Mandela destiny. She had a lamb's head under the divine ax, which suffers from neither fear nor hope. Separated. What is happening to him isn't happening to her, is happening to another.

She too like the people. She doesn't call him Nelson. She doesn't call him this morning, yesterday and tonight are so far away. She calls him tomorrow and in the next century. Between him and her, the crowd and the country. Yesterday you were you. Today him. The world begins with him. He is standing over there where fates are sealed, I am here, at the edge of the world, one step from the door and what unites them separates them. We falls silent. I've always known this densely populated day would come when I would not touch you with my hand, but with the hand of this woman very near to you, very far from me, and beneath my own feet the desert, and I would want it, this day without me. Drop among river drops and tear among tears.

And between my eyes and your eyes, so many faces. Your lips over there I forget having tasted them. All that remains with me is your voice, which no one can see, no one can take in her hands, for roof all that remains with me is your voice, under which my soul slips incognito.

During the exaltation she calls him Mandela. If one day I spoke familiarly to you, in this exact moment I don't remember it, I don't know it, you who are their, he who is lifted onto their shield and I too I carry him above me, I too I lean my life on his voice, and I too I look at him from afar with fervor and without desire, audaciously and with shyness, me a woman among the people, he destiny. And feminine atom, she has shared everything with the people, her dreams, her desires, and this Nelson Mandela who belonged to everyone equally and to all men and to all women differently.

Until Friday evening she called him Mandela and she didn't own him. I don't know who in her was agonizing under the ash. She was missing someone, a part of herself, herself. All she kept hold of were Zeni and Zindzi, one pressed against her left side, the other in her arms, and one inside the other the three are but a same bewilderment. This is how they survive. Beside herself and above herself.

Waiting was a furnace and yet I'm cold and yet this rock that burns in the world's bosom, it is my heart in the middle of me that burns and does not want to cede.

Zami has been walking for forty days in the desert without advancing an inch, walks and walks, determined not to show the slightest emotion. Beneath the tent of fire I burn and I am icy, sand is sprouting beneath my feet but it is really this one, the sand, that will tire.

At noon a silence spread like wildfire throughout the courtroom, over the entire audience inside and out it devoured thoughts, and over the police, and over the countless crowd of people crammed together in Church Square, and unto Zindzi's syllables. It was death, its toneless blank white voice, everyone felt it enter.

In the court Nelson and his people listen to the sentencing, the annulling, swallowing step.[96] A lava of snow descends on Africa. This will be the age of life without life. The snare falls on Mandela, Sisulu, Mbeki, Mhlaba, Motsouledi, Mlangeni, and Kathrada.[97] Condemned to death without dying. The present arrested, the future cast back into nothingness.

Zami thought nothing: she had become a spider suspended above the timeless void and she swayed on the end of her own thread, which she was weaving like a madwoman. Holding on to life by a tenuous thread.

Nelson said: for future centuries and for my descendants' triumph, I renounce and I accept.

Awakened by the first bird awake I will never more awaken my beloved.

My name will be danced in processions, shouted in white letters on walls and branches, painted on the faces of foreign cities, my name will travel without a pass in all unknown languages, I will be called to and nevermore will I have a voice to answer I'm coming,

One Sunday, just like the children capable of forgetting the war during the war, I won't enter the white and black football stadium, I won't dispute the childish victory, but drawn up to my full height up to the excessively high prison porthole, with my hands thrust between the bars I'll applaud.

At our mournings and our marriages I'll be the absent guest, we'll be born and we'll die with between us the abyss.

I shall never return to my native village except in dreams, except in dreams. With my hands of flesh never again shall I open the fresh book of the forest.

They have cast me into the shadows, at the end of the night the night will rise.

My eyes vain agates in their cases,

I renounce and I accept.

Your Creation is turned upside down, the sky is tucked away beneath the stone, hell is sprouting in broad daylight,

My God, I've come to give you back my flesh and my blood, now for this century, but I will take them back again at time's next time around.

Today I enter for a hundred years the strange icy car

For a hundred timeless years, without echo, without telephone

The train that is deporting me is motionless and has no stops,

Penitent of extreme human stupidity, I renounce and I accept.

And Zami as if she were neither mortal nor dying,

As if the fire were not burning, as if one day the snow had awakened black,

And as if there hadn't been in her chest a tear of molten lead roasting her lungs,

As if the roar of the lioness eviscerated alive weren't rising up to the star,

As if she weren't feeling what she was feeling, clinging to the moment like to a boiling bar, as if it were an other, quartered, dismembered, boiled,

As if the gulf were a bush in bloom,

And only as if, in truth, Zami gave birth to a true smile.

Zami living dying and without the help of madness and with only the help of an unprecedented pain. Smiled.[98]

The universe saw this mystery and photographed it.

There was no mystery. Smiling had come all by itself to her silent lips.

For in us there is a strength stronger than are we and all our wills.

What Zami couldn't do, she did: she smiled.

But the last thing she could have done, she wasn't able to

do: she wasn't able to embrace Nelson on June 12 at the Courthouse exit, at the entrance to infernal hell.

Destiny never made her any small concessions. Only very big ones.

They could both of them no longer do a thing except the impossible.

And Zindzi said: what did papa say?

"Where will we see each other, when

"Will we see each other?

"Will we see each other?

"We must let this brainless century go by, century of claws and fangs and three-toothed tails. This musicless century must die.

"And tomorrow, the next world,

"We will see each other, yes, Where and When,

"A where, an impending when a we revived

"Will go unearth the stars

"And see again together the black velvet face of our night with unblinded eyes

"A Where, a When, yes you'll see,

"And nothing will be lost, Nothing has ever been lost, you'll see,

"*Nothing has ever been lost my love*[99]

"But you who think you inhabit the big white cities where the hundred species of automobiles and the icy buildings grow, you who think you grow and move and live,

"You will never live this: the impending future sprouting up through stone and iron in dreams through eternal forests,

"You who are riding around in circles without seeing, without dreaming, without future, without eternity.

"You who are rotting presently, and for every promise in the centuries of centuries, the eternal effacement

"From your seeds sowed in sands and in stones will be born of you but stones sands and purulences.

"You will never live tomorrow."

I think this is what he would have said.

Immediately his rivers are taken from him, nerve by nerve his earth is enervated, his brown-breasted plains are taken from him, his paths are taken from him,

O all the roads and all the paths, his paws are cut off, his wings, his feet, his fins, his racecourses are ripped from him,

—And the turns, O nevermore a turn, when suddenly comes unto me the other face of the earth, nevermore

They take from him the countless surprises the soul cannot breathe without,

—And the muffled murmurs that hollow out the space of night, frogs insects and drums nevermore,

In the train car the air is deafening: not a breath not a squeak. The century will be without note. Absolutely.

What is a man without arms without legs without space, with four walls around his head,

Only a branchless rootless trunk

Only a heart left standing, without arms for howling, without knees for kneeling

They take his watch

The century's sky is without stars

They won't even leave him a thimbleful of sea, not even a fistful of mountain, and barely a handkerchief of sky

They cut his sight off level with his eyelids.

They leave him just enough light to see the world's squared space.

And what is a world without minerals, without crust, without matter, without skin?

He living confined in the pit, this train is endless and without address.

He is poured into cement, monumentalized, nailed inside a box, living fossil of himself.

It is said that the end will never come. The end of his life is before him each day, it is the iron door, the last day's very mask itself.

And yet behind the coffin's cover, each day there is a resurrection, I know it but I don't know how.

———————

It's another language. It writes me a letter.

I don't know how to read it. I only know how to recognize its letters. I don't understand what they are saying, but I recognize the secret.

We cannot penetrate the secret. We have only to let the secret impregnate us with its soundless song.

Where Nelson is now I have never been nor Zami nor anyone from this side.

Nelson is in a foreign land. It's another world. Another era. Another vision of the earth. Another biology we cannot see from here. We other noncondemned souls, inhabitants of our convenient and customary lives, condemned to noncondemnation

Let someone close the familiar doors of the future in our face, and here we are, stuck in the dark and disabled. But Nelson sees through these doors.

For us it's not about seeing what we cannot see. We must merely believe the unbelievable.

———————

There is a poem by Mandelstam. I look at it I do not hear it, I see it, I adopt its gait, letter by letter I follow it, stranger in a strangely foreign street without fear of making a mistake, I don't read it I let it run ahead of me, and without leaving it for a syllable I go where it will lead me. To Leningrad, to Voronezh where I have never been, on board a foreign poem I go, without fearing for a single second not making it there.

What we don't know in our language, we recognize in the other language.

Is Nelson condemned to remaining before the door till his very last day? Every day till his last day and the last day too.

Will he never get out? He'll get out. Does he believe this? He believes it. He also believes otherwise. He can't do otherwise than to believe also otherwise.

Does he hope for a pardon? Not at all. He hopes for nothing. There is nothing to hope for in this Africa of the twentieth century. From here he expects nothing. It is from over there, from abroad, that he believes.

The sail is black. The black sail is white. This is what we must believe, so as not to lose track of Nelson.

Certain nights by chance I see the black sail, I see its shining smile, and I see clearly how white it is. At certain moments, the impossible scintillates with possibilities.

Zami's smile was stronger than she. It reflected an unknown joy. Which I will never know. Mirror of an Africa promised to the whole world except her.

And not a drop of hate that day.

If only I could still hate, my dear heart, and give you drink, if I could become a living knife, if I could slit throats, if I could laugh, crush their tongues beneath my feet like grapes, if I could squelch them in the mud, if I could become harsh submachine gun and shaken by shudders from my flanks to

my head, machine-gun them mow them down, break them
like plates, like old bottles smash them,

decompose them into blank verse, into white worms,
crush their crawling by the thousands upon thousands,

put them to the sword, be a divine machine,

if I could wipe the world's nose and massacre the
tares.[100]

A flash I imagine such a joy, a flash I desire, I think I'm
fooling my pain with my rage and turning Hell upside down
into illumination, not even a flash, an illusion.

Yes, she would give her life to be a thousand lionesses
and with a single maw make of boot-wearing inhumanity but
a single mouthful. But what life, my dear heart? My entire life
is today to be suffered, all my strength is in love's field, and it
is I who am axed and devoured. I don't even have enough of
all my flesh to feel adequate to my agony.

It is not my eyes they wrench from me, not my entrails,
not even the fruit of my entrails, it is the best of myself and the
biggest, it is the body of my body and it is the soul of my soul,
it is my mother for every day and the breast for my dreams, all
my life's pain is not sufficient for suffering this pain, do you
understand, my sister, today I'm learning the other affliction,
the torment of being unable to suffer beyond my doors, beyond my body, up to the mountains' summits, up to the peak
of Ararat.

This high monotonous note of suffering is musicless.

It's a calvary, without the help of a cross. And not even a
drop of vinegar.

From hate, nothing to hope for, if not the brief joy of a
dream.

In vain one wants to avenge oneself, there is no ven-
geance my sister, this is the agony of the just, now you know

it and Nadezhda knows it too. We want, we want, in vain. One can end up dying of this sublime thirsting.

And thus, without bread, without wine, Nadezhda lived thirty years of frozen passion, from December 27, 1938, on,[101] not the slightest flake of hate to warm her veins.

Not that she detested hatred. But was it worth it? No one having ever been worthy of a Mandelstam hatred.

Here below it takes two memories. One for carefully keeping. The other for forgetting everything.

And up above a memory for just the poems.

Each poem by Mandelstam notifying hatred of its short paws and its vanity.

—————

And leaving the space that was my mother, I enter the orphans' garden, the harsh country of hungers, of thirsts, of phantom creatures, of the banished.

Here all distances are suddenly swallowed up, all yesterdays move away immediately. Round about me there is but the faraway, and breaks and separations.

This past year, last year, last winter, all this is so far away today, all is from another life, the last one.

My country is no longer my country, one of us is banished, the other one is banished in return.

I no longer live where I dwell. My life is breathing over there very far from here behind the forbidden door. Exile is passing through my body. I am banished down to my toes, to my knees, to my ovaries, to my lungs. I have become a stranger to myself.

Through which country am I walking, I cannot see with my eyes, my staff watches for me, through which lifeless country toward what house am I wending my way with my body by my side, my house is far away, my house is never

Wherever I go traversing the vain hemisphere, wherever I go I agonize

And it is very far from here under the other stars that I hope.

Through which country am I moving, tripping, with my staff for light, hoping at times that one day I'll find hope.

For the faraway distances over there are still as beautiful, the blue-breasted horizon as clear, the sleepy belly of the veldts as gold,

No, it is I who no longer follow the rhythm of the seasons,

I who dream without finding the door to waking,

I the almond tree Mandela who no longer tolerate the touch of a springtime, I who suffer from too much misfortune and do not want to be separated from it. Suffering has become one of my goods.

It is under my own roof and in my own life that I have become the stranger, the intruder, the plague-stricken, me struck and disfigured, me disfiguring and striking myself, in order to resemble the madness that takes the place of life for me.

It isn't me, it is my mouth that is smiling. It is my mouth that sees what I cannot see with my eyes pierced by blackness.

Everything has become very white, very cold, very mute, very dead in Zami's body, and up above the shining smile, the splendid flat part of the sword and around her body the red crowd, united in a convulsion, that couldn't understand her, that understood her in its blind red breast, that couldn't imagine the immensity of the cry Zami wasn't uttering, even with a hundred thousand united imaginations, couldn't imagine such a powerful cry, so helpless and yet so powerfully guarded held back behind the teeth.

Of this cry she could die, of its pointy end and of its cutting edge, tearing into her entrails down to the entrails of the earth. But she was also dying of holding it back.

214

No one could imagine, and neither could she.

It was this ultimate forbidden joy that made her suffer behind the smile her mouth was brandishing, this intolerable impossibility of dying, this bliss that could have killed everything and pierced the ears of humanity and penetrated up to the clouds and burst her own heart, had she been able to strike.

They remove her bone's marrow they pluck out her heart they cut her life off in her throat, and she wasn't even dying.

And smiling and dissimulating, no one is there to wipe the lips and brow of her tortured soul.

The crowd carries my smile in triumph and I am so very forsaken, so very much alone among all those who cannot hear the enormity of my silence. But don't you see that I am sliced, axed, and ransacked? Entirely cut off from the future behind me the past is razed, and in place of the present the abyss before my feet and in my chest.

And you don't see this night at high noon like a thick covering on the world's face, you don't see this grief that is eating my gaze and only lets me see this hole in the fabric of the day, in its place this sore, this trace of a cry in the mouth of the sky there where the tongue was, and over there you don't see that rocky tomb, slightly opened by the sun?

Because of my blinding smile, my archangel's scales, you can't hear this silence?

And alone he too goes away, Nelson severed alive and all surrounded saluted sipped eaten and sampled, without anyone to suffer the exactitude of his suffering.

For it is here that imagination stops. Here starts the pain of not being able to follow you, of not being followed on the strange paths of pain, here starts the pain of being unimaginable and of not being able to imagine.

She sees Nelson move away, she still knows him, pushed from the back, disappear, does she still know him? still another day another hour, the door that separates the worlds opens wide, the door closes beyond which she knows no more, she follows no more, she is no more.

Here the silence starts, his.

Her lips were left her. But her voice was arrested.

They left some paper, they took the pencil.

———————

I am walking along the Ocean and I cannot hear it. I run endlessly, these are its kilometers its shores of yellow sands its great vigorous waves its herds of manes, it moves, it opens its mouth but soundlessly. Is it me or it, cause of this senseless silence? I utter a great cry of anguish: a black point on the world's white page. It is not from me, it is from the Ocean the monstrous silence rises.

A pity, a terror fill my whole heart.

The sound of Creation has been cut. Never have I felt myself to be as solitary as before this mute giant. Will we never get along again?

As though we were no longer contemporaries.

Myself nevermore contemporary of myself.

The train is stopped in a very distant time.

By the dozens, faceless centuries are passing by without, unless it is within.

Under a same sky our times total strangers.

———————

Here, June 12, 1964, end.

Life was leaving in long slow strides, Zami couldn't see it, she saw it without seeing it, with haggard eyes that cannot swallow, leaving backward, leaving calm, implacable, like the abandoning sea leaves, o how you move away sea and how I stay, and receding backward to the horizon she drags her dress along and lets me see, instead of her, a sinister field of gray and white bones. O life who gives me death to see and I can't not contemplate it.

On the shore, how dark it is before the world's bones. Thus, all moves off and nothing moves. It is this day, this light, that strikes the scene with immobility. The arrest has spread into the Universe's veins: "Here ends." All exits. From now on nothing moves forward. Nothing is left but to descend from flesh to earth, down to the worms, step by step, year after year. That's the story. Life woven erased lived entirely grown old in advance.

So she started on her way with her two little girls.

Each day a step each step a day.

Do we order the almond tree to stop blooming? Yes.

Do we ask the lover to stop nourishing her eyes from the face of her beloved? Madness.

The eyes, the ears, the arms, the skin, the flesh, chased into an eternal winter.

But the trees are still as beautiful, the orange trees as scented, still in flower already in fruit

Everything in nature is following its course except me.

How to flower, ripen, run, how to rise and fall, take a street, a bridge, a telephone, when you who are me you have a wall for sky, a wall for earth, for tree the memory of a tree of old behind the wall.

Africa lost has become intolerably slow and long and fatty and vast for me who am you embedded between two narrow flanks of stone

And what to do with its moons and its ever so populated skies, I who am you with a blindfold of wall upon my eyes?

A life with two faces, one with eyes gnawed by salt, the other with a smiling smile, one with winged eyelids, the other with eyelids of stone.

She lives what she lives and yet unlives everything he doesn't live, she the living.

It's like this: sometimes unfortunately, by good fortune, by surprise, Africa carries her off, and everything Zami doesn't want, everything she doesn't desire is given to her at a blow, in spite of her and even though Nelson . . . and even if for him, no

Neither the animals in the river as at the beginning of the world

Nor the children in the dust at evening, food for grand-mothers' eyes

Nor the crowns of clouds around the mountains' brows,

Nor the jubilation of having risen alive at the same time as the sun in the innocent beginning of a day, before man, before the fall, before memory,

Nor any pure beginning,

Ever reach him will not reach him in the thick-walled pit

However, by earth, by air, by water, inevitable happi-nesses do come to him, by brief exaltations, as a blessed rain falls, as birds come to the window and atop the table

She cannot not take pleasure from a hard lively naked joyous pleasure, without any pity either for him or for herself. And these moments given to her hurt him who doesn't receive them except in her, he who is in her and yet isn't, he who isn't in her, but over there in a strange land behind the door behind the window's pane.

All is well, and all that happens thus has two tastes, one is harsh to the tongue and the other makes her laugh. From each laughter spring tears. Everything that feels good hurts.

————

And the country behind the wall behind the door that opens onto a threshold, only a threshold that opens onto nothing, the country on the threshold of which so rarely Nelson appears, once a year, like a beautiful afar, is there a country behind the prison wall, is the country still there?

From this country neither stories nor news. Rocks and walls, that sums it up. No this is not Hell of the myriad eloquent hosts, of the flying, crawling, buzzing inhabitants, of singing drowning men, of gangs prattling away even in the teeth of flames, of the damned always happy to tell of themselves again and remember, no. It's the country of dry gorges, of memories in flight, the meager country, spoiled, breathless. The island of stuffed birds.

Nelson is the only country in this noncountry. To him alone the mountain, the plain, the river, and all the animals. Africa is now at the bottom of his heart, absolutely earthless, but not without fire and without nerves.

And for eighteen years he remembers the stars.

———————

Frozen June. Doesn't pass. The heart's hands torn out. What time?

This is no longer the time of long paths, it's war. The door to my life is shattered, my life's force is torn from me, I am taken by the marrow and uprooted to the teeth, my great size is slaughtered, my armor is finely chopped, all my alleyways are bombarded, I can't keep anything either around me or on me or in my very self, my soul its moorings cut suddenly flows outside me and like a mist invades the street and soon spreads in a canopy of tears above the city's summit, I am emptied of me.

I am gone mad and naked,

Without being dead I am killed, I am pinned to myself dying and living myself dying and no one to help me, to stop this leak, this sticky spreading, to lift the door back up, to stem this grief.

Ah! how the grief is great. It is the greatest: all the country's griefs, dwarfs compared to mine.

Nothing is anything compared to mine. I drink it and I go mad I am a dog condemned to drink the Red Sea. The Red Sea is black and full of cries. When I drink it it barks heartily, with its wild savage throats in my throat.

I am widowed I am killed I am orphaned I am naked, no hand on my head to be my roof, no hand to hide my face, a great wind blows and besieges me, and carries me off to the last thread.

What none can live, I am living. I am living it with death.

This day without him without me, this day of pale cheeks of skies growing pale, in my Absence I see it. I see my Absence, it is my soul mingled sobbing with the dusts from the sky. I have already known it in dreams, this day separated from me, myself all separation I have already wept for it, on two feet fled, already through all its slow unusable nothingness I have wandered. For in dreams my two feet were still awake to save me.

Behold the day save me. I am wandering alone, endlessly, at the foot of the pale wall the world is putting up against me, everyone is on the other side, there is no door no fault no entry. For me, this wall, space rises straight up before my feet. Wherever I try the wall follows me. Why am I born if I must non-be, arrested, detained, rejected, penned in the narrow passageway between the wall and death, and my life is fettered far from me, at the other utmost end of time?

I fell this June to the bottom of the ladder of beings. Last night I was a woman, I remember this in another memory, this morning thinking ant crumb of being, the world has become too big for me, my paws tremble with weakness, time's giant height throws me onto my back in terror.

What's the use of struggling. Time is impenetrable. As if I were never born. Without a boat put out to sea and in the winds, I don't arrive to myself, I survive superhumanly. I know the horror of not-being-born day after day, over there life is passing by, her sail her stuff her matter, I lean toward her, I want to dart forth, I want to take her I miss her, I cannot raise my mountains.[102] Buried, I am under a landslide of absence. On my back. Under sand, standing up as far as the world's ceiling.

With my paws I scratch eternity.

Misery has laid hold of me with its limitless arms. It is killing me whole, from my mother's womb to my old old-age. It presses me to its hooked breasts, it lacerates me for a hundred years. Today like next year I am moaning. My sight barely dares to leave my eyes: there in front the yellow-toothed terrors are lining up. Their cannons are khaki their trucks are bestial.

Barely weaned I must take up arms and be myself my husband my father and my very own knight. Before my front line the enemy armies are laughing. The more naked I am the more dressed they are. I had a courage, I have it no longer. They have captured my courage, they have gouged out its eyes cut off its curls tied its hands.

I am so cold. I am so afraid.

My teeth are torn out, they shrink me, my reasons and my causes are taken away, I am put into the desert of deserts, neither cloud nor bird nor direction. Every step distances me from every sense. They deliver me up to distance.

My grief is the most robust. It is the youngest of all. My grief and my fear don't leave each other anymore. I have no wings, these things are all I have, my heavinesses, my companions, my sisters.

And no one to cry out to, father mother I am forsaken, all my people are prisoners, all are nobody and nowhere.

Like a foolish madwoman I complain to those with neither ear nor voice.

The telephone crouching a few vain meters away from me, the telephone doesn't listen to me. Useless God, sad toad of cut wires, imitation, minuscule monument. This is what is left me of Nelson. Frozen fountain. Coagulated river. Clotted spring.

I am so thirsty. Whoever has never wanted for voice doesn't know the worst thirst, the ghost. One's entire body is an ear of parched lips.

I listen and I do not hear you, I do not hear you, what I hear is this not hearing, this violent silence of your voice, this uncomingness,[103] this formless, colorless vibration of the empty air. Through this deserted bed the familiar river once flowed. One can no longer even behold its banks.

And yet I cry out toward you tirelessly, through sand through stone and through the motionless air I cry out, I invent in my throat new cords of sonorous timbre, month after month I play the unbreakable music of Job, I know all these songs, hymn to the leprous and the ulcerous, canticle of whoever has lost everything but her voice for counting the inestimable loss, and sitting in the shit of men and God, and scraping off with shards of glass the derma all eaten away by canker sores, singing in forty-two cantos the cruel rich catalogue of calamities, song for canker sores and song for teeth, song for ruin and song for mourning

And when nothing in the world is left her save the skin on her bones, song for skin on the bones,

And if only my bones were left me, I would lift myself up from betwixt my skeleton and I would fashion a last instrument from my bones.

Who would have thought there could be so many resources and so much wine of indignation in such a small human goatskin? God himself didn't guess as much.

This woman knows how to wail. Sobbing over herself as over the body of a murdered bride. This is how she lives on in tears and in salty songs.

Whoever knows how to let themselves be conquered down to the marrow by the trios of Brahms will hear with their bones' ears the violent plaint of Zami.

Rich penetrating theme, nourishing itself on so many many moments still all fresh with life, mysterious state of farewell in colorful accents, there is so much sparkle and munificence in these nothings that come back to our eyes all sprinkled with the marvelous gold of regret.

Theme of jealousy for her own riches hidden then revealed to herself, theme of the marvelous value of the without-value. This is a state of apparently monotonous ache, but with poignant variations: the piano dances lightly, the violoncello sinks to the heart, what is moving past on a wing suddenly tears at the hollow of the soul.

I am the chief mourner for slender human things. Mourning for the shirt I was washing yesterday. I wash I lose I weep I envy me it was I who was washing, I had it, I had everything, nothing of nothings, and without glory without trumpet without pomp

I was pouring a cup of coffee for him, as for a man, as for an ordinary living man,

How ordinary everything was, marvelously, secretly ordinary, and I didn't know, I was washing without knowing it the transparent flag of my mourning come from tomorrow,

The days were teeming with trivialities, morsels of chamber music I didn't notice,

Nothing what a bunch of nothings and I had everything

And behold: everything comes back to me, dipped in the golds of the regret that is lost to me and conserved in the music.

Now she had fallen into the hell of the extraordinary, where there is no thing, nothing without echo, nothing that doesn't resound and cause tears to well, and all that was mute, cup, street corner, shirt, makes music.

Except the telephone. The telephone's silence makes her sick.

All year long she wanders at the far edge of the past, calling for help from No One—I'm so afraid of the new times—calling for Nelson, the one who doesn't answer

Knowing very well this year of 1964 that in vain the voice, the body, rings, and yet one must shout

As if all the bells of the forty forty some odd churches of Moscow, in the year of 1939

As if all the lionesses of the forty forty some odd brush

Were roaring and ringing inaudibly,

For no one on this earth or on the other hears

Who would hear the cry of a wounded ant?

It takes a poet to hear the bush with the broken arms lamenting

And the earth of 1964 is as poetless as the snow of 1939.

Africa has only a deep quaking.

And now in which tense to live? In which tense to desire?

On her knees in the faraway and imploring imperative, this is how she lives, O come O let him come he who cannot come, O grant that one very far off day one day in my lifetime still one day in this century of endless skies he may come to me,

That from space, empty tomb, the bodies the voices may be revived.

And ceasing finally to be the urn of the voice without comingness,[104] may the telephone too be restored.

Thus the first year passes in lamentations. Thus passes the year after. Sometimes the worst is to have to do the cooking.

After that Job lived on for a hundred and forty years and beheld four generations. And why not her too?

She puts on her hat with the highest feathers, woman three heads taller than all the rest, and with the reflection of hoped-for triumph in her face she places a bet. It is May 1, 1986.

How many years still left before after, how many years to lose and to win, after and before, how many years already and how many after already, and yet nothing has ever been lost my love, not a minute, not a tear.

—Nothing has ever been lost my love,[105] it isn't she it is he who can say this, the bigger loser, inhabitant of the unimaginable.

In his cell, all urn, no telephone. No mute trace. Or tree or asperity. Virgin place from before genesis. Or forest fragrance. Not an ant, not yet or ever.[106] And for furniture for country for road for humanity for moon for kitchen for child for lover's womb for living for bridge over the gulf for all ark: a letter.

Time is that of the sandglass: dust, dust, dust.

A Life of Letters

It is a life with death. World almost without earth. Here and there after three oceans every six months a letter to light on, a letter to rest on, to sleep at last, regain a bit of flesh, a bit of me, a bit of consciousness. In order to live with so little life and so much death one has to know how to change bodies, be first a dove then a dream then pure means of transport, soul stiff across the abyss, fleshless feet walking on pebbles of air, six months not looking, not feeling the serrate edges of six-month days, not breathing, endless swimming under time without olive tree and without stopping, holding back from dying, from expiring, not stopping to split the Nothingness, to not be (born),[107] to go, not being, to fly over scanning, searching with one's eyes on the thick surface of the waters for a sign, a branch, a leaf of paper.

It is a life with five hundred words per letter, five hundred breaths per month, and the rest is silence and asphyxiation, and night.

For one birth, ten deaths.

And sometimes in the darkness stretched out between two letters, one no longer knows if it is nonbeing or being born[108] that is being barely written in the dark. Between two letters such inanition.

My wings closed once more here I am standing in the pit,

227

on the lowest step in the world, the sky is so far off, it is only barely that, throwing back my head, I manage to make it out. I am waiting for the single flake of manna to fall from the invisible on high, I have been waiting for six months, I have been waiting for a thousand years. I am writing you the letter that will not leave, the letter I will not write, I am singing to you the letter from the buried alive.

Here time is killing us, cracking our skulls with shovel blows crushing our brains, setting our thousand nerves on fire, spitting us into the mud, sweeping us up in the courtyard grinding our bones between two rocks, but powder, debris, dust, delirium, we never stop suffering and clinging to the date, so distant, of the next far-off mail.

I will not write to you the interletter and the mysteriosities of time,[109] yes, its excesses, its monsters, its terrifying masks.

Here below fifteen days last two years, one has to lift up an earth to be born, but in a day two years go by, no, two years have just gone by, and in these two years I have done nothing but go to bed and get up, I took two years to go from one wall to another wall, I will not write to you the grimaces that for us make up time.

And I too have for face the torment of a grimace. With only the wall for a mirror my face is a wall, a hardened crust that waits for a lava to lacerate it. Or the letter.

Buried beneath the impalpable tons of emptiness, to smile I move the muscles of my mask, and I cleave the crust from the corner of my lips.

The worst torment: this phantom burying, this being mad without madness, this drowning without water, with open eyes this blindness that can see itself. I am a blind man who can see the world's extinction.

This is why I do not write to you: what I see does not exist. Is an inverse version of life. A corpse's nightmare but the dreamer isn't dead. He has only fallen into the interletter, and for six months he comes to know what living on this earth he never knew.

The letter falls. Burying flees. Death was but a six-month dream. Here is notice of life. So light and so strong. And the letter more true than time. So brief and so powerful.

In five hundred words to rebuild the temple, glue back together the boat pieces, render night unto day and North unto South, restore the soul to human time, for some time, for some weeks, a letter! I rise immediately, I throw off the coat of stone, it is I who live and death that dies, my love I was a skeleton, I did indeed receive the five hundred words of your letter, immediately slipping my parched voice into the humid heart of your words, I put your flesh on my bones

Five hundred words, a fleet, I put my body on and I set sail

Manna, sails, wings, tanks and planes on the paper, the curtains of stone fall at the horizon, Africa too leaves its sepulcher, I am in a hurry, I am impatient, I am infinitely patient, I am capable of waiting five hundred more deaths if necessary. *Amandla! Nwagethu!*[110]

I would never have believed that a letter could be my mother and my boat! Look walls, look bars, I know how to pass through your teeth and your irons. And you hysterical century, in vain you shout that I am dead forgotten and erased. Look, I know how to survive you. See my wings opening. It is I who will wake in the future, it is you who will not see it.

A letter, I open, the twenty-first century enters.

I received a letter of five hundred doors. By five hundred pathways it leads to tomorrow. It is a "Ticket to the Universe."

What's in a letter? There is what there is and what there isn't too. There is everything and almost everything and everything that isn't there is there too, is omitted and promised there. Everything depends on you who read it. The Universe in each letter, if you are child enough to receive it. In each letter all the music of all the spheres, if you are musician enough.

Little infinity, to be deciphered from all sides, by the white and by the black, by the leaves of paper and by the secret roots.

The first letter from Zami arrived on January 12, 1965, not a letter, a transfusion of the entire being in two pages of paper, a sea and in each word a pearl, an interlacing of all the legs and all the nights, and in between all the words a world, time, her skin, her hand, bread, it isn't a letter, and it is a letter just the same, not the world and the world just the same in two populated, planted, constructed, irrigated pages,

It was a plant. It was a leaf of paper. It was a closed door on which Zami could feel some keys. It was the mirage of a wall and I cannot find the words that will make it tremble.

But the tension of desires around the leaf of paper delivers it from its servile fetters.

The leaf of paper beneath Nelson's fingers is now the cooing of turtledoves that wakes the lovers. It was a forest, it still stirs from winds and storms. Carrier, kin to the pigeon, the plane, the boat, anciently and always plant and soul bearer.

One can read it. And also not read it. Take it. Barely on board, start it up and cross the city. At dusk a sort of peace rises in Johannesburg. At night peace climbs back up through the net's mesh. Before us in all its sparkling breadth flows the city bordered by pillars of steel. From one building to the other the sky stretches orange-colored tulle. The moon is in its hammock as though there were no danger. And it looks like the announcement of tomorrow. While I write to you, day twists in today's claws, but I can see it tomorrow rolling out its great sparkling boulevards before you, contemporary at last.

To not read it, to follow its footpaths without haste, and sink step by step into its enigmatic breast like a Jew into the

Tora. In the middle of the text is the secret. In the middle of your life there is the key.

And each letter is Bible, promised revelation, problem and deception. Who can say where the middle is, where before ends, where after starts?

Do you know there was a word missing in your letter of May 1?

I carefully counted and recounted, there is one less word, I wonder which one it is.

Or else it isn't missing. This is the word that makes for dreaming and hoping. The last word of this story. The first word of the other century.

O, there are so many letters in the letter and yet so few, and yet there is an extra letter in the letter, always an extra letter in each letter, and once all the letters hidden in the letter have been discovered, reading is a limitless journey, in the letter is all the air in the world and almost all the earth,

— But writing was such a torment my love, this I will not write you. How this letter ran from and provoked me, and how it rose up before me like a wicked army, with its five hundred words mocking me, I do not write this.

Counting the words on my page a hundred times there are too many and not enough, from day to day anxiety mounts, in five hundred which words for saying all I'd like to tell you, and may each word be the right one full and juicy, each word true and not lying, I haven't succeeded, I struggle for weeks surrounded by ten thousand words, my tongue becomes strangely foreign to me, this is not exactly what I wanted to tell you.

And how saying these words to sing, and how with all these words to write the depth of my silences, and how counting the words to kiss your mouth and nose? My head is full of bookkeeping. Neither one more nor one less.

My love I send you five hundred words but I do not tell you from out of what a mass of words I have taken them, and that I am beaten and bewildered. May you manage to read behind the hurdle of hedges all I wanted to write you, in only three words, life, victory, future, and these three words in only one: we.

My love I send you the ashes. I ask you to read the fire.

Happily there is paper, happily there are the hands of paper on my cheeks, on my brow on my chest on my belly, I read your letter with my whole skin and without words, with my whole skin I drank your paper caresses, I rubbed my whole body with your letter of January 12, eyes closed I sipped and sniffed it and it was really your scent I was reading, line by line.

Or else it is "the senseless and blessed word" that Osip talked about, the word he was going to say, the word he would have said, and will no one ever know what it is?

What is it, this marvelous word Nadezhda dreamt of for twenty-six years? For only in dreams can she still hope.

Which is it, what will be the first word to reach his liberated lips when the coffin is taken out? I do not know it. But I know who will receive it.

Without hands, without nose, without tongue, without music, without stars, without sex. But not without letter. And for a moon the bulb of feeble filaments.

The rest is silence. Silence must be learned. It is such a difficult language. We do not speak it. It is spoken in a low voice, so very low . . .

And for the eyes? A life of panes.

The landscape of the prison visit is the dark and icy well, six months deep. In order to depict it as harsh as it is I need the famous rude hoarse raspy tongue of rock, tongue of tusks, of rack and rock, tongue dirtied with dung and daub, of flaking rhymes, this tongue that Dante lacks in the treacherous region number thirty-two, for even his mouth, skilled at making so many different accents resound high and low, dry or soft like butter, pale and strong in color, even his mouth, capable of Tartar, of Greek, of peaks, of worst, and of horrible bursts, would not have withstood the usage of a tongue so cruelly foreign to all human modulation. Without the juice of vowels, of pounding diphthongs, I need a guttur,[111] affricate tongue, with striking dentals and cacophonous orchestra. And up above a thick bed of ice.

For none lives in this heartless circus without first having frozen his nerves of compassion and of shame.

I mean to say, no voluntary inhabitant, no guard. Here in the dark depths of the Universe dwell freely only those who have forsaken all sensation. Prison means refrigeration of the soul's faculties. A guard does not live, he is conserved. For if he were alive he would die of pity. Here is the horror: the condemned man, he, wants to suffer. And it is with all his strengths that he fights to not allow the ice to take his heart and mortally quell it.

Only torture and separation happen here. Separation is scattered everywhere. Nothing escapes it, neither thought, nor body, nor phrase, all that is separable is struck with separation. All is cut out, sectioned off, broken up, dismissed, dispersed, denied.

When, after having crawled for six months between ranges of rocky teeth, Zami arrives within sight of her goal, she is finally going to see him with her eyes of flesh, a day of twenty minutes after six months of shadows, finally the source, a single sip of blessed water for forty deserts, he is going to come, he is coming, he enters, no, he only enters recaptured, refused, in vain the eyes in vain the lips hope for the sip of light.

Through a pane of glass — O why don't I have the tongue of rack and rock so as to try to scratch it — this isn't a window but rather the Cocytus raised up before her before him,[112] a sheer lake a double lake of ice and mud, as if the bottom of the entire Universe were standing straight up like a door, so as to separate them more.

Through a wall of ice — a sliver of Nelson. Like half a fish caught in an ice of tears. Almond tree cut through the middle. A trunk. Twenty years go by. Springtime after springtime recaptured by the ice, half a Zami can see no more than half of Nelson.

Who invented the glass torture? In vain the eyes fold themselves and twist the eyelids, nothing can bite the worst of walls, the most perverse, the one that effaces the hope it has aroused.

Never did the Danube in Austria or the Neva under the January sky, or the Volga beneath the boundless bridge, cover its body with such an opaque crust. It is zero degrees between the gazes. And the glass is voracious of each expression. The voice too is devoured. The timbres shatter on rocks of glass. And like frogs that keep their faces above the infernal water, slivers of livid life visible to the waist and for the rest vanished, thus separated from in front and through the middle, and under the sway of glass metamorphosed into half-batrachians, Nelson and Zami exchange snatches of conversation crushed and splintered by the ice. Trying to see, through the glaucoma that masks them, the unalterable truth. "How beautiful you are, my love, how handsome you are!" They croak. And make of the menacing pane of glass a bizarre bond of ice. All that separates them clandestinely unites them.

Twenty years go croaking by. But I remember Mozart of the well-nourished birds of the rapid arpeggios of satisfaction, I have deep down in my ear, a little transparent but clear, the roundish roulades of your voice, this is why I don't surrender to the pane's argument. Twenty years without milky sounds have not succeeded in killing the music sown in my memory. It is dozing alive beneath the beds of ice. And even if twenty years have passed since my last words rang out in the African air, snow is good for the rosebush, I'm not afraid of winter. Today in the middle of summer we are cold like Russians. Today like the damned enraged by jealousy, the pale century plants its fangs in my throat and keeps me from moving, I look like half a frog, I know it, but I haven't changed a bit, my voice hasn't lost a B.[113] And tomorrow as soon as the pane melts, you will recognize me at the gong of the first word.

I am not of the vitreous species, I am not of the ice age, I will not die by a foreign hand, but under our own stars, by a hand with familiar skin.

———————

And it is in 1981 after seventeen years of panes, that Zami found out at least what Nelson was eating in this year of 1981.

This year of 1982 I saw your body down to your hips.

And I saw your whole left foot through the pane in the year of 1983.

Here is how he comes back to her, through slow and cruel and fantastic evolution, unpredictably, as though reconstituted out of order by a chance naturalist.

Pains riches.

Isis is paralyzed, birds bring Osiris back to her in fragments, without any vision of the whole. Now she has a foot, the right one is missing, the chest is breathing but not the belly.[114]

Waiting for the whole she adores the part. And all the things that Zami didn't know when she was little, when the beauty of the hills, the far-off, blue breasts of the earth, led her to believe her mother the world belonged to her whole, and when the tunic of barbed wire had not yet been placed upon her body,

all the strange ruses our species tirelessly invents for surmounting infernal separation and reclaiming the mother, the air, the blueness, the milk, the honey, the marrowy, and all the goods privation kills in us, all the secrets of survival below zero,

she has discovered through exile and separation.

How so many agonies added to so many angers and so many regrets and so many exhaustions and so many despairs added together produce in the end such an exaltation, the heart's marvelous response to the knife!

And as the child makes child's play out of taking the air by playing with the rubber ball, Zami takes the air by going out with the superb hat. And for bread and wine? For visiting the bottom of the well she has chosen the long earrings that hang down all along her neck to rest upon her breasts. All one has to do is follow them.

The earrings pulverize the pane's ambition and lift the mountains of time, for no matter how deprived of palms and fingers the lovers are, just as it is said that Persian poems are sweet enough to attract the appetite of bees, so the earrings arouse on the forsaken skin the living memory of past caresses. I think I feel I feel caresses caressing me and I don't know how my soul finds this agile magnetic body, capable of passing through the wall and coming to nestle on your chest.

Yes, these are the mysteries that occur in the places where desire outwits the laws of matter.

———————

And from the whale of January 20, 1973, Nelson received the sea he had lost nine years ago, for the second time.

. . . It was a day like the thirty thousand days before, so much the same so gray of sky and sea, and for thirty thousand years nothing new under the sun of Robben Island,

On the island all equally white with dust and all equal in nonhope. No one uses the future tense anymore, and from the word "future" even dreams turn away. One no longer dreams except in the past tense.

Drop by drop of blood the years are lost and one desires shamefully for the exsanguine hour to finally come.

One feels a kinship with the dust. My mother the dust, my sister the pickax, my dog my ankles' chains. And for cathedral without walls and without rose-window a colossal boredom.

And to think that alive I beheld complexly planned cities branching out in all directions, just like my brain and my thoughts used to do. What remains of the universe: the unreadable ocean, a senseless sum of vaguely wavy waves.

If only from the rock we could still see the mountain and its tables furrowed with signs, there would be something to read. But here for books we have this infinite and rumpled rag, forgetful of everything at every moment. On Robben Island we hated the sea.

But suddenly between the coffin and the horizon, over there in the far-off middle of the desert, behold: a fountain bursts forth. Like a dying sailor crying: land! land! like the lost cameleer moaning at the mirage, Walter cried out: a whale! And they all saw the gush the first time, and like a second trumpet blow the second time and at the third burst it was like their gushing tears, shooting forth from the bosom of the earth, up into the closed sky.

A whale! A free whale! a giant dove! someone! a big black mammalian angel.

No one saw the body of the whale from here with his own eyes but they all felt it, and the sea, deserted and the same, which for nine years had never brought them any consolation, as though around Robben Island the sea itself ceased being sea, suddenly the sea was pregnant and good and its belly was full of mystery and freedom and also of play. The whale engendered all kinds of legends. She became a submarine train that whistles three times, she became the mother of all the Xhosa and Tembu ancestors, but for the Indians she was an avatar of Ganga,[115] for all of them she became the black egg out of which the first ocean came out of which came the earth, and for Nelson, the powerful and vulnerable giant to whom he is devoted. No one really saw the whale but none doubted having seen the promise, all the sea's doors having opened before their so ancient so discouraged desire.

And for one day and one night each believed according to his belief, according to his hope and according to his taste.

And none felt the irons the walls the bars.

They were all at sea, swimming and riding and winning the war. And exultant childhood memories were returning from all parts. They had all come out of their coffins like children in pajamas. And there were boastings and delicacies. The whale, the fairy, the woman, the ring that circulates from hand to hand, the queen one only asks for the first kiss. Each one knowing anew how to find the strength to vanquish monsters with a simple nod of the mother's head.

Unfortunately Rolihlahla missed the second whale, the one in 1981, detained as he was on that day by an Australian journalist. Having been deprived of the whale caused him a pain he would not avow. But fortunately there is always Walter to play the part of the ostrich. At night under the thirty-watt moon, Walter said to the air: "Don't regret the whale my son. In two months you'll have a visit from your own whale."

Courage is finding courage when there is no more courage. And where to look for it? When he feels abandoned by hope, aged, with the child inside him dying, Nelson gets up and goes to clean the prisoner Daniels's sanitary bucket. And in the bottom of the bucket he finds courage.

———————

But this infernal torment of bodies, this torture of the pane, Zami and Nelson cannot want it to cease, all one can want is to submit to it again and again for it is all that remains for them to enjoy, yes, it is hewn down to pain out of desire always alive, its bite the ultimate benediction.

Grant that I may not be disembodied by separation. Grant that the ice not seize my soul. Grant that I may be devoured again in my chest and in my belly by the same intolerable hunger, may I go through the veldt my arms full of flames, flayed by the roses of separation, grant that I believe I shall die of pain once again at each visit, before the hour after the hour and at each minute of the hour, in twenty years, in thirty years and when my hair is white,

Grant that I may try in vain to extinguish the fire, grant that I may dream in vain of closing the abyss again,

Grant that harsh tears of mourning roast my eyes,

Grant that I may feel absence uproot my organs, so that lack tears my soul from me like a tooth, may I feel my widowed body turned all tiny and naked, like a dwarfed heart detached from the world's chest that beats crying,

Grant that separation never stop attacking, and may I never begin to bear the unbearable,

keep us forever from all appeasement, give us to taste the bitterness of consolations that come to us under the innocent guise of our grand-children

may each tender morsel of baby that comes in delicate pity to our lips may each kiss turn straight away to glowing embers on our tongues,

if the aurora sky transports our heart in a chariot of red colors, may joy itself dash us to the bottom of pain, once we arrive at the peak of exaltation,

Fill us with happinesses that burn like nettles,

Sharpen our senses, suffocate our throats with beauties, may each magnificent hour be our agony

And when day sets in a concert of crickets and the charivari of birds, may our souls deplore yet another murder, yet another life with its womb full of children and of the little birds they have assassinated inside us, yet another mother yet another child,

Haunt our fleshes with the blind eroticism of the newborn, that seeks, as if its entire life were but a mouth, the absolute breast, and from the strong depths of our bodies may our shouts of fury rise up like irrepressible sap

And may the day of crucifixion be every day, Amen.

For I say to you I want to enjoy the fruits of this martyrdom. At dawn my pain rises its cheeks red and covers my body with a wild and opulent absence of flowers. Everything is lily, lilac, arias of freesia for me, inaudible hymn of iris and trumpet of amaryllis, I have everything I do not have, lack celebrates in me the inexpressible ecstasies of satisfaction, I have your invisible and heavy hands upon my breasts, I am an almond tree that burns without rest, like two tormented bodies closely bound for thousands of years, I inhale eternity through my roots with clutching fingers, up above I end in smoke, under the earth I am born I suck I cling immortally, I am firmly planted with all my fibers I who am doubled by you, in the uterus of the future.

Martyrdom is my placenta. The atrocious bread.

In the bitter kernel the milk seed. The almond is there, in the bitterness. That is the Mandela secret: the manna. Manna come from the heavens hidden under the earth. It has a taste of necessity. *Amandla!*

In the hopelessness hope. One must despair alongside abrupt and rending time, the vertical desert, face against the wall, chest lacerated on the rock's fingernails, eyes wounded by the sand, from step to step, until hope.

The first part of the wedding cake of almonds and honey was blessed and consummated in June 1958 at Bizana in the Pondoland. The second part will be eaten at Qunu[116] in the region of Umtata, at the end of the wall along which Zami trudges, leaning up against Nelson, the link of sand and stone unites them.

A team of two ants is hoisting itself toward the summit of Ararat, the cradle of humanity. This won't take a century.

The Posthumous Poem

"The last day—no—the hour that was to follow, during the night of May 1 to 2, 1938, I was sleeping my ears pricked, vigilant, following Osia's dreams in his forest. He had started to tell me he was starting to see something he had never seen before, starting, a sort of . . .

"And awake under sleeping I was going to see what is finally starting, it's a sort of: —

"but as the falcon falls on the dove and never will the message arrive from the other side, so barely does the word dawn at his lips' door, misfortune throws itself upon him, bites him, breaks his vertebrae and closes in on his flesh. The last word was stopped in mid-breath, on the verge . . . Destiny thrown over the word like a net over the sun. I will never know what is finally starting,

"As if they knew what they were doing these weredogs[117] in suits gray with inhumanity, they killed the seed, they slit the dove's throat, they disemboweled the horse of the honey black eyes, they strangled the word that would have murmured to me the future's address . . .

"And now who will tell me the name of the word they took away between night and day? They stole from me the word that opened walls, as if they knew these weredogs, that it wasn't enough, in order to kill the poet, to ax his throat and mouth, but his shadow too, and the words' neck, and down to the slight wormy murmur of a verse that sadly repeats itself like the memory of a wing."

What stops Nadezhda between life and death is the impossible mourning for this word. Since then something remains in her throat that she'd like to say and that would like to be said and that she doesn't know, doesn't manage to pronounce, a secret that doesn't find her body, a blind seed, the torture of a sound that seeks to soar.

And the dead man himself, so subject may he be over there beneath the snow to the orders from the earths and from his fellow creatures the sands, isn't he tendering, tireless, his shadows of Osia's ears?

———————

"Who knows what the dead man desires when his lips no longer know how to ask, Nadezhda, do you know? You know it yes you know, reread my poem about the train station.

"It was a dream without witnesses. It was already the truth. More than once I have died while I was alive.

"Who's leaving? The train. Me. He. A sky of earth is thrown over him.

"Stars even in his eyes. Mute but agitated. The dead man is cold, I was sure of it. In the meantime. I would have so liked you to place the old Scottish plaid blanket over my body with your hands, flag from a journey that I won't have made. Who is it? Who has died? Who am I? Who is I who recognizes each noise? All the poems dash into the train car, afraid of missing, memory, whistles, last minute, all aboard, I would never have believed I had written so much. Choir in Mandelstam's head. Delighted. How I have lived! Sobs and scuffles, the universe is scrambling about in my nutshell, so much music, quick, before the departure, violins! tousle your hair! to die, and straight away astride the bow. Finally the Earth! I'm dying of curiosity.

"So this is what awaited me: the train, whistleblows, poem cries, and worms of verse for stars.

"Do you love me Nadezhda, do you love me? loveven me? even you, do you loveven me, even mute do you hear me?[118] humming? my lips tumefied, kissed by wormy lines of verse, quick, dictate the last poem, promised you know, dead, I told you, barely dead, will write you, the posthumous poem. I'm sending it to you. Once you will receive it.

"When I was alive more than one dead man came to me, once or often, Dante, Bely, or Batyushkov,[119] I was moved, mute, I would say 'thank you,' it was I who would fall silent, it was he who would speak to me, to me, who was trembling with fever, to my lips would come the flapping of wings, I had lost my tongue, no words supernatural enough, I would murmur: 'thank you' in Russian on a street in Florence, it was on a street in Lublin,[120]

"Call me back I will come, open the door to me, the coat, the notebook, I will enter, finding the key will suffice.

"What key? A word. The word, the one I gave you, I don't know which one anymore, the blessed, senseless word, I only know it used to palpitate, labial perhaps, it had that taste of frenzied rose and egg yolk, do you recognize it? yes you'll recognize it.

"And nothing will have been lost.

"Or else on a street in Kiev, or why not in Sukhumi, where I saw the nuptial cloud of phosphorescent insects dancing? You said to me: a wedding. I saw: my decomposition.

"Seek seek! No bigger than a cochineal, smaller than a pea, difficult to find with the eyes, but with the ear you will find, if not me, at least my breathing.

I whirl around in the meantime, in dispersed particles, multitude in vibration before the ear.

" . . .

"I deny the arrest. I am deceased alive; with my stirring tongue I speak to all the passersby, I had a body, I had myriad, I left you a hundred thousand footprints.

"Let them arrest my blanket, let them deport my plaid, threadbare, it isn't me it's my coat you have entrenched, at the expiration of the year 1938.

"Whoever wants to arrest Mandelstam will have to arrest all the M's all the A's all the N's all the D's all the E's all the L's all the S's all the T's and all the Arthropoda, or more than half the entire animal kingdom, and fireflies and mayflies and twenty thousand species of birds, without counting the unarrestable harmony of all musics.

"Listen Nadezhda, lend me your lips, I'm going to whisper you.

"Look me up. My address is in the Universe. Bring me back, bring me back to life and let's go far away from here. I dream of a nomad's tent at the foot of the Ararat."

Nadezhda takes two lives to search for Osia's remains.

One short, one long. The same one. I told you: one must live from now on in two directions, pell and mell are the parents of this bewildered era, and into the bargain pell is mell, and as we shall see, the skin itself wears foreign signs.

Without Osip at her side, with Osip over here and over there, she is no longer of the world of tramways and straight lines. Like a spider, she comes and goes from her own heart to the very ends of a web that she sprouts and weaves on the warm shores and icy strands of all that was Mandelstam space. Transparent snares for ensnaring the remains. Being the friend of everything that was alive hence of everything, he listened to everything and translated everything, pouring samples of his discoveries from one tongue to the other. Gathering was his art and his rite.

—Whatever are these unimportant pebbles, these dead maple tree leaves for, this endless herbarium, I remember I used to get irritated, why this bizarre shop?

It was so as better to read and hear and better to see the world's child.

And now she takes the yellow straw basket, the one from Yerevan,[121] and she is running too, up to the ten thousand doors. There is almost half the Universe to recapture. Even dead he advances with long strides, never doubting she is following him even dead, and like every day usually since May 1, 1919.

Luckily time has changed its laws. And it no longer knows either night or North or duration.

Where to call him? There exists no house that could swear: here lived Mandelstam. Or tomb, or cradle. But everything has seen him passing: the black sky and the white sky, the grass, the stars in the bucket's ice, the bridge, the rivers, the mountains, Asia, Hell, Paradise. There is barely a street where his step doesn't echo. He has laughed and rhymed from city to city, in each one losing and finding his own town and from Yalta to Astrakhan he must have sown a hundred vows, and at least two curses. Where?

During the day Akhmatova helps her fill her basket. It is she who remembers the *Unknown Soldier*.[122] Already it was Osip, this poem, and it wasn't quite him yet. It was the song of the unknown soldier, himself, in person, and in millions of copies. The dead man's song ended with his date of birth.

I was born in the night of the 2nd or 3rd of January in the untrustworthy year of '92, it said.

As for the other date, Nadezhda, I'll let you decide. The ultimate day of my death will be the day of your death.

As long as poems kept coming no one could say he was dead, isn't that true? Only personally unfindable.

———————

In the night of Thursday to Good Friday, Virgil passes by in a gust of wind before Nadezhda, as always, as eternally, on long light legs.

—Where is Dante? I cried, my voice struck down by emotion in my chest.

I wanted to say: Where is Mandelstam? But this wasn't important. They were inseparable. "I am his wife," I say suffering with all my rags and tatters, "I am his death. His exiled. Do you understand me?"

Yes. In the same way that a dead man can live, in the same way even I standing in tatters, at my feet, scraps of shoes no one after me would want, me whose stomach is rumbling with starvation, I who cry and creak I am dead, dead by marriage and by nationality, dead relative of the dead and my life is but a long parenthesis. This is why Virgil understands me. Between us from now on no strangeness, no difference, other than that his hands are elegantly gloved in yellow leather, my hand naked in its glove, rough and chapped but just as chilly as his.

Virgil is a man in a hurry. I won't tell anyone I find him misogynistic.

He looks through me as through an open window. Maybe I wasn't dead enough or maybe too dead. What does it matter. Courteously without a word, sure-footed and empty-eyed like a chauffeur absorbed by the road, he drives me all over Europe, showing me from West to East the whole of Dante, displayed from wells to mountain peaks, and lets me hear each one of his musical instruments, economically, at the high speed of dreams. And I saw him as distinctly as he saw the inflamed sainted creatures sing to him canto XVIII in winged letters. But I didn't have the time to speak with him. Only the right to geography.

———————

But awake it's longer: she takes ten years to remake Russia, Ukraine, Armenia, Crimea, Abkhazia, Caucasia, Kazakstan,[123] she on the earth and he below, I listen o I listen. Osia speaks to him in all the colors of Russian and in all the tongues forbidden to the Russian mouth, in a meticulous orgy of sounds taken from the trees, from the streams, from the churches, from the terrestrial and human dialects. Hence the chernozem[124] use fricatives, he recites, and hence the streams of rainwater babble in Achtarak, and Armenian is strong like a black tea, and behold how the Cornalines of Koktebel express themselves, in strata, in cutting hard dense sentences, through the piling up of metaphors.

And by dint of rereading the newspaper of the earth and stones, she erstwhile townswoman of towns and reader of printed books, she ends up reconstituting almost all of Mandelstam's *oeuvre*.

All she's missing now are the last words.

Here the story ends. Here the legend begins.

At Tashkent,[125] with Akhmatova, in the street that has its source in the ice and at the end hurls itself into the sky, the room is barely bigger than three coffins. It is here at the far end of the world that they house the witness. The one who heard Mandelstam's last words in the Vtoraya Rechka camp.[126]

The witness has no toes. He doesn't have a cent. No roof. No reason. No pity. Not a memory. Not any. Osip's last words, he heard and forgot them. He pounds the pavement, he pummels women, he prattles, and says nothing.

No this is not by chance. It is good. How could there be another witness? No other witness than Osia. And for remains of pain the remains of a man. It is good.

At the end of winter the witness goes away, Akhmatova's shoes on his toeless feet.

(Meanwhile Osia is root. He descends head down, crawling along the secret axes of Asia, hot on Pallas's heels.[127]

They're exploring the blue Uzbek glebe.[128] Descending he is carried back in time, one meter a year. Now he sees the world with the serenity of a naturalist: this century too will be classed among the quartz.)

No chance in the legend. A logic lovely as a geology orders the events. So behold the man with the shoes. The cobbler that destiny's divinities donate to Nadezhda. All the dust of pity that remains in Uzbekistan has been gathered together to manufacture this man.

For nothing, he makes Nadezhda shoes for traversing winter. From four unpaired shoes he recomposes a solid pair of shoes with mottled uppers, and behold: as at the beginning of memory, the light and very agile *lonza* returns,[129] covered with a spotted skin. She, feeling clearly right away in the room that Mandelstam isn't far. In truth these shoes were made of all the shoes that Osia would have worn. This mosaic composition, isn't it the thousand-faceted eye of Mandelstam? These shoes weren't shoes. They were much surer and more powerful than simple shoes, and without a single doubt they carried Nadezhda above the nights. There are shoes that are alive like poems and that carry us farther than ourselves. There are shoes like dreams.

Everything that we are not, aren't we not it without scandal between the pair of sheets, are not we the limitless and moving sum of all our possibilities?

Last night didn't you sleep lying face down on a dream of dust, under the tent of some sort of raincoat, on the ground before my door, you Dante, you Homer, you male mother, and me with the knees of a girl in love, around thirteen armies old I was sitting on the step sucking my unknown poet's pen, waiting without haste for you to awaken and without surprise at seeing you lying you sleeping, you sleeping off the intoxication of so many books, plastered shamelessly in the mire, under your belly a mire for black sheet, in the simple informal station of all eternity.

He became a drunkard, someone disclosed to me. The news is in the papers, black on not quite white. He is not merely gray and a little tipsy. He is completely black and totally smashed.[130]

Thus by dint of books and verse the celebrated surveyor of all worlds will have ended. Naturally, I told myself, waiting, by suckling time, you slept off the fermenting universe[131] and its countless shelves of landscapes.

———————

Then one night Osip finally wakes up personally in a dream, or rather his essence in person, the poet. Neither Dante, nor Virgil, but Osia young and petulant—for I swear he was young and twenty years old in the beginning—wakes her with in his hand for you, your poem. Nadezhda's poem, the one that didn't exist. This is why I've come. Just as one recognizes the angel, she instantly recognized the dream of dreams. The one that comes once. To announce reveal and repair. The one that gives the dead man back for one instant. It must be done quickly. This meeting of the two worlds occurs in a flash once a century. Quick, for you, a youthful and posthumous poem. Written under the earth. In spite of life, in spite of death. This poem was the strongest. Quick quick listen! The lips open: the title leaps out: Lifebird. And already from the lips escape wormy lines of absolutely new poetry. Brief and colorful, the poem, a flight. She sees and she hears it. She has just enough time to hear it flapping, its wings flee off before her eyes. It's a poem in bird pieces. And in a multiplication of wings the flight tells her the poem. Tells her, shows her. The bird is your voice, the name of your voice Nadezhda, and the clear water of your voice that I can hear down to the most grave and somber strata of burial, the flutelike sharpness that I can hear down to the dried-up heart of the dead trunk. It is the bridge that leads the music down to the deafest part of the stone.

And as a flight of sea gulls veers above the shore, she reads it being written with a tug of wings in the window of the sky, and etching the air with furrows and curls, o I see it, my poem indicated up there disappearing without a trace, I see the *O*, I see the *I*, I see the chain of words faster than my gaze, o the violent speed, breathless, wild-eyed, an *M*, an *N*, a last figure by the whole flight together, and see how they retreat suddenly toward the far end of the earth and nearsighted and alone I remain, dazzled.

A poem was given to me, from the first word to the last! Ah! So this is how they arrive from the front, tilling the entire space, and how just as quickly they fade.

I thought they were arriving from a remote part of the forest, on tiptoe very slowly, behind my left shoulder. And now I understand Osip's face twisted in anguish and his eyes wide and dilated like a prophet's mouth beneath the manna, whenever there was a visitation.

In my chest the ball of fire poetic violence leaves as it passes.

—If one could die of a too good dream I would have died of this grace. And it is to me this miracle came! To my eyes, the vision of what with my nearsightedness I would never see! It is through my stiff and awkward throat that Osip sang the rapid the light the voluble posthumous poem!

"I wonder whom this poem is by," said Akhmatova.

"It truly is Mandelstam's last poem."

"And yet I wonder," said Akhmatova.

"All is well with Osia now. All is found and regained."

And it was true perhaps, perhaps. If one knew what well and true meant.

"Yes, all is well now with Osia's bones, and with the birds, and with the little bird osselets!"

If one knew what well is for a poet. Yes. And what a poet is? Perhaps his poems? Perhaps these bones that live, obstinately, on.

"I too would love to be able to write a poem after my death. But I have no Hope, there is no woman to make my impossible.

"And who knows finally from where poems come to us, by what voices? From sufferings disguised as birds, this is what I believe. One will envy me my sufferings."

"What is there to envy? Did Osip breathe thanks to asphyxiation? Do I limp thanks to the hardness of my shoes? Do you sing thanks to hunger?"

They were going down Pushkin Street, fighting till the very end. Unable to separate. Suffering was fashioning a link of flesh between them. But Nadezhda couldn't survive more than one and Akhmatova didn't have a wife to perpetuate her.

They were walking. And the light wasn't. In truth, after the dream of dreams, Nadezhda ceased being afraid: now she could die.

At the end while crossing the bridge, here is what they saw. Even though the world was so dark. Even though the sky, even though the century, even though the humans, there were those, the inhabitants of languages, friends, side by side, meditating in deep meditation, who would take onto their slender bodies all the world's rare light, for their need was so much stronger than the real possibilities of the universe, for their song was so necessary that they feared neither looks from the police, nor the sky's blindness, nor the deafness of the times, nor absence, nor shadow, but all the good there was in the world they took, they gave it to each other, they kept it between their bodies, exposing themselves without fear for they saw nothing that wasn't the other, they felt nothing that wasn't desire and illumination, being wholly made of passion for each other. Each would recite the other.

And seeing them the two women saw that it was good, they themselves were no longer but love side by side without a single distraction, the gray no longer filled them with gloom.

Sea gulls rejoicing in their pasture were fluttering and diving, etching the water with pale lips and sparkling signs.

And nothing will have been lost.

Notes to the Introduction

1. In *Prisms*, trans. Samuel Weber and Shierry Weber (Cambridge, Mass.: MIT Press, 1981), Adorno states: "Cultural criticism finds itself faced with the final stage of the dialectic of culture and barbarism. To write poetry after Auschwitz is barbaric. And this corrodes even the knowledge of why it has become impossible to write poetry today. Absolute reification, which presupposed intellectual progress as one of its elements, is now preparing to absorb the mind entirely." Rather than placing an ethically motivated prohibition on the writing of poetry in general, Adorno's statement is a reminder of how the perpetrators' abuse of poetry and art as tranquilizers in the service of forgetting their daytime atrocities has rendered any naive reception or production of poetry barbaric and thus impossible. In that view, poetry is possible only if the political is reinscribed in the poetical, if poetry is guided by what Adorno has called a new categorical imperative: " 'I'm thinking of Auschwitz' must accompany all my ideas" (p. 34). (See, for example, *Minima Moralia: Reflections from a Damaged Life*, trans. E. F. N. Jephcott [London: Verso, 1974].) Cixous fashioned her own version of Adorno's imperative in the text from which this essay's title is taken, "Poetry Is/and (the) Political," trans. Ann Liddle, *Bread and Roses*, vol. 2-1 (1980): 16-18: "There must be a poetic practice in the political practice—(Without this the political kills: and inversely.) We need: we must, if we want to be alive, to succeed in being contemporary with a rose and with concentration camps: to think an intense instant of life, of the body, *and* concentration camps."

2. See, for example, Steven Conner, *Postmodernist Culture: An Introduction to Theories of the Contemporary* (Cambridge: Blackwell, 1989).

3. "Interview with Hélène Cixous" in the "Cixous Dossier," ed. and trans. Catherine A. Franke, *Qui Parle: A Journal of Literary Studies*, 3, no. 1 (Spring 1989): 152-79.

4. For an overview of Cixous's life and work, I refer the reader to Susan Rubin Suleiman's introductory essay, "Writing Past the Wall," in *"Coming to Writing" and Other Essays*, ed. Deborah Jenson, trans. Sarah Cornell, Deborah Jenson, Ann Liddle, and Susan Sellers (Cambridge, Mass.: Harvard University Press, 1991), pp. vii-xxii. See as well the beginning chapters of Verena Andermatt Conley's *Hélène Cixous* (Toronto: University of Toronto Press, 1992). Both these illuminating texts are rich in biographical detail.

5. Public discussion at a conference organized by Hélène Cixous, entitled "Exploring the Unexplored," held at and sponsored by the University of Virginia's Commonwealth Center for Literary and Cultural Change, September 26, 1992. Cixous went on to say, "Does poetry make it to the inside of Auschwitz, or does it stop at the door to the camps? My fear was always that poetry have a limit. But later I discovered, in, among others, the work of Etty Hillesum, who was reading Rilke to help her live in the camps just a few days before her death, that poetry did last to the very end, unto the ashes." (For a further discussion of the writer Etty Hillesum, see note 16.)

6. Hélène Cixous, in "A propos de *Manne*. Entretien avec Hélène Cixous," by Françoise van Rossum-Guyon, in *Hélène Cixous, chemins d'une écriture*, ed. Françoise van Rossum-Guyon and Myriam Díaz-Diocaretz (Amsterdam: Rodopovi; Paris: PUV, 1990), p. 225, my translation.

7. For an interesting discussion of the possibility that the politics of this utopia do not work, see Conley, *Hélène Cixous*, p. 111.

8. Published by the Théâtre du Soleil Press, Paris, 1985 and 1987, respectively.

9. "The Parting of the Cake," in *For Nelson Mandela*, trans. Franklin Philip (New York: Seaver Books, Henry Holt, 1987), pp. 201-18.

10. See Sigmund Freud, *Totem and Taboo*, volume 13 in *The Standard Edition of the Complete Psychological Works of Sigmund Freud*, trans. and ed. James Strachey (London: Hogarth Press and the Institute of Psycho-Analysis, 1953-73).

11. For instance, in *Manna*, the ostrich is praised in a way that resembles a Sotho tradition, as described in S. M. Guma, *The Form, Content, and Technique of Traditional Literature in Southern Sotho* (Pretoria: J. L. van Schaik, 1977): "A number of Sotho clans venerate certain animals which serve as their totems. . . . The various animals that were known to the ancient Basotho were praised in various ways. Praises were composed for wild and domestic animals, thus indicating that the praisers were intrigued by them and their habits. Their observed habits and characteristics, such as hunting, and their methods of running, are included in their praises" (pp. 145-47). It is very much in this way that Cixous came to venerate the ostrich. She explains how she discovered this fabulous creature, in "A propos de *Manne*. Entretien avec Hélène Cixous": "I began working on the ostrich

through the [Mandelas' wedding] cake. The cake existed in reality, I began to dream: what kind of cake could withstand the passing of twenty or twenty-five years? So I went to look in a South African cookbook. In this cookbook there were the most beautiful illustrations of South Africa one could ever find. And then there were also the omelettes, the breakfasts, I discovered the ostrich side of things: from one ostrich egg they make a breakfast for twelve. I felt a sort of nausea. I discovered at the same time that ostriches had become these sorts of chickens, raised in these . . . chicken coops? Now that's South Africa! Then I worked on the character of the ostrich with encyclopedias. I discovered fabulous things about ostriches; for example, that our myth about 'making like an ostrich' isn't founded in reality. To the contrary, the ostrich is very keen-sighted and she can see in the sand for miles. We have constructed, as usual, a sort of reverse, negative mythology about the ostrich. On the level of myths, the dictionary tells us the ostrich is a Promethean bird, a bird who is said to have given fire. So, there has been by definition a cover-up, a story transformed into its opposite, and reductive of an extraordinary animal. The putting to death of the ostrich is the metaphor itself of what I'm in the process of recounting [in *Manna*]" (p. 228, my translation).

12. See Catherine Clément's "The Guilty One," in Clément and Hélène Cixous, *The Newly Born Woman*, with an introduction by Sandra M. Gilbert, trans. Betsy Wing (Minneapolis and Oxford: University of Minnesota Press, 1986), p. 6.

13. Referred to in *Poems from Mandelstam*, trans. and preface R. H. Morrison, intro. Ervin C. Brody (Rutherford, Madison, Teaneck: Fairleigh Dickinson University Press; London and Toronto: Associated University Presses, 1990), p. 28.

14. Cixous, "Poetry is/and the Political."

15. Winnie Mandela's nickname, from her Xhosa name, Nomzamo.

16. See, for example, *An Interrupted Life: The Diaries of Etty Hillesum, 1941-43* (New York: Pantheon Books, 1983). All those convinced that Cixous's reading of the lives of the Mandelas and the Mandelstams merely represents a glorification of victimization would read the works of Etty Hillesum with interest. Hillesum thanks God for the spiritual riches of her life in the camps. The books by Winnie Mandela and Nadezhda Mandelstam also confirm that some "victims" do believe they have found a wealth of inner resources as a result of their suffering, and insist on mining this wealth as a form of resistance to their very status as victims. For an analysis of Cixous's relationship to Hillesum, see Conley *Hélène Cixous*, pp. 104-5.

17. "Interview with Hélène Cixous" in the *Cixous Dossier*, ed. and trans. Catherine A. Franke, p. 169.

18. Morag Shiach, *Hélène Cixous: A Politics of Writing* (London and New York: Routledge, 1991), p. 102.

19. Winnie Mandela, *Part of My Soul Went with Him* (New York: Norton, 1984); *Hope against Hope*, trans. Max Hayward (New York: Atheneum Books, 1970).

20. Winnie Mandela describes a paradise that is very much in keeping with the notion of paradise as relative that *Manna* invokes, when she describes her husband's reaction to being moved, in April 1982, from Robben Island to the prison in Pollsmoor: "He said the last time he saw a blade of grass was on the island, as he was leaving. Now he can only see the sky. The prison is in a valley. He must be in a part of the prison that is so enclosed that he can't even have the view of the mountains. Isn't it strange that there can still be a difference between nothing and nothing? That island—which was nothing, which was death itself—suddenly became a paradise . . . The irony of it all! Pollsmoor is a virtual palace when you compare the structure itself to the island. Yet he is certainly worse off there than he was on the island" (*Part of My Soul Went with Him*, p. 142).

21. See Blanchot, *The Writing of the Disaster*, trans. Ann Smock (Lincoln: University of Nebraska Press, 1986).

22. Mallarmé says in "As for the Book: Action Restricted," trans. Mary Ann Caws: "You noticed, one does not write luminously on a dark field; the alphabet of stars alone, is thus indicated, sketched out or interrupted; man pursues black on white." *Stéphane Mallarmé: Selected Poetry and Prose*, ed. Mary Ann Caws (New York: New Directions, 1982), p. 77.

23. The word *vers* in French commonly means both verse, or line of poetry, and worms. The text plays on these two meanings. I have chosen to translate this word variously, context permitting, as "wormy verse," "worms of verse," or sometimes, according to context, simply as "verse," "line," or "line of poetry." Where the text seems to bear the double meaning, I have inserted, so as not to lose, the underside of the metaphor. However, such a translating decision is always an artificial solution, as it does lead to an overevaluation of the weight of the worms when the primary meaning in most contexts is verse, an overevaluation that should be noted as such.

24. I am introducing this term in keeping with Katherine Binhammer's helpful analysis of Cixous's use, in her writing, of a "metaphor that is not a metaphor [and] is a metonymy." See "Metaphor or Metonymy? The Question of Essentialism in Cixous," in *Tessera*, a Canadian literary journal published by York University Press, Ontario (October 1991, pp. 65-79).

25. The word *metaphor* comes from the Greek *metapherein: meta* (over) and *pherein* (to bear). It is, of course, a word indicating a kind of linguistic travel, a transference whereby one word flies over to carry off and replace another.

26. "A propos de *Manne*. Entretien avec Hélène Cixous," p. 223, my translation.

27. See her letter to Mary Benson in *Part of My Soul Went with Him*, p. 44.

28. For example: "Nelson once wrote me a letter about a twig. He can write a whole book just from staring at that twig. He had a few tomato plants and he inadvertently injured one of the plants he loved very much. He wrote two letters (you cannot exceed 500 words). The first letter of 500 words was not enough. He described the beauty of that tomato plant, how it grew and grew, how he was able to give it life because he nursed it, and how he inadvertently injured it and his feelings when it died. He pulled it out from the soil and washed those roots and thought of the life that might have been. He is unable to write to me politically. Out of letters like that, you can sort of get how he feels about certain things" (ibid., pp. 85-86).

29. "A propos de *Manne*. Entretien avec Hélène Cixous," pp. 215-16, my translation. In her recent book, Morag Shiach contends nonetheless that Cixous's rendering of Winnie is politically problematic: "The mythical imagery that already surrounds Nelson Mandela is just much more extensive than that which is available for Winnie. Nelson becomes 'a planet, a temple, a mountain,' while Winnie is a 'doe' or an 'ant.' From *Le Livre de Promethea* we know that Cixous sees the doe as a powerful image of the grace and beauty of the feminine. Yet, when applied to a contemporary historical figure, such imagery has meanings that cannot be confined to the intense personal imagery of Cixous's texts" (*Hélène Cixous: A Politics of Writing*, p. 103). Might I add, for the purpose of clarification and to contribute to what I'm sure will be an ongoing and interesting topic for discussion around this text, that there is an interesting tension at work when a European or American critic (and I do not mean to refer only to Shiach; I have heard comments of concern from others regarding Cixous's depiction of animals in this text) takes it upon herself to defend Africans and Africa against an association with animals, when indigenous and other peoples of color all over the world have often had a history of deep respect for and interest in animals, as well as a tradition of using them symbolically to depict people and various human traits in their storytelling. For example, Daniel P. Kunene writes in his essay "Metaphor or Symbolism in the Heroic Poetry of Southern Africa" (in *African Folklore*, ed. Richard M. Dorson [Bloomington and London: Indiana University Press, 1972]): "The poet's intimate knowledge of the natural phenomena around him facilitates his use of metaphor for the hero and his qualities. The metaphor may be universally intelligible, as when the hero's bravery transforms him into a lion. . . . For here we have something akin to the fable, where qualities (even though not all of them illustrated from the animal world) are constant, and universally give man parallels against which he measures his own reasonably comparable characteristics" (p. 318). Harold Scheub writes of another, oral tradition in *The Xhosa* Ntsomi (London: Oxford University Press, 1975): "The

Xhosa *Ntsomi* . . . is a performing art which has as its dynamic mainspring, a *core-cliché* (a song, chant, or saying) which is, during a performance, developed, expanded, detailed, and dramatized. . . . A general theme seems to govern the development of the *core-images* (core-images are composed of the basic core-clichés plus allied and supporting details). This theme centers on the need for order in the human community, an order that finds its perfect metaphor in Nature. . . . *Ntsomi* performance moves easily back and forth between the reality of the contemporary milieu to the worlds of Nature and fantasy, with their talking birds and beasts. . . . This use of *parallel sets of images* to embody a theme is a basic structural device in the construction of a *Ntsomi*. . . . It is thus not possible to speak of 'animal' and 'human' narratives. The division is artificial and not very helpful, because the performer is interested in the metaphorical nature of her characters. . . . She therefore spends little time detailing the features . . . emphasizing instead, through actions, those elements that help to describe the nature [of the trait] itself" (pp. 3, 80). I would argue that, in keeping with the literary traditions *Manne* in many ways parallels, Cixous's descriptions of Africa and its animals are neither cliché nor problematic, but powerfully encomiastic, performative devices.

30. In French, "Poésie e(s)t Politique." This text appears in English translation; see note 1.

31. For a discussion by Cixous herself of her use of these two terms, see Conley's exchange with her in Conley, *Hélène Cixous: Writing the Feminine* (Lincoln and London: University of Nebraska Press, 1984), pp. 129-61.

32. And this especially on the level of writing, where psychic pain can be transformed into poetic pleasure. Cixous explains: "I receive what could be called 'a wound,' but which, at the same time as it is displaced by making a text, is the cause of a poetic *jouissance*, it is there that there is something that makes me speak, suffer, or take pleasure." "A propos de *Manne*. Entretien avec Hélène Cixous," p. 214, my translation.

33. James Joyce, *Ulysses* (New York: Vintage Books, 1961), p. 34. My thanks to Alexandra Bloom for reminding me of this reference.

34. Hélène Cixous, speaking at San Francisco State University in 1988.

35. "Exile prevents speaking / Exile makes for earth." Cixous, speaking at San Francisco State University in 1988.

36. "A propos de *Manne*. Entretien avec Hélène Cixous," p. 219, my translation.

37. Here I am paraphrasing Diana Fuss's evaluation of Adrienne Rich's notion of a "lesbian continuum." See her important book *Essentially Speaking: Feminism, Nature, and Difference* (New York: Routledge, 1989), p. 44.

38. Ibid., p. 37.

39. Ed. Peter Connor, trans. Peter Connor et al. (Minneapolis: University of Minnesota Press, 1991).

40. Conley, *Hélène Cixous: Writing the Feminine*, p. 96.

41. *Essentially Speaking*, p. 36.

42. See, for example, the excellent collection *Making Face, Making Soul, Haciendo Caras: Creative and Critical Perspectives by Women of Color*, ed. Gloria Anzaldúa (San Francisco: aunt lute, 1990); Teresa de Lauretis, *Feminist Studies/Critical Studies* (Bloomington: Indiana University Press, 1986); and, for an overview of the problematic of difference as it impacts feminist, queer, and African-American studies, see Diana Fuss, *Essentially Speaking*.

43. *Canadian Review of Comparative Literature/Revue Canadienne de Littérature Comparée*, March/June 1992, pp. 25-36.

44. This link is noted in Conley, *Hélène Cixous*, p. 106. Cixous herself has told me she is not familiar with the Polynesian mana. Of course, to remark on the similarity between the two words, "manna" and "mana," and to marvel at how well the notion of good fortune adds to the reading of Cixous's text, is an acceptable and even inspired critical gesture. Nonetheless, the biblical word "manna" is the only possible *translation* of the title of Cixous's text: it is to this substance Cixous was referring when she wrote *Manna*. In French, the word *manne* has yet another, secondary, meaning altogether, that of basket or cradle, which has its echoes in this text as well, seen in the Mandelstams' special basket from Yerevan, and in the fleeting references to Moses, the baby in the basket.

45. One English version of this poem appears in *Poems of Paul Celan*, trans. and intro. Michael Hamburger (New York: Persea, 1988), p. 189:

> *In the almond—what dwells in the almond?*
> *Nothing.*
> *What dwells in the almond is Nothing.*
> *There it dwells and dwells.*
>
> *In Nothing—what dwells there? The King.*
> *There the King dwells, the King.*
> *There he dwells and dwells.*
>
>   *Jew's curl, you'll not turn grey.*
>
> *And your eye—on what does your eye dwell?*
> *On the almond your eye dwells.*
> *Your eye, on Nothing it dwells.*
> *Dwells on the King, to him remains loyal, true.*
> *So it dwells and dwells.*

Human curl, you'll not turn grey.
Empty almond, royal-blue.

46. From Cixous's 1988 speech at San Francisco State University.

47. Milton, another guardian of Manna, wrote of Belial in *Paradise Lost*: "His tongue / Dropt manna, and could make the worse appear / The better reason."

48. P. 76.

49. See Roman Jakobson's "Linguistics and Poetics," in *Style in Language*, ed. Thomas Sebeok (Cambridge, Mass.: MIT Press, 1960); and Jacques Lacan's *Ecrits: A Selection*, trans. Alan Sheridan (New York and London: Norton, 1977).

50. This is the famous Jakobsonian example of the poetic function.

51. And here I am applying Diana Fuss's analysis (*Essentially Speaking*, p. 64) of the functioning of Luce Irigaray's writing to the writing of Cixous, in a way I hope is helpful.

52. To paraphrase Julia Kristeva's notion of the semiotic as it functions in poetic writing, in, for example, *Desire in Language: A Semiotic Approach to Literature and Art*, ed. Leon S. Roudiez, trans. Thomas Gora, Alice Jardine, and Leon S. Roudiez (New York: Columbia University Press, 1980).

53. Cixous's *doctorat d'état*, which she completed in 1968 at the age of thirty-one, making her at that time the youngest recipient of the degree in France's history, was on the works of James Joyce.

54. *Economie libidinale*, or "libidinal economy," is a term coined by Jean-François Lyotard in his book by the same name (Paris: Minuit, 1974). Cixous uses this term to refer to an energetic and economic model of the libido as a drive of desire that basically can be either spent or retained. *Ecriture féminine*, or "feminine writing," is a term in common usage (but not coined by Cixous) that has been used to describe the explorations into femininity practiced by the writing of such French authors as Cixous, Annie Leclerc, Christiane Rochefort, Chantal Chawaf, Madeleine Gagnon, and, in philosophy, Luce Irigaray. For a discussion by Cixous herself of these terms, see Conley's exchange with her in *Hélène Cixous: Writing the Feminine*.

55. In trying to understand the sometimes confusing and subtle relationship between what Cixous calls the "feminine" and biological females, the Anglo-American reader might find it helpful to recall Adrienne Rich's use of the notion of a "lesbian continuum" in her classic article entitled "Compulsory Heterosexuality," which appears in the collection *Powers of Desire: The Politics of Sexuality*, ed. Ann Snitow, Christine Stansell, and Sharon Thompson (New York: Monthly Review Press, 1983). Lesbianism

for Rich is to all women what femininity is to all people according to Cixous's use of the word: we all, men and women, participate in its economy to some greater or lesser degree. Although she has often been cited as a perpetrator of that new feminist crime of essentialism, Cixous herself has characterized her use of the adjectives feminine and masculine as qualifiers, and she issued a critique of the ideological dangers of essentialism as early as 1975, in her essay "Sorties," translated as "Sorties: Out and Out: Attacks/Ways Out/Forays," in *The Newly Born Woman*: "I make a point of using the *qualifiers* of sexual difference here to avoid the confusion man/masculine, woman/feminine: for there are some men who do not repress their femininity, some women who, more or less strongly, inscribe their masculinity. Difference is not distributed, of course, on the basis of socially determined 'sexes.' On the other hand, when I speak of political economy and libidinal economy, connecting them, I am not bringing into play the false question of origins—a story made to order for male privilege. We have to be careful not to lapse smugly or blindly into an essentialist ideological interpretation, as both Freud and Jones, for example, risked doing in their different ways. In the quarrel that brought them into conflict on the subject of feminine sexuality, both of them, starting from opposite points of view, came to support the formidable thesis of a 'natural,' anatomical determination of sexual difference-opposition. On that basis, both of them implicitly back phallocentrism's position of strength . . . It is impossible to predict what will become of sexual difference—in another time (in two or three hundred years?). But we must make no mistake: men and women are caught up in a web of age-old cultural determinations that are almost unanalyzable in their complexity. One can no more speak of 'woman' than of 'man' without being trapped within an ideological theater where the proliferation of representations, images, reflections, myths, identifications, transform, deform, constantly change everyone's Imaginary and invalidate in advance any conceptualization. Nothing allows us to rule out the possibility of radical transformation of behaviors, mentalities, roles, political economy—whose effects on libidinal economy are unthinkable—today. Let us simultaneously imagine a general change in all the structures of training, education, supervision—hence in the structures of reproduction of ideological results. And let us imagine a real liberation of sexuality, that is to say, a transformation of each one's relationship to his or her body (and to the other body), an approximation to the vast, material, organic, sensuous universe that we are. This cannot be accomplished, of course, without political transformations that are equally radical. (Imagine!) Then 'femininity' or 'masculinity' . . . would no longer amount to the same thing. No longer would the common logic of difference be organized with the opposition that remains dominant. Difference would be a bunch of new differences" (pp. 81, 83).

263

56. See Freud's "Three Essays on the Theory of Sexuality," in *The Standard Edition*, vol. 7.

57. See also Cixous's essay "The Author in Truth," in the same volume, where she again writes of her take on this topos: " 'An economy said to be F.,' 'an economy said to be M.'—why distinguish between them? Why keep words that are so entirely treacherous, dreadful, warmongering? This is where all the traps are set. I give myself poetic license; otherwise I would not dare speak. It is the poet's right to say something unusual and then to say: believe it if you want to, but believe weeping; or, as Genet does, to erase it by saying that all truths are false, that only false truths are true, and so on" (p. 150).

58. See "Introjecter-Incorporer: deuil *ou* mélancolie" by Nicolas Abraham and Maria Torok, in the *Nouvelle Revue de Psychanalyse*, no. 6 (Fall 1972): 111-22.

59. In *"Coming to Writing" and Other Essays*, pp. 150-52. For a discussion of the Cixousian paradigm linking pleasure and knowledge, as it relates to Kant's distinction between knowledge and the senses, see the chapter in Conley, *Hélène Cixous: Writing the Feminine*, pp. 95-124, entitled "Accord Koré to Cordelia."

60. In the original Russian-language version of her memoirs about her husband and their life together (see Suggested Further Reading), as well as in the French translations (although, unfortunately, this is not carried over by the English translator), Nadezhda Mandelstam refers to Osip as "OM" throughout, and Cixous often uses this same device in *Manna*.

61. Unless you are a reader of poetry in the German, and are familiar with Paul Celan's translations of and poems about Mandelstam. See, for example, *Poems of Paul Celan*.

62. The title is taken from Ovid, who, like Pushkin and later, ironically, Mandelstam himself, was exiled to the Black Sea steppes.

63. *Osip Mandelstam: 50 Poems*, trans. Bernard Meares, intro. Joseph Brodsky (New York: Persea Books, 1977), p. 9.

64. The other truly major poets referred to most often as being Marina Tsvetayeva and Boris Pasternak.

65. Introduction by Clarence Brown, in *Osip Mandelstam: Selected Poems*, trans. Clarence Brown and W. S. Merwin (London: Oxford University Press, 1973), p. ix.

66. Ibid.

67. Quoted in the introduction to *Poems from Mandelstam*, p. 17 (see note 13).

68. In 1935, Mandelstam wrote his own version of what he thought would be his official fate:

> *What street's this one?*
> *—This is Mandelshtam Street.*
> *His disposition wasn't "party-line"*
> *Or "sweet-as-a-flower."*
> *That's why this street—*
> *Or, rather, sewer*
> *Or possibly slum—*
> *Has been named after*
> *Osip Mandelshtam.*

Mandelstam has been "rehabilitated" in Russia, but there is still no street named for him. The preceding poem is to be found in the translator's preface to *Osip Mandelshtam: The Eyesight of Wasps*, trans. James Greene, forewords Nadezhda Mandelshtam and Donald Davie, intro. Donald Rayfield (Columbus: Ohio State University Press, 1989), p. 17.

69. Exile has long been a major theme in Cixous's study of the coming to writing in others, and in her own writing. It was, for example, the central critical strand of her earliest theoretical work, her doctoral dissertation on James Joyce, available in English translation under the title *The Exile of James Joyce*, trans. Sally A. J. Purcell (London: John Calder, 1976). The theme of exile is ever present in *Manna*, on a literal, political level, as well as on the poetic, mythological level of the weave of writing. Cixous has said about the writing of *Manna*: "I had never noticed that fundamentally, exile was inscribed in my texts from the very beginning. Which means it is always new, which means it is always happening to me. It comes back like a kind of state, it is a human state." "A propos de *Manne*. Entretien avec Hélène Cixous," p. 215, my translation.

70. Quoted in the introduction by Clarence Brown to *Osip Mandelstam: Selected Poems*, p. xii. During this time, Mandelstam turned to prose and translation, completing his "anti-memoir," *The Noise of Time*, and his novella *The Egyptian Stamp*, which explores the effects of the Russian revolution on the naive poetic persona. Both appear in *The Prose of Osip Mandelstam*, trans. Clarence Brown (Berkeley, Calif.: North Point Press, 1967).

71. One English version of the complete poem is as follows:

> *We live without feeling the country beneath us,*
> *our speech at ten paces inaudible,*
>
> *and where there are enough for half a conversation*
> *the name of the Kremlin mountaineer is dropped.*

His thick fingers are fatty like worms,
but his words are as true as pound weights.

His cockroach whiskers laugh,
and the tops of his boots shine.

Around him a rabble of thick-skinned leaders,
he plays with the attentions of half-men.

Some whistle, some miaul, some snivel,
but he just bangs and pokes.

He forges his decrees like horseshoes—
some get it in the groin, some in the forehead,
    some in the brows, some in the eyes.

Whatever the punishment he gives—raspberries,
and the broad chest of an Ossete.

From *Osip Mandelstam: Selected Poems*, trans. David McDuff (New York: Farrar, Straus, Giroux, 1975), p. 131.

72. "Osip Mandelshtam: An Introduction," by Donald Rayfield, in *Osip Mandelshtam: The Eyesight of Wasps*, p. 31.

73. For a look at Hélène Cixous's seminars on these themes and poets, see *Readings*, ed. and trans. Verena Andermatt Conley (Minneapolis: University of Minnesota Press, 1991).

74. Shiach, *Hélène Cixous: A Politics of Writing*, p. 102.

75. Ibid.

76. Mandelstam was greatly influenced by his reading of Lamarck's original *Philosophie zoologique* of 1809. He felt that Lamarck's imaging of the evolutionary process as a ladder echoed Dante's nine circles of hell. Mandelstam saw Lamarckian correspondences in Ariosto's poem "Biology" as well as in Petrarch's sonnets.

77. Even before exile, he had written as the first line to his poem "Tristia": "I have studied a science of good-byes." (See Clarence Brown and W. S. Merwin's version of this poem in *Osip Mandelstam: Selected Poems*, p. 23.) This sentiment could be said of *Manna*, the Mandelas, or the Mandelstams.

78. Shiach, *Hélène Cixous: A Politics of Writing*, p. 102.

79. In Nadezhda Mandelstam, *Hope against Hope*, p. 378.

80. The preceding discussion of Osip Mandelstam is greatly indebted to my reading of the introductions to and the translations of the works cited.

81. See, for example, the figure of Saint Georges ("Sein-Georges") in

Cixous's *Le troisième corps* (Paris: Grasset, 1970), and the Jean Genet ("Jenais") figure in Cixous's *Souffles* (Paris: Editions des femmes, 1975).

82. For an analysis of *Souffles*, which marked the beginnings of the Cixousian thematic of the breath, *le souffle*, see Susan Rubin Suleiman, *Subversive Intent* (Cambridge, Mass.: Harvard University Press, 1990), pp. 128-30.

83. My thanks to Professor Christiane Makward of Pennsylvania State University, who brought this passage and its relevance to my attention.

84. This might be as good a moment as any to contend that since Nelson Mandela's release from prison on February 11, 1990, Winnie Mandela has been pushed aside and maligned, her heroism gone unrecognized because of errors that, if committed, were committed as if by a war veteran. Or, as Jill Smolowe wrote in her article "Winnie's Walk into Obscurity," which appeared in *Time* magazine (April 27, 1992, p. 47): "Now comes the word that Winnie and Nelson are separating. Were they any other couple, the real news would be that their marriage lasted as long as it did." It is sad and eerie to read Cixous's love story in the light of what we now know comes after: more separation for the couple, and a seeming lack of generosity of spirit shown by the international community toward Winnie Mandela, one of the many casualties of the struggle against apartheid and a woman who was once seen by many, and still is by some, as the mother of black South Africa.

The preceding is the translator's opinion. Cixous herself has called any questions about the current fate of the "real-life" Mandelas irrelevant to her work. She pointed out, when speaking of *Manna* at the conference "Exploring the Unexplored," that the Mandelas poeticized here "are my Mandelas, not the 'real' Mandelas," in the manner of Marina Tsvetayeva's essay *My Pushkin* (see *Marina Tsvetayeva, a Captive Spirit: Selected Prose*, ed. and trans. J. Marin King [Ann Arbor: Ardis Books, 1980]). In "A propos de *Manne*. Entretien avec Hélène Cixous," Cixous says of *Manna*: "If I were writing a political work, I would be obliged to take into account a thousand other factors. Including that the Mandelas, the heroes of my story, have adversaries not only among the whites but among the blacks. The blacks themselves are prey to division and exclusion . . . If I were writing a play, I would take this into account. Here I am writing a fictional text, like a great poem, and, in this space, reflection on the political machine doesn't interest me, because it is a machine" (p. 217, my translation).

85. See Suggested Further Reading for listings of their works.

86. Conley, *Hélène Cixous*, p. 93.

87. What I go on to offer here is another way of reading what Morag Shiach has called Cixous's "version of Winnie as the patient, passive, and silent woman, whose identity has no significance apart from her relationship with Nelson. At times, indeed, [Cixous] sees such self-obliteration as part of

the power of Winnie, which allows her to sustain the loss and separation of so many years. . . . there are echoes of *Promethea* in this intense, erotic intersubjective relation, but when applied to a relationship between a man and a woman, who live within the structures of contemporary political struggle, such representations can only be uncomfortable in their familiarity" (*Hélène Cixous: A Politics of Writing*, p. 103).

88. Again, Morag Shiach reads the text otherwise: "Cixous uses Winnie's African name, Zami, in order to suggest the complexity of her identity as one caught between the tribal relations and the political structures of modernity. The version of her African identity we are offered, however, seems to reinforce many myths that serve to place Africa 'outside' the political space of the contemporary, and to associate it with the mysterious, the ancient, and the natural" (ibid., p. 104).

89. P. 70.

90. To recollect the myth, see Virgil's *Eclogues and Georgics*, trans. T. F. Royds (New York: Dutton, 1965). Blanchot, *The Space of Literature*, trans. Ann Smock (Lincoln: University of Nebraska Press, 1982), p. 175. The poet Rainer Maria Rilke has also written about Eurydice, in his *Sonnets to Orpheus*, trans. M. D. Herter (New York: Norton, 1962). And Cixous wrote her own version of this myth in her 1970 fiction *Le troisième corps*, in which she explores the position of the woman writer with regard to Orpheus.

91. Blanchot, *The Space of Literature*, p. 172.

92. The book's epigraph reads: "A book, even a fragmentary one, has a center which attracts it. . . . He who writes the book writes it out of desire for this center . . . here, towards the pages entitled 'Orpheus's Gaze.' "

93. See Conley, *Hélène Cixous: Writing the Feminine*, p. 107.

94. Blanchot, *The Space of Literature*, p. 176.

95. Ibid., p. 172.

96. Statement made at her seminar at the University of Paris-VIII on December 1, 1979; my notes.

97. (Paris: Editions des femmes, 1980).

98. See Conley, *Hélène Cixous: Writing the Feminine*, p. 114.

99. To reread the myth, turn to Ovid's *Metamorphoses*, trans. Mary M. Innes (Harmondsworth: Penguin, 1955). Cixous has often chosen to rewrite mythic stories, particularly those whose female figures have proven unreadable to the paternal representatives of phallogocentrism as anything but signs of silence, weakness, treachery, or death.

100. See Conley, *Hélène Cixous: Writing the Feminine*, p. 97.

101. This is Conley's formulation (ibid., p. 103). I owe my reading of *Illa*, and my understanding of Cixous's work in general, in part to Conley's groundbreaking first book.

102. See, for example, Jacques Derrida's essay "Differance," in *Margins of Philosophy*, trans. Alan Bass (Chicago: University of Chicago Press, 1982), pp. 1-27.

103. Hélène Cixous, *With ou l'art de l'innocence* (Paris: Editions des femmes, 1981), *Le livre de Promethea* (Paris: Gallimard, 1983), and *La Bataille d'Arcachon* (Québec: Trois, 1986). Shiach, *Hélène Cixous: A Politics of Writing*, p. 101.

104. Here I am informed by Carolyn Burke's responses to criticisms of similar tropes of the body in the work of Luce Irigaray. See "Irigaray through the Looking Glass," *Feminist Studies*, 7, no. 2 (Summer 1981).

105. See *The Standard Edition*, vol. 14.

106. There may be a partial correlation between Cixous's notion of the maternal as linked to life and Julia Kristeva's study of the Virgin Mary, who, Kristeva says, represents "the conviction that death does not exist . . . an unreasonable but unshakable maternal certainty, upon which the principle of resurrection must have rested for support." See "Stabat Mater," trans. Arthur Goldhammer, in *The Female Body in Western Culture*, ed. Susan Rubin Suleiman (Cambridge, Mass.: Harvard University Press, 1986), p. 110.

107. "Interview with Hélène Cixous," in *Cixous Dossier*, ed. and trans. Catherine A. Franke, p. 167.

108. "The Laugh of the Medusa," *Signs: A Journal of Women in Culture and Society*, 1, no. 4 (Summer 1976).

109. Critical theorists might wish to ponder the positions posed here in relation to the well-known "series" of position papers on reading and writing in or from one's place: Peggy Kamuf's "Writing Like a Woman," in *Women and Language in Literature and Society*, ed. Sally McConnell-Ginet, Ruth Borker, and Nelly Furman (New York: Praeger, 1980), pp. 284-99; Jonathan Culler's "Reading as a Woman," in *On Deconstruction: Theory and Criticism after Structuralism* (Ithaca, N.Y.: Cornell University Press, 1982), pp. 43-64; Robert Scholes's "Reading Like a Man," in *Men in Feminism*, ed. Alice Jardine and Paul Smith (New York: Methuen, 1987), pp. 204-18; and Diana Fuss's "Reading Like a Feminist," in *Essentially Speaking: Feminism, Nature, and Difference*, pp. 23-37.

110. "Interview with Hélène Cixous," in *Cixous Dossier*, p. 178.

111. Ibid., pp. 178-79.

112. Deborah Jenson, "Coming to Reading Hélène Cixous," in *"Coming to Writing" and Other Essays*, p. 185.

113. In a television interview on the CUNY channel in New York City, Octavio Paz contended that there is a "religious substance" found in many twentieth-century artists, and he cited Kafka, Neruda, and Matisse as examples. We would have to add Hélène Cixous and the great twentieth-century Brazilian writer Clarice Lispector to this list, as well as many others, and my emphasis in taking up this Pazian category would be on the word "sub-

stance." For manna, like Clarice's cockroach, is a food. (For a discussion of the cockroach in Lispector's novel *The Passion according to G.H.*, trans. Ronald W. Sousa [Minneapolis: University of Minnesota Press, 1988], see Cixous's essay "Clarice Lispector: The Approach," in *"Coming to Writing" and Other Essays*, pp. 59-77.)

114. Jenson, "Coming to Reading Hélène Cixous," in *"Coming to Writing" and Other Essays*, p. 189.

115. In lowercase in the text.

116. "Interview with Hélène Cixous," in *Cixous Dossier*, p. 176.

117. In discussion at the conference "Exploring the Unexplored," Cixous answered her own question in this way: "To invite real historical characters into one's political texts is a terrible risk, but I have taken that risk. One is accompanied by these risks, like by swords, all the time of the writing. But the fear is of the reception, not of the writing. On the other hand, there is no privileged hell. We are all allowed to go to hell. We are all allowed to enjoy the sublime sufferings of hell. We all have a permit for hell—and this is our blessing. 'Our soul is our aptitude for suffering,' as Tsvetayeva said. This is our common lot."

118. Conley, *Hélène Cixous*, p. 132.

119. Conley's formulation, from *Hélène Cixous: Writing the Feminine*, p. 106. Morag Shiach is left with a different feeling after reading *Manna*, and, in *Hélène Cixous: A Politics of Writing*, concludes her comments on this text with the following provocative criticism: "Despite [the] difficulties, *Manne* is a courageous text. Such public identification by a writer with the armed struggle of the ANC is far from usual. The implications of such a commitment, however, remain unclear, precisely because of the strong parallel Cixous draws between the Mandelas and the Mandelstams as figures of resistance. Writing poetry and waging a guerrilla war are not the same, yet *Manne* deals with both at a level of abstraction that renders such distinction almost irrelevant. We are thus left with a slight feeling that some important questions have been evaded by the sheer virtuosity of Cixous's metaphorical associations" (p. 104).

120. In Betsy Wing, "A Translator's Imaginary Choices," Hélène Cixous, *The Book of Promethea*, trans. Betsy Wing (Lincoln: University of Nebraska Press, 1991), p. vii.

121. It is interesting to note that in the somewhat controversial *New History of French Literature* (ed. Denis Hollier [Cambridge, Mass.: Harvard University Press, 1989]), which has been accused of having "shrunk" the canon by including previously marginalized (women) writers and excluding more problematic rightist ones, Cixous's *writings* only figure in the essay entitled "French Feminism"(although she is mentioned by name only in two other essays). In that essay, Cixous, an extraordinarily prolific and creative writer, who has produced over thirty texts of poetic fiction in the last thirty

years, is only mentioned as a "feminist" and proponent of *écriture féminine*, although her major contribution has not been primarily of that order. Furthermore, only two of her texts are mentioned specifically, "Le Rire de la Méduse" and "La Jeune Née," neither of which fully represents her enormous production and strength as a writer of avant-garde fiction and poetry. As Morag Shiach puts it, "Cixous's writing . . . cannot be reduced to one 'position,' or summed up by reference to one or two of her texts" (*Hélène Cixous: A Politics of Writing*, p. 2). (For an overview of the polemic surrounding the Hollier volume, as well as an insightful analysis, see, for example, Naomi Schor, "The Righting of French Studies: Homosociality and the Killing of 'La pensée 68,'" "*Profession 92*, MLA Publications, 1992, pp. 28-34.)

122. This is a Cixousian construct, inspired by Kleist's essay "The Puppet Theatre," found in *An Abyss Deep Enough: The Letters of Heinrich von Kleist, with a Selection of Essays and Anecdotes*, ed., trans., and introduced Phillip B. Miller (New York: Dutton, 1982). See, for example, Cixous's essay "The Last Painting or the Portrait of God" in *"Coming to Writing" and Other Essays* (pp. 104-31) where she writes of a second innocence: "I call 'poet' any writing being who sets out on this path, in quest of what I call the second innocence, the one that comes after knowing, the one that no longer knows, the one that knows how not to know."

123. See *Hélène Cixous*, p. 103.

124. Derrida, *The Ear of the Other*, trans. Peggy Kamuf (New York: Schocken, 1985), p. 122. Quoted in Diana Fuss, *Essentially Speaking*, p. 83.

125. In Wing, "A Translator's Imaginary Choices," p. viii.

126. See Cixous, "Without End no State of Drawingness no, rather: The Executioner's Taking Off," trans. Catherine A. F. MacGillivray, *New Literary History*, 24, no. 1 (February 1993), p. 91.

127. It is interesting to note the extent to which *écriture féminine* is embedded in music and the voice, similarly to current African-American literary criticism's association of the black "vernacular" with its own auditory vocabularies. See, for example, Houston A. Baker, Jr., *Blues, Ideology, and Afro-American Literature: A Vernacular Theory* (Chicago: University of Chicago Press, 1984). Diana Fuss has suggested that "the key to blackness is not visual but *auditory*" for critics like Baker (*Essentially Speaking*, p. 90). Perhaps the same can be said for critics and writers of "femininity."

128. For a reflection on the question of voice in translations of Cixous's work, see Betsy Wing's excellent analysis in "A Translator's Imaginary Choices," pp. viii-xi.

129. In "A propos de *Manne*. Entretien avec Hélène Cixous," p. 227, my translation.

130. Katherine Cummings, *Telling Tales: The Hysteric's Seduction in Fiction and Theory* (Stanford, Calif.: Stanford University Press, 1991), p. 8. See Shoshana Felman, "To Open the Question," in *Literature and Psycho-*

analysis. The Question of Reading: Otherwise, ed. Felman (Baltimore: Johns Hopkins University Press, 1982), p. 9.

131. In *Selected Writings*, vol. 2 (The Hague: Mouton, 1971).

132. As quoted in the translator's preface to *Osip Mandelshtam: The Eyesight of Wasps*, p. 15.

Translator's Notes to Manna

The following notes are offered to provide quick definitions of lesser-known geographical and other proper names, to give insight into some of the translation choices in relation to the original, and as an aid to those interested in exploring the intertextualities at work in the weaving of the text that is Hélène Cixous's *Manna*. I wish to stress that the notes mark an intertextuality, and nothing more or less, for any referentiality in relation to a particular "reality" is not operational here. The companions to this text are other texts: memoirs, biographies, autobiographies, oral histories, and poems. In providing these notes I do not mean to contribute to any illusion of referentiality, for *Manna* is a fiction, "which then, however, in its turn, acquires a degree of referential productivity," as de Man has said. (See Paul de Man, "Autobiography as Defacement," *MLN* 94, MLA Publications, 1979, quoted in Nancy K. Miller, "Facts, Pacts, Acts," *Profession* 92, MLA Publications, New York, 1992, pp. 10-14.) Or, to quote Foucault, who said of his own writing what could be said of the texts that fed the writing of *Manna* and of *Manna* itself: "I am fully aware that I have never written anything other than fictions. For all that, I would not want to say that they were outside the truth. It seems plausible to me to make fictions work within truth, to introduce truth-effects within a fictional discourse, and in some way to make discourse arouse, 'fabricate,' something which does not yet exist, thus to fiction something. . . . One 'fictions' history starting from a political reality that renders it true, one 'fictions' a politics that does not yet exist starting from a historical truth." (See *Michel Foucault: Power, Truth, Strategy*, ed. M. Morris and P. Patton [Sydney: Feral, 1979], p. 75. Quoted in Linda Hutcheon, "Response: Truth Telling," *Professional 92*, MLA Publications, New York, 1992, pp. 18-20.) Indeed, we must wonder if this statement by Foucault isn't an excellent definition of all writing, to the extent that the impossibility of ever escaping the figurative in any system of representation can be said to hold "true."

---

1. "And as birds, risen from the shore, as if rejoicing together at their pasture, make of themselves now a round flock, now some other shape, so within the lights holy creatures were singing as they flew, and in their figures made of themselves now *D*, now *I*, now *L*." *The Divine Comedy*, trans. Charles S. Singleton (Princeton, N.J.: Princeton University Press, 1975). See the introduction to this volume for a reference to this canto of the *Paradiso*.

2. A black-earth steppe region in south-central European Russia; also, its capital. When Mandelstam was arrested on May 13, 1934, he tried to commit suicide in a mental hospital in Cherdyn. Thanks to the intervention of Nadezhda and others, Stalin himself agreed to allow Mandelstam to choose another place of exile. He chose Voronezh, because of its associations with Russian poetry, and because it lay in the European part of Russia. The Mandelstams were in exile in Voronezh for three years, until 1937. The poems Mandelstam wrote there, referred to as the "Voronezh cycle" or the "Voronezh notebooks," are considered among his finest. See the Introduction for a further discussion of these poems.

3. See note 23 to the Introduction for an explanation of the juxtaposition of worms and verse.

4. Reference to the biblical story of Samson and Delilah (Judges 16:21). Samson was blinded by the Philistines in Gaza for having lain with Delilah. Later, Samson killed himself and the Philistines when he caused their house to fall down around them (Judges 16:30).

5. Winnie and Nelson Mandela's African heritage and native language is Xhosa (see note 19).

6. Maat is the ancient Egyptian personification of the world order, incorporating the concepts of justice, truth, and legality. She is the daughter of Ra, creator of the world. *Pharaoh* means "beloved of Maat, he who lives in her through his laws." A favored venue for judicial hearings was before her shrines, and judges were regarded as her priests. In Egyptian art, Maat is depicted with an ostrich feather in her hair.

7. Winnie's nickname, from her Pondo name Nomzamo. Her full name is Nomzamo Winnie Madikizela Mandela.

8. Zami's native village, Bizana, is in Pondoland, near the Cape-Natal border, close to the Umtamvuna River. Meaning "a small plot," Bizana was an independent territory until 1894, and has historically been the scene of many tribal battles. Zami has described her homeland thus: "The part of Pondoland where I come from is still totally tribal; tribesmen still congregate on the hills, wearing their traditional blankets." (See *Part of My Soul Went with Him* [New York and London: Norton, 1984], p. 46.)

9. "And as their wings bear the starlings along in the cold season, in wide, dense flocks, so does that blast the sinful spirits; hither, thither, downward, upward, it drives them. No hope of less pain, not to say of rest, ever comforts them." Dante's *Inferno*, canto V. The "sinful spirits" referred to here are Paolo and Francesca (see note 89).

10. A province of South Africa, on the Indian Ocean. Its capital is Pietermaritzburg.

11. In French: *je suis*, meaning potentially both "I am" and "I follow." Cixous often calls upon these two meanings in a single context, so I have chosen to include them both in English. See notes 18 and 53 for other examples of this polyvalent use of *je suis*.

12. Nelson's Tembu name. The common shortened version of his name is Nelson Rolihlahla Mandela.

13. The phrase "on the island" has only one meaning for most South Africans, that of the prison on Robben Island, where Nelson spent the first eighteen years of his life sentence, before being moved to a maximum security prison on the mainland. There are many references in *Manna* to the metaphor of the island itself as representing a geographical prison, with its limited land patch surrounded by a seemingly endless sea and a barely visible sky.

Nelson is of the Madiba clan or family of the Tembu group. His great-great-grandfather was King A-a-a Dalibunga! of the Madibas. He sometimes signed his letters to Winnie "Madiba." (See *Part of My Soul Went with Him*, p. 139.)

14. Steve Biko founded the South African Students' Organization, an all-black group that rejected any commitment to multiracial movements,

and the Black Consciousness movement when he was a student at the University of Natal in the late 1960s and early 1970s. After being expelled from the university in 1972, he worked with the Black Community Program in his hometown of King William's Town, to which he was restricted. In 1976, he used his testimony in the trial for treason of nine Black youths to broadcast his philosophy of Black Consciousness. He was arrested on August 18, 1977, and died in police custody on September 12, 1977.

15. Reference to Dr. J. O. Loubser, chief state pathologist, who conducted the postmortem on Steve Biko's body on September 13, 1977. He and a team of two others determined that Biko had died, in contradiction to the police account, as a result of head injuries, which, he went on to say, could have been self-inflicted.

16. From the Arab word for infidel, a pejorative name used by whites to refer to a South African Black or "Bantu," Bantu being the name and the categorization used by whites to designate a large group of indigenous tribal peoples living in central and southern Africa, including the Tembu and the Xhosa, all of whom use the root *ntu* (hence "Ba*ntu*") to mean "a person," and whose languages have other linguistic similarities.

17. Said by the ghost, Hamlet's father, in Shakespeare's *Hamlet*, act 1, scene 5.

18. In French: *je te suis* (see note 11).

19. The Xhosa are a pastoral people living in Cape Province, South Africa. Their language is widely spoken and is characterized by the use of clicks. Winnie Mandela is a Xhosa from the Pondoland. Nelson Mandela learned the Xhosa language in the mission school in Qunu, where he was educated.

The Swazi are the Black African tribe of Swaziland, in southeastern Africa. Their language is SiSwati, and like Xhosa it is a click language. They are part of the Nzuni group within the Bantu subfamily of the Niger-Congo group. The Swazi are primarily farmers, producing corn and millet. Livestock raising confers higher prestige, with cattle serving as an index of wealth and status.

The Tembu are a people of the Eastern Cape Province, who today are settled in Tembuland, a region lying mainly between the Umtata and Mbashe rivers in the Transkei. The Tembu farm this fertile area, growing maize, grain sorghum, and tobacco; they also raise cattle, sheep, and goats. Nelson Mandela is a Tembu, and he is of their royal family, a descendant of the great Tembu warrior-kings Shaka and Dingaan. (See note 13.)

The Zulu are the great Black African nation, also of southeastern Africa.

The Sotho-swana are the western Sotho peoples, comprising more than fifty groups and known as the Tswana. The Tswana live in the northern Cape Province, the western Transvaal, and Botswana; some are also scattered in small numbers throughout South Africa. Among the largest and best known family groups are the Kwena at Molepolole, the Mangwato at Serowe, the Ngwaketse at Kanye, and the Kglata at Mochudi. They speak dialects of the Tswana language, including a dialect called Sotho. There is much ethnic, religious, and traditional diversity within Tswana tribes—anyone found to be of good character may be granted Tswana citizenship by the chief. Tribal chiefs are believed to represent the spirits of ancestors and are endowed with much political power in their towns, despite the impact of white rule. Today, hunting has virtually disappeared, and as a result the sexual division of labor has lessened. Entire families participate in cultivating their land as subsistence farmers.

The Venda are the people of the traditional Venda homeland of South Africa. The Venda became self-governing in 1973.

The Zulu, Pondo, Tembu, and Xhosa are all "families" descended from the same people, the Niguni. In *Manna*, the author refers to Winnie Mandela as a Pondo, subfamily of the Xhosa, and to Nelson as a Tembu, and a Xhosa speaker. In other writings, Nelson is frequently referred to as a Xhosa, although he is specifically descended from the Madiba clan of the Tembu.

The Tsonga are a Tswana people, descendants—from as far back as the Iron Age—of the same people as the Sotho.

20. In French, blood, *le sang*, is masculine, and although I have chosen not to maintain this gender specificity, which is awkward in English, in French the blood is clearly also a "he."

21. Umtata is the name of both a district in Tembuland and the capital town of the Transkei, located in the Umtata district. Umtata was founded as a "buffer zone" between the warring chiefs of the Pondos and the Tembus, thereby establishing colonial privileges for white settlers. Today, Umtata is a powerful legislative, administrative, and commercial center in the Transkei and home to the Commissioner-General of the Xhosa.

22. In the following two paragraphs there is a subtle and complex intertwining of subjects and object pronouns at play that is lost in English, between the masculine and feminine, with the Beast, *la bête*, and the almond, *l'amande*, representing the feminine pole and the animal, *l'animal*, the lover, *l'amant*, and the name, *le nom*, representing the masculine pole in Nelson.

23. In December 1956 Mandela was one of 156 men and women of all races arrested on charges of treason. The trial, which came to be known as the Treason Trial, took place in a court that was once a synagogue. On March 29, 1961, the defendants were found not guilty.

24. Reference to Ferdinand, Prince of Naples, central character in Shakespeare's *The Tempest*.

25. In French, the car, *la voiture*, is feminine, and there is a play throughout this passage with the feminine pronouns, suggesting perhaps that the car's fidelity is due in part to "her" femininity.

26. In French, the neological portmanteau word *voudrage*.

27. The traditional Xhosa bride price.

28. South African pet name meaning "grandmother"; from the Dutch.

29. A grain commonly eaten by the Xhosa.

30. A separate municipality, but under the jurisdiction of Johannesburg city; this is the township where Winnie and Nelson were initially to make their home.

31. In French, the antelope is feminine (and the crocodile is masculine, as is the hippopotamus), and I have chosen to inscribe this gender distinction in English so as to maintain the ambiguity and proximity between the subject antelope and the subject Zami.

32. Table Mountain is just south of Cape Town, overlooking the city of Table Bay. Its summit is flat and often shrouded in a white mist, referred to as its "tablecloth."

33. B. J. Voerster became the Minister of Justice in South Africa in the early 1960s. It was he who passed the well-known and internationally protested "ninety-day law" giving the South African Security Police the right to detain people for interrogation without formally charging them, even in solitary confinement and without access to counsel, for up to ninety days. This law immediately led to thousands of arrests and to the first deaths in prison believed to have been caused by torture during interrogation.

34. In lowercase in the French.

35. Bloemfontein is a South African city located southwest of Johannesburg; it is the capital of the Orange Free State, which was founded in 1854 as an independent Boer republic.

36. An Orlando police officer. Winnie wrote of him, "I can't remember any junior court finding me not guilty except when I had assaulted Sergeant Fourie. The irony of it — the things I have not done, I've been found guilty of, and the only thing I did to my heart's satisfaction, I was not guilty of." (Winnie Mandela, *Part of My Soul Went with Him*, p. 88.)

37. The African National Congress, founded in 1912 at a conference of tribal leaders.

38. "From the Hebrew, meaning 'help of God,' the angel of death, who, in ancient Jewish and Moslem belief, parts the soul from the body" (*Webster's*).

39. In French, *la vie*, "life," is feminine, as it is in Russian, and here "she" is anthropomorphized.

40. In French: *sans air sans aile, sans aime sans o sans l sans o . . .*

41. The Transkei is an area in South Africa bounded by the Great Kei, Tembuland, and the Indian Ocean.

42. In Danakil, a northeastern coastal country home to the Afars and Issas, Hamitic peoples who inhabit this arid region due east. Also known as the Danakil, they speak a Cushitic language. Their official religion is Islam. They number about 110,000 and are divided into two classes: the nobles, or "red men," and the commoners, or "white men." Pastoral nomads, they wander the desert with herds of camels, sheep, goats, and donkeys. They also mine salt.

43. Pondoland, Zami's homeland, is a part of the Transkeian Territories and is bounded by Tembuland, Griqualand, Natal Province, and the Indian Ocean. Its capital is Port St. Johns. Its chief products are citrus fruit, bananas, and tobacco; dairy farming, stock raising, and forestry are also carried out there.

44. Nelson and Zami's daughters, Zenani and Zindziswa.

45. Father Leo Rakale of the Anglican Church, who was a great help and comfort to Winnie in the worst of times, including during her seventeen months spent in solitary confinement at Pretoria Central Prison.

46. Brandfort is a small South African town, located in the west-central region of the Orange Free State, northeast of Bloemfontein. Before Winnie Mandela's banishment there, Brandfort was best known as the town that shaped the Afrikaner Nationalist identity of Dr. Hendrik Verwoerd, architect of apartheid. The Afrikaner Nationalists came to power with their policy of apartheid in 1948. Brandfort is located in the typical South African *platteland*, at the very center of the Afrikaner territory. Winnie Mandela has referred to the Orange Free State as the "kingdom of the Afrikaner" (see *Part of My Soul Went with Him*, p. 27). The local black African language is Sotho. (For a description of the Sotho, see note 19.)

47. In French: *seul bien*, which can also be translated as "sole possession." I have chosen to translate *bien* as "good," because in this way "wrath" is qualified, as it is in French, as both a last possession and a positive attribute. This choice of the word "good" or "goods" will occur again as a translation for *bien* or *biens*, and the reader should be aware of the semic tensions at work around these words.

48. The word for "moon" in French is feminine, *la lune*, and here, "she" is anthropomorphized.

49. Reference to the arrest that led to the Mandelstams' three-year exile in Voronezh (see note 2).

50. A poet and friend of the Mandelstams, whom they met in 1933 in Koktebel. Bely, whose real name was Bugaev, was one of the greatest of the Russian Symbolists, and his book, *Symbolism*, greatly influenced Mandelstam's generation of poets and intellectuals.

51. Reference to the poem by Mandelstam "10 January 1934," the date of Andrei Bely's burial. One English version of this poem, translated by

Clarence Brown and W. S. Merwin (*Osip Mandelstam: Selected Poems* [London: Oxford University Press, 1973], pp. 72-73), is as follows:

I am haunted by a few chance phrases,
repeating all day "the rich oil of my sadness."
O God how black are the dragonflies of death,
how blue their eyes, and how black is that blue!

Where is the rule of the first-born? Or the felicity of
    custom?
Or the tiny hawk that melts deep in the eyes?
Or learning? Or the bitter taste of stealth?
Or the firm outline? Or the straightness of speech?

honestly weaving back and forth,
a skater into a blue flame,
his blades in the frosty air braiding
the clink of glasses in a glacier?

Ahead of him solutions of three-layered salts,
the voices of German wise men,
fifty years of the glittering disputes
of the Russian first-born, rose in half an hour.

Suddenly music leapt from ambush—
a tiger was hiding in the instruments—
not to be heard, not to soften a thing,
it moved in the name of the muscles, of the drumming
    forehead,

of the tender mask just removed,
of the plaster fingers holding no pen,
of the puffed lips, of the hardened caress,
of the chrystallized calm and goodness.

The furs on the coat breathed. Shoulder pressed shoulder.
Health was a red ore boiling—blood, sweat.
Sleep in the jacket of sleep, that held once
a dream of moving half a step forward.

And there was an engraver in the crowd
proposing to transfer onto pure copper
what the draftsmen, blackening paper,
merely sketched in split hair.

So I may hang on my own eyelashes,
swelling, ripening, reading all the parts of the play
till I'm picked.
The plot is the one thing we know.

52. This clause plays on the homophonic relationship in French between "I'm not writing," *je n'écris pas*, and "I'm being born," *je nais*.

53. This whole passage plays on the ambiguity of the French enunciation *je suis*, which means currently both "I am" and "I follow."

54. In French, the noun for truth, *la vérité*, is feminine, and here "she" is anthropomorphized.

55. Russian city, located on a narrow watershed between the right banks of the Volga and the Sviyaga rivers, southeast of Moscow. Renamed Ulyanovsk in 1978, after Vladimir I. Ulyanov Lenin. It is a major port for the manufacture of trucks.

56. Mount Ararat is the highest peak in Turkey, near its borders with Iran and Russia. It is traditionally considered to be the landing place of Noah's ark. The Ararat region is identified with Armenia in many ancient records. Mandelstam refers to it in his long poem *Armenia*, written after his sojourn there in 1930. This cycle of poems, published posthumously, represented Mandelstam's first effort at writing after five years of silence and was a direct result of his visit to the region. See the Introduction for a further discussion of this period in Mandelstam's life.

57. Emma Gerstein was a literary scholar and a close friend of the Mandelstams and of Anna Akhmatova. She was the author of *Lermontov's Fate*.

58. Russian city where the Mandelstams were exiled before being moved to Voronezh (see note 2). Located on the right bank of the Kolva River, Cherdyn was an important trading center in the nineteenth century.

59. Russian river that flows west to the Gulf of Finland, forming a delta mouth at the port of Leningrad. A canalized channel is navigable from April to November. It is connected to the Volga River and the Caspian and White seas.

60. Nijni or New Novgorod is a Russian city located on the Volkhov River, southeast of Leningrad. The Volga is the largest river in Europe; located in Central European Russia, it is Russia's principal navigable water

artery. It has a total length of approximately 2,290 miles and forms its delta below the city of Astrakhan, located near the Caspian Sea. Astrakhan is the major Caspian port.

61. The Taiga are the coniferous forests in the far northern regions of Eurasia and North America. Taiga, also spelled Tayga, is also a city on the Trans-Siberian Railroad.

62. Adelaide Joseph was a close friend of Winnie Mandela's who worked alongside her in the FSAW (see note 80). She was Indian and was married to Paul Joseph, one of the original Treason trialists with Nelson.

63. In French, the word for voice, *la voix*, is feminine, hence its feminine personification in this instance.

64. Koktebel was a resort in the Crimea, popular with writers in the 1930s (see note 50).

65. The poem referred to here is Mandelstam's famous satirical epigram against Stalin, which cost him his freedom and eventually his life. One English version of the text of the complete poem can be found in the notes to the Introduction.

66. A native of the Ossetic region in the Russian Caucasus, bordering on Georgia; Stalin was, in fact, a Georgian. Osip Mandelstam often called him "the Osset."

67. Reference to the character of the Prince in Dostoevski's novel *The Idiot*.

68. In French, "death," *la mort*, is a feminine noun, as it is in Russian, and in this passage it is anthropomorphized; therefore, I have chosen to inscribe death as a female allegorical figure in English as well, although this rendering is less subtle than in the original.

69. It seemed to me important here to maintain the French so as to maintain the letter *V*, which is picked up again in the flight pattern of the birds three paragraphs down, and in the first letter of several of the Russian cities mentioned, including the city of Mandelstam's death, Vladivostok. An English version of these two words could be: Ali*v*e . . . Arri*v*e, words that are in evidence in the translation throughout the rest of the next section, and which in French give the visual impression that the entire section is covered with scattered *V*'s, an impression I have tried to inspire in English too.

70. Vladivostok is a Russian city located on the southern tip of the Muravyev-Amurski Peninsula between Amur and Golden Horn bays, southeast of Moscow. This was Mandelstam's last address, where he was sent after being sentenced to five years in exile for "counterrevolutionary activity" by the Special Tribunal. He was first sent to Butyrki Prison in Moscow, from where he was transported by train on September 9, arriving in Vladivostok on October 12. The letter to his brother Alexander Emilievich Mandelstam, referred to farther down, was written sometime between October 20 and 30, 1938, approximately two months before his death. This was the first exile

Osip had to endure alone, and it is widely believed that had Nadezhda been allowed to accompany him, she could have seen to his survival.

71. Reference to one of Mandelstam's poems from the Voronezh cycle, written in exile sometime in 1936 or 1937. One English translation is as follows:

> *Into the distance go the mounds of people's heads.*
> *I am growing smaller here — no one notices me anymore,*
> *but in caressing books and children's games*
> *I will rise from the dead to say the sun is shining.*

From McDuff, trans. *Osip Mandelstam: Selected Poems*, p. 133.

72. In Dante's *Inferno*, canto XVII, Geryon appears as the monster of Fraud, who will carry Virgil and Dante on his back and fly them down to the part of Hell that houses the Fraudulent and the Malicious. Dante gives Geryon, usually depicted as having three heads and three bodies, the general shape of a dragon and the capacity to fly.

73. Mandelstam carried a copy of Dante's *Divine Comedy* around with him in his jacket pocket for many years. According to his wife, Nadezhda, this was "just in case he was arrested not at home but in the street." (See *Hope against Hope: A Memoir*, trans. Max Hayward [New York: Atheneum, 1970], p. 228). Mandelstam referred frequently to Dante and *The Divine Comedy* in his own poetry. One of Mandelstam's prose sketches is entitled "Conversation about Dante." This sketch appears in English translation in *The Prose of Mandelstam*; see Suggested Further Reading.

74. In the preface to his translation *Osip Mandelstam: Selected Poems* (New York: Farrar, Straus, Giroux, 1975), David McDuff quotes the description of a reading Mandelstam gave in Leningrad in 1933, written by E. M. Tager, in "O Mandel'shtame" (*Novy Zhurnal*, no. 81 [1965], pp. 172-99). Tager tells how after reading about his journey through Armenia, Mandelstam was asked "to give his opinion of contemporary Soviet poetry, and to determine the significance of older poets who had come to us from the pre-revolutionary era. Thousands of eyes watched Mandelstam grow pale. . . . The poet was being subjected to a public interrogation — and had no means of avoiding it. . . . Mandelstam strode to the edge of the rostrum; as always, his head was thrown back and his eyes sparkled. 'What is it you want of me? What answer? [In a stubborn, singing voice]: I am the friend of my friends!' Half a second's pause. In a triumphant, ecstatic cry: 'I am the contemporary of Akhmatova!' And — thunder, a storm, a tornado of applause" (pp. xii-xiii).

75. In French, the neologism *venance*, formed as a substantive for the present participle "coming."

76. The *Fourth Prose* is a pamphlet that Mandelstam began writing at the end of December 1929 and finished on his way back from Armenia in 1930, about the campaign against him and the deteriorating atmosphere in Soviet literature. It has been called "a blend of autobiography, criticism, and sheer excoriation."

77. A variation on the famous proclamation by Louis XIV, "L'état, c'est moi," and on Flaubert's "Madame Bovary c'est moi."

78. See note 69.

79. Reference to Dante's *Inferno*, canto I. According to most interpreters, Dante figures the wolf as a symbol of the sin of incontinence, and the greyhound as a symbol of the person, probably his contemporary, the great Italian leader Can Grande della Scala, who would deliver Italy from its political strife.

80. The Federation of South African Women was founded in the early 1950s. It developed as a multiracial women's organization committed to the struggle for women's rights and the liberation of men and women from the oppression of apartheid. Although independent from the ANC, the ANC's Women's League worked to establish the FSAW and had many members in common, including Winnie Mandela.

81. Zami's father taught her history; he was a history teacher in government service.

82. ANC leader Walter Sisulu met Nelson Mandela in Johannesburg in 1941 and introduced him to the ANC. Several years older than Nelson and self-educated, Sisulu was imprisoned with him in 1964. He was released on October 15, 1989, along with seven other ANC leaders, at the age of seventy-seven. He is currently the deputy president of the ANC, second to Nelson.

83. Capital city of the South African province of Natal, on the Umsunduzi River. It was here that Nelson gave the keynote speech at an All-African Conference, attended by 1,400 delegates from all parts of the country. This event immediately followed his acquittal in the Treason Trial and was the first time in nine years that Nelson found himself no longer under a banning order, and so able to speak freely in public.

84. Reference to the Keiskama or Kei River in southeastern Cape Province; this river rests in the Amatola range and flows past Keiskmahoek to the Indian Ocean.

85. In French, the neological portmanteau word *petigre*.

86. Winnie was banned from wearing her traditional dress to the Rivonia trial.

87. In the winter of 1938, the Mandelstams were sent from Moscow, all expenses paid by the Union of Writers, to a rest home in the village of

Samatikha. They took this to be a sign that the Union was finally preparing to accept Mandelstam into its favor, but instead it was a setup and a chance to spy on Mandelstam, who, on the first of May 1938 was arrested and deported into exile for the last time.

88. Illicit lovers killed by Francesca's jealous husband; this couple figures prominently in Dante's *Inferno*, canto V.

89. Bridge in Moscow renamed in honor of Mikhail Ivanovich Kalinin, a prominent figure in the Communist party and the Soviet government until his death in 1946.

90. A fiacre is a small carriage for hire, named after the Hotel St. Fiacre in Paris.

91. See note 72.

92. The ancient Egyptian god of the lower world, judge of the dead, husband and brother to the goddess Isis.

93. Helen Joseph is a British-born social worker who has long been an opponent of apartheid in South Africa. She was a founding member of the multiracial Federation of African Women, among other things, and has been a friend of the Mandela family since the 1950s. Winnie Mandela calls her "granny" and has said she became a mother to her during Nelson's imprisonment. She is now in her eighties and remains active. Joseph published her autobiography in 1986. See Suggested Further Reading.

94. The Bush people are a nomadic tribe of southwestern Africa in the region of the Kalahari Desert, notable for their unusually small size.

95. Date of Nelson Mandela's trial for attempting to overthrow the government, in which he was found guilty and sentenced to life in prison.

96. In French: *le pas ensevelissant*, a play on the word *pas*.

97. Seven of the Rivonia men, all ANC leaders, were condemned with Mandela at this time.

98. A journalist present at the Mandela trial the day the verdict was rendered described the scene this way in Winnie Mandela's book *Part of My Soul Went with Him*: "I fully expected to see a shaken Mrs. Mandela emerge from the courthouse. But no. She appeared on the steps and flashed a smile that dazzled. The effect was regal and almost triumphant, performed in the heart of the Afrikaner capital in her moment of anguish, and the crowds of Africans thronging Church Square . . . loved it. They cheered, perhaps the only time black people have ever summoned the courage to cheer in that place" (pp. 79-80).

99. In English and in italics in the French. Taken perhaps from Mandelstam's poem to the poet Batyushkov (see note 119), in which this same line appears in the English version of this poem as translated by Clarence Brown and W. S. Merwin, *Osip Mandelstam: Selected Poems*, p. 64.

100. Biblical word meaning noxious weeds, from Matthew 13:36, "separate the wheat from the tares."

101. Presumed date of Mandelstam's death, in exile.

102. See note 39.

103. See note 75.

104. See note 75.

105. In English in the French text.

106. The "ant" may be a reference to *Part of My Soul Went with Him*, where Winnie writes of the loneliness of her seventeen months in solitary confinement and describes it thus: "I remember how happy I was when I found two ants, how I spent the whole day with these ants, playing with them on my finger and how sad I was when the warders switched off the light" (p. 99).

107. In French, *nêtre*, a play on the French for "to be born," *naître*, and the negation of the verb "to be," *n'être pas*.

108. In French, *n'être ou naître*.

109. In French, the neologisms *entrelettre* and *mystériosités*.

110. *Amandla* means "power," and this is what Nelson Mandela cried to the crowd at his trial, and they answered him, *Nwagethu!*, which means "to the people."

111. In French, *gutture*, a neologism.

112. In Dante's *Inferno*, canto XXXII, the Cocytus is the huge frozen lake of the Ninth Circle. Fixed in its ice are the sinners guilty of betraying kin. The smooth ice resembles glass, and only the necks and heads of those trapped inside it show above the surface.

113. In French, this phrase reads: *mais je n'ai pas changé d'un cil, ma voix n'a pas perdu un si.*

114. According to Egyptian mythology, the god Osiris (see note 92) died by dismemberment, and his sister-wife, the goddess Isis, Great Mother goddess of civilization and fertility, collected his body parts, which had been scattered all over the world, and founded a shrine at each spot.

115. Ganga is one of the manifestations of the Hindu Great Goddess. The Ganges River and mountain range are both named for her.

116. Qunu is a village in the Umtata district where Nelson Mandela grew up and went to school as a child.

117. In French: *chiengarous*, a play on werewolf, *loup-garou*.

118. In French, this series of questions reads: *Tu m'aimes Nadejda, tu m'aimes? tu mêmes? même tu, tu m'aimes, même muet tu m'entends?* The play is on the homophonic relationship between *tu m'aimes*, "do you love me," and *tu mêmes*, "even you." I have tried to suggest the intermingling of these two phrases with my invention of the word "loveven."

119. Konstantine Nikolaevich Batyushkov (1787-1855), great nineteenth-century Russian poet, a contemporary of Pushkin, who served in Italy as a diplomat and was a translator of Tasso. Mandelstam wrote a poem for him, entitled simply "Batyushkov," in June 1932.

120. Province in eastern Poland; its capital city of the same name is located southeast of Warsaw.

121. Capital city of Armenia, where Mandelstam sojourned. This city is referred to in Mandelstam's long poem *Armenia*, published posthumously (see note 56).

122. Mandelstam's poem *Lines about the Unknown Soldier*, written February-March 1937, in Voronezh. It is his longest poem, and he destined it for publication by giving it a title that could lead one to think it is a lament for the victims of the First World War; it is more obviously a song for the unsung victims of Stalin's purges. One English version of the full text is as follows:

1

Let this air be a witness:
his far away beating heart,
even in dugouts all-poisonous, active,
is an ocean, a substance without a window.

How denunciatory are these stars:
they need to see everything—why?
To convict the judge and the witness,
into the ocean, the substance without a window.

The rain, unfriendly sower, remembers
his nameless manna,
how the wooden crosses marked
an ocean or a battlefield.

Men will grow cold and sick,
will kill, be cold and hungry,
and in his notorious grave
the unknown soldier is laid.

Teach me, sickly swallow
that has forgotten how to fly,
how shall I master this airy grave
without a rudder or a wing?

And for Lermontov, Mikhail,
I will give you strictly to understand

how the grave instructs the hunchback
and the airy chasm attracts.

2

These worlds threaten us
like rustling grapes,
and they hang like stolen cities,
golden slips of the tongue, slanders—
like berries of poisonous cold—
tents of tensile constellations,
the constellations' golden oils.

3

Through the decimal-pointed ether
the light of speeds ground down to a ray
begins a number suffused
with bright pain and a mole of zeros.

beyond the field of fields a new field
flies like a triangular crane—
the tidings fly along a road of light-dust—
and it is bright from the battle of yesterday.

The tidings fly along a road of light-dust—
I am not Leipzig, not Waterloo,
I am not the Battle of Tribes. I am the new,
from me it will be bright.

In the depths of the black marble oyster
the light of Austerlitz died—
the Mediterranean swallow frowns,
Egypt's plague-ridden sand ensnares.

4

An Arabian jumble, medley,
the light of speeds ground down to a ray—
and on its squint feet
the ray stands in my pupil

The millions of those killed on the cheap
have trampled a path in the emptiness,
good night, good wishes to them
from the face of earthen fortresses.

Incorruptible sky of trenches,
sky of mighty, wholesale deaths,
behind you, away from you—whole one,
I move my lips in the dark.

For the shell holes, embankments and screes
over which he lingered and glowered,
the gloomy, pockmarked and
living genius of overturned graves.

5

The infantry dies well,
and the nightly choir sings well
over the smile of flattened Schweik
and the bird-spear of Don Quixote
and the chivalric birdlike metatarsus.
And the cripple makes friends with the man:
work will be found for them both.
And around the outskirts of the age
the family of wooden crutches goes knocking—
Ah, comradeship—globe of the earth!

6

Must the skull be unwound entirely
from temple to temple,
so that the troops cannot but pour
into its dear eye sockets?
The skull is unwound from life
entirely—from temple to temple—
it teases itself with the purity of its seams,
gleams like an understanding cupola,
foams with thought, dreams of itself—
cap of caps and motherland to motherlands—

289

a cap sewn like a starry scar—
cap of happiness—Shakespeare's father.

7

The clarity of the ash and the sycamore's vigilance
barely red rush to their home,
as if with fainting fits addressing
both heavens with their dim fire.

To us is allied only that which is superfluous,
before us there is not a dead gap but a measurement,
and to struggle for air on which to live—
this is a glory beyond compare.

Is the package of charm
prepared in empty space
so that the white stars,
barely red, should rush back to their home?

And addressing my consciousness
with a half-fainting existence
I will drink this brew without choice,
I will eat my head under fire!

Do you sense, stepmother of the starry bivouac,
the night that will be now and later?

8

Aortas stiffened with blood
and in rows there sounds as a whisper:
"I was born in the year 'ninety-four,"
"I was born in the year 'ninety-two . . . "
And, squeezing the worn
year of my birth in my fist en bloc *and wholesale*
with my bloodless mouth I whisper:
"I was born in the night of the second and third
of January in the untrustworthy year
of 'ninety-one, and the centuries
surround me with fire."

From David McDuff, trans. *Osip Mandelstam: Selected Poems*, pp. 151-59.

123. These are all republics of the former Soviet Union. Ukraine is in the southwestern European part, on the Black Sea; its capital is Kiev. Armenia is in the Transcaucasus; its capital is Yerevan. Crimea is in the Crimea, a peninsula that extends into the Black Sea. Abhkazia is on the Black Sea; its capital is Sukhumi. Caucasia is on either side of the Caucasus, between the Black Sea and the Caspian. Kazakstan is in western Asia; its capital is Alma-Ata.

124. This Russian word refers to the belt of rich black topsoil found characteristically in the grasslands of Russia, which stretch from the Carpathians and the Black Sea to the Altay Mountains. Mandelstam wrote a poem about this soil, called "Black Earth." What is lost in translation here is that in French the verb meaning "to use fricatives" is *grasseyer*.

125. Capital of the Russian Republic of Uzbekistan, in central Asia. Economically, this is the most developed Soviet central Asian republic. It is the principal producer of cotton, rice, and silk.

126. Reference to the journalist Kazarnovski, who was in the camps at Vladivostok with Mandelstam just before his death. Nadezhda hid Kazarnovski from the police in the 1940s after he returned from exile, in order to try to learn more about Mandelstam's last days alive.

127. Another name for Athena, Greek goddess of wisdom.

128. Of Uzbekistan. *Webster's* defines *glebe* as a poetic word for soil or ground.

129. Italian for leopard. This is a reference to a beast that appears in canto I of Dante's *Inferno*. Many interpreters believe the spotted leopard symbolized fraud, the worst of the three major categories of sin.

130. In French, a play on the expressions *être gris* and *être noir*, to be gray (a little drunk) and to be black (completely drunk), which refer back to the newspaper printed black on gray.

131. In French, *cuver l'univers*, a play on the expression *cuver son vin*, which means to sleep off one's drink, and *cuver du vin*, which means to ferment wine.

Suggested Further
Reading

The Mandelas

Benson, Mary. *Nelson Mandela: The Man and the Movement*. New York: Norton, 1986.

Derrida, Jacques, and Mustapha Tlili, eds. *For Nelson Mandela*. New York: Seaver Books, Henry Holt, 1987.

Joseph, Helen. *Side by Side: The Autobiography of Helen Joseph*. New York: William Morrow, 1986.

Mandela, Nelson. *No Easy Way to Freedom*. London: Haneman, 1986.

Mandela, Winnie. *Part of My Soul Went with Him*. Edited by Anne Benjamin, adapted by Mary Benson. New York: Norton, 1984.

Meer, Fatima. *Higher than Hope: Mandela*. Durban, South Africa: Madiba, 1990.

"The Ordeal and Triumph of Winnie Mandela." *Ebony*, vol. 45 (May 1990).

"Peace on Trial." *Maclean's*, vol. 103 (October 1, 1990).

"Winnie's Walk into Obscurity." *Time*, vol. 139 (April 27, 1992).

The Mandelstams

Brown, Clarence. *Mandelstam*. Cambridge: Cambridge University Press, 1973.

Brown, Clarence, trans. *The Prose of Osip Mandelstam*. Berkeley, Calif.: North Point, 1967.

Greene, James, trans. *Osip Mandelshtam: The Eyesight of Wasps*. Fore-

words by Nadezhda Mandelshtam and Donald Davie; introduction by
Donald Rayfield. Columbus: Ohio State University Press, 1989.

McDuff, David, trans. *Osip Mandelstam: Selected Poems*. Introduced by
David McDuff. New York: Farrar, Straus, Giroux, 1975.

Mandelstam, Nadezhda. *Hope Abandoned*. Translated by Max Hayward.
New York: Atheneum, 1981.

———. *Hope against Hope: A Memoir*. Translated by Max Hayward. New
York: Atheneum, 1970.

Morrison, R. H., trans. *Poems from Mandelstam*. Introduced by Ervin C.
Brody. Madison, Wis.: Fairleigh Dickinson University Press, 1990.

Hélène Cixous was born and raised in Oran, Algeria, and attended university in Paris. She is currently head of the Centre d'Etudes Féminines and professor of English literature at the experimental University of Paris VIII–Vincennes, which she helped to found. Her celebrated seminars attract students of literature and women's studies from the world over, and are held at the Collège de Philosophie in Paris. She has also lectured in the United States, at Harvard, the University of California at Berkeley and Irvine, Cornell, and the University of Virginia, among others. Although best known in North America as a writer of "French feminisms," Cixous is primarily a poet who has published more than thirty works of fiction in forms as varied as the avant-garde novel, plays (a number of which were especially commissioned by the renowned Théâtre du Soleil), prose poetry, essays, and a hybrid genre that might be called poetic theory. Her most recent publications in France include the fictions *Déluge* and *Beethoven à jamais ou l'existence de Dieu* and the play *On ne part pas, on ne revient pas*. The University of Minnesota Press has published her *Newly Born Woman* (1985, coauthored with Catherine Clément) and other works.

Catherine A. F. MacGillivray studied with Hélène Cixous at the University of Paris–VIII from 1980 to 1984, where she completed a *Licence* and a *Maîtrise* in *Lettres Modernes* and *Etudes Féminines*. She received her doctorate in French Literature from UC Berkeley in 1993, and has taught French, English, and women's studies at UC Berkeley and in New York City. She has published translations of a number of Cixous's essays and shorter texts, and is currently translating another volume of Cixous's poetic fiction for the University of Minnesota Press, *Jours de l'an*.